W9-CFK-715

The
Ragtime Kid

Also by Larry Karp
First, Do No Harm

The Ragtime Kid

Larry Karp

Poisoned Pen Press

Poisoned Pen Press
6962 E. First Ave., Ste. 103
Scottsdale, AZ 85251
www.poisonedpenpress.com
info@poisonedpenpress.com

Printed in the United States of America

This one's for

Dorrie O'Brien   *and*   *Barbara Peters*
of   *of*
Write Way Publishing   *Poisoned Pen Press*

They wave magical blue pencils,
clouds clear,
and a writer sees
just how to make a manuscript into a book

History never embraces more than a small part of reality.
—La Rochefoucault

*So very difficult is it to trace and find out
the truth of anything by history.*
—Plutarch

There is properly no History; only Biography.
—Emerson

The Invocation/Dedication Prayer offered at the dedication of the Scott Joplin Memorial Park in Sedalia, MO, on June 1, 1999, is reprinted with the kind permission of the Reverend Dr. Marvin G. Albright, Pastor of the United Church of Christ in Sedalia.

Acknowledgments

Many people helped me construct the historical framework for *The Ragtime Kid*. Special thanks to Betty Singer, the cheerful and indefatigable researcher, who replied with lightning speed to my endless email requests. Betty's information about everyday life in Sedalia in 1899 was instrumental, and without her research, the characters of Dr. Walter Overstreet and P. D. Hastain never would have asserted themselves, nor could I have properly represented the Pettis County Jail. Mark Forster worked his way through impressive genealogical tangles to find critical information about the Stark and Higdon families, including John Stark's army record. The Reverend Dr. Marvin G. Albright, of the United Church of Christ in Sedalia, was generous in permitting me to reproduce the moving and eloquent prayer he offered at the dedication of Sedalia's Scott Joplin Memorial Park. Rhonda Chalfant steered me toward invaluable reference reading regarding social and political affairs in Sedalia a century ago. Richard Egan helped me locate material on the life and music of Brun Campbell. Nora Hulse certified a pivotal piece of information concerning Will Stark. And the staff at the Carnegie Library in Sedalia were patient far beyond the call of duty, as I pestered them for days on end to dig out century-old newspaper microfilm and locally written historical material.

Thanks to Jeanne Dams for telling me the secret of the geographic accuracy and verisimilitude in her fine Hilda Johansson series: Sanborn historical maps.

A particular thanks to my friend John Wright for permitting me to poach a line from the title poem in his collection, *The Beginning of Love*, that leaped into my story and excluded any other possibility.

I apologize to anyone I should have mentioned but didn't.

If you find merit in the historical aspect of my novel, much of the credit goes to those who gave me so much help. If you find errors, the blame is all mine.

Chapter One

Oklahoma City
August, 1898

Brun Campbell heard a piano, and that was all she wrote. Any time Brun heard a piano, that was all she ever wrote. The piano was Brun's one true love, and when it called him, the boy dropped whatever he was doing and attended.

When this particular piano summoned Brun, he was walking down the main street of Oklahoma City with his friend Sam Mueller. The afternoon before, Brun had dared Sam to run off with him for the day and go to the fair in Oklahoma City, thirty miles down the road from El Reno, where the boys lived. Sam's father, the town doctor, was forever warning his son he'd find trouble associating with that Campbell boy, and you know what the effect of that was. For his part, Brun figured Dr. Mueller for a decent old guy, and saw no reason to make him a liar.

So early that morning, Brun and Sam hopped a freight. Brun had been bringing home good money, playing piano for tips in restaurants and hotel lobbies, and he and Sam could have ridden in the passenger coach like gentlemen. But no point throwing away money you could otherwise spend at the fair.

The wooden sidewalks in Oklahoma City looked solid with people. As the boys worked their way through the crowds toward the fairgrounds, Brun set his mouth into just the right degree of sneer so as not to gawk. More plug hats and swallowtail coats than he'd ever seen before in one place at one time, and though it was only eleven in the morning, some women were gussied up so you'd think they were on their way to a fancy ball. The boys walked past a hotel grander by degrees than anything in El Reno, saw restaurants with white linen, gleaming glasses, and silverware shining in the sunlight. Shops of every sort, groceries, coffee and tea, shoe stores, leather goods, men's clothing, women's. "Hey, Brun," Sam shouted. "I bet you can buy anything you'd ever want in Oklahoma City."

That's when the piano sang to Brun. Soft, but loud enough to drown out anything more Sam might have had to say, and Sam right with it. The music made the shops disappear, the hotels, the restaurants, the crowds of people. Picture a string between the piano and Brun's neck. The boy crossed the street, came close to getting hit by a horse and wagon, never heard the old farmer up behind the horse cuss him out for a young whippersnapper, never realized that by the time Sam got across, trying to follow, Brun was already lost in the crowd.

He trailed the melody to a large music store, ARMSTRONG-BYRD in white letters on a glittery black background above the door, then stood a moment and goggled through the open doorway like the half-grown Reuben he was. Rows of shiny brass horns, clarinets, accordions ran down the sides of the store; guitars, banjos, mandolins and fiddles covered the back wall. Music stores in El Reno couldn't hold a candle to this. And all the while, the piano called.

Just inside the door, a woman considerably ample in the bosom and hindquarters, and a little older than women like to say they are, struggled to play a religious dirge on the house piano. Brun walked inside to get a better look. The woman's cheeks were on fire; water ran down in front of her ears. The boy nearly laughed out loud.

At the counter, to Brun's left, a clerk held up a small wax cylinder under a customer's nose, then slipped the cylinder onto a tiny mechanical contraption. Brun had heard tell of these talking machines, but this was the first he'd seen. He edged a couple of steps closer. Music, a band playing a snappy two-step, poured through the little black and gold horn, scratchy and thin, but to Brun it seemed a miracle. The customer, a stringy man with arms and legs at odd angles that made him look like some sort of human spider, pushed his wide-brimmed leather hat back off his forehead and shook his head side to side in wonder.

The woman finished playing her hymn, gathered up the sheet music like it might've been Holy Scripture, and waddled toward the counter to pay. Brun quickly moved sidewise, sat on the bench, and began to play the same tune he'd just heard coming through the phonograph horn. People all around stopped talking and looked at the boy. The spider-man laughed and poked a finger into the clerk's vest. "How about you sell me that kid, Marcus? He sounds a whole lot better than this here phonograph of yours."

Brun briefly considered that his playing might be a bother to the clerk, but when somebody praised his piano work, he likely wouldn't have stopped if his pants were on fire. With all his energy, he swung into "Hot Time in the Old Town," playing it march-style, pounding the keys for all he was worth. People commenced to sing; he saw men nod approval. A pretty young woman in a frilly white blouse slipped him a wink that nearly threw him off the beat. When he hit the final notes, there were loud whistles of approval, and everyone in the store applauded. But if Brun Campbell had any say, the show was not over. A quick transition, and now he was playing "You're a Good Old Wagon But You Done Broke Down."

All commerce in that Armstrong-Byrd ceased.

Brun had an audience of nigh-onto twenty. A man and a woman beside the piano kicked up their heels. Brun gave them "The Band Played On"; people whooped and shouted and clapped their hands. The boy already had his next two tunes in mind, but when he felt a sharp tap on his shoulder, his hands froze on the keyboard. The dancers stared over their shoulders.

Likely the shopkeeper, Brun figured, aggravated at the way sales had gone south since he'd sat down at the piano. He turned half-way around on the bench, ready to cut and run. But the tall, slim man standing behind him was smiling, friendly as could be. He looked to be in his twenties, light-skinned but not altogether white. A quadroon, maybe even an octoroon. Dressed to the nines in a pinky-gray suit and vest, diamond collar-studs, no kink at all in the black hair below the derby hat, and every hair slicked right smack in place. The man turned up his smile. "You play pretty good, boy. How old you be?"

"Fourteen."

The man raised his eyebrows and reached inside his suit jacket, whereupon Brun commenced to feel a bit uneasy. Those days, in that part of the country, nice as a man may seem, when he reaches inside his coat, you'd better keep watch. "Mmmm, on'y fourteen, huh?" The light-skinned Negro looked impressed. "Well, you pretty good right now, and you got a passel of years ahead to get better. You play any syncopation? Know what syncopation be?"

If his schoolteachers' questions were that easy, Brun thought, he'd be class valedictorian. He swung back around to face the piano and played a little of "Mr. Johnson, Turn Me Loose." The Negro nodded in time with the beat; his smile worked up into a soft laugh. He brought a sheet of paper out of his pocket, unfolded it, and set it on the music rack in front of Brun. "Let's see how you do with this, boy."

Brun stared at the pen and ink manuscript. It looked like no music he'd ever seen. He put his fingers to the keys.

For the rest of his life, Brun told anyone who'd listen that before he'd played ten measures, he knew he was in the grip of something powerful. Like the music was playing him, not the other way round. Mr. Johnson, turn me loose? The notes seemed to reach down from the manuscript, place Brun's fingers, push them down, then move them along. As if from somewhere far off he heard the Negro say, "That's good, boy, good. But you playin' it too fast. Scott Joplin ever hears you play his tune so fast, he ain't gonna talk pleasant to you. Slow it down, now…yeah. That's better."

As long as Brun played, that room was dead-quiet, but the instant he stopped, all Niagara broke loose. People whistled and cheered and pounded their hands together. The Negro opened his eyes wide; one corner of his mouth moved upward just a little. "You mighty good, boy," he said. "That is no easy piece of music to play, for sure not the first time. *An'* for sure, not for a white boy. Why, you only made two mistakes! One day you gonna be a great piano player." He reached for the music, folded it, started to put it back into his pocket.

"What *is* that?" Brun whispered the words.

"That," the Negro said, then stopped like he was waiting for a trumpet to play a fanfare. "Is called 'Maple Leaf Rag.' Composed and written down by Mr. Scott Joplin. You ever hear of him? Mr. Scott Joplin?"

"Not until now," Brun said, in a strange, strangled voice. "But I'd sure like to know what other music he wrote."

The spiffy quadroon sized the boy up and down. Brun didn't stop to think how his youth was all to his advantage. If he'd been a grown man, the Negro would never have dared take such personal liberties with him, and definitely not in that very public place. "I be Otis Saunders," the man finally said. "Scott Joplin's my friend. Lives in Sedalia."

"Missouri?"

Saunders laughed. "Ain't no other Sedalia I know about." He took Brun by the elbow. "Come on, boy, you look like you could do with some lunch. I'll tell you all about Scott Joplin, an' Sedalia too."

It occurred to Brun that if his mother were there, she'd already have two arms around him, hustling him away from this colored stranger who was going to take him God knew where to do God knew what. But Mrs. Campbell wasn't there, and Brun followed Otis Saunders out of Armstrong-Byrd, onto the wooden sidewalk, down a block, around a corner, through a doorway into a hole-in-the-wall where he found himself face to face with a huge sable-skinned woman in a tent of a white cotton dress, grease stains all across her white apron, and a dirty towel over one shoulder. Below a red polka-dot bandanna, she had a face on her that would have frozen the bogeyman in his tracks. But Otis Saunders just smiled and motioned with his head and eyes toward the back of the room.

The woman glared at Brun, then led the way to a table all the way in the rear, and snapped a curtain shut to close off Brun and Saunders from the rest of the room. "Thank you, Minnie," Saunders said, polite as if she was the queen of England. "Fix us up, if you please."

Minnie walked away without a word. Saunders rolled himself a cigarette, his long, slender fingers swift and agile.

"Bet *you* play a mean piano," Brun said.

Saunders laughed. "You pretty quick. Yeah, a man live in Sedalia, he play *something*. Most musical town in the country." He passed tobacco and paper across the table. Brun managed to roll a smoke without spilling too much tobacco.

They lit up. Saunders smoked his cigarette the way he seemed to do everything, smooth, easy, and cool. Brun was more deliberate, taking care not to embarrass himself by choking on the intake. Saunders looked just this side of amused.

In a few minutes, Minnie was back. Still without saying a word, she set a platter of ribs on the table, then a bowl of collards. As she started to walk away, Saunders chirped, "Hey, now, Minnie. You done forgot the beer."

The woman turned back, eyes bulging. Brun stopped breathing. But Saunders just laughed in an easy manner. "You don't expect this young gentleman and myself to be eatin' our ribs without no beer, now, do you?"

Minnie took a moment to glare at Saunders, then pulled the stained towel off her shoulder and snapped it into the mulatto's face. Saunders lurched back, shrieking with mock fear. He jumped out of his chair and threw both arms around the big woman. "Me an' Minnie, we goes back a long, long way," he said to Brun. "She always take good care of us young boys. Don'tcha, Minnie?"

The woman gave Brun another hard look, then pulled away from Saunders and started toward the door. "An' don't you be forgettin' the corn cakes," Saunders called after her through a giggle.

Once Minnie was past the curtain, Saunders said, "She a good woman. I likes teasin' her when I can."

"She doesn't say much," said Brun.

"She don't say nothin'. Eight years old, they went an' cut out her tongue. 'Cause her massa's li'l daughter say Minnie sassed her."

Minnie was back directly with a plate heaped with corn-meal bread, and a pitcher of beer. Brun forced himself to look the woman straight in the eye. "Thank you," he said. Minnie nodded, then walked off. Saunders grabbed a rib off the plate and motioned for Brun to do the same. And for the next two hours, while they ate and drank, Saunders told Brun about Scott Joplin and Sedalia.

No story in any book Brun had ever read came even close to the yarn Otis Saunders spun him that day. Sedalia was built on music, Saunders said, all different kinds of music. Walk down a street where white folks lived, you'd hear girls and ladies practicing their Mozart and their Chopin, or playing waltzes by Strauss. Night after night, bands and small orchestras played concerts in the park, or on street corners. Jig bands played one competition after the last. Clubs, white and colored, held dances. There were wonderful musical shows at the grand Wood's Opera House. And every night except Sunday, of course, a man could walk down West Main Street and just listen to the music. Every bar, saloon and parlor on West Main had a piano man, and what they played, they called ragtime. "Ragtime music been with us colored forever," Saunders said. "When white folks first really hear it was in 'ninety-three, Chicago, at the World-fair, and you shoulda seen their faces. Scott Joplin and me, we were there—fact, that's where we first got ourselves acquainted. Afterwards, we go to Sedalia, and Scott study composition at the George R. Smith

College for Negroes, an' what he learn, he show me. Mark me, boy—one day you and everyone else gonna see his name and mine on music sheets in that Armstrong-Byrd, and every other music store in the country besides."

Brun swallowed a mouthful of collards. "George R. Smith College for *Negroes?*"

Saunders wiped at his mouth with the edge of the tablecloth. "Oh yes. Yes, indeed. Mr. George R. Smith founded Sedalia in 1860, an' it was a big outpost for the Union all through the war. Afterwards, the railroads come on through, so they need plenty of workers, don't they, good hard workers. Colored come up from the south, bring they music with 'em. An' when Mr. George R. Smith die, he leave money in his will for a school for colored, supposed to teach all the subjects, but most of all, music. I say if a man don't like music a whole lot, why, then he best go'n live someplace else besides Sedalia."

Brun left Minnie's that day feeling like he'd walked inside a building, then come back out the same door to find himself standing on a road he wouldn't find on any map, in a world he never knew existed, You might think the beer had something to do with that, and you might wonder if it was just tobacco the boy smoked with Otis Saunders. But Brun always insisted it was "Maple Leaf Rag" working on him, more powerful by a long shot than any drink or smoke. The notes barreled through his head, rearranged his every thought, made whatever he saw or heard or touched or smelled or tasted seem somehow different.

On the sidewalk in front of Minnie's, Otis Saunders said good-bye. "Now, you be sure'n keep up your piano work—do that, an' maybe one day I be comin' to hear you play in a big concert hall. But before we go our ways, you let me give you one li'l piece of advice. Okay?"

"Sure."

"All right, then. When you in a city, you got to be careful of some things. Like best you leave your money in your front pants pocket. Or in your shirt pocket, 'neath your coat or vest. But never—not ever—in the back pocket of your trousers."

Brun frantically slid a hand into his back pocket, where he'd put some twenty dollars' worth of folded bills that morning. At the sight of the boy's face, Saunders laughed, then reached behind his vest and came out with a wad of money, which he placed into the boy's hand. "They's bad people in cities, young Mr. Piano Man. You don't want to be helpin' them to help themselves, you get my drift."

"I'd be pretty dumb if I didn't," Brun said, though his voice shook considerably. Saunders, still laughing, put out a hand; they shook. The boy pushed his money down as far as it would go into his shirt pocket.

Brun told me he could never remember what he did the rest of that day, or how he managed to get back home. But he had no trouble recalling the hiding his father gave him. "You worried your mother," Mr. Campbell shouted, as he swung the thick, black razor strop. "You had both of us worried to death." Brun did feel a little bad about that, but having met Otis Saunders and learned to play "Maple Leaf Rag," he would not have taken the day back for the world. That strop his father laid again and again across his bottom seemed to be hitting another boy. It inflamed Brun's mind a whole lot more than it did his butt.

Chapter Two

Sedalia, Missouri
June, 1899

A dull pounding sprang up behind Scott Joplin's left eye. Why didn't Saunders write his own damned music, and quit bothering him about the trio section in "Maple Leaf Rag"? "I appreciate you wanting to help, Otis," Joplin said. "But 'Maple Leaf' is done. You know I've got a bigger fish to fry right now, but I can't fry him unless I catch him, and I can't catch him if I don't throw him a line."

Like he hadn't said a word. Saunders went right on grinning like a fool. "Yeah, Scott, but just you listen for a minute, okay? Just one little minute. The way you startin' that trio right now…"

The hammer in Joplin's head beat harder. He closed his eyes. That was his way when he was among people and needed to develop a musical idea. Out of sight, out of hearing, out of mind. He lived in a lively boardinghouse, earned his living playing piano at taverns and dance clubs. If he could write music only when he was alone, he'd never write music.

During the summer, weekday afternoons were quiet in the Maple Leaf Club, a large room up on the second floor at 121 East Main. Joplin had come here today, hoping for some time to himself. Walker Williams, one of the club's owners, stood behind the bar, talking quietly over mugs of beer with Tom Ireland, a colored newspaperman who played a first-rate clarinet in the Queen City Concert Band. They knew why Joplin was there, so they'd done no more than smile and nod a hello as he and Saunders walked over to the piano and sat side by side on the bench. Joplin sighed. If he didn't get *The Ragtime Dance* down on paper pretty soon, the whole kit and caboodle might just float right out of his head, gone forever. Music did that. Like a woman who thought her man wasn't paying her enough mind. He'd lost other half-composed pieces that way; he didn't want to lose this one.

Saunders was a magpie, near impossible to shake, thoroughly impossible to shut up. But it wasn't in Joplin's nature to just out and tell the man to go away. Instead, eyes closed, ears blocked, he directed his mind toward the passage in *The Ragtime Dance* he'd been working at. Saunders' words became a hum in the background. The breeze through the open window put a damper on the throb in Joplin's head. He heard the music. His right hand twitched. Left hand up. Fingers struck ivory and ebony. He corrected the chord, played on for a few seconds, then snatched the pencil off the music rack and wrote down what he'd just played.

Saunders said something, no more than a blur in Joplin's ear. If the man said one word, just *one* word, about the "Maple Leaf" trio…

"Gettin' company, Scott." Saunders aimed a hitchhiker's thumb toward the doorway, across the room.

Joplin turned and saw two white men standing just inside the door. His headache mounted a comeback. Beethoven didn't have to put up with anything like this. When he wanted to write music, he locked himself away in a room with a keyboard for hours at a time. And when Beethoven played his music of an evening, it was for audiences who appreciated his art, not for a roomful of men who liked a little lively background to get drunk to, or a bunch of prostitutes and johns who wanted a bit of musical foreplay. Why couldn't Scott Joplin find a patron with money? The last time he'd seen Mr. Weiss, Joplin had complained to that effect, which had set the old German to waving a finger under his pupil's nose. "Scott, you got more talent in your little finger than any other student I ever taught got in his whole body. What you *don't* got is time to waste feeling sorry for yourself. Least you got a chance, which your mama and daddy never did."

The two white men began to walk across the room toward the piano. Walker Williams glanced under the bar, where his pistol lay on a shelf within easy reach. Ireland shifted on his stool so as to keep the white men in sight without giving the appearance of looking or listening.

As the men approached them, Joplin and Saunders swung their legs over the bench, then stood. "Trouble?" Saunders whispered from the corner of his mouth.

Joplin answered with an almost imperceptible shrug. His face was a poker master's dream. He stared at the younger of the white men, a slicker not much over twenty, with wide-set brown eyes above a friendly enough smile, snappy in a dark tailored suit and rakish derby. "Good afternoon, Mr. Daniels," Joplin said.

"Good afternoon to you, Scott."

Joplin extended a hand; Daniels gave it a brief pump. "Mr. Daniels, my friend Otis Saunders. A fine pianist and musician. Otis, this is Mr. Charles Daniels. From Carl Hoffman Music Company in Kansas City."

Saunders' eyes went wide. He nodded to Daniels, who returned the slight bow.

Joplin turned his attention to Daniels' companion, a heavy-set man of forty-some years, with light skin and blue eyes. Some kind of Swede or Norwegian, Joplin thought. White suit, wide blue tie with a fake-diamond stickpin, boater set a little cockeyed on his head. He sweated freely, but his smile dazzled, lots of teeth, and he leaned forward from the waist to bring that smile right up to Joplin's face. Joplin thought of alligators. "Scott, this is Mr. Elmo Freitag, my associate," Daniels said.

Right there, Joplin knew something was out of whack. A man with a boss half his age is like a man with a wife half his age. Joplin looked directly at Daniels. "What can I do for you?" Daniels' smile extended. "Why, I've come to see *you*, Scott. I hear you're working on a full-score ragtime ballet—*The Ragtime Dance*? You'll be needing a publisher, won't you?"

Anger bubbled up from Joplin's chest; the skin of his face felt like it might catch on fire. But that emotionless mask didn't change, not a trace. "I guess that's true," he said, mild as you please.

"We've done well with 'Original Rags,'" said Daniels. "And we can do just as well with this music, maybe better. How many tunes are there in your ballet?"

"It's not yet finished, Mr. Daniels."

Daniels' smile gave him the look of an appealing little boy. "Oh, now, Scott, why do you want to play games with me? I'm interested in your work. You can tell me more than 'It's not yet finished.'"

Joplin swallowed hard. "All right. I'm trying to work it out with an introductory section, then a preparation for the dance, and after that, thirteen dances with a caller, over maybe five to ten strains—"

"Well, that sounds just wonderful. Fifteen pieces altogether. I'll arrange them for separate publication. And then if they catch on, we can put out a folio of the entire work. I'd say that would make your reputation."

My reputation and your fortune, Joplin thought, but he said, "I'm sorry, Mr. Daniels, but with all due respect, I'll never publish a piece of music again that credits someone else as arranger."

Seeing Daniels' cheeks go red gave Joplin pleasure, malicious and satisfying. "Now, Scott—I know you didn't like seeing my name as arranger on 'Original Rags.' But that's just the business. Everyone knows that."

Which means, Joplin thought, most white people think they can't play music by a colored man unless a white man makes it over for them. So just put a white man's name on the cover, even if that white man didn't change a single note. Joplin shook his head. "I mean what I say. I do my own arranging, and will not under any circumstances publish another piece of music that says otherwise."

The expression on Freitag's face set off a chuckle inside Joplin's head. But he kept silent, his face indifferent.

"Wait a minute, Scott…" Daniels looked to be in pain. He stared, tightened his lips, then finally let out a little laugh. "My God, you *are* a stubborn man. Well, all right. All *right*. If you insist, we'll do it that way. Your name will be the only one on the cover, composer *and* arranger. I'll give you my word on that."

"Will you put it in the contract?"

Daniels looked thoroughly buffaloed. "In the…*what* contract, Scott? What do we need a contract for? You deliver me all those tunes, I'm prepared to pay you three hundred dollars, cash."

Joplin heard Saunders suck in his breath.

"I'd say that's pretty generous." Freitag's first contribution to the discussion.

"I'm sure you think it is," Joplin said. "But I don't intend to sell *The Ragtime Dance*, or any more of my music, outright. I'd want a contract that provides for royalties, and if that's not acceptable to you, I really don't want to waste your time."

Daniels pressed his lips together until they were bloodless. "Oh, come on, Scott. You know Mr. Hoffman would never agree to that. If you don't want to publish with us, why don't you just say that. Then, I'll ask you why not, and maybe we can make some headway."

"That is not what I'm saying. I said exactly what I meant. Full credit for composing and arranging. And a contract providing for royalties and specifying that I would keep all rights to put on performances."

Daniels exploded. "Rights to put on…*Damn*, Scott, what in hell are you thinking? A colored man, producing his own performances? If you want to lose your shirt, why don't you just take it off and throw it away, and be done?"

"Cole and Johnson didn't lose their shirts. And neither did Cook and Dunbar. Two all-colored shows in New York last year, and they both did pretty well. I don't see why I can't do it, too."

Daniels wiped the back of his hand across his mouth. "Scott, I don't mean to insult you, but you're not Cole or Johnson or Cook or Dunbar, at least not yet. When you get yourself that well known, then I'd say maybe you could pull it off. But nobody—and I mean *nobody*—right now is going to give Scott Joplin a royalties contract with performance rights reserved."

"Then nobody is going to publish this music." Joplin's tone was as mild as his face. "But I've been talking to Mr. Will Stark, and he said he'd consider it."

"Will Stark?" Daniels looked at Freitag, who shrugged.

"Mr. Will Stark's in business with his father. Stark and Son, on East Fifth."

"Old Man Stark? For the love of heaven, Scott, that's a music store. They're not publishers."

"Mr. Will Stark is looking into expanding," said Joplin, stolid as the Sphinx.

The men stared at each other. Daniels looked away first. Then, he said, quietly, "You're serious, Scott? You really mean all this?"

"I would never fool around in any way with my music."

Daniels' cheeks went pasty. "All right, then. I guess we don't have anything more to say. Thanks for your time."

Joplin watched the men stamp to the doorway, then vanish. As they clumped down the stairs, Saunders let out a low whistle. "Whoo-whee, Scott. You just got two buckras mighty displeased with you."

"I was polite," said Joplin. "I said no, but I said it in a civil way. You know what I got for 'Original Rags.' How much money do you think Carl Hoffman made?"

Saunders looked doubtful. "Did Will Stark really say he'd give you a contract with royalties?"

Joplin swiveled on the bench to rest his hands on the keyboard. "We talked about it. Now, I'm sorry, Otis, but I need to get back to writing this tune. I've wasted more than enough of my time today."

Saunders grinned wide. "Well, I guess I can take a hint. See you for supper? I'll come by for you." He tipped his tan straw hat and strode across the room to the bar. Joplin bent his head forward, played a chord, then another.

Walker Williams slid a pint of Moerschel's Sedalia Brew across to Saunders, who took a long pull at the glass, then set it down and groaned. Like someone had given a signal, the three men looked back at Joplin, hunched over the keyboard, scribbling at the papers on the music rack. Williams shook his head. "Don't even know we's here."

"Boy's got music in his head," said Tom Ireland. "And not much of anything else."

Williams snorted. "Sometimes I think he don't even know he's a colored man."

Saunders leaned forward, spoke low. "Scott tell me one time, back a few years, he was in the Texarkana Minstrels, and they give a show there for the Confederate Veterans to raise money to build a monument for Jeff Davis."

"No!" Williams put his hand to his mouth, too late. Three heads swung around as one, but if Joplin heard, he gave no sign.

Saunders went on in a whisper. "Made a real fuss among the colored, and not just in Texarkana. Scott and them minstrels caught all manner of hell in the colored New Orleans papers. But Scott, he just say he figured Jeff Davis was dead, an' long as the minstrels got their forty percent of the gate, what's it matter to them if people want to be fool enough to spend money to carve Jeff Davis' name on a stone?"

Ireland shook his head. Williams refilled his glass.

"Colored man don't dare forget for one minute that he be colored," the bartender said. Ireland nodded agreement.

"Scott had this white man in Texarkana, teach him piano," said Saunders. "Professor Julius Weiss. A *real* professor, out of a school in Germany."

Williams' smile went sly. "Julius Weiss. Clipdick, huh?"

"Don't know for sure," said Saunders. "But Scott say Mr. Weiss always tell him he just as good as anybody else, never mind white or colored."

Tom Ireland set down his glass. His face was sad as eternity. "That man must've been straight over from the old country. They hear we got set free, but past that, they don't know a thing. He didn't do Scott any favor."

"Mmmm-*mmm*." Williams nodded sharply. "Boy's gonna find himself some real trouble one day."

Ireland got up to leave, pulled a five-dollar bill from his pocket and laid it on the counter. Williams laughed. "What you think, three o'clock in the afternoon, I got anything in the till to change that?" He cupped a hand to his mouth. "Scott! Hey, Scott. *Joplin!*"

Joplin finally looked up. Like a man coming out of a coma, Ireland thought.

Williams motioned him toward the bar. "Hey, Scott, I hate botherin' you, but can you break a fin for me so I can give Tom here his change?"

Joplin walked slowly to the bar, trying to hold the elusive musical strain in his mind. Robot-like, he fished a money-clip from his pocket, gleaming yellow metal in the shape of a musical lyre. He peeled off five singles, gave them to Williams, took the fiver, and slipped it into the clip. But before he could return it to his pocket, Tom Ireland held out his hand. "Let's see that a minute, Scott."

Joplin placed the clip in Ireland's hand. "Nice," Ireland said. "That's enamel-work on the front, isn't it?" He rolled the clip over, then stared at it.

"Push that little button," Joplin said.

Ireland pressed his thumb against a tiny bit of metal sticking out from the back of the money-clip, and straightway a tune began to play, a faint tinkle that lasted about ten seconds. Ireland smiled. Williams stared. "Scott, what *is* that thing?"

"A kind of little music box, from Europe. The best friend I ever had gave it to me as a token of his regard. You have no idea how I treasure it." Joplin pointed at the clip, near the metal play button. "That's where you wind it—just pull up on that little key head, and give it a couple of turns."

Tom Ireland clearly had no intention of even touching the key head. He placed the money-clip gently into Joplin's hand. Saunders waved a general good-bye and headed for the door. Joplin strode back to the piano, sat on the bench, took a deep, deep breath. Then he shot his cuffs and began to write.

Late-afternoon business was slow at the John Stark and Son Music Store. A few customers browsed the sheet-music racks, and two colored men toward the rear of the shop looked over a banjo. Behind the glass counter just inside the doorway and to the right, the proprietor sat drowsing, regretting the big slice of apple pie he'd added to his lunch. He glanced down at the bulge beneath the lower part of his vest. Of all a man's appetites, he thought, only the one for food stays with him as he gets older. Damn! In just two years, he'd be sixty. He'd heard it said that sixty-year-old men should be chloroformed. Maybe there was something to that.

He blinked his eyes open as two men came through the doorway into the shop and walked up to the counter. The younger man tipped his derby, showing a full head of thick, dark hair, parted directly in the middle. "Afternoon, sir."

Stark blinked one more time, then nodded. "Good afternoon to you."

"My name is Charles Daniels," the man said. "I'm with Carl Hoffman, Kansas City. And this is my, uh, associate, Mr. Elmo Freitag."

Stark shook the outstretched hands, first Daniels', then Freitag's. "I am most pleased to meet you, sir," the big man said. His voice was full and melodious, but the hint of magnolias was more than offset by an unmistakable whiff of second-hand booze.

Stark turned back to Daniels. "Hoffman, eh? We sell a great deal of your music. New salesman, are you?"

Freitag let go a hootch-scented guffaw. Daniels didn't seem bothered. "No," he said. "I'm a sales agent and demonstrator for Hoffman—"

"'Margery,'" Stark broke in. "You're the young man who wrote 'Margery' last year, aren't you? Fine tune. We sold a great many copies."

Daniels looked pleased, no surprise to Stark. "I'm glad to hear that. I do write music, yes, but my first responsibility is to find good tunes for Mr. Hoffman. That's why Mr. Freitag and I are in Sedalia. We're looking for your son. Will."

"Will's in St. Louis now," said Stark. "So I guess you're stuck with me."

At that point, the two Negroes walked up from the back of the store. One, an older man, slightly stooped and favoring his left foot, wore torn overalls and a ragged blue shirt; he carried the banjo the two had been examining. The other colored man, darker by several degrees than Otis Saunders but lighter than Scott Joplin, was slim, about fifty, with shiny, tightly kinked black hair, and was dressed neatly in an open-collar white shirt and black trousers. He walked behind the counter, to the register, took money from the man with the banjo and rang up the sale.

As the customer limped through the doorway into the street, Daniels and Freitag looked at each other. Freitag laughed again. "Times must be mighty good in Sedalia," he boomed. "If a nigger can afford to buy a banjo in a white man's store, and another nigger has a white man's job, waiting on him."

Stark wondered if the day would ever come when he would not have to listen to that talk. "This is Mr. Isaac Stark," he snapped. "*My* associate. Mr. Stark, these are Mr. Daniels and Mr. Freitag, from Carl Hoffman in Kay Cee."

Daniels reached to clasp Isaac's hand. Freitag kept his hands at his sides. "Isaac *Stark?*" he growled.

"That's right," John Stark said. "*Mister* Isaac Stark. We have the same last name."

Isaac smiled through tight lips.

"Where I come from," Freitag said, "there ain't no niggers get called Mister."

"Then you'd better go back where you come from," said John Stark.

"Would if I could." Freitag's tone was surprisingly affable, almost off-handed. "But where I come from ain't there no more, thanks to Mr. Lincoln and Mr. U. S. Grant."

"That's a good thing, I'd say, and not something I can help you with. Nor would I if I could." Above the edge of his beard, John Stark was livid. "Now, you'll please remember that in my store, this man is Mr. Stark. And that he's a Negro, if you need to comment on that at all."

Daniels jumped forward, in front of Freitag; Stark saw him kick the big man on the shin. "Mr. Stark, as I said, I came to talk with your son, but if he isn't here, I would like to talk to you."

Stark noticed the change from we to I.

"The actual reason I came out to Sedalia was to see Scott Joplin. Do you know him?"

"Certainly. He's a fine young man, and a very talented musician."

"He's also a very talented composer. You may know, we brought out a piece by him earlier this year, 'Original Rags,' and we'd like to publish the work he's doing now, a ballet called *The Ragtime Dance*." Daniels leaned forward and lowered his voice, like he was about to pass along some important secret of state. "Ragtime's the coming thing in popular music, Mr. Stark—you must hear people talking in your shop. Joplin's got maybe fifteen different rag tunes in this ballet of his. I want to set them up into separate pieces and publish them one at a time. If they catch on, maybe someone will stage a performance. And then Hoffman could put out a folio."

Stark wondered if he'd missed an important point somewhere. "That's well and good, but I don't understand why you're talking to me about it. Why don't you discuss the matter with Mr. Joplin?"

From behind Daniels, Freitag let go another snort. Daniels gave him another, backward, kick. "I just did. Or, maybe I should say I tried talking to him. I offered what I thought were generous terms, three hundred dollars for the whole work. But Scott said he won't publish unless he gets a royalties contract and retains performance rights."

Stark smiled more widely than strictly necessary. "Well, good for him. Sounds like he wants a cut of the profits. What's wrong with that?"

Freitag pushed past Daniels. "What's wrong is that Hoffman ain't about to give royalties to some piss ant Knee-grow composer who thinks he's the whole cheese. And anyway..." A sly smile spread across his face. "Joplin's got himself a bug up the ass on account of Charlie's name was on 'Original Rags' as the arranger. Dumb coon, he ought to fall down on his knees and kiss Charlie's feet for all the time Charlie spent making those chicken-scratches over into something a white man could read and play."

Stark glanced at Isaac, then leaned across the counter and stuck his face right into Freitag's. "A man who talks like that is not welcome in my store. You come in stinking of liquor, insult my associate, who is your superior in every respect I can imagine...now, sir, you will apologize." He swept a hand toward Isaac. "Or you will get yourself out of my store, right now. I may be twenty years older than you, but I'm capable of giving you the thrashing you deserve. And I'd be only too glad to do it."

Charlie Daniels sighed, deep, loud, long. That old man was built like a tree trunk. Daniels didn't doubt for an instant that he could and would pound Freitag, that moron, within an inch of his life if matters didn't get squared away fast. And that would be the end of any possibility of hitching horses with Will Stark over Joplin's music. Daniels had his mouth open, ready to apologize for his associate's talk, but Freitag, who'd taken a step backward, out of Stark's immediate reach, spoke first. His piggy eyes shone with cunning. "Now, then, Mr. Stark, let's not get ourselves all hot under the collar. War's been over near-on thirty-five years. Time to get yourself out of that blue uniform."

Stark didn't miss a beat. "Nor will I ever. Not while there are such as you still contaminating the earth with your claptrap."

To Daniels, the air in the store felt heavy, like right before a major storm. Freitag grunted, or maybe he was trying to cover over a belch, but then, of all things, he laughed out loud. "You really did fight in that war, didn't you, Pops."

"I most certainly did," Stark snapped. "I enlisted right after Fort Sumter, and I wasn't mustered out 'til January of '66. Indiana, Company B, First Heavy Artillery. Now, sir, I am still waiting for you to apologize to my associate here."

But Freitag all of a sudden looked like a man having an attack of apoplexy. At the mention of Stark's military service, the salesman's face went near-purple. A blood vessel pounded over his left temple; his eyes bugged. He swallowed hard, a choking sound. "Indiana, Company B... You were in Mobile, then."

"At the end of the war, yes."

"My daddy died in Mobile. Right about the end of the war."

Stark thought the man might be accusing him personally of causing his father's death. "I'm sorry about that, Mr. Freitag. Many good men died in that war...because some of those men believed it was right and moral to keep human beings as slaves."

Freitag bit at his lower lip. Finally, he seemed to get hold of himself. He swallowed again, then set his skimmer straight on his head and thrust his chin into Stark's face. "Wasn't just men who died, Mr. Stark. We had us a way of life where every man and woman knew what was their place, and did their proper part. Emancipation? Might as well have passed a law that said you had to set your farm animals free and let 'em fend for themselves. A whole lot of good Emancipation did for these poor colored. On my daddy's farm, they had work and a roof over their heads and good food to eat. They got took damn good care of. They were safe and they were happy."

He's serious, Stark thought. He believes every word he's saying.

But Freitag wasn't finished. "All kinds of scientists've proved that brains from colored're smaller than a white man's. Colored can't any more look after themselves than a horse or a dog could. Turnin' 'em loose in the world was a cruel thing to do." He pointed at Isaac. "Take your boy there—how's it come to pass that he's gotta work for you, huh? Why doesn't he have his own store…and maybe you work for him? I say he's lucky he found you, 'cause if you weren't looking after him, he'd be dirty and hungry and begging on the streets. That's what my father died for, Mister! To try and stop Mr. Lincoln from destroying a good way of life."

"If it was so good," Stark said quietly, "why did slaves run off whenever they could?"

Freitag's face asked how Stark could be so thickheaded. "Sometimes children run off, right? 'Cause they don't understand. And then you gotta bring 'em back and give 'em such punishment so they don't think of doing it again. I'll warrant you didn't let *your* children run wild as they pleased when they were small, now, did you?"

Stark felt worn out. Years ago, that talk enraged him, but now it seemed like his bucket had gone dry. He privately dismissed his own demand for an apology to Isaac; even if it came, it wouldn't mean anything. He waved a weary hand. Enough.

Daniels picked right up, took Freitag by the shoulders, steered him toward the door. "Go get yourself a drink, Elmo," Daniels whispered. "The train's at six-thirty-three. I'll meet you at the depot."

As the big man disappeared out the doorway and around the corner, Daniels blurted, "Listen, Mr. Stark, I'm sorry. Elmo doesn't speak for me, not in any way." He turned to face Isaac. "He works under me, so *I* will apologize for what he said. That's not the way I talk to anyone, colored or white, and I'm sincerely embarrassed. My first job in the morning will be to talk to Mr. Hoffman, and if Freitag's still working for him after that, I won't be."

Isaac nodded. "That's generous of you, Mr. Daniels, but a man don't need to apologize, except for what he says or does himself. But I do appreciate what you say."

Stark looked around at the big clock up on the wall behind him. "We close in ten minutes," he said to Daniels. "Perhaps you can tell me just why you're here, and how I might help you."

Daniels took in a big breath, then let it out slowly. "Joplin was firm about royalties, and not having anyone's name but his own on the cover. He said he'd been talking to Will, and that Will is inclined to give him the sort of arrangement he wants. But I didn't know you were into music publishing."

News to Stark, though he was not about to let Daniels know that. "Well, a good businessman always looks for opportunity, Mr. Daniels; isn't that so? But to tell the truth, I'm not sure just what arrangements Will might have made with Joplin. You know how it is with young men."

Daniels' cheeks flamed. Isaac chuckled.

"I guess you really do need to speak to Will when he's back from St. Louis."

"I'd like that very much, Mr. Stark. If he really is considering publishing Joplin's music, he might be better off cooperating with a firm as well established as Carl Hoffman, rather than competing with us. I think it would be to everyone's benefit, Joplin's included."

"I will tell my son you were by." Stark looked almost amused. "And I'll give him your message."

Daniels tapped a finger on the counter. "Thank you, sir."

Stark extended his hand, and they shook.

The two Starks watched Daniels walk out. "Guess Will and I need to have a talk," Stark said.

Isaac flashed him a big grin.

"Publishing music's a tough affair." Isaac thought Stark sounded like he might be talking to himself. "We did print up a couple of tunes once, didn't we, back when Will first got the notion to publish. And I don't remember that they did awfully well."

"No, they didn't." Isaac frowned. "But them two tunes... Mr. Stark, you know you ain't never gonna make good cheese outa chalk. Not to mention, we didn't exactly give those tunes any great push."

"Well, but that's part of the problem. It's not enough for a music publisher to figure out what pieces to print and how many copies, he's got to go out to shops and push his line, one day after another. Today's hit is tomorrow's history. We've already got a music publisher in town, and I don't see Austin Perry moving into a mansion. Let Perry—or Daniels there, for that matter—do all that doggoned leg work and take those risks. I'll just go on selling their sheets, and we'll see who comes out better. This store's done very well for my family and me. Won't be long and I'll be retired, and then it'll all be up to Will. If he's got publishing fancies, then *he* can take that fling."

"We both of us know he's gonna do just that," Isaac said. "On'y question is when. All of the time he spendin' in St. Lou these last few months, talkin' with printers and pokin' around in the big music stores? That Will's a real go-getter, always was. He ain't never been satisfied walking on a trail somebody else cut out."

Little chuckle from Stark. "I'm afraid you're right, Isaac. He's not thirty yet. Lord, when I was his age…"

Isaac noticed that suddenly Stark stood straighter, all the slump gone from his shoulders, his blue eyes bright and clear. He seemed to drop twenty years the way a man might take off an overcoat. But then he sagged again. "I'm coming up on sixty, Isaac. That's not when a man ought to be taking new risks in life."

"Oh, stop that talk now, Mr. Stark." Isaac was disgusted. "You got plenty good years left."

"Go on." Stark waved Isaac's words out the door into the street. "Old people need to make room for the young, not get in their way. Another year or two, I'll be ready for the rocking chair."

Isaac seemed ready to argue the point further, but then changed course. "Did you see how that man looked when you told him where you served in the War?"

Stark nodded, but didn't speak.

"I hate sayin' it, Mr. Stark, but I hope we ain't got us some trouble."

Stark glanced at the shotgun under the counter, then turned weary eyes on Isaac. "Maybe not...I hope not. Blast it, I'm too old for any more trouble."

Silence between the two men. Then Isaac said, "Mr. Stark, ain't nobody in this world too old for trouble."

Chapter Three

El Reno, Oklahoma
Sunday, July 16, 1899,
early morning

Brun Campbell found himself sitting up in bed, wide awake. The little alarm clock his father had gotten him so he wouldn't be late for work told him it was a few minutes past one. As suddenly as he'd awakened, he realized he'd somehow come to a decision, a big one. He was going to run away.

Close to a year now since he'd met Otis Saunders in Oklahoma City, and it had been the worst year of his life. Schoolwork, chores, his old friends—none existed for him any more. There was only ragtime music. He played "Maple Leaf Rag" on the piano, over and over and over, struggled with rhythm breaks, fumbled with shifted and shifting accents, fiddled with the bass line. And the more he worked over the tune, the more he heard himself falling short. Like starting to read a book about something you figure is pretty well cut and dried, but the further you get into it, the more you see you really don't know.

All through that long winter of 'ninety-eight into 'ninety-nine, Brun bought every ragtime music sheet he could find in El Reno, not a whole lot. "Mississippi Rag," by someone named William Krell, couldn't hold a candle to "Maple Leaf." But he liked "Harlem Rag," a tune with a good driving bass, written by a colored man from St. Louis, Tom Turpin. He worked his way through *Ben Harney's Ragtime Instructor*, but in the end he felt disappointed. Harney's exercises were no more than a bunch of different songs decked out in syncopation, and "Annie Laurie," even with her beats shifted, could not begin to compare in Brun's mind with "Maple Leaf Rag." Come spring, he found a copy of "Original Rags," by Scott Joplin, published by Carl Hoffman Music Company in Kansas City. He couldn't run home fast enough, but when he played the music, he felt a bit disappointed. Not quite up to "Maple Leaf," he thought, but a fair bit of likeness, and both tunes different somehow from Tom Turpin's piece.

Evenings, Brun usually went out and listened to the colored piano men who played in restaurants and bars. Sometimes an owner let him fill in while the professor went for a stretch, and some nights the boy came home with a dollar or two in tips, which he hid in a poke under his mattress. Once, he got up the nerve to catch one of those professors on his break and ask for ragtime piano lessons. The professor, a hulk named Ollie the Bear, shook his head and rumbled, "Ragtime ain't your music, boy, never will be. Ragtime is colored music. An' until you gets to be a colored boy, you ain't never gonna be able to play it. *Never.* You try an' take my music…" Ollie spluttered, flung his cigar to the ground, pushed his stubbled face into Brun's; the boy recoiled from the spray of saliva and the reek of stale tobacco and whiskey. "*Our* music. *Nigger*-music. You think you wanna steal it huh? Uh-uh. Not offa me, you ain't." Ollie raised one leg, and blew out a long crescendo of a fart. "Now, go on, boy. Get you'self away from here, an' leave me be." Ollie snatched up his cigar, then stomped back into the saloon. Brun dragged his humiliated self home and up to bed.

His performance in school, never anything to write home about, dropped off to nothing at all. In June, just before the end of the school term, his teacher, Miss Logan, a dried-up little spinster with a face in eternal mourning, called in Brun's parents and told them in his presence that he had more brains than any other boy in his class, and if he'd only apply himself, he could be a great success. "Music is all he seems to care about." Miss Logan's voice left no doubt as to just what kind of music she meant.

About that time, Brun commenced to think seriously about running away to Sedalia. Find Otis Saunders and Scott Joplin, get one of them to teach him ragtime piano. The idea raged in his brain like wildfire.

Then, summer. Brun's father got him a job on Calvin Utley's farm just outside town. "Time you learned what the world's really like," Mr. Campbell said. "Farming's tough work. It'll make a man of you." For more than a month, Brun spent six days a week milking cows, feeding horses, slopping hogs, pulling weeds in the corn patch, and being pecked by chickens who didn't cotton to the idea of him taking their eggs. After supper, he took a bath and went directly to bed, too fagged to even think of playing piano, and sorer than boils at the looks his parents gave each other.

One steaming Saturday afternoon, Mr. Utley caught Brun behind the barn, flopped in a shady spot, lollygagging about what it might be like to play piano for a living. Fancy clothes, good money, pretty girls to spend it on… The farmer gave the boy's ears a cuffing like none before, then sent him off to shovel out the pig stalls. At the end of the day, Brun got no more than one foot inside the house before his mother hustled him out to the back yard and made him strip buck naked while she drew a tub of hot water. He scrubbed himself raw and put on clean clothes, but there was no getting rid of the stink inside his nose. Straightway after supper, he dragged himself up to bed, lowered his head onto the pillow, and became insensible.

Next he knew, he was awake, clear-minded, at one in the morning. Out of bed in a flash, into his clothes, muscles complaining every which way he turned. But the exhaustion from the day before was gone. Take a little care, he told himself, go easy. It wouldn't do to wake his parents.

He sat at the wooden table in the kitchen long enough to write a note. "Dear Ma and Pop. It is not that I don't love you, or that I'm ungrateful for what you have done for me." He stopped to think. If his father and mother had any idea where he was headed, the police would likely be waiting to pick him up the minute he arrived. Brun closed his eyes, thought harder. Those stories in the newspapers the old man had been going on about, every night at supper, six months running? Pencil back to paper. "Pa, you always say a man has to strike while an iron is hot. Well, I'm old enough to make my own way now, and I don't aim just to strike, I mean to strike it big. I'm going to Seattle, then up to the Klondike. When I see you again, I'll have enough bags full of gold that none of us will ever have to work again." He signed the note, "Your loving son, Brun." That would do it. He laid the pencil on top of the note, carefully slid the chair away from the table, got up, slipped a couple of loaves of fresh-baked bread out of the breadbox, and wrapped them in a kerchief. Then he slipped out the back door.

The summer night air was warm and fragrant; a three-quarter moon sat low on the horizon. Brun's heart pounded as he followed that moon to the railway depot. He'd hop a freight to Oklahoma City, change there, go through Tulsa and on to Kansas City, then change again for Sedalia. Easy.

But by the time he finally rolled out of Kay Cee, he was feeling a whole lot less enthusiastic. In Oklahoma City, he'd gotten chased by yard bulls, jumped aboard the wrong train, and found himself in Amarillo, not Tulsa. Coming back, he made a worse mistake, climbed into a car where two 'boes lost no time in relieving him of his bread and the little poke in his pocket with more than thirty-five dollars in it, every cent of his tips from playing piano. After the bums shoved him out, he settled himself into a blind baggage car, but as the train rolled out of Tulsa it pulled up short, and a little wooden box full of lead shot flew off a pile and delivered the boy a blow to the ribs that left him gasping and clutching at his side for several minutes. Now, chugging across Missouri out of Kansas City, he huddled behind stacks of lumber, and tried not to think of food. When he had to relieve himself, he turned sideways, opened his pants, and let fly against the wall. He willed himself to stay awake, crawled over to the door, cracked it. Raindrops pattered onto his face.

When he felt the train slow, he stretched his legs and peeked out the crack. In the glow of streetlights, he made out city buildings. Sedalia. He felt dizzy, whether from excitement or hunger, he couldn't have said. Just before the train pulled into the station, he slid the door open far enough for him to squeeze through, then jumped to the ground, a good clean four-point landing.

The rain had stopped, though the air felt heavy enough to swim through. Brun wiped his wet hands on his pants, then started walking toward the buildings and lights he'd seen a few minutes before. All right, he'd lost his food and money, but now his luck was going to change. He knew how to play piano; he wouldn't be hungry or broke for long. He'd get a job and find lodging. And then he'd look up Scott Joplin and somehow talk piano lessons out of him.

But right then, food seemed like the first consideration, and after that, a place to sleep. He even thought a nice tub of hot water didn't sound too bad, and laughed out loud, thinking of his mother's face if she could've heard that particular thought.

Clouds sailed across the dark sky, but a full moon shone uncovered. Brun figured it was probably a little after midnight. His side ached where the box of shot had caught him; he stretched his arms over his head. Hobo life wasn't for him, no sir. Dress in rags, all filthy and smelly? Live by train-hopping and begging food and money? He shook his head. Playing piano, a man could make real good jack, and if he didn't drink it away, he could eat high off the hog, wear spiffy clothes, and when he felt sand in his shoes, travel like a sport inside the passenger coach of a train. Brun was so caught up in his fancies, he didn't notice a log in the weeds at the side of the street. He stumbled, staggered comically, all the while misusing the Lord's name in a most serious manner. Finally, he recovered, and aimed a kick at the log, just to show it who was really boss. As he landed the blow, it occurred to the boy that the log was soft. It shifted just a bit, and by the light of the moon, Brun saw that this particular log wore a long white dress and petticoats.

◇◇◇

Dr. Walter Overstreet wondered just how long this goddamned meeting would go on. Why in all hell had he ever let Bud Hastain sweet-talk him into running for mayor of Sedalia? Overstreet's prize for winning that race was two years of political shit to shovel off his desk every single day, never mind he had an active medical practice to keep up. Today, he'd started with a breech delivery at six in the morning, and what with the usual hospital rounds and house calls, afternoon office visits, a meeting with a bunch of irate citizens, two kids with firecracker burns, and a City Council meeting, he'd gone nonstop until ten that night. By then, he thought he might just be home free, but no. Martha Smith, daughter of George Smith, the founder of his fair city, was having one of her so-called spells. If Sarah Cotton, Martha's sister, had heard what the good doctor said after she'd hung up the phone, he never again would have been allowed to set foot inside the Smith mansion in any capacity. Wearily, he grabbed up his bag, and was off to the huge stone house on East Broadway to dispense smelling salts, a touch of laudanum, and close to two hours of gentle sympathy and encouragement. By the time he dragged himself back, Bud Hastain and John Bothwell were waiting for him in his office, directly below his bachelor apartments. "No," Bothwell told him. "This can't wait until tomorrow. I have appointments all day tomorrow."

Dr. Overstreet slung his bag into a corner, pulled a decanter labeled SCOTCH and three glasses from a little cabinet next to the red-leather armchair behind his consultation desk. Hastain and Bothwell sipped at their drinks, but Overstreet threw his down in one swallow, then refilled his glass.

His visitors glanced at each other, then Bothwell spoke. He was a good-looking man just past fifty, with a full head of dark hair, pompadoured in front, long sideburns and a thick mustache. Dark eyes peered out from below craggy, bushy brows. His bearing and tone of voice never left doubt that if he was not getting his way right then, he shortly would be. "Sorry to keep you up, Doc, but we need to keep moving forward on this State Fair business. We've got to be good and goddamn sure we don't lose the Fair the way we lost out on the Capital."

Hastain, a stocky, light-haired man a few years younger than Bothwell, nodded.

For a moment, Overstreet gave serious thought to asking the two men to leave, then resigning as mayor. Doctors had no business being in politics; he had no trouble imagining what his father would have had to say about that. Two of Overstreet's patients had died that day, one from a heart attack, another from a railyard accident, and now he was supposed to get all worked up about Sedalia's having lost out on the Capital and maybe losing the State Fair as well. But Bothwell and Hastain owned considerable real estate in Sedalia, were officers in banks, operated lucrative farms in the area; if Sedalia failed, the two of them would be just another couple of dime-a-dozen lawyers. That's why Bothwell had got himself elected State Representative from Pettis County, and Hastain had served two terms as mayor. But Bud wasn't allowed to stand for a third term in 1898, so he persuaded his friend, Dr. Walter Overstreet, that it was Walter's civic duty to run for mayor. No worry, Hastain and Bothwell would give him all the help he needed. Some help. When Jefferson City managed to hold onto the State Capital, Sedalia was left holding a large plot of land where the capitol building was supposed to go, and Bothwell and Charlie Yeater, the Pettis County State Senator, were bound and determined that the state legislature would vote that fall to use Sedalia's available acreage as the site for the Missouri State Fair. Not as good as getting the Capital, but a decent consolation prize, one that would bring considerable business into town, year after year. Overstreet had heard so much palaver about cows and sheep and horses, he thought he'd be better off had he gone into veterinary medicine.

"Walter, God *damn* it. Are you listening to me?"

Overstreet, blasted out of his reverie, nodded. "Yes, John, I'm listening to you."

"Well, then, what the hell *do* you intend to do about getting the merchants to support the September street fair? We've gotten off to a good start—even with the rain, we drew a nice out-of-town crowd for the Fourth. But we need to do something big right before the legislature meets to show them we *will* get people to come to the Fair from all over the state. Don't those damn fools on Ohio Avenue understand that?"

Overstreet looked at Hastain, who quickly looked away. The doctor had known Bud a long time, and no question, he was a good man. Hastain knew it shouldn't be up to Overstreet to try to squeeze money out of businessmen to underwrite a street fair. But Bud was not about to take on John Bothwell, not over an issue so important to the senator, and certainly not in public.

"If they don't have the sense to contribute willingly, then get a general assessment passed," Bothwell stormed. "You should be able to talk that through the City Council. If you need help, Bud will give you a hand."

Clear to Walter Overstreet what Bothwell thought of a mayor who'd need help to ram a general assessment through a city council. The doctor set his jaw the way he did when he was about to give holy hell to some drunken yard man who'd beaten up his wife. "Listen to me, John. Most of these businessmen on Ohio, and on Lamine and Osage and Kentucky and every other street, for that matter, are just scraping by. They work from sunup to sundown, and barely make enough to feed and house their families. They're already taxed heavily, and I'm not going to lay another burden on them. It's as simple as that."

Bothwell balled both fists. He lowered his head, the better to glare at Overstreet from beneath his massive brows, a look that usually brought anyone from a naughty child to an erring employee directly into line. But Overstreet had nothing to lose beyond his mayoral office, hardly a deterrent. "Pick out the merchants who are doing well," he said evenly. "Talk to them. Show them it would be to their advantage to sponsor the street fair. But do it yourself. I'm not your errand boy."

Bothwell let out a noise, half-grunt, half-growl, and jumped to his feet. Hastain moved quickly to position himself between the two men. "John, he might have a point. Voluntary contributions from the bigger companies probably would be better. We don't want word getting around that smaller businesses are leaving Sedalia because they're getting taxed past the limit. Besides, Walter really doesn't have the time…" Hastain looked over his shoulder at Overstreet, winked, and turned back to Bothwell. "…or the talent for drumming up contributions. Leave it to me. I'll take care of it."

Bothwell's face contorted in disgust. He glanced at Overstreet, then nodded several times, like he was trying to convince himself. Then he gave Hastain a heavy dose of his famous glare, and said, "All right. I'll be out of town most of the rest of the summer, drumming up support around the state, so I'll leave you in charge here. Just remember, if we don't get that Fair, we might as well board up the city. All the time we've put into the Build Factories Drive, all the calls and letters going out all over the country to convince businesses they should move here, or at least expand? Without the Fair, what are we going to have to bring in that trade? You think the whorehouses down on West Main are going to get respectable businesses to relocate in Sedalia?"

Overstreet worked to keep a smile off his face. He spent a fair bit of time down on West Main, attending to knifings and shooting victims, or a prostitute writhing on her bed, feverish with abdominal gonorrhea, and he could have told John Bothwell about quite a nice number of respectable businessmen he'd spotted on West Main late at night. The doctor liked the lively, syncopated piano music he heard through the open doorways of the saloons and brothels—but then, he was an acknowledged nonbeliever, a member of no church, so why shouldn't he appreciate the music of the devil?

"I think we ought to just close those damn places down," Bothwell snapped. "Battle Row! The clergy all over town are getting louder and louder about it. Hell, even the colored preachers want Main cleaned up."

"Even the colored preachers," Overstreet thought. Jesus!

Bothwell wasn't finished. "Maybe we should listen to them. Until we get that Fair locked up and delivered, this needs to be the cleanest town in the Union."

"Be that as it may," said Overstreet. "You might make the preachers happy, but not a whole lot of other people. Shutting down West Main is probably the best thing you could do to cause trouble." He flashed a sly smile at Hastain. "What do you say, Bud?"

Hastain's face colored, but he laughed. "He's right, John. Get the parlors off West Main, you'll still have the fights and the killings, but they'll be going on all over town instead of just on one street. People will be screaming about how they can't walk out of their houses at night."

Bothwell snorted. "All right, all right. But Walter, you talk to Chief Love, you hear? Make good and goddamn sure he's got cops watching those places."

Overstreet sighed, then nodded, and watched his visitors out the door, then poured himself another belt of scotch and knocked it down. He trudged upstairs, all the while trying to shut out his father's longwinded sermon about sons who stray from their proper medical duties to sully their hands and good names by taking part in filthy political schemes and intrigues. Overstreet shucked his shirt and trousers onto a straightbacked chair, and fell into bed. He was more than weary. He'd been more than weary for a long time.

Young Brun Campbell dropped to his hands and knees, and begged pardon of the woman he'd just kicked. Icy water popped out all over his skin. When the woman didn't respond, Brun wondered had she fainted. Women did that, he knew, with a fair degree of regularity; he'd seen many such performances. A man properly responded by cradling the head of the stricken lady, rubbing her wrists, and giving her smelling salts and sips of water. Brun had neither salts nor water on his person, but he set out to do the best he could. Tall weeds scratched at his hands and face, so he slid an arm beneath the woman's head, and carefully pulled her into the open. Her head flopped like a rag doll's against his chest. Long, dark hair, wet and tangled, fell across her face.

Brun wriggled out of his jacket, folded it and shoved it under the woman's head, then reached for her hand. It felt like putty. He rubbed at her wrist, troublesome because he needed to work around a small locket on a chain. Once again he misused the name of the Lord, then snapped the locket free and without a conscious thought, slipped it into his pocket. He patted the woman's palm, kneaded her wrist hard as he dared. "Wake up, Lady," he whispered. "Please."

Right about then, it began to dawn on him. To look straight into her face, he'd had to twist himself into a most uncomfortable sidewise attitude. The woman seemed to be looking to the right, upward and backward, and when Brun tried to move his own head the same way, he couldn't even come close. He reached a hand behind the woman's head and lifted, whereupon chills coursed through his body. That head felt like it was attached to the rest of the woman only by skin. Any small way Brun moved his hand, the head lolled in a different direction, and the boy got a terrible feeling if he let go too quickly, the woman's head, pretty hair and all, might just come loose and go rolling down the street.

Fighting a strong inclination to cut and run, Brun pulled a lucifer from his pocket and snapped a shaking thumbnail across the tip. On the third try, light flared. Brun brushed the woman's hair to the side, and looked closely into her face. Once, she had been pretty, and not all that long ago. But her gaping mouth and bulgy, staring eyes did a fine job of ruining her appearance. If more was needed, the dark bruise marks over her neck took care of that.

Maybe Brun was never much of a scholar in the classroom, but he had not the least trouble seeing what a disadvantageous situation he'd fallen into. A stranger in town, looking not even close to reputable after his boxcar rides, caught kneeling over the body of a woman very recently choked to death? Didn't take much imagination to see himself looking at the inside of a jail, maybe even at a noose. Best to put as much space between that woman and himself in the shortest possible time.

He blew out the lucifer, grabbed his jacket, whispered a hoarse, "Sorry, Miss," and scrambled to his feet. But as he turned to run, he noticed something gleaming in the moonlight at the edge of the weeds. He sprang past the woman and picked it up. It looked to be some three inches long, in the shape of a musical lyre, and it held small pieces of paper. A money-clip. Brun looked around, no one in sight. He started to shove the clip into his pocket, hesitated, then went through with the act. What were the chances that money-clip would get past the next person who tripped over the body, or the copper who got called when the body was found? Leaving clip and money made less than no sense.

Brun commenced slapping leather along the dirt road. At the first corner, he turned left, then kept close to the edge of the street as he flew past dark houses and vacant lots. A sudden loud noise froze him for a moment, but then he realized it was just a horse tethered in a back yard, and he took off afresh. A couple more blocks brought him to the business section of town. To his left were dark buildings, shops and banks; to his right, lights and the sound of human voices. He turned right and slowed his pace to a rapid walk. A half-block along, just past an alleyway, he came up on a saloon, Boutell's, according to the gold block letters on the window. Maybe he could sweep up or wash some dishes for food. He took just long enough to smooth down his hair, then pushed through the swinging doors.

Boutell's Saloon was a small room, occupied right then by five men at the bar and another twenty or so sitting around five oak tables, drinking and playing cards. Customers and bartender were all white. A couple of geezers in blue shirts and overalls stood at the far end of the bar, nursing glasses of whis-key and taking turns feeding nickels into a little counter-top slot machine. No dice, no girls. Just a quiet watering hole for Sedalia's working men.

Against the far wall stood an upright piano, no one at the stool. Brun's spirits took a sharp turn upward—that piano was not there for decoration. Just about every refreshment parlor had its piano player, but they were not what you'd call steady citizens. Odds were at least fair that Boutell's was in the market for a musician.

Brun started toward the piano, but then considered that a bit of discretion might be in order, so he reversed direction and ambled to the bar. The bartender, a hefty man in his fifties, slouched against a keg as he wiped his face on a towel. A sparse crop of stringy gray hair crowned his head, and he was permanently stooped to the right, as if to accommodate to his work. He sized Brun up over the towel in his hand, then said, "Out a bit late, ain't you, sonny?"

One of the graybeards in overalls at the slot machine let out a rheumy cackle. Another man, well-dressed, with dark hair and a neatly trimmed Vandyke beard, studied the new arrival from his stool at the bar. Brun figured him for some kind of drummer.

"These are my customary hours," the boy said, as boldly as he knew how. He pointed at the silent piano. "I play, and am looking for work."

The barman's lips twisted into a crooked smile. "You're not from here."

Brun cursed himself mildly for not having considered this question in advance. For one thing, the bartender might know at first hand any place Brun mentioned; for another, a lot of people paid close heed to a man's speech. The War was over some thirty-five years, but in Missouri or Kansas, the way you spoke a sentence might still get you either a pat on the back or a dose of lead in the belly.

"Arkansas City," Brun said, which was where the Campbells had lived before El Reno. "I played piano in hotels and saloons."

The barkeep tipped his head and gave the boy a long, hard stare. "You're how old?"

"Almost seventeen." Brun stuck out his hand. "My name is Brun Campbell. I was a student for a little while of Otis Saunders. You know him?"

Brun's hand disappeared inside the bartender's paw. "Gaylord Boutell," the man said. "Sure I know Otis Saunders. Didn't know he ever was to Arkansas City, though."

Brun told himself not to talk too fast. "Actually, I met him one day last summer while I was in Oklahoma City. He showed me how to play a tune by Scott Joplin. Now, I'm bound to meet Scott and get him to give me lessons. But I'm going to need work."

Boutell wagged a hand toward the piano. "Let's hear that tune Saunders taught you."

As Brun strode to the piano, his stomach growled. He sat, stretched his back and fingers, then commenced to play.

All through the smoky saloon, people stopped drinking, talking, playing cards. When Brun wound up "Maple Leaf" with a little flourish, there was great general whistling and shouting. The boy heard an old man's voice carry above the crowd, "My eyes must be goin' bad. I swear that's a white kid, but way he plays, he's gotta be a nigger."

Brun once told me that no compliment he ever received pleased him more. Boutell called out, "Pretty good. What else can you play?"

"Whatever you want to hear," Brun called back.

"'Old Oaken Bucket,'" someone shouted.

Brun swung around and played that awful song, but he ragged it, the way he'd learned from Ben Harney's folio. "Damn hottest oaken bucket I ever heard," somebody shouted. "Betcha can't do that with 'In the Baggage Coach Ahead,'" someone else hollered.

"You're going to lose your money, sir," Brun called over his shoulder, and swung into that sloppy little tearjerker about a man on a train, taking his wife's body home for burial, who gets help from the other passengers in caring for his crying baby. But written as the tune was, in straight waltz-time, it was no trick for Brun to ring in some syncopation, and the longer he played, the louder got the hoo-ing and the hah-ing and the wow-ing. That gang in the bar thought Brun was some kind of sweet onion. When he finished "Baggage Coach," people fell all over themselves calling out their favorites, and the boy played every one, lively cakewalks, grand marches, mush even more sentimental than "Baggage Coach." Finally, Boutell called him back up to the bar. As Brun shoved his way through the crowd, men slapped his back and shoulders. Some pushed coins into his hand. By the time he reached the bar, he was giddy with pleasure. "Yes, sir?" he asked Boutell.

"You play all right," the barkeep said. "How long you been in town?"

"Not two hours, sir. First thing I came in, I saw your lights and the piano, so I figured to strike while the iron was hot."

Boutell grinned. "Well, son, I got to say, I admire your get-up-and-go. But I got a regular player. He's just off tonight."

"I'm sorry to hear that, sir," Brun said, thinking he'd never spoken truer words. But he shut up in a hurry when Boutell slid a thick ham sandwich across the bar. "What'd you say your name was again?" the barkeep asked.

"Brun. Brun Campbell."

"Okay, Brun. You look like you could use a meal." He pushed the plate with the sandwich right under the boy's nose, then drew a beer and set it next to the plate. "Like I said, you play all right. But even if I was looking for a piano man, a boy your age…" He stopped just long enough to let on he knew Brun was younger than almost seventeen. "…shouldn't oughta be playing piano nights in a saloon. He oughta have a right job. Now, I happen to know that Mr. John Stark needs a boy to help with sales in his music store. Over to East Fifth, across from the courthouse."

Brun couldn't hold off one second longer. He grabbed up the sandwich and ripped off a huge bite. His mouth filled with saliva, his eyes teared. Boutell talked on. "Mr. Stark will treat you right. I know him well—been coming around for a beer and some talk just about every afternoon after work for, oh, fifteen years. Go to his shop tomorrow, it's Number 114 Fifth, if I'm not mistaken." Boutell stopped long enough to watch Brun chew. His eyes softened, and that crooked smile broke out again. "Here, I'll write it down for you." He pulled a piece of paper from a small pad, scribbled on it, laid it on the counter next to Brun's plate. "Tell Mr. Stark that Gaylord Boutell sent you."

Brun took up the paper, said, "Thank you," then pointed at the sandwich and the beer. "What do I owe you?"

The saloon-keeper shook his head. "My players get tips *and* food."

Brimming with food, beer, and his good luck, Brun thanked Boutell again. "I'll go talk to Mr. Stark in the morning, I definitely will. But can you tell me one more thing? Where can I find Otis Saunders and Scott Joplin?"

Boutell laughed. "Easy enough. Just go to the Maple Leaf Club." He pointed back over his shoulder. "Down Ohio, the other way from Stark's, turn on East Main, then one block across. Club's pretty much closed down for the summer, too damn hot up on that second floor for dancing, even at night. But most days, late in the afternoon, you'll find your friends there, playing piano. Sometimes just the two of them, sometimes with other colored. Something you oughta know, though…"

"What's that?"

Boutell chewed at his lip. "Main Street gets pretty rough after dark, Brun. Any kind of action a man wants, he can get it there. Daytime, you got no worries, but down on Main after sunset, you watch what you say and what you do. You watch, period. And north of Main, past the tracks, that's Lincolnville, where the colored live, so you don't go beyond Main after dark. Don't get me wrong, white and colored get on well here, always have. Never been a riot in Sedalia, never one single lynching. But you know how it is. Takes only one bad apple."

"Thanks," Brun said. "I'll be careful. It's pretty much the same in Arkansas City."

Boutell raised an eyebrow. "Yeah, I guess. Just one more thing…" The barkeep picked at a fingernail. "I know it ain't the usual, but seeing you're as young as you are, I think if you want piano lessons off Scott Joplin, you'll be smart to call him Mr. Joplin. Not that he'd ever tell you to, no colored'd do that.

But if I was you, I wouldn't go calling him Scott right off. If that wouldn't bother you."

"Doesn't bother me the least," Brun said. "I sure do appreciate your help."

Boutell went back to serving customers; Brun went back to his sandwich. But as the boy chewed, he started feeling uneasy. He turned and found himself looking into the face of the man on the stool to his right, the one he'd figured for a drummer. Nice, finely checked suit, ascot tie nice and straight, celluloid collar still stiff, even that late in the day. Not a scuff on his black shoes. A real dandy. But his eyes were gentle, not like most drummers'. "If you don't mind, young man…Master Campbell, you said?"

His voice was mint juleps and honeysuckle. He looked to be in his middle-forties, not old enough to have fought in the war. But if he had, no question what color he'd have worn. "Yes, sir. Brun Campbell." He stuck out his hand.

The dapper man swiveled on the stool to face Brun directly, then grasped his hand. "Edward Fitzgerald. I'm pleased to make your acquaintance. I gather you're newly arrived in town?"

"Couldn't be much newer, sir." Brun began to wonder and worry just a bit as to just what the man was after.

"You're a runaway, aren't you? If you don't mind my asking."

Was he a Pinkerton? In town on some other business, a Pink would've been glad to pick up a runaway boy, return him to his family, and walk away with his wallet a bit fatter. Brun regretted having told the man his actual name, but seeing he'd already given it to Boutell, he was caught between a rock and a hard place. "No, sir," Brun said. "Not a runaway. I can't exactly say my parents liked having me leave, but they knew I was bound and determined to—"

"Take piano lessons from this Mr. Scott Joplin?"

Brun fought a strong inclination to tell Fitzgerald to mind his own damned business. But without knowing just what that business might be, he figured better to play along. "Yes, sir," he said quietly.

"That's good," Fitzgerald said. "I'm glad to hear your parents are not worrying, fearful of what might have happened to you. Though of course they always *will* worry anyway." He laughed lightly, a gentle breeze off the Swannee River. "I have a son, myself, not nearly as old as you. But I pray he'll never run off from home, leaving me no idea where he is or what he's doing. Please do keep in touch with your parents."

The sadness that appeared in and around Fitzgerald's eyes gave him the look of a man who'd given up all hope of ever coming face to face with the happiness he'd once expected to find in his life. The boy felt a catch in his throat, quickly took another bite of sandwich, chewed slowly. "I will, sir."

Fitzgerald took several seconds to look Brun up and down. "I should guess you haven't been traveling in a passenger coach."

"No, sir. I might've done that, but truth, a couple of 'boes robbed me two nights ago, took every cent in my poke. So I had to make my way here best as I could. Boxcars."

By the pain in his eyes and the little smile that struggled around the corners of his mouth, Brun thought Fitzgerald looked like he himself was the one who'd been robbed. "Well, Master Campbell, I declare. You *are* a most determined young man."

Brun put the rest of the sandwich into his mouth, chewed, swallowed. "I am that, yes, sir."

"But nevertheless," Fitzgerald went on. "You have just arrived in town, and you have no money. Where do you propose to spend the night?"

Uh-oh. All of a sudden Brun thought he might know why Fitzgerald was showing all this interest in him. Just the year before, a man in El Reno had earned himself a tar-and-feather suit and a one-way ticket out of town because of what he did to a boy he'd coaxed into a hotel room. "It's warm enough, sir," Brun said. "I can sleep out-of-doors, maybe in a field, or I can find me a barn. At least until I make enough money to get a room in town."

Fitzgerald threw back the last of his drink, set down the glass, then looked squarely at Brun. Brun glanced at Boutell, but the bartender was talking with a customer. "Y'all come with me," Fitzgerald said. "The YMCA is just down the block. For a quarter a night, you can get a decent bed there." He lowered his voice. "And a bath. I'll see you to a week's lodging. With your spunk and resolve, I expect by then you'll be able to attend to your own needs."

"I couldn't permit you to do that, sir," Brun said, talking considerably faster than his usual.

But Fitzgerald waved him off. "I admire your courage." He pronounced the word coo-rage, and drew it out to several seconds. "If you wish, you may consider it a loan, payable without interest when your circumstances are comfortable. It's what I'd hope someone might one day do for my own son." He slid off the stool.

Brun was surprised at how short the man was, not more than five-seven, though he stood very straight. "Let us not discuss it further, Brun. The Y is just a short way down the block. I'll take you there and get you your room."

Brun figured if the man tried anything funny, he could handle him. Fitzgerald was not only small, but slender, and clearly not heavily muscled. And behind those fine Southern manners, there was such a tiredness about him. What if the guy really was on the level? Wouldn't it be a whole lot better to sleep that night in a YMCA bed than in a hayloft, or between rows of corn?

Brun slid off his stool, and said, "Are you local? If you don't mind me asking."

Half-hearted chuckle. "One must consider a little turnabout to be fair play, isn't that so? No, I live in Buffalo, New York. I'm here to investigate certain prospects for my employer."

"But you don't hail from New York. Not the way you talk."

Fitzgerald pulled himself even straighter. "No, of course not. I'm proud to say I hail from Maryland. My family there goes back to the sixteen hundreds."

And, he said without actually saying it, every one was a fine and upstanding gentleman, or a noble and gracious lady. Which Brun thought probably went a long way toward explaining his appearance. Trying to live up to that sort of heritage every minute of every day *would* get to be exhausting. Maybe better to have at least a few horse thieves among the heroes in your ancestry.

In the end, Brun's concern turned out to be unnecessary. His Southern-gentleman benefactor walked him up to the desk at the YMCA, put down a dollar and a half (twenty-five cents off for a week's payment in advance), then bid him good-bye and wished him good luck. As he left, he pressed three dollar-coins into Brun's hand. "A young man looking for work needs to eat well," said Fitzgerald. "You will make a far better impression if you don't look as if you're starving. And…" That tired little laugh again. "Your piano teacher just might expect you to pay for your lessons." Brun watched him out the door, then took the key from the bald, scaly-faced little desk clerk, went up to his room, stripped down, wrapped a towel around himself, and walked down the hall to the bath room.

With some reluctance, Brun admitted to himself that the bath actually did feel good, cold though it was at that hour. And the bed was far more comfortable than the floors of the freight cars he'd stretched out on for the past couple of nights. He fell directly into a heavy sleep, so satisfying that when a bell commenced a terrible clanging, he managed to bury his head under the pillow and put the noise aside. But a while later, a steam whistle showed no mercy whatever, just blasted the boy up and out of bed. The clanging, as Brun shortly found out, was the courthouse bell, which rang six days a week at six in the morning. The whistle came from the MoPac railroad shop, and blew seven.

Brun yawned and stretched, then pulled the chamber pot from under the bed and relieved himself. Too early to go talk to Mr. John Stark, so the boy wandered down to the communal room and sat through morning prayer service, not out of piety or anything resembling sincere interest, but because it was the price of the Y's egg and pancake breakfast, payment in advance. The boy's attention wandered; he gazed out the open window at the growing crowd along Ohio Avenue. A man working a slow route on a horse cart called out, "Rags! Old iron! Bottles!"

The junkman stopped long enough to say a word to a colored man playing an accordion on a street corner, then dropped a coin in the musician's cup. Which set Brun to thinking about the change he'd gotten in tips the night before at Boutell's. He'd never counted it. He reached into his pocket, his fingers touched a little metal object—and his empty stomach lurched. Sitting there on a hardwood bench, half-heartedly joining in "Abide With Me," he remembered the locket and the money-clip. What with the excitement of playing his way into a meal, hearing about the possibility of a good steady job, and meeting Mr. Fitzgerald and getting the room at the Y, he'd forgotten that strangled woman at the side of the road and her possessions he'd made off with. Now, they burned in his pocket like they'd been heated red-hot in an oven.

He downed his breakfast considerably faster than he'd planned, then ran back to his room, locked the door, and laid his booty on the bed. The money in the clip looked like found treasure, two tens, a five, and three singles. Twenty-eight dollars, not a fortune, but a comfortable cushion until his first payday. He heard his mother's voice: "A thief never profits from his ill-gotten gains," but as Brun studied the money-clip, the voice faded. That piece of jewelry interested him no end. It was shaped like a musical lyre, a clever piece of work, about three inches long, half an inch thick. A bit of delicate blue enamel work decorated its base. At first, Brun thought it was gold, but then took notice of the few flecks of gold plating still remaining on the brass body. The boy's fingers picked up on a small irregularity on the back; he turned the clip over, and saw a tiny winding key, like for a watch. He gave it a tentative turn, and felt the pressure of a spring winding; then he pushed a metal button next to the winding key. A simple little tune began to play.

He'd never seen such a thing. He listened until the music stopped, then turned the key and pushed the button again. His first notion had been what the money-clip might bring from a pawnbroker, but now the possibility of pawning his find went altogether out of his thoughts. Women didn't carry money-clips, men did. That poor woman must have struggled, and in the fight, the money-clip probably fell out of her killer's pocket. As musical a city as Sedalia was said to be, the clip could have belonged to any number of people, but since the item would indict its owner as a killer, Brun knew he'd be foolish to pawn it, then have to worry that the wrong person might trace it back to him.

His attention turned to the little gold square, the locket. Brun flipped it open, found himself staring into the wide-set eyes of a blond man with a big round face and a smile that looked forced. The woman's husband? Brun closed his eyes, tried to remember. Yes, there *was* a plain gold band on the fourth finger of her left hand, the hand he'd been massaging like a fool. Did her own husband kill her?

It occurred to Brun that he should go directly to the police station and turn in the money-clip and the locket. He could say he'd been scared the night before, didn't know what to do. But he shook his head. A kid from out of town, a runaway, just arrived on a freight? The cops would give him the third degree, and like as not, by the time they were done, he'd be getting free lodging, courtesy of the county jail, for stealing valuable property off a dead person, maybe even for killing that dead person.

But the money in the clip was no problem. Twenty-eight dollars, not a fortune, but add in the three dollars from Mr. Fitzgerald, and he was close to what he'd left home with a few days before. Didn't his Ma always tell him a person should trust in the providence of the Lord?

Brun thought about stashing the locket and clip somewhere in his room, but the idea made him uneasy, so he put them back into his pocket. Then he washed his face in the basin, went out, locked the door, marched past the communal room and out into the street. While he was going about his business, he'd keep his eyes and ears open, see what he might learn about the murdered woman.

Chapter Four

Sedalia
Wednesday, July 19, 1899, morning

They say the devil once spent a week in Missouri in July, then went back and set up hell to specifications. Only ten in the morning, but the air was already a sopping blanket as Brun worked his way across Ohio Avenue through a steady parade of one- and two-horse wagons, then walked half a block down Fifth, and stopped under a black sign with squared white letters: JOHN STARK AND SON. He took a moment to stare at the window display, then put a swagger into his step and went inside.

Not very different from the Armstrong-Byrd store in Oklahoma City where he'd met Otis Saunders. To his left, racks of music sheets and books ran the length of the store. Two pianos stood toward the rear, flanked by a cabinet organ in a fancy walnut case inscribed with gold designs, and a little pump organ that could be folded up into its own wooden carrying case, like a street preacher might use. The right side of the shop was all instruments. Guitars, mandolins, banjos hung on the wall, brass of every description, a piano-accordion and one with buttons, New Orleans style. All the way in back, behind and to the right of the pianos and organs, a stairway took off and vanished through the ceiling, likely into Mr. Stark's living quarters. Brun's attention quickly focused on a beautiful mahogany grand piano, its lid open, standing just inside the doorway so that any tune an employee or a customer might play would carry out to the street.

A man looked up from behind the counter, greeted Brun with a polite hello, and asked how might he be of help. "I'm looking for Mr. Stark," Brun said.

"You're looking *at* Mr. Stark," said the man.

Brun figured him to be pretty old, about sixty, with the appearance of a successful businessman of that day, neatly groomed hair going gray, and a full, bushy beard that took off southward from the edges of an equally bushy mustache. He wore a dark vest and proper dark bow tie. Deep lines at the corners of his eyes, but those light-blue eyes fixed so intensely on Brun that the boy had the uncomfortable feeling Stark might be able to see inside of him, maybe even right through him, like with those X-rays some German doctor had discovered a few years before.

"What can I do for you, young man?" Stark asked.

Brun thought Stark's voice, a full, deep baritone, was most agreeable. "My name is Brun Campbell, sir," the boy said, smartly as he could. "I'm newly arrived in town, and I met Mr. Boutell last evening. He recommended me to you for a job."

"Oh, he did?" Stark looked amused, ran fingers over the thick hair at the corners of his mouth. "Where do you come from...Brun, is it?"

"Yes, sir. Short for my middle name, Brunson, it's a family name. Brun is what everyone's always called me. Pop once told me I got Sanford for a first name because Ma thought Sanford Brunson Campbell sounded like a justice of the Supreme Court. But truth, I don't think that's ever going to happen."

Stark stifled a grin. Fresh kid, but he had a way. "Well, you never know, Brun. Life's a funny proposition, and you've got plenty of time. How old are you?"

"Sixteen, sir."

"And you are from?"

"Arkansas City."

Brun's heart whacked against his ribs. Those eyes… Quickly, the boy added, "Actually, my family has lived in a lot of places, mostly in Kansas and Oklahoma. We were even in St. Joe for a while, Missouri."

"That's all right, Brun. It really isn't my business, is it? What makes you think you're suited to work in a music store?"

"Music's what I've always liked the most, sir. I play a pretty mean piano, and one day I hope to play piano for my living. And I do get on with people pretty well."

Which clearly tickled Stark. "Yes, I'll own you do. And I'll bet you do play a pretty mean piano. What kind of music can you play?"

"Anything you like."

"That a fact?"

"Yes, sir."

Stark laughed, then pointed toward the piano and stool behind Brun. "All right. Let's hear you play something."

Brun sat himself at the piano, rolled his sleeves, and commenced to play "Maple Leaf." By the time he finished with his customary flourish, hands high above the keyboard, three men and a couple of women who'd wandered inside to listen, clapped and made complimentary remarks to Stark. Which, naturally, Brun appreciated no end. One of the men was colored, an older fellow with a great deal of white wool up top, and a raggedy plaid shirt and overalls. "Hey, Young Mister," the colored man called. "Where you learn jig-music from?"

Brun smiled at the old man. He was getting used to that sort of question, and didn't mind in the least. "That is 'Maple Leaf Rag.' Taught to me by Otis Saunders, and composed by Mr. Scott Joplin. Right here in Sedalia."

"My, my, *my*." The old man raised his eyebrows, protruded his lower lip, and nodded vigorously. "You play as good as any colored I ever did hear."

"Do you have the music for that?" one of the women asked Mr. Stark.

Stark shook his head. "I'm sorry, no."

Brun slid off the stool; the little crowd drifted out the door. Stark stared at Brun, then finally said, "You say Scott Joplin composed that piece?"

"'Maple Leaf Rag'? Yes, sir. At least, according to Otis Saunders." The boy noticed Stark's hands shook. "Did you like it okay?"

"Okay? I should say so, and then some. It's extraordinary. But tell me now, Brun, do you have any experience selling music?"

On the point of lying, the boy stopped himself. Those eyes would pick him right up. "No, sir," Brun said. "But I am a quick learner."

"You are, you say?" Stark pulled at his beard. "Yes, I'll wager you are. You seem a clever young man…perhaps even a little sly? But you've got to be reliable. If you're not, don't waste your time and mine. If you are, I guess I can use you."

"I can be as reliable as required, sir."

Again, Stark tugged his beard. The corners of his mouth bent upward. "Very well, then. If you are both reliable and responsible, I'll employ you part-time, at least to start. One o'clock to five, six days, twelve dollars a week. You'll wait on customers and play piano as needed. If you work out well, we'll talk about full-time employment. How does that sound to you?"

It sounded so good to Brun, it took him a moment to answer. He remembered the way his friends in El Reno fought with each other over jobs in penny-candy stores and bakeries, but picturing himself working in this music shop, he felt envy of no boy or man. "It sounds very good, sir," he said. "Thank you. You won't be disappointed."

"I trust not. And I also trust that since this is a music store, not a music hall, you can play songs I have on sheets to sell."

"I can play whatever you like, sir. And I can play it so people won't be able to take a step out the door without carrying away a sheet."

Stark's eyes opened wide. He laughed aloud. Then he pointed toward the piano and stool. "Let's see."

Brun quickly sat back at the piano and by way of a warmup, knocked out a medley of Stephen Foster tunes, "Old Folks at

Home," "Jeannie With the Light Brown Hair," and "Camptown Races." Then he did a real barnburner of "The Glendy Burk," and, without stopping, turned it up a notch for "Daisy Bell." People walked in off the street, one at a time and in pairs. Brun swung into a lively cakewalk he'd learned a few months before off sheet music from the music store in El Reno. The crowd around the piano buzzed and pointed, and a young woman asked the name of that tune. "It's called 'At a Georgia Camp Meeting,' ma'am," Brun said. "By Mr. Kerry Mills, and it's the hottest new tune around. You can't walk down a street in St. Louis or Kansas City, and not hear it."

The woman turned to Stark and asked him for a copy of the music. Two men said they wanted sheets as well.

After the audience wandered back outside, Stark turned a look on Brun that told the boy he'd sold more than three copies of sheet music. "You've got a mouth on you, but you can deliver the goods. You'll do. But you can't work in my shop looking like you just walked off the last freight into town. Go back to Ohio, turn right, then go three blocks to the corner of Second, the St. Louis Clothing Store. Tell them to fix you up with a decent suit, shirts and a tie. Put it on my account."

Brun was two steps to the door when Stark called after him. "One more thing—where are you lodging?"

"I've got a room at the Y," Brun called over his shoulder.

Stark nodded. "All right, go on, then. Get yourself suited up. I'll see you at one o'clock."

At five minutes to one, Brun walked back through the door and up to Stark, who stood beside the piano, talking to a slim dark colored man in a worn, but clean, white shirt and black trousers. The two men caught sight of Brun at the same time, and the way they suddenly stopped talking and gapped the boy, he knew he had trouble. Stark made that plain in a hurry. "This is a music store, Brun. A respectable establishment."

"I'm sorry, sir," Brun said. "I thought I looked pretty sharp."

The colored man laughed, which did not appear to do anything favorable for Stark's frame of mind. "Sharp, is it, eh? Pink silk shirt? Patterned necktie so loud it could make me hard of hearing? Yellow and black checkered suit bright enough to blind me? Patent-leather shoes with pearl buttons? I guess you'd be just fine if you were going to work in a house of ill-repute, but you're not going to work in *my* store looking like a pimp. Now, get yourself out of here. Go on back to St. Louis Clothing, and…who the hell waited on you, anyway? I'll bet it was Felix, wasn't it?"

"That's right." Brun's voice quavered like an organ pipe. "Mr. Felix Kahn. Big man, tall, very fine manners. Talks like a Frenchman—"

"Blast it, he *is* a Frenchman," Stark shouted. "So are his brothers, but they've got more sense than to sell an outfit like this to one of my employees. Get yourself back there PDQ, and tell Felix to take back these bordello duds and give you a proper outfit to work in my store." He pulled out his watch and glanced at it. "If you're back here and looking decent by one-thirty, you'll still have a job."

In less than two minutes, Brun was inside the St. Louis Clothing Store. Felix Kahn laughed when he heard the problem. "Ah, Meestair Stark, he is so vairy tradeetional, yes? Well, come, come, young man. It would not do to have you lose your new job." He pushed Brun back into the try-on room, and while the boy got himself out of his unrespectable threads, Kahn went off, then came back with two armfuls of dark cloth that Brun thought could in no way have given offense to an undertaker. "Put them on, young man, hurry," Kahn said. "If you or Meestair Stark is not hoppy with ze fit, just come back and we will make adjustments."

The fit was fine, though the dark English worsted suit was heavier than Brun would have cared to wear in the Missouri summer. He tugged at the celluloid collar, then caught himself. For four hours a day, he could handle it. He'd wear his old clothes whenever he could, though it might be a good idea to get the dirt and hay out of them, and have a tailor stitch the holes.

When Brun hustled back into Stark and Son, the clock on the wall behind the counter said one twenty-eight, but John Stark neither looked at it, nor did he check his watch. Just nodded at the colored man, and said, "Well, that's a little better, isn't it?" "Um-hmmm." The colored man was grinning, clearly enjoying the situation. "Looks like a proper young gentleman now, don't he?" He extended a hand to Brun, who gripped it. "I be Isaac, I work for Mr. Stark too."

"Brun Campbell."

Stark raised his eyebrows. "You cleaned up pretty good, Brun. Now, let's get you to work."

Even with the door open, the mid-afternoon temperature and humidity in the store were both well up into the nineties. Still, Brun always remembered that day as one of his happiest ever. He waited on customers, sold some guitar and mandolin strings, a couple of picks, and several pieces of sheet music. He showed a pretty little girl of about nine or ten how to work her way through a Beethoven piano sonata, then said, "Here's what you can play when you finish your regular practice time," and got her and her mother laughing to beat all through a lively "Buffalo Gals." Afterward, Stark patted the boy on the back and said, "You're a natural salesman, Brun. I'm bound to admit, you've got *me* sold."

Toward closing time, Stark gave his new clerk an eye-opener. The boy was showing a low-priced parlor guitar to a young woman of Raphaelitic proportions, when all of a sudden, Stark strode up, took the guitar from his clerk's hands, and commenced to play a very creditable medley of "Old Dan Tucker" and "Weevily Wheat." The old man sang along in that fine baritone voice, "I won't have none of your weevily wheat, I won't have none of your bar-ley." Then he took a second guitar off the wall, and played the same tunes. "You hear the difference?" he asked the woman. "This guitar was made by the C. F. Martin Company, back in Nazareth, Pennsylvania, and it's the best, bar none. For just an extra few dollars, your investment will come back to you many times over in musical pleasure and satisfaction." The Martin guitar went out the door with the woman.

"You're a pretty good country salesman yourself, sir," Brun said. "You sounded darned fine on that guitar."

"Huh! I've been playing those songs for fifty years and more. Don't ask me to play any up-to-date tunes, or I will embarrass myself severely."

"Meaning no disrespect, sir, but I'd bet a man who plays guitar like I just heard could learn any song he set his mind to."

During the exchange, Isaac had walked to the front of the store. Stark scratched at his forehead, and chuckled. "I guess I've always had a knack for bringing music out of an instrument. I grew up on my brother's farm in Indiana, learned banjo and guitar from the free colored, and piano from my sister-in-law. One day I found an old bugle in town, and I figured out how to make noises on that, well enough that when war broke out, I enlisted as a bugler. After the War, I homesteaded a while in northwestern Missouri, and if there's a more dreary life on this earth, I don't ever want to live it. Without my guitar to play of evenings, it would have been unbearable. I finally gave it up, and peddled Jesse French organs, so I had to learn to play those, too. There was a time I aspired to play music for a living, or perhaps teach at some academy, but my skills on any instrument were modest in respect to those goals. Which, I suppose, explains how it is I'm here today, running a music store."

"You was a mighty fine bugler." Brun thought Isaac's face said there was more to the matter, but Stark just coughed, walked over to the register, slipped on his spectacles and began going through receipts.

A little after five, Brun helped Stark and Isaac close up, then took off toward the Y at a gallop. Not that he wanted to take the time, but he thought he'd be foolish to risk wearing his new suit outside the music store. Better to change into his old clothes before going down to the Maple Leaf Club to meet his piano teacher.

Ohio Avenue, which divides east from west in Sedalia, had been a-bustle during Brun's sprints back and forth between Stark's and the St. Louis Clothing Store, but now all the banks, stores and offices were closed for the day, and the street was considerably more quiet. As Brun walked past the sandstone Missouri Trust Building on the corner of Fourth, a clattering caught his attention, and he turned to see a small dog shoot by, a tin can tied to his tail. He made a lunge for the pooch, missed, landed face-down on the sidewalk. Good thing he'd changed out of his suit.

He turned right at Main, hustled past Archias' Seed Store, dodged a wagon to cross over in front of Big Callie's Grocery, then stood and gawked at Number 121. Blocher's Feed Store on the ground floor had closed for the night, but up a story, windows stood open, and bits and snatches of piano music floated out and tickled Brun's ears. No tune he could recognize, but knowing who was likely up there playing it got his legs moving double-time.

The narrow paneled door at the corner of the building stuck, but he tugged it open and ran inside, up the stairs to a landing, then up another flight. Even before he reached the top, butterflies zipped full speed around in his stomach, and ants crawled inside his shirt and trousers. He was hundreds of miles from home, primed to go into a colored social club and ask for piano lessons from a colored man he'd never met. Nor could he know how many colored men he might actually be facing, or how inclined they might or might not be to let a white boy learn their music. What if they were all like Ollie the Bear?

He stood on the landing, listened. Those piano notes and chords didn't sound at all like music. More like the noises Brun used to make himself, his first year of piano lessons. A few melody notes, once, twice, then the left hand came in with a discordant crash, and after that, a few seconds of muffled voices. Then came that same short melody, but a little different now, with a D where the first time he'd heard a G. The idea of doing a quick turn-and-run entered the boy's head, but he said, "No," right out loud, and walked into the room.

Fifty years later, Brun could describe that scene as if he'd been there just the day before. The Maple Leaf Club filled the entire second story of the building. Four great gas chandeliers hung off the ceiling. To Brun's left was a massive bar, all carved walnut, practically covering the northern wall; to his right, three pool tables and several smaller tables for cards and dice. Between Brun and the pool tables, wooden tavern chairs were set around six square oak tables. Straight ahead, Brun saw what he'd come for. A black man sat on a bench, his back to Brun, fingers on the keyboard of an upright piano. Around the player clustered five men, two of whom were white. That pumped up Brun's courage. If he did get sent away, less chance it'd be at the point of a knife.

All five men looked to have their full attention on the piano keyboard. In no particular order, they reached out to hit a note or play a chord, and all of them seemed to be talking at once. Brun had been part of such groups himself. The minute an itinerant piano player landed in a new city, he'd be off to trade music and ideas with the locals.

The air in the room was oppressive, not a puff of breeze coming through the open windows. The thousands of cigarettes and cigars smoked over endless years worked with the mildew on the flaking plaster walls to create a bouquet you'd give only to a girl you wanted to get rid of forever. Brun drove his mind hard to come up with a line Scott Joplin could not possibly refuse, but before he could get his thoughts in line, he unleashed a holy whopper of a sneeze. The piano playing stopped as if Brun had fired a pistol. Five pairs of wide eyes stared at him. The boy stared back, dumbstruck. That sneeze had blown every sensible notion in his head straight out his nose.

The man on the piano stool was very dark, the kind they used to call a blueskin. Close-cropped hair retreated back from his temples. His black suit fit him just so, tie to match, and his collar was spotless. Despite the heat, he looked cool and comfortable. His face asked a dozen questions, but he didn't say a word. The two men to Brun's right, now that he looked closer, were actually boys not much past his own age. One was almost as dark as the man on the piano bench, and with his ragged plaid shirt and ratty overalls, he looked like he'd just come in from farmwork. He sat open-mouthed, his forehead splattered with drops of water. The other boy was lighter-skinned, hair neatly trimmed and parted cleanly in the middle. He had a delicate look about him, lips sharply formed, and eyebrows that could've been painted on. Directly to the left of the piano player stood an older man, hard for Brun to guess his age. Could've been forty, might've been sixty, dark-skinned, with great gleaming teeth and an impressive bay window. Under his jaw lay a huge swelling, but that caught less of Brun's attention than the man's fingers, which looked a good six inches long. Next to him, leaning against the edge of the piano, was a white man, easily the oldest in the group, about John Stark's age. No hair at all up on top, but a thick mess of gray curls on the sides and in back, such that Brun could not have sworn in a court that the man actually did have ears. His face was round and red, lips thick. What with his soiled white shirt, tails hanging free over baggy gray trousers, Brun thought if he saw the man on the street, he might give him a nickel or a dime.

The last man in the group, dapper in a light suit and red-banded straw hat, chuckled. "Well, well, what *do* we got here? You sure got yourself a light step, boy. I didn't even begin to hear you comin' up them steps."

He looked white but talked colored. Recognition dawned in Brun's mind, but before he could say anything, the big man with the goiter and long fingers spoke up. "Sheet, Crackerjack. Noise we was makin' on this poor piano, we wouldn'a heard the U. S. Cavalry comin' up them steps."

Brun strode the few steps to the grinning, duded-up man, and stuck out his hand. "Glad to see you again, Mr. Saunders."

The other men looked back and forth from Brun to Otis Saunders. Saunders squinted hard as he might, then finally took the boy's hand and gave it a ceremonial shake. "Well, young sir, I'm afraid you've got me at a disadvantage. You do look familiar—"

"Oklahoma City, Mr. Saunders. Last August. The Armstrong-Byrd Music Store."

A smile started across Saunders' face.

"You stood me to a fine lunch at Miss Minnie's after you taught me to play 'Maple Leaf Rag.'"

"So I did. So…I…*did!* Well, Mr…"

"Campbell. Brun Campbell."

"That's *right*. Mr. Brun Campbell, make no mistake, a fine young piano player. Now, whatever is it brings you to Sedalia, and how did you chance to find me?"

"Not chance at all," said Brun. "Mr. Saunders—"

Saunders cut Brun off with a wave. "We being friends of some considerable standing, you will please to call me Otis."

"An' when you gets to be his goooood frien', you can call him Crackerjack." That from the big man with the goiter. The others chuckled, all but the black man on the piano bench. He didn't crack a smile.

"Okay," Brun said. "Otis. Like I was saying, it's not chance that I'm here. I ran off from home, just especially to find you. *And* Mr. Scott Joplin."

Everyone looked at the man on the piano bench.

"Are you Scott Joplin?" Brun hoped that what was flying around inside his stomach didn't show on his face.

Joplin nodded. "What do you want with me?"

No fear in Joplin's voice, no antagonism. The man's face was impassive. Just a shirt-sleeve question, and Brun gave him a shirt-sleeve answer. "I want to take piano lessons from you. I want to learn how to play colored ragtime."

Joplin looked up at the older white man, and to Brun's great surprise, the white man commenced to laugh. Joplin's expression didn't change; he seemed to be thinking. But Brun couldn't keep his mouth shut. "Please, Mr. Joplin. Ever since Otis there taught me the 'Maple Leaf,' it's had me by the neck. I played it all winter and spring, I went out and bought all the other ragtime music I could find, and I played and I played, but I just couldn't seem to get any better. Otis told me last year that you and he lived here in Sedalia, so I ran off, just got in yesterday. Today, I got me a job, working afternoons for Mr. John Stark, at his music store."

"You don't waste time," Joplin said. The others laughed again.

Joplin's face stayed a mask, but his voice sounded kind, which heartened Brun. "What do you charge for lessons?" the boy asked.

Joplin held up a hand. "Let's not go quite so fast. You said Otis taught you 'Maple Leaf'? And you've been playing it almost a year now?"

Brun thought Joplin's speech was a thing of wonder. The boy had heard tell of Paul Laurence Dunbar and Booker T. Washington and George Washington Carver, colored who'd gone to school and were making their mark, but he'd never heard any of them talk. Joplin sounded like some kind of college professor who ought to be wearing a fine suit, and have a monocle in front of one eye. Where did he learn to talk like that? Brun finally managed a mumbled, "Yes, sir."

Joplin got up from the bench, and motioned Brun down. "Play it for me, then. Play me 'Maple Leaf.'"

Brun settled onto the hard wooden seat and began to play. He cruised through the A and B strains of "Maple Leaf Rag," no mistakes, but as he swung into the trio section, Joplin said, "Stop." The boy had no trouble making out the intensity of the displeasure in that one word.

Joplin settled himself on the bench beside Brun, then commenced to play "Maple Leaf" exactly as Brun had. The men standing around broke into laughter, all but the old, fat white man. The big colored man with the goiter guffawed so hard, Brun thought he might split wide open.

"Do you hear that?" Joplin asked.

Hear what, Brun thought, and was suddenly soaking in sweat. "I'm sorry, Mr. Joplin, but I don't know what it is you want me to hear."

"I want you to hear just how I played that tune." Joplin swung back to face the piano, then banged out an overdone version of Chopin's "Funeral March," and sang along, "Da, da, da-da, da, da-da-da-da-da-*da*!" Again, everybody laughed, except for the old man. And Joplin. And Brun Campbell.

Brun glanced at Saunders, then turned back to Joplin. "When I played it for Otis there, he told me if you ever heard me play it so fast as I was doing, you were not going to talk pleasant to me. All this last year, I must've played that tune five thousand times…" The boy's voice petered out.

Joplin glanced at Saunders. Saunders' grin wavered. "Working by yourself, you can develop bad habits," Joplin said quietly.

Again, the boy took encouragement from the gentleness of Joplin's tone. "No one would help me. No regular piano teacher would give ragtime the time of day, and none of the professors in saloons and restaurants would give *me* the time of day. Besides, the ragtime those professors played wasn't really like 'Maple Leaf Rag.' I liked it good enough, but…"

Otis Saunders smiled openly, put a hand to Brun's back. "You remember how you played that music before I said you was playing too fast?"

"Yes. I played it like all the professors played *their* ragtime."

"Well, then, show the man. Go on, now."

Brun thought he might rather just crawl out the door on his hands and knees, but he went to work and hammered out "Maple Leaf Rag," somewhere between double and triple-time. After only six or seven measures, Joplin tapped his shoulder. "All right, that's enough. Let me show you something." Just for a second, Joplin stared at his friends, a warning, Brun thought. Then the composer looked directly at the boy. "My ragtime *is* different from barrelhouse ragtime. My ragtime has form—it is classical music. Of course there are syncopations and flatted sevenths, but they are set into a structure as well defined as any waltz Strauss ever wrote."

He stopped just long enough to shoot a glance at that fat, smiling old white man, who then said the first word Brun had heard from him. "Pre-cisely." With some kind of foreign accent.

Joplin spoke on. "And just as you would not play a Strauss waltz in either rapid-march time or funeral-march time, you should not play ragtime too slow *or* too fast. Do you remember the time signature I wrote at the top of my manuscript?"

Brun shook his head.

"*Tempo di marcia*! Spirited and lively, but closer to *allegretto* than *allegro*. Certainly not *presto*. And you should not accent the beat to the point of a march. The music itself will carry you along, if you only let it." Joplin played a few bars, banging the bass as Brun had, then said, "Watch my left hand closely." Then, he replayed the passage. "You see?"

"Yes. Your left hand does strike harder. But only a little."

"And you hear the difference?"

Brun nodded. "Yes."

"Look at it like this, boy." The man with the goiter talked like he had gravel in his throat. His grinning face was smeared with mischief. "It be like with a woman. You don't wanna go an' rip off her beautiful clothes, now do you? Nicer, you open up that dress, one button at a time."

Brun felt his face go red. He'd done a bit of fumbling with buttons behind barns and in cornfields, but had never been permitted to go exploring below the equator. The two young black men smiled, and made a point of looking anywhere but at him. Otis Saunders snickered. "Hey, now, Froggy—what you think this li'l boy know about women, huh?"

Scott Joplin's expression never changed. Brun wondered if the man ever smiled.

Saunders clapped Brun's shoulder. "Now, I am just coming to see, we ain't got us no manners, do we, young Mr. Campbell? You know me, and you just met Mr. Scott Joplin. And this here is

Mr. Arthur Marshall and Mr. Scott Hayden." Saunders pointed first at the dark young man in the ragged clothing, then at the lighter one. "They both fine piano players, even if they still be wet behind they ears. Mr. Joplin's showin' them how to play and write his kind of ragtime music."

Envy such as Brun had never felt clutched at his throat and his temples. But he managed to smile and shake hands with each of those fortunate boys, and tell them he was pleased to know them. First Marshall's face, then Hayden's, told Brun how unaccustomed the colored boys were to exchanging social pleasantries with whites.

"And then this great philosopher here..." Saunders stuck a finger into the fat man's belly, and wiggled it with fake malice. "This here's Big Froggy. Plays Number One piano at Miss Nellie Hall's, over to West Main...where they th'ow you out in the street if'n you try'n open up more'n one button at a time."

Brun's smile left Joplin as the only person in the room with a straight face. The composer pointed at the mussy white man. "This is Professor Julius Weiss, my teacher and my friend." Joplin's tone was one a person might use to introduce a king, or at the least, a duke. "Without Professor Weiss' help, I would not ever have—"

Weiss waved his hand back and forth like he might've been chasing a pesky horsefly. "Nah, nah, nah, Scott. That is not true. A genius like yours would have succeeded with or without any help from me."

"So what you say, then, Scott?" Saunders talking now. "You gonna take on this boy?"

Joplin stared at Brun, not a word. Impossible to know what was going on behind that mask of a face. Then he glanced up at Weiss, who turned a smile on him like the sun bursting out from behind a cloud.

"Boy lef' his home and come all this way, just to take lessons from you," growled Big Froggy. "How old was you, first time you go on the road?"

Joplin held up a hand to Froggy. "I didn't say I wouldn't take him on." He fixed his eyes on Brun, eyes so black, deep and burning, that the boy struggled not to squirm. "You will have to work hard. Before and after you go to work at Mr. Stark's, you'll need to practice regularly...*religiously*. If I ever see you are less than serious, that will be the end of our association."

"If I can learn how to play ragtime your way, and maybe write it... Mr. Joplin, I never even dreamed of writing it. But if I could do that, well, I think my life will be worth living."

Brun surprised himself no end by that speech. He didn't know he had words like that in him. Maybe Scott Joplin had a knack for pulling such out of people.

"What hours will you be at Mr. Stark's?" Joplin asked.

"One in the afternoon 'til five, sir."

Mutters rumbled through the group, but no particular words. Probably the first time anyone in that room had heard a white call a colored "sir." But Brun would have sworn on anything holy that he was not trying to curry favor with Joplin. The word just came out. Whatever color the man was, his dignity was overwhelming.

Joplin didn't seem to notice, just nodded and said, "All right, then. Morning is the best time for lessons. I'll meet you here at eleven, Tuesdays and Fridays. My fee is a half-dollar per session, payable at the time." He made a point of looking at the hole in the right knee of Brun's trousers. "Is that agreeable?"

Brun barely managed a blubbery "Yes, sir."

"Where will you practice?"

Now, there was something Brun hadn't thought of. He'd need a piano, one that would not be in use, and where he'd have privacy to work out troubles without embarrassing himself. "Maybe Mr. Boutell would let me in his place mornings so I could play," Brun said. "And Mr. Stark might let me stay in the store after hours."

Scott Hayden spoke for the first time. "Where you stayin'?" His voice was soft as any girl's.

"Got a room at the Y."

Big Froggy burst out laughing. "Guess they wouldn't be much inclined to let you play there."

"Not the devil's music, no way." Saunders looked as amused as Froggy, but then his face went serious and he said, "Wait, now. Wait a minute. Mr. Robert Higdon…don't him and his sister got a couple empty rooms in that house of his? And he sure got a piano. If you ask him, Scott, I bet he'd take in our boy as a lodger. He could practice there after supper, and mornings, when Mr. Higdon's to work."

"Don't Mr. Higdon got his niece stayin' there over the summer?" asked Arthur Marshall.

"What if he does?" Saunders looked like a kid who'd got the cookies out of the jar and the lid back on before his mother walked into the kitchen. "That's not a bad-sized house. Oughta be enough rooms for four people without crowdin' em. An' anyway, I don't expect the close company of a nice young lady would trouble our new friend very much, do you?"

Everyone looked away from Brun. Froggy cleared his throat. Not at all smart those days for a colored man to say anything even remotely complimentary to or about a white woman. Even Joplin wiggled a bit on the piano bench. Brun smiled hard, then said, "I don't guess that would trouble me at all. And it'd be swell to have a piano right there."

Joplin gave Saunders a short, stern look, then turned to face Brun. "I'll talk with Mr. Higdon tomorrow, at his office. Then, I'll stop at Mr. Stark's to let you know what he says. In any event, I will expect you here Friday at eleven." He paused, glanced at Professor Weiss, then went on. "There are some who say a white man can never play proper ragtime, but I don't believe that. I hope that you and I can prove how wrong it is."

"I won't make you sorry, sir."

"You don't need to call me sir." Joplin reached into his pocket, tugged, and came out with a red rubber ball, which he put into Brun's hand. The boy looked him a question.

"This will help your technique," Joplin said. "You can get one at Mr. Messerly's General Store, over on Osage. Put it into your pocket, and whenever you're just walking or sitting around, take it out and squeeze it, first with your right hand, then with your left. Then hold the ball between your hands and push them together. Start off easy, and squeeze harder and harder as you go. That will build the muscles in your forearms, hands and fingers. You've heard of Bernarr McFadden, haven't you? The physical culture man?"

Brun nodded. "Well, sure. I guess everyone has."

"He grew up here in Sedalia," said Joplin. "And while he was back for a visit a couple of years ago, I went by and asked him whether he could give me some exercises that might improve my playing. I'll admit, I did wonder when he told me to squeeze a rubber ball, but inside a month I could see a real difference in my piano work. So I recommend it to all my students."

Hayden and Marshall looked at each other, grinned, then each pulled a rubber ball from his pocket and held it up for Brun to see.

Curious, Brun thought. Joplin was a good deal younger than Froggy, and not all that much older than Saunders, but he was without question the leader of that group.

Joplin put out a hand; Brun dropped the rubber ball into it. "I'm sorry, but I need to get back to work now," Joplin said, and turned back to the piano. "I'll see you Friday at eleven." He was already hitting keys by the time Brun said, "I'll be here."

Chapter Five

Sedalia
Thursday, July 20, 1899, noontime

Next morning, Brun's four wild days and nights finally caught up with him. When he opened his eyes, bright light filled his room, and when he peered out the window, he saw the sun was close to straight overhead. He hadn't heard the courthouse bell, had slept straight through the rail yard whistle. The boy jumped out of bed, washed up, dressed in his new suit, and hurried up Ohio to the Boston Café, where the clock on the wall behind the counter told him he'd be late for work in thirty-five minutes. He took a seat, ordered a stack of pancakes and a cup of coffee, then picked up a newspaper someone had left on the counter, and commenced to read. On the first page, between an account of Admiral Dewey's lawsuit asking pay for destroying the Spanish Fleet, and an editorial chastising the city's merchants for not supporting an upcoming street fair, a short article caught the boy's eye. A young woman had been found the morning before on Washington Avenue, apparently murdered by strangulation. There was no identification on her body, and no one in Sedalia had reported a missing person of that description. Chief of Police J. E. Love asked anyone with information about the woman to come forward.

As the young waitress set Brun's food in front of him, he quickly snapped the paper closed. The girl flashed him that smile unmarried young women have always given attractive and apparently unattached young men, then said, "Sorry if I gave you a start. You must've been real interested in what you were reading there."

"Nah, not really." Brun fingered the outside of his trouser pocket. "Kinda daydreaming, I guess."

The waitress' smile broadened. "You're new in town, aren't you?"

Brun nodded. "Just got here a couple of days ago. I'm working at Stark and Son, music store on Fifth."

"Sedalia's a nice place to live."

The girl was far from unattractive, probably about his own age, shiny black hair, blue eyes, nice clear skin, but right then, Brun wanted only for her to go away. He broke off a chunk of pancake with his fork, shoveled it into his mouth, chewed, swallowed, willed a smile. "Y' got good pancakes in Sedalia." Then, he picked up the paper in his left hand, and began to read, this time an article about a Negro man, Frank Embree, accused of outraging a young white girl, then escaping to Kansas, where the governor refused to extradite him without a guarantee he'd get a fair trial, and not be lynched.

The waitress' smile faded. "Let me know if you need anything else."

Brun nodded to the girl's back. He slipped a hand into his pocket. What was he going to do with that locket and money-clip? Go out of town after dark and bury them in the woods? That wouldn't help anyone, himself included. How about sneaking off to another town and pawning the things there? But when? Between his job and piano practice, his available daytime hours were pretty well spoken for. Maybe best right now to sit tight until they either catch the killer or get interested in something else and forget about the dead woman. Then, Brun could do as he pleased.

That afternoon, business was slow, so Stark set Brun to learning the stock, which the boy found slow and tedious. Much more fun to play piano or wait on customers, but remembering

Mr. Utley's pig troughs was more than enough for the boy to set himself hard to his task.

Toward midafternoon, he was standing before the mandolins on the wall, reading the manufacturers' hype and hustle papers, when he heard a woman's voice behind him. "Excuse me, sir. Can you please help me?"

The words came on a wave of gardenia. Brun turned around and found himself face to face with a vision in blue cotton and lace. Not much over twenty, curly ash-blonde cascades down over her shoulders and a smile he imagined he might see in his dreams that night and for nights to come. Gray eyes soft as velvet, white teeth, and blooming cheeks. The young woman's lipstick and face powder were applied with more enthusiasm than was customary those days, and she wore eye shadow, a daring advance. Brun thought of a ripe juicy apple, just ready to be bitten into.

"Well, hello," the vision said. "I haven't seen you here before...oh, I hope I haven't made a mistake. You do work here, don't you?"

"My second day," Brun said, and looked around. Stark was inside his little office back of the counter, and Isaac was nowhere to be seen. Probably delivering an organ or a piano, or out on a break. The boy worked to keep his pleasant smile from stretching into an idiot's grin. "What can I help you with, Miss?"

She pointed toward the racks of piano folios and lesson books. "I'm looking for *Wiley's First Piano Studies*, it's usually right up in the rack over there. I have two new students starting this afternoon."

"We ran out," Brun said, then, before the young woman could do more than look concerned, he added, "but we have new copies, still in the carton. I'll get them for you."

Brun considered that knowing the stock might actually be a good idea. The books had just come in that morning's mail, and he had intended to put them on the shelf once he'd finished looking over the stringed instruments. He hustled up behind the counter, grabbed a couple of books from a carton on the floor, laid them on the glass between the girl and himself. She smiled, flicking the tip of her tongue between her teeth. Brun's knees shook. "I'm so glad you have them," she said. "Imagine, my new students and their mothers coming in for their first lessons, and the teacher doesn't even have the lesson books. I think first impressions are so important, don't you, Mr. ..."

"Campbell. Brun Campbell. Oh yes, of course. First impressions are very important."

Just as it occurred to him that he was shamelessly dogeyeing the girl, Brun realized John Stark stood beside him at the counter. "Good afternoon, Miss McAllister," Stark said. "I trust you're finding what you need."

"Why, yes, Mr. Stark, thank you." Miss McAllister pointed at the books. "Your new young man has been so very helpful. Do you play, Mr. Campbell?"

Before Brun could do more than clear his throat, Stark said, "Brun is a fine pianist. You'll have to come back some time when he's not quite so busy, and I'm sure he'll be glad to play for you. But right now, I have him working the inventory."

Clear enough to Brun. A polite, "Pleased to meet you, Miss McAllister," and the boy was on his way back to the strings. Stark rang up the sale.

A few minutes later, Brun once again found Stark at his side. "You did fine, Brun, but I think a bit of caution around Miss McAllister would be in order. She came to town last fall, moved into a little house out on East Sixth, and set up as a piano teacher for children. Nobody really knows where she came from, except that she'd been a circus performer. Not the most respectable life for a young woman."

"Maybe she was orphaned," Brun said. "Or her father was a drunk and the family had no money. I've known such back home, sir, and sometimes there was not any respectable work a girl could do so as not to starve."

The earnestness on Brun's face took Stark back forty years. "Well, yes, that may be," he said softly. "Perhaps I should have more sympathy. But her behavior isn't...well, what you might hope. She's had any number of beaux, and there have been fights over her affections, one quite a serious affair where a young man suffered a bad injury to his head. And aside from giving piano lessons, she's involved herself in a business venture with a particularly disagreeable man. Had I not come out when I did, I expect she'd have had you talking for a good while, and then suggested she might like to get to know you better. That would, of course, be your business, though on your own time. But I'd suggest you keep your eyes open and your wits about you."

Brun remembered the story about the fox and the sour grapes. He thanked his boss, who then went back to his office, leaving Brun to his work and his thoughts.

A little before three, Stark sent Brun out to the bank to make a deposit. When the boy returned, he was surprised to see his boss and Isaac in the office, heavy in conversation with Scott Joplin. As soon as the men saw him, they came out, Stark and Isaac smiling, Joplin's face as serious as ever. But by now, Brun had decided that was not something to be concerned about.

He was right. Joplin told Brun he'd been to see Mr. Robert Higdon, and Mr. Higdon was willing to take the newcomer as a boarder, with permission to use his piano for practice. "Mr. Higdon expects to see you at his office after you're done working this afternoon," Joplin said. "Katy Building. 223 South Ohio."

"I'm sure you'll be comfortable there," Stark said. "Bob Higdon's a fine young man, very congenial and smart as a whip. He just opened his own law office. Last year he clerked for Bud Hastain, and Bud can't say enough good about him.

Isaac smiled. "Be one sight better than the Y."

Joplin nodded, placed his black bowler onto his head, and started to walk out. But Stark called him back. "Brun played me a tune of yours yesterday—'Maple Leaf Rag'?"

"Yes…that's my music."

"Would you play it for me?" Stark gestured Joplin toward the piano. "I'd like to hear it again."

Without a word, Joplin sat, put his fingers to the keys, and played "Maple Leaf Rag." Brun looked from his boss to his teacher, and back again. Stark stared like a man in a trance.

When Joplin finished, the shopkeeper blinked, then smiled. "That's one glorious piece of music. Thank you."

You couldn't have told from Joplin's face that he'd received a supreme compliment. "I'm glad you enjoyed it," was all he said; then he was out the doorway.

Isaac shook his head. "That Scott Joplin, he sure be one serious boy."

Stark said, "What he must hear inside his head, none of us will ever know." Brun would've sworn his boss sounded envious.

At five o'clock, Brun left the music store, walked to the corner, then up Ohio. At Fourth Street, a bunch of small boys crowded around the little red and yellow popcorn and peanut wagon. The squat vendor yanked at a string, whereupon a shrill whistle sent the boys into a frenzy of shrieking and clutching at their ears. Brun smiled, but felt a little sad.

A sign in a window at the Katy Building announced that Mr. Robert Higdon took general law cases and lent money at five percent. Brun opened the door, looked around inside, then walked in. Higdon's waiting room was empty, the air warm and close. A faint scent of violets around the small secretary's desk next to an inner door told him the secretary had left not all that long before. Brun knocked at the inner door, no answer. A moment's hesitation, then he turned the knob and pulled the door open just enough to peer inside and see the room was empty. He shut the door, walked back across the waiting room, settled into a homey brown sofa opposite the desk, and rested his head back against the cushion. Next he knew, he heard, "Mr. Campbell, I presume."

Brun scrambled to his feet before he was full-awake, and blinked up into Robert Higdon's face. The lawyer was about thirty, a good six feet tall, with a broad face and wide-set brown eyes. His ears stuck out like jug handles, and the lines of his full lips were soft, just a trace of a smile at the right corner. He wore a neat, well-tailored three-piece light worsted suit, with a red and green plaid bow tie set around a crisp white collar. Mr. Higdon didn't buy clothes on the cheap.

"I apologize for keeping you, Mr. Campbell. I was called out unexpectedly."

"That's all right, sir. I suspect the lawyer business can be unpredictable. And please, if you'd like, call me Brun."

"Good. I'll do that." Higdon draped an arm over the boy's shoulders. "Come on inside, and let's get better acquainted."

They sat and talked for about half an hour, mostly Higdon asking questions about Brun, and Brun replying, mostly with the truth, and when not, close enough to do. All in all, the boy's answers seemed to satisfy Mr. Higdon, who agreed that Brun could lodge and take meals in his home, and practice on the new Steinway grand in his living room, so long as that practice didn't take place too late at night or too early in the morning. Terms would be a sawbuck a month. Higdon laughed at the look that came over Brun's face. "Aren't those terms satisfactory to you, Brun?"

"Well, no—I mean, yes. I'm sorry, sir, I guess I'm just surprised. They're way more generous than I'd ever thought."

"I don't think you'd make a very good business negotiator."

"I'm sure that's the truth, Mr. Higdon. I hope I'm a lot better on the piano than I'd be in a business office."

Higdon's grin went wry. "Well, touché, Brun, and fair enough. I play piano myself, though with far more enthusiasm than skill. But I do love music. I get to most of the shows at Wood's Opera House, and the dances Saturday nights in the hall at Second and Ohio, above the St. Louis Clothing Store. You might enjoy those yourself. Scott Joplin provides the music—that's where I got to know him. The fact that he's willing to have you as a piano student means a lot. And Mr. Stark told me that as well as he could tell in a day, he was favorably impressed with your abilities and thought you were of sound character. If both Scott Joplin and John Stark are willing to take a chance on you, so will I."

"Well, Mr. Higdon, I sure am grateful for that."

Higdon pulled a gold pocket watch from behind his vest, flipped it open, frowned. "I think we'd better be heading home. My sister gets annoyed when I'm late for dinner. You can pick up your things at the Y later, if that's all right."

More than all right with Brun, who'd had nothing to eat since his pancake breakfast. He kept time with Higdon down Ohio, then west onto Sixth, and along to a two-story white frame house, recently painted, with a wide wraparound porch and well-tended flower gardens in front. Higdon pointed. "That's it. Will it do, do you think?"

"It looks more than ample, Mr. Higdon."

Higdon laughed. "Good. I hoped you wouldn't be disappointed. Come on inside and meet the ladies. They're expecting you."

They walked under a bower so thick with morning glories Brun couldn't see but a bit of the trellis, then up a short path, onto the porch, and inside. From somewhere out back, Brun heard a pretty two-part soprano harmony on "Love's Old Sweet Song." Higdon called a hello, and like they'd been waiting for the summons, the music stopped mid-phrase and two young women hustled through the doorway. The lawyer kissed the older on the cheek, then the younger, and then made introductions. "Mr. Brun Campbell, my sister Belle Higdon and my niece Luella Sheldon. Louie."

"Miss Higdon, Miss Sheldon, I'm pleased to meet you." Unfortunately, Brun's stomach picked that moment to make a loud and rude sound. Miss Higdon bit on her lip but couldn't keep from smiling. Miss Sheldon giggled.

Least I've got on my new suit, Brun thought, then said, "I do beg your pardon, but it smells so good in here, I couldn't help myself. We ate pretty plain back home, and except maybe on Christmas, my ma never got the house smelling anything like this."

Miss Belle smiled again. "Well, then, I suspect we'd do well to sit ourselves down. We can get acquainted over dinner."

Brun warned himself to watch his manners and not eat to excess, but as to the latter consideration, he found he had no worries. The Higdons were big people, Miss Belle being a good couple of inches taller than Brun, while Miss Luella, at thirteen, looked directly into Brun's eyes. Considerably often, in fact, he couldn't help but notice, and he found himself thinking she was regarding him in much the way he had regarded Miss McAllister at the music store, though for his part, he felt a great deal more interest in the roast chicken, dumplings, garden vegetables and pie. Not that Miss Luella was ugly, just she was at that funny point between being a girl and a woman, all gawky and sharp angles, not much yet in the way of soft curves. Her face was long, with big brown eyes and thin lips, and she had a nice mane of chestnut hair, tied back in a blue ribbon. Miss Belle was more womanly, but like her brother, she sported an impressive pair of jughandle ears, which she tried to hide under her long brown hair. All said, neither Higdon female came off too well by comparison to Miss McAllister.

Along with their big ears, the Higdons seemed to have a family trait for hospitality. They asked all about Brun, and he told them what he'd told everyone else, where he'd come from and why he was in town. In turn, they told him about themselves. When Higdon had come to Sedalia the year before to read law with Mr. Hastain, Miss Belle came along to keep house for him, at least until she married a Mr. Campbell (no relation, so far as Brun could say) from St. Louis. Mr. Higdon himself had a fiancee, a Miss Selover, who lived right there in Sedalia. Miss Luella was Mr. Higdon's and Miss Belle's niece, and was staying with them for the summer.

After they made a peach pie and a pot of coffee disappear, Higdon offered to help clear the dishes. Brun jumped to his feet, but Miss Belle told the men they'd only be in the way, and shooed them off to the back porch, a nice, screened refuge from summer bugs, with comfortable wicker chairs and a table in the middle. Higdon lit a pipe, took a few puffs, and sat. Brun followed suit, then thanked Higdon for the fine dinner. "Do you eat like that every night?" the boy asked.

Which sent Higdon into a full-fledged laughing fit. When he finally got himself in hand, he said yes, theirs was a family of big-boned farmers, and ample provisions at the dinner table was part of the way they lived. "The farm's over near Clifton City; that's where I grew up. Belle, too, of course..." Higdon's face went serious and, for the first time Brun had seen, sad. "And Luella—that's to say, my sister, Luella, this Luella's mother. She died in childbirth, back in '88, when Little Louie was just two. Her father's a good enough man, but my sister's death affected him badly, and the fact is, he's not much of a parent."

Brun thought that might be Higdon's polite way of saying that Miss Luella's father had been trying those eleven years to replace his wife with a bottle of whiskey.

"So we do all we can to make Louie feel like one of us. She's spending the summer here, and frankly, Brun, that's one reason I'm glad to have you board with us. Louie's a shy girl, doesn't make friends easily. The Fourth of July, while every other boy and girl her age was having a time of it, she just sat on the porch here, doing needlework or reading her Bible. As much attention as Belle and I give her, I think it will be good for her to have someone near her age right here in the house. And I would take it as a personal favor if you can find time to escort her to some events—say, a concert in the park, a show at the Opera House. I'll be glad to bear the expense, though of course you needn't tell her that."

Brun thanked Higdon and said he'd be more than happy to try to make Miss Luella's summer more enjoyable. "But truth, Mr. Higdon, most of the girls back home who read Bibles when no one was making them do it would never go to a show or a dance. They thought music and dancing were sinful."

Higdon shook his head. "Preachers can be pretty sharp at spotting a lonely girl and putting a Bible into her hands. I suspect if Louie got out more and did some of the things young people do, the Bible might not look all that interesting. But I hope I'm not offending you, Brun."

"No, sir, not at all. I'll take a sheet of lively music anytime in preference to a Bible."

Higdon puffed a mouthful of smoke, then grinned. "Well, then, I guess we're in full agreement, though you are more fortunate than I." He held up a finger, teacher-like. "'Sentimentally, I am disposed to harmony, but organically I am incapable of a tune.' That was said by Charles Lamb, and it applies at least as well to me. But I won't complain. Practice of the law is stimulating and provides me a good living, and my evenings are free to savor the musical pleasures. Not many men get to enjoy the compatible companionship of a practical wife and a lively mistress."

Brun would've bet a gold eagle that Higdon could talk a lion into a dentist's chair. The man's wide-set brown eyes always seemed to be asking questions, his friendly manner invited confidence. He knocked his pipe with the palm of his hand, then looked at Brun over the bowl. "If you smoke, feel free," Higdon said. "Just not in the house. Belle has an asthmatic condition, and smoke bothers her lungs."

Brun thanked him, took out his little pouch of tobacco and papers, rolled a cigarette, and leaned forward to take the flame from the lucifer in Mr. Higdon's hand. "You're an enterprising fellow," Higdon said, as Brun blew two streams of smoke out his nostrils. "Only two days in town, and you have a job, a piano teacher, and a place to lodge and practice your music."

Brun grinned, and through the smoke cloud said, "I never did like to cool my heels."

"Then you should do well here. It's a young city, not a lot of history to get in the way of a young man with drive. You can make it more on your own merits than on who your family happens to be. But keep in mind, every coin's got two sides. Sedalia's a wide-open town, and things can get unpleasant at times, particularly around Main Street at night. You're bright, you're sharp, you're a real go-getter, but you need to know when to keep your mouth muzzled. Get careless in the wrong place, at the wrong time, with the wrong person, you may find yourself more trouble than you can handle. In Arkansas City, you at least had the advantage of familiarity. I hope you'll be judicious here."

"Thank you," said Brun. "I'll be sure to take proper care."

Higdon smiled. "I hope so." He extended his hand. "You have the freedom of my house, and welcome. Now, would you like me to come along and help you get your things from the Y?"

"No need, sir. There's not anywhere near that much. I'll just run on over, shouldn't take me long at all."

A few minutes before eleven next morning, Brun whipped up the creaky wooden stairs to the Maple Leaf Club, two at a pace. Arthur Marshall sat on the piano bench, Scott Joplin to his left, and the round German, Professor Weiss, to his right. It looked to Brun like Weiss and Joplin were both talking at once, and Marshall couldn't figure which way to turn. As the floor creaked under Brun's step, Joplin glanced over his shoulder, then nudged Marshall. "Time's up, Arthur, Mr. Campbell is here. Take your papers, come back this afternoon. We'll have to work on that passage."

Marshall gathered up manuscript pages from the piano rack, nodded in Brun's direction, then started toward the door. "Don't worry, now," Joplin called after him. "You're doing fine. Writing a good classical rag is no easy thing." Then, without so much as a hello or a how do you do, Joplin pointed at the piano stool. "Let me hear how you play 'Maple Leaf' today."

Brun thought he understood. It wasn't that Joplin was unfriendly, or had no manners, just that his mind was so full of music, there wasn't room left over for some of the usual things most people carry around with them. The boy said hello to Professor Weiss, then plunked himself onto the bench, still warm from Marshall's behind, and started to play. As he went along, he got that feeling of having something smack on, right as rain, and just for sport threw in a little run up and down the keys. But before he'd finished, Joplin had his right wrist in a painful grip. "Where did you get that from?"

Brun forced himself to look his teacher in the eye. "I just thought—"

"Was it in the score?"

The score? Like a symphony? "No, sir. But when I hear people play ragtime, they usually put in a passage here or there that they think will go well. Back home, I could tell who was playing before I even went inside."

Joplin drew in a deep breath, then slowly blew it out. "All right. Now, listen. My ragtime is different from the ragtime you hear in hotels and saloons and parlors. Those tunes *develop*—usually start from a melody that's been around forever, then as people play it, they add a little of this, a little of that. Like the songs minstrels sang in Europe, no two singers the same, and the song as it was sung in 1700 was not even recognizable in 1800. But my music is composed. It is high-class music, no different from a song by Schubert, a concerto by Mozart, or a Beethoven symphony. You know the opening of Beethoven's *Fifth Symphony*, don't you?"

Brun nodded.

"Would you put a run in between all those Ba-ba-ba-boms?"

"No."

"Then, kindly do not put any into my tunes. I don't consider a piece of music finished until I can't see how it could be improved by adding or changing a single note. You will play it as it is written. Now, go ahead. Start from the beginning of the second A-section. Up to there, you were doing well."

Brun felt a heavy hand on his shoulder. He turned, saw Julius Weiss smiling down on him. "Don't worry, Brunnie. This is part of learning. You will do fine."

As Brun played on, Joplin listened and watched with fierce concentration. "Good," he said. "You've got the tempo right. Go on, now. *Play* that tune."

When the boy finished, Joplin sat beside him. Though the teacher's eyes were gentle, something about the way he looked made Brun uneasy. "You know the notes," Joplin said. "But before you can play a classical rag properly, you must *feel* it, and that you are not yet doing. Let me show you." Joplin swung into a hustling performance of "Maple Leaf." After about ten bars, he looked around at Brun. "Hear that? It might be one of those player-piano rolls, just pump with your feet and there's your tune, da-da-da-da-da-da-da-da. Now, listen to this." Again, Joplin played the opening bars of "Maple Leaf," slower now, but every bit as mechanical, and all the while watching Brun's face. "You see? Simply slowing the tempo is not the answer. Unless you can actually feel the music, your performance will be superficial. When you play classical ragtime, try thinking of a bright sunny day, just a perfect day. But somewhere, far in the back of your mind, you know that sooner or later, the lovely day will have to end. All right? Listen to this."

Music filled the room, hung in the air like a puff of breeze, scent of fresh-mowed grass. Brun stopped breathing. Every now and again, a cloud seemed to slide over the sun, but not for long. The driving bass, beautifully melodic in its own right, played counterpoint here and there with one or another voice in the syncopated treble. Every hair on Brun's body stood at attention. Why didn't anything like this happen the day before, when Joplin played the very same music at Stark's? The boy felt lightheaded, then suddenly reached past Joplin to strike the keyboard, right over his teacher's fingers. At the crash of the chord, Joplin stopped playing and cocked his head to look at Brun out of the corners of his eyes.

"I'm sorry," Brun said. "I couldn't hold back."

Joplin came as close to a smile as Brun had yet seen. "No call to be sorry," Joplin said softly. "Maybe you're just a real ragtime kid." The corners of his mouth twitched. "Mr. Brun Campbell, The Ragtime Kid."

Brun's head couldn't have swollen up more if Queen Victoria had called him to London, touched a sword to his shoulder and made him a knight.

"Try it again," Joplin said. "From the beginning."

Brun had just about gotten into the first go on the D strain when Joplin said, "All right, now. Hold up a minute." The boy sat, fingers suspended over the keyboard. "That's better," Joplin said. "But listen to me play that same passage."

Brun didn't have to listen long or hard to hear the difference. The music he'd played was a thick slice of his Ma's pound cake, certainly not anything to turn down. But Joplin made the music into a charlotte russe. Brun stared at the black hands, gliding gently from key to key, then looked at Joplin's face. As always, no clue there. The man could've been reading a book, overhearing a conversation, sweeping a floor. "But...how...?" Brun stammered.

"You hear it?"

"Sure. But I don't have any idea how you're doing it. What makes it sound like that?"

"I can't say. I can only show you. You can't translate a properly written ragtime piece into words. Take Beethoven's *Pastoral Symphony*—here, listen." Joplin began to play again, and if Brun hadn't been watching, he'd have sworn this was a different pianist. "You see," Joplin murmured over the music, "Beethoven himself said that this music should not be thought of as a painting of country scenes, but as an expression of feeling."

Without warning or even a musical bridge, Joplin swung into more violent music, fingers no longer dancing, but pressing firmly at the keys. "Wagner," he shouted. "From his opera, *Gotterdammerung*. You don't see anything in particular when you hear this, do you? But what do you feel?"

Then in a trice Joplin was back to "Maple Leaf Rag." Like hearing a man speak a sentence flawlessly in one language, then switch to another tongue, and then go right off into a third. "Where did you learn to play Wagner and Beethoven?" Brun asked.

Something flashed in Joplin's eyes. "You think a colored man can't learn European music?"

"Mr. Joplin, please don't take offense—that's not what I meant. I've listened to lots of piano players, white men and colored, and you are the first I've ever heard who played this kind of music and ragtime, both."

Joplin's face relaxed. He looked past Brun to Weiss, who smiled and said, "Tell him, Scott."

Joplin turned sidewise, leaned an elbow on the keyboard, and looked Brun square in the eyes. "I apologize for taking offense where none was intended. I should have known better. It bothers me that so many people, Negroes as well as whites, think that the colored have something in their bones or their blood that permits them to play, compose, and appreciate ragtime, but leaves them deaf to European music. When I play Beethoven, I feel as if he and I are not only personally acquainted, we are on the very best terms of friendship."

He glanced again at Weiss. It's not coming easy for him, Brun thought.

"My mother was a...laundress. She worked for the Rodgers family in Texarkana, where I grew up. Professor Weiss lived in their house and taught their children. He heard people in town talk about me, how I was just a small boy who'd never had lessons, but how well I could play piano. He got me to play for him, and told my parents I had talent which should be encouraged, and that he would give me lessons free of charge. Then when Colonel Rodgers bought a new piano for his children, Mr. Weiss arranged for my father to chop wood to pay for the Rodgers' old piano, so I could practice at home. It's because of Mr. Weiss that I know classical music and have some familiarity with opera. He taught me Beethoven and Wagner. And he also arranged for me to listen when he tutored the Rodgers children in mathematics, science and history."

Now Brun knew why Joplin spoke such a fine tongue. Have him and me talk, the boy thought, and a blindfolded listener would point at me and say, "That one there's the nigger, sure enough."

"Scott is like my own son," Weiss said. "He is a true genius. Maybe why God sent me to Texarkana was so Scott would have lessons and tutoring. When I left Texarkana, I gave to Scott a gift, a little money-clip I had brought from Europe, it played music. I wanted it would be a reminder for him about what a great talent he has got, and he must not ever stop trying to get better and better."

Joplin wiped his hand across his mouth, but said nothing. Brun worked fiercely to keep his face as straight as Joplin's. He didn't want to ask the question, tried not to. But out it came. "Could I...see it? That money-clip that plays music?"

Joplin shook his head. "I'm sorry, but I don't have it with me. But now you understand, Brun, why I'm pleased to have a white pupil." Joplin pointed to a disorderly stack of music on the floor to the right of the piano. "That is a full-length performance in ragtime, a ballet, like Tchaikovsky's *Swan Lake*, or *Sleeping Beauty*. I call it *The Ragtime Dance*, and I'm working to put it on later this year, at Wood's Opera House. But first, I want to present the music at the Emancipation Day Festivities. People will come from all over Pettis County and beyond, a tremendous audience. There should be enough talk afterward that I think a lot of Negroes—and I hope whites as well—will come to Wood's for a full performance."

As smoothly as Joplin had moved the talk off the money-clip, Brun figured he could take a lesson from the composer in more than music. "I guess that'll be a real barnburner," the boy said. "Emancipation Day is when?"

"August the fourth."

"But that's less than two weeks off."

"That's why Professor Weiss is here. I sent him a letter and asked if he could possibly come up and help me."

"Hah! As if I would ever say no. I would not miss this performance for anything."

"If it weren't for Professor Weiss," said Joplin quietly, "I would be in Texarkana right now, pounding away with a hammer in a railroad shop." Then he swung around on the piano bench with such suddenness, Brun jumped. "Now," Joplin said. "I was trying to show you something, wasn't I?" He held his hands lightly above the keyboard. "This ragtime tune has nothing at all to do with maple leaves. I could as easily have called it 'Etude in Ragtime Number Two,' by Scott Joplin, and maybe I should have." Joplin's fingers drifted back and forth along the keys. "It is not a musical painting of a sunny day, or a beautiful woman, or a fresh-baked sweet-potato pie. It is how you feel on that sunny day, seeing that woman, smelling that pie. But despite yourself, you know that inevitably the sun will set. That woman will grow old and bent and wrinkled. The pie will get eaten or moldy. While it lasts, though… You need to listen to the music with more than your ears. You and I may play the same notes, but there *will* be a difference between our performances, just as there will be differences in the way two singers perform a Schubert song. Beethoven and Schubert speak to the performers, and the performers tell the audience what they hear. Listen to 'Maple Leaf Rag,' Brun. Then, speak it through the piano. All right? Now, let me give you some exercises that might help."

The hour-lesson lasted an hour and a quarter by the clock, if only about five minutes by Brun's reckoning. When the boy put his half-dollar piece into Joplin's hand, Joplin said a polite thank-you, and slipped the coin into his pocket. "Go and practice now. Come back eleven o'clock next Tuesday."

The boy was halfway to the door when Joplin called after him, "Are you working with your rubber ball?"

Uh-oh. "I'm sorry, Mr. Joplin. Just haven't had time yet to get one."

"If you do not have it by Tuesday—"

"I'll have it in five minutes. I'll go right from here to Messerly's."

Brun skipped down the stairs to the door; outside, the midday sun hit him smack in the face. He shaded his eyes. Across the way, a stoop-shouldered colored man worked a broom across the wooden sidewalk in front of Callie's Grocery. East Main looked like a washed-out man after a night of carousing, getting too old for that kind of thing. But Brun Campbell was fifteen years old, on his own tack in Sedalia, Missouri, far away from Mr. Utley and his cursed farm, taking lessons in ragtime music from Scott Joplin. If he was going to go to hell for playing that music, he was in heaven now, and bound to enjoy every minute.

A brief stop at Messerly's Dry Goods Store, then he ran through the heat back to Higdon's, squeezing the red, cast-rubber ball at each step.

Miss Belle and Miss Luella were nowhere to be seen, probably out grocery-shopping for supper. Brun sat at the piano, played "Maple Leaf Rag" and Joplin's exercises until close to one o'clock. Then he ran upstairs to his room, changed into his good suit, and ran all the way to Stark and Son's. Never gave even a passing thought to lunch.

Toward midafternoon, traffic at Stark's was light, and the proprietor told Brun to go down to the Boston Café and have a phosphate. The boy took off running. But as he flopped into a chair at a little table, he heard metal clink on metal in his pants pocket, and straightway his conscience commenced to hammer at him without mercy. He sucked halfheartedly at the straw in his phosphate. That money-clip, twenty-eight dollars and all, belonged to Scott Joplin. Brun tried to imagine Joplin, that shy and quiet man, with his calm, intelligent face and gentle voice, savagely throttling a woman, then leaving her body in a clump of weeds at a roadside. It didn't add up.

But Brun knew that if you push any man hard enough, there's going to be trouble. The hidings his Pop dispensed for misbehavior were generally pretty moderate, but once, when the boy was seven, he got caught with his hand in the penny candy jar at Mr. Munson's store, and no pennies in his pocket to pay. Pop, who admired Honest Abe Lincoln to considerable excess, was embarrassed by Mr. Munson's tattle, and that night, Brun got a switch on his bare bottom to end all. "*That's* for trying to take something not yours," Pop shouted as he whaled away. "*That's* for a hand that goes where it has no business. *That's* for being a humiliation to your mother and father." When the old man finally quit and stomped out of the shed, Brun looked around through two lakes of tears to see whether his butt was bleeding.

And how long had Brun known Scott Joplin? All of two days. "Still water runs deep," Ma used to say. Maybe that dead woman kept after Joplin about something or other until he couldn't take another minute of it, so he grabbed her, and choked and choked and choked. Joplin might not even have realized what he was doing until it was too late. Maybe he panicked and ran, didn't give a thought to the money-clip. So Brun could hardly give it back, then sit on a piano bench and concentrate on playing music with Joplin standing behind him.

Could he walk on down to the Maple Leaf Club after work, give Joplin the clip, tell him he'd found it on the floor at Boutell's? Or on the wooden sidewalk in front of the St. Louis Clothing Company? Would Joplin swallow that? Not likely.

How about sneaking into the Maple Leaf Club and leaving the clip and the twenty-eight dollars on the piano? But someone else might come in first and pocket it all. Worse, someone might see Brun sneaking in, and tell Joplin or the police.

Nothing he could think of sounded right. But one thing he knew, and for sure—he was going to take piano lessons from Scott Joplin. And that being the case, he needed to make certain neither he nor Joplin could be tied to that dead woman. He had to hide that money-clip in a safe place, maybe somewhere in his room at Higdon's…

"Well, hello, there, Mr. Campbell. How is it you're not working at Mr. Stark's today?"

Brun snapped around, and found himself looking at Miss McAllister. Before he could answer, he heard a deep voice announce, "Maybe Stark gave him the can."

Brun shifted his eyes to take in the speaker. A big man, familiar round face, smiling, but not in a pleasant way. Then it hit Brun. This was the man on the little picture inside that locket, and he was a dandy, a sight to behold in pearl-gray ice-cream pants and a swallow-tail jacket, blond pompadour neatly combed under a straw skimmer. Brun knew the type, a big talker, particularly with the ladies. So why was his photograph in a locket on a dead lady's wrist? "No, he didn't give me the can," Brun said. "Just a break to have a phosphate."

"Pays you pretty good, does he?"

The big man was still smiling, but his face had the look of a costume mask. "If you don't mind me saying so," the boy said, "I don't think that's any of your business."

Now, the man laughed out loud. "Well, now, this young man's got a backbone, don't he, Maisie? I like that."

Maisie McAllister, Brun thought. He repeated it in his mind. Maisie smiled at him.

The man swept his arm grandly in front of Brun's face. "Let me explain," he intoned. "Then, I think you'll see that it just *might* be my business, and that your business and mine could be the same. First, let me introduce myself. I'm Elmo Freitag, from Kansas City. I'm in music publishing, and more."

Give the man a chance? "Pleased to make your acquaintance," Brun said, then half-stood to shook hands. Like shaking with a catfish just hauled out of the river. The boy pulled free as quickly as he could. "Brun Campbell."

Freitag pulled out the chair to Brun's left for Maisie, who smoothed her white skirts and sat; Freitag took the chair to Brun's right. Brun noticed people staring from all around the café, and they weren't looking at him or Freitag.

"Now…" Freitag gestured with his hat. "I used to represent Carl Hoffman Music Publishers in Kans' City, and if you know the business at all, you know there's no bigger name in the game. But I'm striking out on my own now, and I'm going to blow every other outfit right out of the water. You know what's the coming thing in music sheets…Bert, was it?"

"Brun."

"Right, Brun. Sorry. Not a usual name. Well, let me answer my own question for you. It's colored ragtime, and it's going to make certain people rich."

None of them colored, Brun thought, but he kept his counsel.

"And I don't mind telling you, I'm going to be one of those people. Sedalia's got more colored music than any place in the country, and that's why I'm here."

Brun's attention had wandered back to Maisie McAllister. Freitag picked right up. "I had the great fortune to meet Miss Maisie here, and she knows a good thing when she sees it. She's signed on as secretary and general assistant. Now what I was saying, Brun…"

Freitag leaned in close. Brun had no trouble deciding that the man had already held a serious business meeting that day with John Barleycorn. "A man has to know when the right moment is at hand," Freitag said. "By the time I'm done, I'm going to have me a box two feet thick with colored ragtime music, and when I do, I'll take the next train to Kay Cee and have a little talk with a printer I know. And before the year is out, I'll have the hottest ragtime sheets in every store from New York to Topeka. But that's not the whole story."

All the while Freitag talked, Brun sipped at his phosphate. "I guess that's good," he said. "But I don't see what it has to do with me, and I need to get back to work."

He pushed his chair away from the table, but Freitag arrested him with a fleshy hand to the shoulder. "Hold on just a minute, there, Brun. I did tell you, didn't I, that I believe your interests and ours might just coincide."

Brun went on alert. The man sounded like any number of two-bit country preachers he'd heard, warming up to the heart of their Sunday message to the flock just before they passed the plate.

"I said that wasn't the whole story. As much money as there is in music publishing, there's more yet in performing. And Freitag Enterprises is going to be right there, too. I'm not just going to put this music on paper, I'm going to start up a colored troupe to play that music, sing and dance it on the stage. That's what they're good at. I'll take care of all the business arrangements. Colored'll just need to write down their music, play it on pianos and banjos, and sing and dance. They won't have to bother themselves about where their next meal's coming from, or the rent money. Just like in the old days, not a worry in the world, everybody's happy. We'll start in Kans' City, then when we've got us a name, take it on the road. To New York. Give me two years, and Elmo Freitag's gonna be the biggest name in show business. All the gold to be mined ain't in the frozen north… Well, Brun, that's an odd look you've got on your face. I bet you don't believe me."

That odd look was because Freitag had reminded the boy about the note he'd left his parents just a few days before. "No, sir, I don't disbelieve you," he said. "It's just you were talking about music publishing, then all of a sudden you're onto the Gold Rush. I'm not sure I follow your drift."

"Ah, the young—so impatient." Freitag shot Maisie an arch glance. Brun slurped down the last of his phosphate and made to slide sideways off his seat, but Freitag shifted to block his exit. "Now, Brun, you'd be smart to pay me mind. I've been in music publishing nearly twenty years. Ragtime music is going to take this country by storm, and I'm bound to ride that wave to my fortune. Maisie here…well, her dream is to have a singing career, and what with all these ragtime tunes I'm going to get, that little dream can't help but come true. And so can yours. All you got to do is help me get Scott Joplin's music, and bang, like magic, you're vice-president of Freitag Enterprises. How does that sound?"

Brun thought it sounded like the man was a nut case. Brun Campbell, of all people, was supposed to get Scott Joplin to give him music?

Freitag's laugh filled the café. "Listen up, I'll explain it to you. I got to know Joplin at Hoffman, from when we published his 'Original Rags,' and he's a whole different kind of nigger. Don't drink hardly at all, don't fool around—the man's a ragtime-writing machine, that's all he ever thinks about. Now, if I've got his music, I've got the best that's being written, and on top of that, with Scott Joplin in my company, every nigger in Sedalia and for miles around is going to come in line. Problem is…" Freitag stopped long enough to snicker, then wiped the back of his hand across his mouth. "Joplin says he'll only publish under a royalties contract. A nigger talking royalties, can you imagine that? Where'd he ever *get* that idea from? You ever meet a nigger who could tell you what a percent is?"

Brun's impatience rose like a creek in flood time and washed over the banks. Mr. Stark was going to give him hell for taking too long on his break. "Truth, Mr. Freitag, I've met more than my share of white men in Kansas and Missouri who'd hear the word percent and figure you were probably talking Latin or Greek."

Freitag ignored the wisecrack. "Now, Brun, I do know you're in a hurry to get back to your job, but just give me two minutes—not a second more—of your time, and listen to my idea. I don't think you'll regret it."

Many years later, Brun told me he knew he should have just said a nice-to-meet-you to Freitag and gone out the door, fast as he could walk. But he looked at Maisie McAllister, in her lace-trimmed turquoise silk waist and bright plaid skirt, smiling and blinking her eyes at him, and asked out loud what he would better have just kept wondering about. "Why do you need *me* to get Scott Joplin to publish with you?"

"Joplin seems well inclined toward you," Freitag said. "So take your lessons with him, learn to play his music. *Learn* his music. Get so he trusts you. Then, maybe you can persuade him that his future lies with Freitag Enterprises. But if you can't, well, that wouldn't really be all that much of a problem. Once you've learned Joplin's music, what's going to stop you from writing it down and bringing it to me? And then..." Freitag spread his arms grandly. "Then, it will be Mr. Brun Campbell, the Boy-King of Ragtime. You'll be on Easy Street right there with Miss McAllister and me. How does that sound, my lad?"

For answer, Brun pushed away from the table, gave Freitag a hard shove to the chest, and stamped across the floor and outside. His brain was hotter than the thermometer next to the door, and that read ninety-six. Steal Scott Joplin's music? Bad enough he'd made off with a money-clip and a locket from a murdered woman. But if he ever stole Scott Joplin's music, he'd have to crawl out of Sedalia on his stomach the next time Joplin even looked at him.

But how did Freitag know he was taking piano lessons from Scott Joplin? Miss McAllister? He hadn't said anything to her the day before. He was sure he hadn't.

Chapter Six

Sedalia
Friday, July 21, 1899, afternoon

From behind the counter, John Stark watched with no real interest as a man and two women browsed the sheet music racks. Time was, he'd have been out there, asking them what they might be looking for, and had they tried the newest hit from St. Louis or New York, but now, more often than not, he just let browsers be. How many years had he been selling, selling, selling? Stark wasn't a rich man, never would be, but he was comfortable. His wife and children always had what they needed, and Stark himself had the luxury, nights, of reading whatever he pleased, history, theology, science. Will was looking to branch into music publishing, but the idea of learning a whole new business, once an exhilarating notion to Stark, now just made him feel tuckered. And the thought of risking everything he'd worked for all those years just scared the bejesus out of him. A rocking chair and a book, with a glass of lemonade in the afternoon and whiskey after dinner, sounded better to him every day. He was almost sixty. An old man.

He breathed a sigh of bravura proportions, then glanced at the big clock up on the wall behind him. His new boy was taking himself a pretty good break, twenty minutes already. Probably saw a sweet little girl at the Boston, bought two phosphates, sat himself next to her, and started talking. The boy had the kind of mouth that would likely bring him either success or an early grave; Stark hoped it would be the former. Brun was a likable kid, willing and eager, didn't act like the world owed him a living. You couldn't exactly call him a liar, just that he was not overly inclined to let truth stand in the way of convenience. Like telling his real age, or where he'd really run off from. Still, Stark thought when chips were down on the table, Brun could be counted on.

Just then, the object of his musings burst through the doorway and up to the counter. Stark took him in with a mild squint. "I'd say you're looking a bit worked up."

"Just thought I might've overstayed my limit." Through teeth zipped tight.

Stark smiled without changing the expression on his face. The girl must've turned him down, or maybe her boyfriend happened to walk in on them. "Well, perhaps you did, just a bit—but here." He pointed at a fair-sized carton on the floor. "You can make up for it by getting these guitar strings into the display case *molto vivace*. Isaac's out delivering a piano to a farm past Smithville. He'll be gone all afternoon, so you and I are it."

As Brun hustled off, Stark lowered himself onto a stool behind the counter, and mopped at his face with a handkerchief. He looked up to see two colored men walk into the doorway, then just stand there, looking all around like they were a little unsure of themselves. Stark cleared his throat, slid his hand down to the shelf behind the counter, gripped the shotgun. He stiffened as he saw Brun stride up to the men. The boy was bright, but he still had a lot to learn, and if he didn't learn caution in a hurry, he wasn't going to live long enough to learn the rest. Stark heard him say, "Hello, there," then ask how he could help.

The bigger man smiled. He had on a black coat, a wide-brimmed black hat, and a neat white shirt and black tie. Heavy dressing for a day like this, and his near-black skin shone with sweat. "Thank you, young sir," the big man said. "I means you no disrespect. But I think we needs to speak directly with Mr. Stark, yonder."

The man started toward the counter, moving in the slightly rolling, shambling gait of an old man with arthritic hips. The younger man followed him, staring all the while at Brun. Stark folded his finger around the shotgun trigger. As the older man closed in on the counter, Stark suddenly took his hand off the shotgun, and stood. "Mr. Weston, welcome. I'm sorry, I didn't see it was you out there."

"Well, now, that's no trouble," the man said. "Sun's bright outside, does make it harder to see."

Stark smiled, but his eyes were sad. "And at our age, our sight's not what it once was, now, is it? What can I do for you, Mr. Weston? By the way, this young man is my new clerk, Brun Campbell. He's just gotten to town from Arkansas City."

Weston looked Brun up, then down, seemed to approve of what he saw. "Welcome to our city, Master Campbell. What is it brings you to Sedalia?"

"I came to take piano lessons from Mr. Scott Joplin." Brun looked at the young man who'd come in with Weston, and who now seemed to be looking anywhere but at Brun. "Well, hello, there, Scott Hayden," Brun said. "Don't you recollect me? From the other day, when Mr. Joplin agreed to give me lessons? Remember, he introduced us, said he was teaching you and Arthur Marshall to write ragtime, and…"

The dismay accumulating on Hayden's face shut down the flow of Brun's words. Stark glanced at his clerk, rolled his eyes. The older colored man looked fit to explode. From the scowl he turned on Hayden, you might have thought the young man was a loathsome bug that had just crawled in under the door. "Scott Hayden! Is this true?"

"Well…yes, sir." Hayden scraped the floor with the toe of his right shoe, held one hand with the other. "But Scott Joplin is a fine pianist, the best teacher in Sed—"

Weston slammed down his huge fist; the counter shook and rattled. "That is the music of the devil! And you want to be our church organist? When you walk out of God's house and consort with Satan's followers?"

Stark reached out, took Mr. Weston's arm in his hand, and immediately regretted the move. The big, angry Negro seemed to shrink in size, the customary reaction of a colored man when a white took hold of him in the midst of an altercation. Stark released his grip. Weston, all his anger safely locked away, at least for the time being, said quietly, "I do apologize, Mr. Stark, for creating a commotion in your store."

Brun was astonished at the sudden mildness in Stark's blue eyes. "Not at all, Mr. Weston," Stark said. "I just wanted to say that I fear you're making a mistake, abandoning such a fine young man to the darkness. Do you suppose our Lord Himself would have cast him out?"

Mr. Weston looked at the floor.

"Besides…" Stark chuckled. "If I'm not severely in error, the older generation has always thought their offspring were going straight to the deuce. Didn't your own father ever have concerns about you, Mr. Weston?"

Severity drained out of Weston's face, replaced by an odd mixture of embarrassment and humor. What the man might have been going to say, we'll never know, because Stark didn't wait for an answer. "All right, then, Mr. Weston. What was it you wanted to see me and only me about?"

A skinny old white man in a shabby blue shirt and torn overalls, who hadn't had acquaintance with a razor for some time, shuffled into the shop on bowed legs. He tipped his leather hat and said, "How dee, Miz Stock," showing teeth like a picket fence splashed with kerosene. "I need me a new C string, I do."

Stark nodded, then motioned to Brun. "Brun, meet old Clete the Fiddler, he's been my customer since the day I opened. Can you please get him a C-string? Put it on the tab."

Brun was back with the string in almost no time. Clete shook his hand to some excess, told the boy how obliged he was, then left Brun to watch the rest of the drama. The matter of Scott Hayden and ragtime seemed to be in the past. Weston pointed toward a folding suitcase organ, all shiny varnished tiger-striped oak, sitting like a sovereign among a display of five or six of those little twelve-note organs that play paper rolls when you turn the crank. "Something like that li'l Bilhorn would do us just right—that's a real organ. Got itself a fine sound, and when we ain't usin' it, we can fold it up and keep it safe under lock and key. An' in fine weather, it could go down to the river with us for baptisms, or on a Sunday church picnic."

Stark nodded, then looked at Scott Hayden. "Before Mr. Weston makes a decision, why don't you play him some music. Make sure you're both satisfied."

Hayden looked doubtful, but walked over to the Bilhorn, stopping on the way to pick up the piano stool. He sat at the keyboard, pumped the sustain lever with his right foot, checked the swell lever outside his right knee. Then he shot his cuffs, wiggled his fingers, stretched his head all the way back, then forward again. Putting on a bit of a show, Brun thought. Mr. Weston called out, "Don't you dare play no ragtime now, hear? Play us a hymn."

Stark picked up on the smile that flickered across Hayden's face before the young man began to pump the pedals and move his hands. Like Scott Joplin's, Brun thought, fingers gliding over the keys, gently pushing one here, three there. He wondered whether he'd ever be able to play like that, rather than banging away like those piano keys had done something to insult him.

It took just a couple of measures for Brun to recognize "The Battle Hymn of the Republic." Mrs. Howe generally gets credit for that tune, but she was a poet, not a composer, and just plugged her words into the popular Civil War anthem, "John Brown's Body." Hayden played it soft and slow, but then, on a second go-round, he commenced to pump more air. Mr. Weston smiled broadly. Brun heard him whisper to Stark, "There, now!"

Stark, though, seemed not to hear him, just stared at Hayden, who at that point did something with the music that Brun couldn't quite figure. But when he saw his own foot tapping, he realized Hayden had shifted the beat. He was syncopating. Playing the Lord's melody to the devil's rhythm. Just a hint at first, but the further Hayden went, the more the music seemed to carry him along; he stepped up the tempo, pumped the pedals ever faster, moved his knee into the swell lever to put even more emphasis on accented notes. Now his left hand played a clear barrelhouse rhythm. Faster and faster, louder and louder. Hands crossed over, back and forth. On a piano, this would have been an impressive performance; on the organ it was past belief, put to shame any playing Brun ever had done. The boy felt sick with envy. He heard applause behind him, someone clapping time with the music. He glanced back and saw it was Weston. "Isn't that *something*," the preacher called out. "Why, he'll have them jumpin' in the aisles in the church."

Lest Weston catch sight of his face right then, Brun quickly turned away. He saw Stark's lips move, then realized his boss was singing, but as if to himself. "John Brown's body lies a-mould'ring in the grave. John Brown's body..." The pain weighting Stark's eyes moved Brun so, he began to sing along, and then Weston joined in. "John Brown's body lies a mould'ring in the grave. But his soul goes marching on." Scott Hayden finished with a flourish, the fingers of his right hand dancing from key to key, finally winding up in a big, bass-supported, "Ah-*men*."

Hayden swung around on the stool, dripping sweat, a sly smile all over his face. A few people who'd gathered at the doorway cheered and clapped; then, as they saw Hayden move away from the organ, they went along their way. Weston was almost dancing with pleasure, but Stark looked like he was just barely holding back a flood of tears. Seeing Brun staring at him, Stark swiveled to face Weston. "I guess that organ is going to the right place."

Whereupon Weston's smile faded. "I hope so, Mr. Stark, sir. I truly do. But of course. I need to ask the price."

"Well, of course," Stark said. "Let's see, now... That's the best of the Bilhorn Telescope Organs, Style C, double reeds and four full octaves. It lists at seventy dollars, but for ecclesiastical use, we would give a discount of ten percent."

Weston took off his hat and fanned himself, exposing his bald pate and looking some twenty years older. He stared into space and his fingers twitched, as if trying to calculate sums. Then he looked at Stark with great seriousness. "I don't wish to offend you, sir, but the fact is, our congregation simply does not have that much money to spend. But would you consider a time payment?" He reached into his pocket, pulled out a handful of bills and coins, and laid them on the counter. "Say, thirty-six dollars and eighty-two cents down, and five dollars each week?"

Stark now looked fully recovered from whatever had been ailing him. "That would be just fine, Mr. Weston. We do offer time payments, and considering the situation, in addition to the ten percent discount, there will be no interest charged on the balance."

"Why, bless you, Mr. Stark." Weston had Stark's hand between the two of his own, and was working it like he hoped to fill a pail with water from the shopkeeper's mouth. "Bless you, sir! My congregation will pray for your well-being, and your family's."

Stark managed a reasonable-enough smile. "Well, then, Mr. Weston, I suppose we're both getting a good deal, aren't we?"

After Weston signed a time-payment agreement, he and Scott Hayden folded up the organ and began to carry it out, Weston in front, Hayden bringing up the rear. As Hayden walked past Brun, Stark heard his clerk half-whisper, "I sure hope one day I'll be able to play hymns like you."

For a moment, Hayden seemed to consider the wisdom of answering, but his grin wouldn't be denied. "Glory hallelujah an' a-men, brother," he said to Brun.

Once the Negroes had navigated the doorway and passed out of earshot, Stark turned a good hot eye on his clerk. "That was wicked of you, Brun."

"Yes, sir." Stark thought the reply sounded more triumphant than repentant.

The boy went on. "Mind if I ask a question, sir?"

"That is the only way to learn. Say on."

"I was wondering…when Scott Hayden played that tune, you looked mighty severe. Didn't you approve of his playing?"

Stark looked away. He saw files of blue-coated soldiers, a young blue-eyed bugler at the edge of the first rank. The Indiana Twenty-first Infantry Regiment, late in the summer of 'sixty-one, marching southward toward Baltimore to the tune of "John Brown's Body." Stark felt as though Brun had gone trespassing on private property, but he could hardly fault the boy. There had been no signs posted.

"I apologize if I talked out of turn," he heard Brun murmur.

Stark shook his head, couldn't shake away the vision, finally fought his mind back to the present. "No, it's all right, Brun." He checked the clock, then strode around the counter, shut the front door and locked it, hung the CLOSED sign, and motioned Brun toward the office. Once inside, he sat behind his desk and motioned the boy to a chair opposite him. "You've heard of John Brown, I suppose," Stark said.

"Old Osawotomie Brown?" Brun shouted. "Well, sure. I grew up mostly in Kansas."

Stark smiled. "Then you've heard plenty."

"But everyone says different. Some say he was a saint and a martyr, and others say he was just a cold-blooded killer. And some say he was just plain bughouse."

"He was all that," Stark said. "And then some. But most important, more than anyone else, he was responsible for starting the Civil War. He believed slavery was an abomination, and prophesized that the crimes of this guilty land—as he put it—would be purged only with blood. Well, for five years, Brun, I saw more blood shed than ever I could have imagined."

All the pain Brun had seen earlier flooded back into Stark's eyes. The old man went on speaking, softly. "That was a long time ago…near-forty years. And now I'm a businessman in Sedalia, Missouri, I've got a good business, an even finer family, a good home. I'm respected here. I'm respectable."

Brun thought Stark made respectability sound just a bit unseemly. But he said, "Yes, sir."

"My daughter Nell learned piano, I sent her to Europe for two years to study with Moszkowski. You know of him, of course."

Brun nodded. He'd never heard of the man, but it sounded like he should've.

"And now, my son Will wants to go into music publishing. He's spending so much of his time in St. Louis, looking into possibilities, that I've had to hire a part-time boy for the shop."

"Which I'm not going to complain about, sir."

Stark felt surprise at how fond he'd become of this boy, and how quickly. He was just close enough to smart-alecky to be endearing. "No, I'm sure you're not. But *I'm* concerned. Will thinks we can do better in music publishing than selling instruments, but I just don't know. Music publishing wouldn't be the first business to flame up, then burn out like a comet. I suppose if it did, Will's young enough; he can start something else. But what about me? I'm fifty-eight years old."

Stark saw Brun open his mouth, motioned for the boy to close it. He shook his head slowly, denial of all possibility. "You're a live wire, Brun, and you do have real musical talent. I've been giving it some thought. You might be the right man in the right place. If Will decides to go ahead with publishing, he can't go it alone, and maybe you'd be the man to work with him. The store should support Mrs. Stark and me the rest of our days. After I've gone, Will could decide what to do with it."

Brun could hardly believe his ears. Thinking he might have been summoned into the office for a stern lecture about minding his own beeswax, he was being all but offered a junior partnership in the Stark Music Publishing Company. Well, when you're being praised for a live wire, no point trying to pretend you're a shy violet. "I'd be real interested in that, sir."

"Well, you think about it, then," said Stark. "And I will do the same. Now, I'll tell you what. Sunday, you come by and have dinner with us, one o'clock. Mrs. Stark would like to meet you."

"I'd be pleased, sir," Brun said, but pleased didn't even begin to cover what he felt. If Stark was considering him for bigger things, he'd need to be sure his Mrs. cottoned to the new boy. Brun vowed he'd make certain she would. For now, he'd show Stark he was on the ball. "I've got another question, sir. About that time payment—does it worry you? I mean, since you let them take away the organ."

"Good thought, Brun. But no, it doesn't worry me. You heard what Pastor Weston said about young Hayden having them jumping in the aisles? I'm sure he's right. What do you suppose the pastor will do directly after that?"

Brun couldn't help laughing. "Pass the plate."

"So will I get paid sooner or later because they already have the organ in the church?"

Answer enough. Brun nodded.

Stark, though, was not finished. "And with everyone in that congregation knowing where the organ came from, and that John Stark and Son was willing to trust them, where do you think the men will go when they want a new banjo or a guitar? Or strings? Where will the mothers go when they want lesson books for their children? Will they go to Perry's or Stark's? The best salesman profits beyond his sales figures because he takes care that his customer is more than satisfied." Stark stood and stretched. "All right, that's enough for one day. I need a beer before supper."

They were outside, re-locking the door, when a young man who'd been sitting in the doorway got to his feet, a human rail in a light blue shirt with red sleeve holders, and baggy brown worsted pants held up by red suspenders. He picked up a basket, shifted it onto his left shoulder, then shuffled up to Stark and Brun, tipped a tattered wide-brimmed straw hat, and said a polite, "H'lo, Mr. Stark."

"Hello yourself, John," said Stark. "Is there something we can do for you?"

"Yes, indeed." The man pointed at Brun. "I got a message for your boy. I seed him and you in there, so I sat down here to wait."

"You should have knocked. We'd have let you in."

"Well, I thought not to disturb you, Mr. Stark. B'sides, this time of day, I grab whatever chance comes along for me to take a li'l rest."

Stark smiled, then went on tiptoes to peer into the man's basket. "Your oranges look good today."

"They is," John said. "Sweet and juicy. Better in the apples, but tomorrow, who knows?"

Stark dug into his pocket, dropped twenty cents into John's hand. "I'll take one, and another for Brun here—he's our new boy. Brun, this is Mr. John Reynolds, Apple John. He sells the best fruit in Sedalia."

Apple John considered his new acquaintance. "He's the very one I come here to see. But whatever kind of a name is that, Brun?"

"Short for Brunson." Which seemed to satisfy Apple John. He took off his hat, brushed lank, sweaty black hair off his forehead, then plunked the hat back on. "Mr. Boutell over by the saloon, he ask me to come tell you his piano man's sick and can you play for him tonight?"

"Well, sure. *Sure.*"

"Mr. Boutell say be there nine o'clock. You get tips and food and beer." Apple John made a face as he spoke the last word. "But you listen right to me, you take the tips and the food, but just you leave the beer. Any kinda liquor, it ain't good for you. That and those cigarettes, they's the worst kind of thing for your body. Cause liver troubles and consumption. Now, me, I walk to Smithton every day, pick up my eggs and butter and fruit, maybe fifty pounds, and I carry it back to Sedalia. Then I walk up and down the streets all day, sellin' it. You think I could do that if I drank liquor, or smoked an' chewed tobacca?" John cocked his head to give Brun a severe look. "I hope you pay heed, but 'course, I can't no more than warn you, can I? Now, you gotta go tell Mr. Boutell yes or no yourself about tonight, 'cause I ain't no messenger boy. Don't mind doin' a man a favor, he asks, but I got my own work, and I got to be on my way now."

"I'll go right over," Brun said. "And thank you. I'm real glad to get that job."

John shuffled off down the street, calling, "Apples and oranges…apples and oranges." Stark and Brun walked to Boutell's, where Stark lowered himself onto a stool at the bar, ordered a mug of Moerschel's, and lit a cigar. So much for Apple John's counsel, Brun thought. He told Boutell he'd be there at eight, then said good-bye to Stark, and set off back to Higdon's.

Scott Joplin ran a handkerchief over his forehead, then shoved the soggy cloth back into his pocket. He looked up at Julius Weiss, then toward the bar, where two colored railroad workers had just sat down. As Walker Williams drew beer into glasses for them, all three suddenly burst out laughing. A joke, Joplin thought, or more likely, something to do with a woman. "I suppose we'd better quit for now," he said to Julius Weiss. "The whole lot of them will be in, and then we won't be able to hear ourselves think, let alone talk."

Weiss shook his head sadly. "Scott, Scott…why you gotta be so fussy, you need such peace and quiet to write your music? Don't some of your friends make up their music in saloons and…other places?"

Joplin pulled the red rubber ball from his pocket and began to squeeze, slowly, first with the left hand, then the right, then back to the left. "Of course you can write barrelhouse music in a barrelhouse." The composer's tone was that of a patient teacher, one he'd heard for enough years to pick up and make his own. "But I write classical music. Respectable music. I can't do that with drunks shouting foolishness and obscenities into my ears.

"But, Scott—if you want to write 'respectable,' then why are you writing this ragtime? Why don't you write symphonies? Operas? Ball—" He stopped mid-word as he saw the trap he'd stepped into.

"That's exactly what I'm doing," said Joplin. "*The Ragtime Dance* is a ballet. And one day I *will* write operas and symphonies—"

"In ragtime."

"Yes. *Classical* ragtime." Joplin squeezed with the right hand, then the left.

Weiss had to use all his restraint to resist an urge to grab that ball out of his protegé's hands and throw it as far as he could. "Scott, if you want so bad to write like Beethoven, then why don't you just *write* like Beethoven? Like Boone does."

"Blind Boone makes his living performing in concert halls, so he plays Strauss' waltzes, Chopin's polonaises, and Liszt's etudes. And when he writes waltzes and polonaises and etudes, they sound like what Strauss, Chopin, and Liszt might have written after a trip to Africa." Squeeze left, squeeze right. "But I intend to succeed on my own terms. What I hear in ragtime, rough as it is, I will make over into art. Into a classical music no one in Europe has ever heard."

"And no one in the United States, either. Scott, let me tell you. Most people don't take right away to something what's new. It'd be hard enough for a white man to make music from the parlors respectable."

"That's one reason I agreed to take on the boy from Oklahoma as a pupil." Joplin's voice was soft, but Weiss couldn't miss the fiber in his words. Squeeze right, squeeze left, squeeze right. "He has the talent, but I don't know whether he has the ear. The way he plays…if I can teach that white boy to play my ragtime like a proper classical music, it might be the making of us both. If I need a pair of white hands to help me lift ragtime out of the gutter and put it into the drawing room and the concert hall, I will get those white hands. There's no need for another Beethoven or another Lizst. Fifty years from now, mark my words, music critics will talk about Beethoven, Lizst and Joplin."

Amazing, Weiss thought. From anybody else, that would sound like a ridiculous conceit. But from Scott Joplin… A rush of emotion flooded the old man's head, as if this ink-black colored man might actually be his son. "But you need to get known, Scott. Even if you teach Brunnie to play right, if nobody knows *you*, neither one of you is ever going to get anywhere. Music sheets are so popular now, every day a new tune for people to buy and play. You should let someone publish your ragtime."

Cramps ran up Joplin's arm from his right hand; he relaxed his grip on the rubber ball. "I'd be glad to have my ragtime published on sheets, but only as *my* ragtime, composed and arranged. And under a royalties agreement."

"Scott, that is just foolishness, you must know that. Even some white composers only get an outright purchase."

"But many of them get royalties." Joplin slipped the ball back into his pocket. "And if I want the public to take me seriously as a composer of classical music, I need to insist that publishers take *me* seriously." Joplin's face tightened. "As long as I'm willing to take their ten or twenty dollars, let them list someone else as arranger, and not object when they put out a cover with Negroes who look like monkeys with razors in their back pockets, no one will respect me *or* my music. I made a mistake last year with Carl Hoffman, but I won't make it again."

Weiss felt beyond defeated, guilty as sin itself. How many times had he drilled into that young colored boy's head that he was as good as anyone, and in regard to music, better than anyone, the white Rodgers children included? How was Weiss supposed to argue with the man who'd grown from that boy? Weiss had planted the seed, watered and fertilized it, and now the mature plant was rooted more firmly than any oak tree. Despite his anguish, Weiss smiled. If he'd had a child of his own, he could never be prouder of him than he was of Scott Joplin.

The old German pulled at the composer's arm. "Come on, Scott. It's been a hot day and we've worked hard. Let's go over by Mr. Williams there and have us a beer. It won't hurt you to drink a beer every now and then."

As Brun ran in through the front door, the smell of dinner cooking hit him full blast. A quick lean-through the kitchen doorway to say hello to Miss Belle and Miss Luella, then up the stairs to his room, shut the door. He took the locket and money-clip from his pocket, laid them on the bed, then picked up the locket, clicked it open, and looked hard at the picture.

No question, Elmo Freitag. The boy cursed himself for running off with that locket, not leaving it for the police to find on the dead woman's body. *Was* she Freitag's wife? Which brought up a terrible notion in Brun's mind. Would Freitag have put his own wife onto getting Joplin's music to publish? Sure he would've. And no telling just what Mrs. Freitag had tried. Did she make Joplin so sore that he killed her?

So Brun couldn't take the locket to the police any more than he could the money-clip. At best, his father would be on the next train down from Arkansas City; at worst, Freitag would tell a story about how he'd sent his wife to sweet-talk Joplin out of his music, and hadn't seen her since. And a story like that would end with Joplin in a jail cell, or worse, hanging from a tree outside town.

Better hide the clip and locket where no one could possibly find them, then sort out what to do. Brun stared through the window into the back yard. No. Someone might hear him digging. Dresser drawer? Not nearly safe enough. Same for the writing table and under the armchair cushions. Under the mattress? He might break the money-clip, or set it to playing, by lying on the bed. The closet… Brun opened the door, stood on his toes, felt around above the door, found a little floored recess between beams, behind the top of the jamb. Perfect. He ran back to the bed, snatched up the money-clip and locket, carefully slid them into the cubby, then took off downstairs for dinner.

Higdon laughed when Brun told the dinner company about his evening's engagement to play piano. "The way you're going, Brun, by this time next year you'll own the city, and we'll all be working for you."

Miss Belle clucked and told her brother he shouldn't tease Brun, that it was good to see a young man these days willing to work so hard. Then she turned Brun's way and asked, "Is your engagement for just tonight?"

"Belle!" Luella had been sitting there like a mouse, but all of a sudden she looked mightily distracted.

Brun remembered how his father used to say it's not easy to put up a shelter when you don't know which direction a storm's coming from. "Far as I know," he said. "Mr. Boutell told me his regular player got bit by a kissing bug last night and went all swollen up. He's better today, but not better enough."

"Well, then, I'd guess he'll be all right by tomorrow night. If he is, would you like to escort Luella to the young peoples' church social? I thought that would be a nice opportunity for you to make some new friends here in town."

Brun hoped with all his heart that what was in his mind was not showing on his face. He'd been looking forward to his first Saturday night in Sedalia, going down to West Main Street, maybe dropping into Miss Nellie Hall's establishment and hearing how Big Froggy played. But he smiled at Luella, her face by now redder than the ripest raspberry in the bowl on the table, and looking everywhere but at him. "Why, I'd be real pleased to do that," he said. "That is, if Miss Luella would agree."

Luella instantly stopped looking flustered, and commenced to gaze at Brun like he was the grand prize in the Fourth of July raffle, and the number stamped on her ticket was also stamped across his forehead. "What time is the social and what church is it at?" Brun asked.

"Eight o'clock," said Luella. "At the Central Presbyterian Church, on the corner of Sixth and Lamine." Then, a concerned look came over her face. "You're not a Catholic, are you?"

Brun laughed. "Truth, Miss Luella, I'm not much of anything when it comes to religious faiths. But I'm sure not any Catholic."

"Oh, good. My friend, May O'Brien, says the nuns tell her she must never go into a Protestant church, else she'll burn in the flames forever."

Brun laughed. "I guess I'll take my chances, Miss Luella. Somehow, I figure if I burn in the flames, it won't be because I went to a social in the basement of a Presbyterian church."

Chapter Seven

Sedalia
Friday, July 21, 1899

A little past ten that evening, a big man with more muscles than teeth and hair, and way too many drinks under his belt, wobbled up to Brun at Boutell's piano and bellowed, "Play 'Silver Threads Among the Gold.' And play it straight, y'hear? Not like it was some kinda nigger tune."

In a saloon the customer was always right. Beer on whiskey can be very risky, and piano players who ignored requests were likely to get themselves permanently silenced. So Brun played "Silver Threads" straight as any arrow, and tried not to watch the man snuffle and honk into his glass of brown lightning. Then, the drunk demanded "Aura Lee," and after that, "When I Saw Sweet Nellie Home." He snorted and sobbed his way through all three of those Godawful tear-jerkers, and by the last lines of "Nellie," you could hear discontent grow in the room like a swarm of yellow jackets coming closer and closer. When the drunk demanded "Sweet Genevieve," another voice boomed out, from the opposite side of the piano, "Fuck 'Sweet Genevieve.' Play something with some life in it, boy."

A piano player's nightmare. Very slowly, Brun edged off from the piano, but then saw Gaylord Boutell hustling full-bore out from behind the bar, and up to the sniveling drunk. "Come on, now, Horace, let's you give somebody else a chance, huh?"

He put a lock on Horace's arm and wrestled the man off in the direction of the bar.

Brun eased back onto the stool, but before he could put hands to keys, he heard from behind him, "Hey, there, Young Mr. Piano Man, takin' lessons from Scott Joplin. You play 'Harlem Rag'?"

If Brun had been chewing gum, he'd have swallowed it. He looked up, up, up at the tallest person he'd ever seen, a young colored man not much older than himself. The man's dark flat cap sat a good seven feet off the ground. Skin like milk chocolate, thick brows, a nose more Roman than negroid, surprisingly thin lips stretched over white, even teeth. The Negro was all angles, hands and fingers like twin brown daddy-longlegs, face skinnier than any horse's. His was the first brown face Brun had seen in Boutell's Saloon. Not that anybody seemed to care. "Hey, Henry, how y' be," hollered an old Reuben with a beard halfway down his shirtfront. From back near the bar came, "Well, if it ain't High Henry—ain't seen you in a coon's age." Everybody laughed.

Including High Henry. If the joke bothered him, he didn't show it. "Go on now, Young Mr. Piano Man," Henry crooned at Brun, that long face near-split by a friendly smile. "You jes' play 'Harlem,' and I show you something I guarantee you ain't never seen before."

"Yeah, Henry," someone shouted. Someone else yelled, "Show him your stuff, Henry." "Play that boy his music," called a third voice.

The men backed off from the piano and formed a wide circle around High Henry and Brun. Young Mr. Piano Man was more concerned than curious, but when he saw Boutell calm behind the bar, grinning, he turned back to the piano and commenced playing "Harlem Rag." The crowd whooped and clapped, and in a quick glance over his shoulder, Brun saw Henry dancing, a kind of buck and wing, but in the most frantic manner. Henry's legs bent, then straightened. His feet slapped the floor; his arms flew every which way but Sunday. And then without the least warning he fell forward, like a tree just cut down. Brun thought for sure he'd passed out from his exertions, was going to smash his face to bits and scatter those pearly teeth from one end of the saloon to the other. In one quick motion, the boy left off playing, jumped up from the stool, and ran to catch Henry before he hit ground. But as the colored man's elbows touched the floor, up he bounced again, the felled tree going backwards, just like there was some sort of big spring between his chest and the floor. Then Henry stood and stared at Brun like that white boy was some kind of fool.

Brun realized the whole room was laughing, then laughed himself. "How the hell you do that?"

Henry wiped at his eyes. "Don't exactly know, but it's a thing I been doin' since I was little. Guess I just kind of got me a knack."

The men drifted away from the piano, back to their card games and drinks. Time for the piano player to take a break. "Buy you a beer?" he asked Henry.

The Negro shook his head. "Mr. Boutell's a good man, but best a colored boy don't go drinkin' in a white 'stablishment." As Henry began to edge toward the door, he leaned down to whisper, "Long as I do my dance, I be all right with white mens, but now I done with the dancin', so time I take my colored face someplace else. I just wanted to hear you play. Arthur Marshall be my friend, an' he tell me you be playin' here tonight."

"That's how you knew I'm taking lessons from Scott Joplin."

Henry grinned.

"And you wanted to see if I'm any good."

Henry's grin widened.

"Am I? Any good?"

"You got promise, Young Mr. Piano Man, I'll sure say that much. Now, I'd best be on my way."

Brun thought a beer would go well, never mind Apple John's warnings. As he pushed through a knot of men drinking and arguing local politics at the bar, he caught sight of Mr. Fitzgerald, so he walked over and said hello.

Fitzgerald studied the boy over the top of a whiskey glass. "Well, Master Campbell. I'm pleased to see you again, I surely am. How are you coming along?"

"Couldn't be better, thanks to the start you gave me." Brun told Fitzgerald about his good fortune since that time, then added, "And since I'm boarding with Mr. Higdon, I got back a dollar from the Y when I left. So I can pay you back what I owe you."

He reached for his pocket, but Fitzgerald stopped him with a gentle touch. "If I'm not mistaken, you've not yet received your first pay."

"No, that'll be tomorrow. But with the tips I got here the other night and the ones I'll be getting tonight—"

"There's no such hurry." Fitzgerald's voice was firm. "You just wait 'til you're more comfortable, and then you can repay me, if you'd like."

It occurred to Brun that he might just need a little money the next night. Bad idea to have empty pockets when you go out with a young lady, to a church social or anywhere else. So he thanked Fitzgerald, and asked how much longer he expected to be in town.

"Another few days, at least. Perhaps a week. I'm making very satisfactory progress with my business."

"Would it be okay for me to ask what your business is?"

Fitzgerald took a swallow of whiskey, then looked at Brun like the boy might have told him a joke that was moderately amusing. "Well, of course, Master Campbell. It's not as though I were here on a secret mission. Since the end of the Great Conflict, my endeavors have been entirely above-board." Another belt from the glass. "I work for Procter and Gamble, in Buffalo, New York. It's a big company, getting bigger, and they are looking to expand their production into other areas of the country. Sedalia is attractive, a new city, growing and booming. There's a Build Factories Drive here, and they're prepared to make some attractive concessions to companies willing to locate in Sedalia. And there *are* advantages to a place where both raw materials and labor are much cheaper than on the east coast. My superiors have sent me to negotiate because, well…I speak the language." He stopped talking just long enough for one of his sad little smiles to work its way across his face. "And I'd be telling less than the truth if I didn't say that success would represent the finest sort of personal opportunity for me. So, there you have it."

"I wish you luck," Brun said. "And I will definitely pay you back next week."

Fitzgerald took another sip. "You are a young man of honor," he said. "You'll go far in the world."

Brun wondered, as he walked back to the piano, whether Mr. Fitzgerald's ideas about honor had brought him far in the world, or whether that was just one of those things people say because saying it makes them feel better. Like drinking whiskey for hours in a saloon does.

Next time Brun looked around, Mr. Fitzgerald was gone, but there was Elmo Freitag, at a table with Maisie McAllister. He didn't seem conscious of Brun, but Miss McAllister slipped the boy a wink that came close to disconnecting his fingers from his brain. Then he caught a glimpse of someone else he knew, carrying three glasses of whiskey up to the table. Otis Saunders. Saunders set down the drinks, slid onto a chair, and the three commenced to talk like old friends who hadn't seen each other in years.

Brun realized he'd lost his place in the music. Quickly, before he made a complete fool of himself, he swiveled back to face the piano, and commenced banging out "Good Old Wagon." What on earth were those three discussing with such energy, and what in *hell* was Otis Saunders doing, drinking in a white saloon, at the same table with a white woman, never mind a white man? Then Brun realized—Saunders was doing a bit of passing. But why?

Brun was still trying to dope the trio as he played a wild "Down Went McGinty," when he heard, "You play a good piano, kid. Too bad that's all you'll ever do—play piano in a third-rate saloon and sell my music sheets in a fifth-rate store. When I'm on Easy Street, and Miss Maisie's right there with me." Sneered from Brun's left through a heavy cloud of secondhand scotch.

Brun glanced sidewise, and there stood Freitag. "Talk's cheap," Brun said. "Cheap enough so even you can afford it. If

Mr. Boutell's third-rate and Mr. Stark's fifth-rate, I can't count high enough to figure where you stand."

Freitag laughed. "You talk big for a squirt. Think John Stark's such a hero, do you? Well, fact is, he deserted from the Union Army, yes, he did. Just last month I went and looked up his record. His officer ordered him to shoot a nigger, been spying on them, and what do you think that hero of yours did? He ran off, just flat-out deserted. Six weeks later, back he comes with a cock and bull story about how him and the nigger got caught by a band of rebels, and they hung the nigger, but Stark got away. What do you think of that?"

For answer, Brun sang at the top of his voice, "Down went McGinty to the bottom of the sea."

Freitag made a clucking sound. "You don't believe me, go ask him. That is, if you ain't afraid."

After Freitag left, his taunt echoed in Brun's ear, and no matter how hard the boy banged at the keys, or how fast he played the tunes, the voice in his head got louder and clearer. He played until two in the morning, and in the process of trying to shut Freitag up over the course of the long evening, Brun found out for himself that beer on whiskey was in fact very risky. When he reeled out the front door of the saloon, for the first time in his young life he was truly three sheets to the wind. At the corner of Ohio and Sixth, he stopped long enough to empty into the gutter what poisons remained in his stomach, after which he felt enough better to make it to Higdon's without falling down. He watched carefully as he came up to the house; it would not have done to have Mr. Higdon see his niece's escort for the coming evening drunk as a skunk. But all was dark, so he carefully removed his shoes, tiptoed up the stairs to his room, closed the door, then fell onto the bed, fully clothed. All night, Elmo Freitag's voice echoed in his head. "You don't believe me, go ask him. That is, if you ain't afraid."

◇◇◇

Next he knew, bright sunlight streamed through the window into his face. He wiped sleep from his eyes, drool from his cheek. To put it mildly, he'd seen better mornings. Pounding eyes and churning stomach, the calling cards of Mr. Beer and Mr. Whiskey, led the boy to promise himself he'd never again in his life get drunk, not ever. He willed himself out of bed, navigated his way downstairs. No one home, good. He staggered out back to the privy, relieved himself of his night's accumulation of coffee and beer, then made his slow way up Sixth to Ohio, to the Boston Café.

He blinked at the clock on the wall, a little past eleven. Good thing he didn't need to be at work until one. He took a seat at the counter, and threw himself on the mercy of Mr. Walch, the owner, a kindly old gent whose white chin whiskers, thin face, large ears and bright brown eyes gave him an amazing resemblance to a goat. Mr. Walch nodded with sympathy when Brun told him his story. "I treat more hangovers than any doc in town," the old guy said, then went off and came back in a moment with a glass full of tomato juice, and a little bowl. Four raw eggs in that bowl, yolks swimming around in the gooey uncooked white. Brun felt his stomach go upside-down, and he estimated how long it would take him, if necessary, to make it out into the street. Mr. Walch pointed at the juice. "This'll fix you up. Go on now. Drink it down."

Brun swallowed half the glass, then grabbed at his throat, which felt like it had caught fire. "Rooster shit," he thought he heard Mr. Walch say, but then the old man repeated, "Worcestershire. Go on, boy. Drink the rest, fast."

Brun did as he was told, then managed to get down the raw eggs. Mr. Walch nodded, all encouragement. "Good boy. Now, hang on here, and I'll get you some coffee and toast with jelly. No butter." He squinted at Brun. "Maybe you'll remember how you're feelin' next time you've got a notion to get yourself plastered."

Brun winced. "I already took the pledge."

Mr. Walch smiled benignly. He'd heard it before; he'd hear it again.

By the time Brun got back to his lodgings, it was coming up on twelve o'clock. Still no one home. He went upstairs, washed his face and brushed his teeth. Then, he changed into his new suit and spent an hour at the piano, practicing the exercises Joplin had given him. Finally, a little before one, he went out the door to work, squeezing his red rubber ball, right hand, left hand.

Saturday afternoon was busy time in a music store. When Brun walked in, Stark and Isaac were hopping, looking after two and three customers at once. Brun jumped to, couldn't even think of trying to push music sheets by playing them, but no matter, there was a six-person wait at the piano. Guitar picks, fiddle bows, rosin, clarinet reeds flew out of racks and cabinets faster than the men could ring up sales.

All of a sudden it dawned upon Brun that he was listening to something a little different on the piano. Beethoven's *Moonlight Sonata*. And who was the pianist but High Henry, the incredible seven-foot dancing fool from the night before, playing off a sheet, note-perfect, no hesitations, never a missed key. Brun listened with one ear as he rang up purchases, heard applause as Henry played the final notes. Then a man said, "Well, I'll be. Say, friend, I never would have believed a nigger could play that kind of music. You are mighty good, you know that?"

Brun recognized the voice. Elmo Freitag, and dressed flashy enough to give even Brun Campbell pause. Yellow checkered suit, pink silk shirt, white boater with a wide red band, black patent leather shoes with pearl buttons, and a tie like a rainbow somebody took an eggbeater to. Stickpin in the right lapel—glass, Brun figured—and a big four-in-hand with a monogrammed *F* in the jacket pocket. The Swede patted the pianist on the shoulder, all the while grinning like a 'gator.

Miss McAllister was with him. In her white summer dress and wide-brimmed hat, Brun imagined her as St. Cecilia, though with a good deal more powder, lip paint, and rouge than he imagined he'd see on the phiz of the patron saint of music.

Freitag shook his head, pulled out a gold coin from his pocket, dropped it into High Henry's hand. He took care, Brun thought, that their fingers did not touch. "There's your dollar, boy, fair and square." The big man flashed his reptile grin at Brun. "I told him a dollar said he couldn't do it, but I was sure as the deuce wrong."

All the time Freitag talked, Miss McAllister dog-eyed Henry. Now she said, "I declare—I teach piano, and I've never seen… where on earth did you learn to play classical piano like that?"

Brun saw Stark turn from showing a guitar to a customer. His body was tense, pale blue eyes firing electrical discharges.

But High Henry didn't seem the least bothered. Just smiled shyly, blinked up at Maisie, and said, "Thank you, ma'am. And sir, too. I can't tell you rightly how I came to play. Just been doin' it since I was a li'l boy."

"But you can read music!" said Maisie, like that might've been the Eighth Wonder of the World.

Henry smiled the smile of someone about to pass along a major confidence. "Many colored can, but they don't usually let on. Just say they play by ear."

Don't usually let on *to whites*, Brun thought. Old ways die hard. Before emancipation, it was bad enough for a colored man to have his owner find him with a gun, but even worse if Massa caught him with a book.

Freitag laughed like a hyena, then gave Henry's arm a light punch. "I like you, boy, you got yourself a good sense of humor. But now, tell me something, okay? A smart nigger like you, can read music—"

That was as far as he got. Stark had left his customer at the back of the store and marched up to face Freitag across the piano. "See here," he barked. "I told you once before—that word does not exist in my establishment. I meant it then, I mean it now."

Freitag's face went like raw beef. He looked back to the young colored man. "Hey, now, boy, you know I didn't mean you any disrespect, right?"

High Henry looked from Freitag to Stark and back again. Finally Freitag spoke up. "Well, see now, Mr. Stark? If he ain't got no complaints, why should you."

"This is my store," Stark snapped. "Not his, and certainly not yours. And if you use that word again, I will throw you out, and I doubt you'll land on your feet."

A buzz ran through the little crowd around the piano. Customers stopped browsing music sheets or looking over instruments, and turned their attention to the front of the store. Brun thought for sure he was about to see a battle royal, but Freitag surprised him. "Okay, Mr. Stark, now just calm yourself. I don't mean any insults. I come to Sedalia to get me some good colored ragtime music to publish, and this talented young knee-grow piano player...sorry. What was it you said was your name, boy?"

"Henry Ramberg. High Henry."

Freitag looked up at Henry the way he might've regarded a hot lunch, fresh out of the oven. "Okay, then, Henry, tell you what. You told me you've got some nice ragtime tunes you could write down for me. You do that, and I'll do a neat little magic trick for you." Freitag made a presto-changeo motion, fumbled in his pocket, then came out with a gold coin. "I'll turn a piece of paper with music notes on it into gold. Five dollars, free and clear. Just as soon as the music's published."

High Henry laughed, then rubbed his fingers across his mouth. "I guess that's nice an' all, sir, an' not to sound ungrateful, but most of the boys be gettin' twenny-five or even fifty dollar' for their music. An' they don't gotta wait 'til it gets published, neither."

If that bothered Freitag, he didn't show it. He squeezed Henry's shoulder and stood beside him like a proud papa. "Well, now, Mr. Stark," he boomed. "You hear that? This boy's a first-class musician, and a solid businessman to boot. If he don't got a drop or two of white blood in him, my name's not Elmo Freitag. All right, Henry, what say you play me one of those tunes right now. If it sounds anywhere near as good as that Beethoven piece, I just might give you twenty-five dollars for it."

"Just a minute."

The tone of Stark's voice quieted everyone in the store.

"Mr. Freitag, if you want to audition music for purchase, I think you'd do well to use your own piano."

Henry started to move off, but Freitag put a hand to his back and pushed him toward the stool. "Well, I would do that," Freitag said. "I surely would. But my piano hasn't been delivered yet. And I thought…" He stopped just long enough to flash that toothy grin. "I thought that considering your fond feelings for members of the colored race, you wouldn't have any objection to letting Henry here play me a song or two."

Brun couldn't take his eyes off Stark's hands, balled into fists. "Oh, it's all in his interest, is it? Mr. Freitag, it's Saturday afternoon, and as you can see, there are people waiting to try music on this piano. *My* piano. In *my* store."

Freitag did a quick scan of the crowd around the piano. "Oh, I see," he said. "You talk mighty big about how you love the knee-grow people. But if white folks want to play a piano, then a knee-grow man is just tough outa luck. He's got to make his money some other time, when no white man wants to play."

A young woman, next in line with a sheet in her hand, said, "Mr. Stark, he plays so nice, I don't care if you let him do one more tune." The man behind her chimed in with, "Way he played that *Moonlight* thing, let's all of us hear what he's got in his hip pocket."

Freitag looked like a balloon freshly pumped full of hot air.

Stark sighed, then said, "Very well," without moving his lips. "Go ahead, Henry. Play your tune."

Brun didn't think High Henry looked convinced, but he sat on the stool and started to play. Brun felt well short of impressed. Henry's tune had at least passable syncopated melodies, and some halfway-decent bass drive, but by comparison to "Harlem Rag," it suffered considerably; next to "Maple Leaf" it was pathetic. Brun was surprised at the applause when Henry finished playing. Freitag looked even more like a hungry 'gator.

Stark said, "That's very good, Henry. Lively. Why, I could hardly keep myself from dancing, right here behind the counter. It should be a big hit."

Freitag nodded hearty agreement. Brun couldn't believe his ears.

"I'll bet that tune'll make Mr. Freitag a whole lot of money," Stark said. "Thousands of dollars for sure. Maybe hundreds of thousands."

Freitag went off like a cherry bomb on the Fourth of July. He stormed over to Stark, cocked a fist, but Stark didn't budge, didn't even flinch. Freitag paused, then pulled back his hands. "Hey, Stark," he bawled. "You know what? You'd do good to keep your nose out of other people's business."

Brun thought he sounded like a little girl, somebody was trying to run off with her dolly.

"This is my shop," said Stark. "And my piano. And what goes on in my shop, at my piano, is my business. Henry has a nice tune there, you and I both know that. It should make a good deal of money for its publisher. I say you should share the wealth with the composer. Fifty dollars on delivery of the manuscript, and a penny a sheet royalties sounds about right to me. Oh, and with a legal and binding contract, of course. I'm sure you could get Mr. Higdon, over in the Katy Building, to draw one up for you."

Henry's eyes bulged. The fifty dollars alone, Brun thought, was likely as much money as the colored man would make in a month, whether at the railway yard, in construction, or by sweeping a floor. But royalties? Was Stark serious, or was he playing a game with Freitag?

The Swede stepped away from Stark. "Listen, Henry, he's just talk. How many colored you know who get royalties, huh? What you really want to think about is that my music sheets are going to be in every music shop from New York to Kansas City, and my troupe's gonna be performing those tunes on every stage from Kay Cee to New York. Fact, you can be up on those stages, playing your own tunes. Sign up with me, and by this time next year, people all over the country will know who High Henry Ramberg is." Freitag snickered, leaned in close, stage-whispered, "Pretty women'll be falling over themselves to get next to you. Now, tell you what. You go and write down that tune, give it to me, and we're in business."

Henry tipped his cap, and got up from the piano bench. The young woman next in line sat at the piano, smoothed her skirt, set her music sheet on the piano rack, and began to play. But Freitag wasn't finished with High Henry. "You're gonna write me that tune, and bring it on over soon as you can, right? I'm in Room 201 at the Commercial Hotel. You know where that is?"

"Yes, suh. Out West Main, right 'cross the street from Miss Nellie's whorehouse."

Brun almost laughed out loud at the smile in his boss' eyes.

"Okay," Freitag said. "I'll see you later." Then he led Maisie through the doorway.

Stark turned to High Henry. "You'd be a fool to give that man any music."

Henry laughed, a musical sound. "Sure, Mr. Stark, you don't need to tell me. That man think it still be slavey-time, but I do believe we's free. He been askin' all over town, but ain't nobody gonna give him a tune. We know we wouldn't never see a plugged nickel."

Brun deliberated a moment, then said to Stark, "You don't mind me saying so, sir, but I suspect you've made yourself an enemy."

Stark's face went dead-serious. "I hope so, Brun. A man's character can be gauged at least as well by his enemies as by his friends. You'll do well to keep that in mind."

Fritz Alteneder stared out the window of Boutell's Saloon. He bit off a chunk of his beef sandwich, washed it down with an immoderate swallow of beer, then looked across the table. "Hey, Pa—wanna go shoot squirrel 'safternoon?"

His father shook his head. "Damn, boy, I already told you. We're goin' over to Widda Folsom's, gonna shoe her new horses. Mr. Fehr gives me a half-day off, we ain't gonna waste the time and a bunch of shot besides. Anyways, you got to start learnin' the business. Make a little money yourself."

Fritz laughed, not an agreeable sound. "Who says I want to be a blacksmith, huh? But if I ever do go an' be one, I sure ain't gonna work for some other man, got to ask his permission to take off long enough to have a piss. I'd have my own shop—"

Emil Alteneder cut his son short with an open hand across the cheek that brought tears to the boy's eyes. "You talk pretty good, let's wait an' see how you do when it comes to workin'," Emil growled. "You ain't got no call talkin' like that. Your sandwich there, the beer you're drinkin', they was bought with money I earned and Mr. Fehr paid me. You wanna bite the hand that feeds you, go someplace else."

Behind the counter, polishing bar glasses, Gaylord Boutell shook his head. The saloon-keeper wished the Alteneders would take their business elsewhere. Not only did no one ever sit with them, no one would take a table to either side of them, so disgusting as it was to see them eat, so foul their smell. Boutell swore he'd rather spend time on Hubert Marshall's pig farm east of town than have to breathe the air around Emil and Fritz. Father and son had identical broad, flat noses and thin lips. Bullet-shaped heads sat directly on their shoulders, same barrel chests, same bay windows below. They looked at the world through brown piggy eyes behind slitted lids, as if forever squinting into a low sun. Fritz had more spiky hair than his father, but the kid was only sixteen, give him time. Word in Sedalia was that the Alteneders were as they were because they lived without the civilizing influence of a woman, Emil's wife having died years before in some sort of accident. But Boutell figured people had the story backward: would any woman be desperate enough to take up with those two cavemen? Bad enough they looked and smelled the way they did, but Fritz was as quick as his father to settle a problem with a fist, and a woman in that household would have a body perpetually covered with bruises. "Look at Doc Overstreet," was Boutell's usual observation on the subject. "He ain't never been married, and is he anything like them?"

Emil went back to attacking his food, but Fritz sat and sulked. Somebody's going to get it, Boutell thought. Somebody smaller and weaker than Fritz's old man is going to pay for that slap.

Emil leaned across the table to poke a finger into Fritz's ribs. "That there's lunch," he snarled. "When I'm done, we're leavin'. You get hungry later, gonna just be too bad."

Fritz picked up the sandwich, rested his head against his palm, nibbled a few bites. He swallowed some beer, gazed through the window. A couple went by, the man carrying a suitcase in each hand, real leather, nice. They were headed in the direction of the railway station—on their way out of Sedalia, lucky them. Fritz's stupid old man thought Sedalia was the beginning and the end of the world, but one of these mornings, he was going to wake up and find his son's bed empty. Fritz Alteneder wasn't about to spend *his* whole life in Sedalia, sweating blood in front of an open fire, burning his fingers, saying 'Yes sir,' and 'Thank you, sir' to Mr. Herman Fehr, who wasn't no better in any way than him, and didn't deserve…

Fritz dropped the last uneaten bit of sandwich onto his plate, smiled, snickered. He pointed through the window. "Hey, Pa, lookit there."

Emil shaded his eyes. "What the hell you talkin' about, boy? All I see's a bunch a people."

Fritz pointed. "Li'l pickaninny there, lookit her. You think niggers ought to be walkin' around all dressed up white?"

Emil studied the small colored girl walking past Boutell's, hair in two neat braids that bounced with each step. Her dress was almost blindingly white. Then he looked back at Fritz, and like on cue, the two jumped up from the table and ran outside. Emil pulled Fritz by the arm. "Come on, boy, move it along. Get her 'fore she makes it to the corner." Father and son took off running, shoved past Apple John, spilling fruit from his basket. The peddler knew better than to complain.

Freitag and Maisie walked the half-block from Stark and Son to Ohio, Freitag storming at every step about the way he was going to fix Stark's wagon, just wait and see. Maisie didn't say a word.

When they got to Ohio, she turned south. "See you later." Her voice was just a touch sharp.

"I'll walk with you—"

"Elmo, you can't come over now. I've got a piano lesson in five minutes, little Henrietta Holmvig. Her mother's the biggest gossip in town, never mind that the Holmvigs have more money than God. Now, go get yourself a beer and cool off. I'll be free in an hour."

He watched her strut away, his eyes fixed on her backside. Some woman. Sallie was no cold potato, but this Maisie was something else altogether. Freitag frowned. Just like Sallie, wasn't it, to try to put the kibosh on his game. Lucky he'd caught her in time. He did an about-face, walked slowly up Ohio. Have a beer, Maisie said? Well, why not?

As he crossed the street at Fourth, he noticed a small crowd of men clustered around two stocky yahoos and a little colored girl in a white dress. The girl was in tears. Freitag watched her try to get past the rednecks, but whichever way she moved, the younger one shifted so as to block her path. "Hey, Pa," he called to the older man. "This pickaninny don't give way no matter what."

Pa laughed. "Them people ain't got the brains of an ape." He pointed a finger at the girl. "Think you're as good as a white man, do you?"

The girl let out a honker of a sob, then moved right and tried to get past her tormentor, but he blocked her path. "Well, gol damn, if she don't move every which way I do, Pa. Listen, pickaninny—you're supposed to give way to a white man. Didn't your mama teach you that?"

A horse tethered to a post picked that moment to relieve itself, tail up, loud splashes into the street, a couple of plops.

"Her mama was prob'ly too busy at Lottie Wright's or Nellie Hall's to bother teachin' her anything," said the older man. "Guess it's up to us to give her lessons."

Freitag watched the little girl turn, then start running back the other way, but before she'd taken three steps, the boy was in front of her. "I…beg your pardon," the child sobbed. "Won't you please let me pass."

"She got her some manners, Fritz," called the older man. "Now, if she'd only give way, she could go along."

Fritz gestured with his hand to the open space next to him, but as soon as the girl moved sideways and tried to go forward, he had her blocked again. "Maybe she got talkin' manners, Pa," Fritz shouted. "But that's all. I think maybe we got to learn her some manners 'bout how a nigger's supposed to behave with white folks."

He grabbed the front of the girl's dress and pulled. Freitag heard the rip, then the girl split the air with a screech. Fritz slapped her, hard, on the cheek. "You learnin' something, pickaninny? Well? You think you can just go 'round town in a white dress an' that makes you good as me?"

Pa walked up to Fritz and the girl, a sneer all over his face, hands full of steaming horse droppings. Freitag scanned the circle of men. Some were grinning, others looked consternated, but no one moved forward to stop what was clearly going to happen. The girl screamed, wriggled, tried to run, but Fritz grabbed her from behind and held her still while his father smeared the girl's dress from top to bottom, then wiped his hands on her hair.

A man walking smartly up Ohio did a double-take, then rushed into the crowd and snatched the girl away from Fritz. The man was smaller than either Fritz or his Pa, but what he lacked in size, he made up in passion. "You cowards," he spat. "Is this all you can think to do of an afternoon?" He worked the little colored girl behind him; she clung to his coat-tails. The man seemed not to notice or not to mind that his coat would shortly be in need of a trip to the cleaners.

Pa jabbed a finger at the intruder. "Looks like we got us a nigger-lover, Fritz."

"Indeed you do not." Freitag noticed the man's thick Southern pronunciation. "How dare you call me that? When I was younger than that boy there, I was taking spies around Washington during the War. Did *you* lift arms in support of the Confederacy?" The man swept a look around the crowd. There came a chorus of coughs; then singly and in small groups, the men began to move away. "Cowards, all of you!" the furious little man shouted. "To just stand there and permit two grown men to torment and begrime a child—a girl child, no less! When the newspapers up North print this story, and the Yankees tell us we still haven't learned how to behave like civilized people, not a one of you can dare say a word in opposition." He looked at Fritz and Emil. "Now, get along with you," he snapped. "You Neanderthals."

Neither Emil nor Fritz had ever heard that word before, but they knew it was no compliment. Emil spat, motioned to Fritz, then the two started northward on Ohio. As they stomped past Apple John, the peddler moved out of their path.

Freitag watched the southern gentleman bend down, wipe the girl's face with a handkerchief, then turn the cloth over and dry her eyes. She raised a hand and pointed in a southwesterly direction, past the courthouse. The man stood, put an arm around the girl's shoulder, started walking her across Ohio.

Freitag took off after Fritz and Emil like he'd been shot from a cannon. "Hey, there, wait up a minute."

The men stopped and stood, glaring suspiciously at the man in the yellow checkered suit, pink shirt and white boater. As Freitag rushed up, he wrinkled his nose. "Good afternoon, gentlemen," he said. "My name is Elmo Freitag, and I have a business proposition for you. Can I buy you a beer while we talk about it?"

◇◇◇

Brun barely took notice of Mr. Fitzgerald, leading a little colored girl into the shop and past him, toward Isaac, who was stringing a guitar for a young woman. As Fitzgerald and the girl went by, Brun got a strong whiff of horse manure, but it didn't distract him from talking to the fourteen-year-old girl with black hair and cute dimples who wanted some hot new sheets to play after she finished her daily classical piano practice.

Brun was capping the sale, five sheets, when he sniffed horse shit again. He turned to see Isaac and the little girl standing beside him, and the look on the colored man's face was one Brun never again in his life wanted to see. The girl held onto Isaac's hand with both of hers, as she launched one gasping sob after another. Isaac bent to wipe her face with his handkerchief, then said, "Brun, when you done ringin' up your customer, you think you can finish stringin' this guitar? I got me some urgent business."

Isaac's voice was low and calm. Brun remembered a few years back, when a tornado blasted through El Reno, how still and heavy the air was just before the wild wind hit. "Sure, Isaac."

The cute girl on the other side of the counter moved a few steps away. Isaac didn't say another word, just put the guitar and strings into Brun's hand, and disappeared out the doorway with the little girl. Brun looked toward the back of the shop, saw Fitzgerald in a highly animated conversation with Stark, but couldn't make out any words.

Miss Dimples was through the doorway right behind Isaac, no chance any more of making time with her. Brun turned his attention to Isaac's customer, not a bad looker herself, and no engagement or wedding ring on her finger. He smiled. "I'll get your guitar strung for you right quick."

As Fitzgerald left the store, he paused just long enough to tip his hat to Brun, who called a hello as he set the C-string into place and began winding it on the peg.

With Isaac gone, Brun and Stark ran double-time. When he needed to talk to his boss, Brun thought Stark's answers were clipped, just this side of uncivil.

After a bit more than an hour, Isaac returned with the girl, who was now considerably improved. Her face was clean, she'd stopped crying, and she had on a different dress, a blue one, not nearly so fancy as her white dress, but in far better condition. She carried a small blackboard and a couple of pieces of chalk.

Isaac walked her up to Brun, and said, "Brun, this is my li'l girl, Belinda. Lindy, can you say a good afternoon to Mr. Brun?"

The girl was all eyes. She stared at Brun, then up at her father. He gave her a little push. Finally, she managed a curtsy around her blackboard, and piped, "Good afte'noon, Mr. Brun."

"Well, a good afternoon to you, Miss Belinda." Brun exaggerated a low bow. The little girl giggled and buried her face against her father's leg. Isaac smiled, if a little grimly. "You really do got yourself a way with the ladies, don't you, Brun?" Then he herded Belinda into Stark's office, sat her down at the desk, and she started at work, head low and cocked to one side over the blackboard, gripping a piece of chalk in a fist. Isaac came back out, said thank-you to Brun, and went right to work, not another word.

Well, I guess none of my business, Brun thought. It was getting close on to four o'clock, and the crowd had slackened, so he sat down at the piano, and began to play "Original Rags." He'd just about finished when he noticed a man standing at his side, a heavy-set yap in a dirty blue work shirt and overalls to match, bald in front, but with spikes of black hair that Brun would've warranted had not seen a brush in weeks. Thick arms bent at the elbows, both fists balled, and snorting like a bull on a short chain with a cow in clear sight. He pointed toward the back of the store at Isaac, who was showing a lady a mandolin. "Boy, you go on back there, and tell that nigger to get up here, fast."

Brun considered running Stark's knee-grow routine past the clod, but knew that would be foolish at best. "Isaac's waiting on a customer," Brun said. "He'll be done pretty soon, and then you can talk to him."

The man reacted like Brun had put a cattle prod to his hindquarters. "Well, gol *damn*," he shouted, at which point everyone in the store turned to look. "What kinda place is it you run, boy, you tell a white man he's gotta wait on a nigger? Ain't no wonder he's the kinda nigger he is, him an' his whole fam'ly." Then, the man cupped his hands around his mouth, and shouted so loud it seemed to Brun he'd been whispering before. "Hey,

Snowball—you get your black ass up here, and I mean now. *Right* now. 'Fore I come back there and drag it up."

A couple of girls stopped looking over music sheets, glanced at each other, then made a beeline for the door. Isaac left his customer and started toward the piano, but Stark got there first. Brun noticed he was limping slightly, but he still covered ground in a hurry. "Just what do you mean," he shouted at the angry man. "Coming into my store like this, shouting obscenities and chasing my customers away? Get yourself back outside, and don't ever set foot in here again."

Whatever the man might have said or done by way of reply, Brun never got to hear, because Isaac was now up front as well, and the man turned all his attention in that direction. He waved a fist in Isaac's face. "Nigger, I hope you know, you just done bought yourself more trouble than you'll ever know what to do with."

Isaac turned a fiery eye onto the yahoo, but said not a single word. Which seemed to make the man even sorer. "Gol damn, Rastus, cat got your tongue or something? I ask you a question, I expect I'm gonna get an answer! Talkin' to my boy like you did? Pushing his face in the dirt? Why, no colored *ever* dast do such to a white boy. You're in line for some big-time trouble, and I mean right now."

Brun looked hard, but best he could tell, the man wasn't carrying a gun. Neither did he seem about to pull a knife.

"That boy's lucky I didn't jes' break botha his arms." Isaac's words seemed to hang, shimmering, in the air. "Scarin' a li'l girl half-outa her mind, rippin' up her dress and smearin' her all over with horse shit? That boy of yours ever gets a notion to try anything like that again, you'll be goin' to see him in the hospital. That, or be goin' to his funeral."

The spike-haired man howled, jabbed a finger to the sky. "Okay," he roared. "I couldn't for the life of me figure where a pickaninny comes off sassin' a white boy, won't step aside when he's comin' down the sidewalk, not even when he tells her to move. Well, now I guess I see what's what. She gets it right from her daddy. An' if anybody was lucky, nigger, it was you. Walkin' right inside of a white saloon, grabbin' a white boy away from a respectable gen'lman he's talkin' to, draggin' him out in the street… Hadn't been I was out takin' a piss right then, you'd already be dancin' off a tree. Now you an' me gonna settle this matter." The man jabbed a finger toward the doorway. "Outside."

Isaac took a step toward the doorway. Brun clutched the edge of the counter. Stark said one word. "Don't."

"Best I do," Isaac called back over his shoulder. "If it ain't now, it's gonna be some other time."

The big man laughed. "You're a sassy nigger, all right, but you sure ain't dumb, I give you that. You're likely smarter than that nigger-lover boss of yours."

Brun let go of the counter and ran after the men. Isaac was no more out the doorway before four men surrounded him. Aside from the spike-haired lunk who'd caused the commotion in the store, there was Elmo Freitag and a smaller, younger version of Spike-hair. The fourth man, Brun had never seen. The boy looked all around, but saw no ropes or horses, and no pot of tar, which reassured him, though only moderately. Across the street, Apple John stood and watched, his basket on the courthouse lawn.

The men maneuvered Isaac off the wooden sidewalk into the street. People passed by quickly, made sure to look in some other direction. "Okay, nigger," the spike-haired man shouted. "We gonna start by havin' you tell Fritz here that you're sorry for what you did, and you're gonna make it right."

Brun stood on his toes to see over the heads of the circled men. Fritz was a boy about his own age, with a dirty, pimply, scratched-up face. His right eye was discolored, swollen nearly shut. Easy to see he'd been blubbering at least as much as Belinda had.

Isaac drew himself upright, then took a half-step toward Fritz, who, to Brun's amusement, took a full pace backward. "Only way I could make it right'd be to break his arms," the colored man said. "The coward. Pickin' on an eight-year-old girl."

At that point, Brun noticed sunlight gleaming off a blade in the hand of the man on the far side of the circle. But then he heard Stark's voice, behind him. "All right, all of you. Move away from that man."

Stark stepped forward, pointed a nasty looking sawed-off shotgun at the gathered men. He sighted down the barrel. "I won't warn you again. Get away from that man or I'll shoot."

Freitag moved off, then the other three men shuffled a safe distance away from Isaac. Stark put up the gun, glared at Spike-hair. "Emil Alteneder, you're the worst kind of redneck bully and coward, and your son's just like you. If *I'd* seen Fritz mistreating that little girl, he'd have come off a whole lot worse than he did." Stark waggled the shotgun toward the fourth man. "Marty, if you had anything better to do than hang around Boutell's all day cadging drinks, you wouldn't get into messes like this. Give me that knife."

Stark held out his hand. Marty set his feet. Stark raised the gun. "Slowly," he said. "Handle first, that's it." He took the knife from Marty, then retreated to the edge of the sidewalk. "All right. This ugly game is over. Now, beat it, all of you."

But Freitag wasn't finished. A huge smile split his broad face as he looked at Emil Alteneder. "You gonna let him talk to you like that, Mr. Alteneder? Trash like him is why there's trouble in this country, why the colored don't know their place. A nigger rubs a white boy's face in the dirt and blackens his eye, why next you know, a white man's gonna have to move aside to let a nigger go past." He jerked a thumb in Isaac's direction. "I was you, I'd make dang sure that nigger knows if he don't apologize right to your boy, he's gonna have to keep his eyes on that li'l gal of his twenty-four hours out of every day, forever."

Isaac stiffened. Brun held his breath. The colored man moved toward Freitag, who looked him square in the eyes. "You heard me right. Ain't no way you're gonna be able to watch that child every single minute of every day. And both of us can figure out what kind of thing could happen to a li'l pickaninny girl whose daddy don't keep close enough watch on her. Can't we, now?"

Brun thought Emil Alteneder looked like a man resurrected. Fritz made a sound somewhere between a snort and a giggle. Freitag talked on. "Now, I say it's way past time you apologize to Master Alteneder there. You tell him, 'I am truly sorry, young Master Alteneder. I am sorry all the way down to my sorry black ass, and I do most sincerely apologize to you.'"

Isaac took a deep breath. He glanced toward the music shop, where he'd left the little girl and her chalk. Slowly, he repeated the words, sounding like each one was drawn out of him with hooks and wires.

"Well, now, that is a good start," said Freitag. "Next thing, you are going to get down on your knees and say, 'Young Master Alteneder, I beg your forgiveness.' Then you kiss his feet. Both of them."

A terrible look came over Isaac's face. Stark leveled the shotgun. Isaac took a couple of steps toward the music store, but stopped when Emil Alteneder shouted, "That sure is a cute li'l gal you got. Be a real shame how she's gonna look when you find her. Just might be she's still alive, but both you an' her'll be wishin' she wasn't."

Isaac put a hand atop the barrel of Stark's gun, lowered it, then walked back, knelt slowly, and begged young Alteneder's forgiveness. He kissed one filthy shoe. But as he shifted to kiss the second, Fritz delivered a kick to the side of his head. Isaac rolled over, clutching his temple.

Brun never could remember running up to Fritz Alteneder; his first recollection was hauling off and giving the boy a punch that sent him straight to the ground, spitting blood. "You kiss *my* foot," Brun shouted, and aimed a kick at Fritz's head. But Emil quickly pulled his son back, and Brun came within a hair of falling on his face. Instantly, Stark was at his side, swinging the gun stock in all directions. "One more word from any of you," he shouted. "And I swear by all that's holy, it will be your last. Now! If I don't see your backs in three seconds, I will shoot. One...two..."

As the retreating men reached the corner of Ohio, Stark lowered the gun. "All right, Brun, enough for them. Let's get Isaac inside."

Brun and Stark each took one of Isaac's arms, lifted him, walked him into the store. All the way, Brun kept thinking something was not adding up. Wasn't Elmo Freitag supposed to be in town to get his hands on colored ragtime to publish? Then it occurred to him. If Freitag couldn't get music by flattery and playing the con, maybe a little strong-arm might do the job.

Inside the store, they sat Isaac on the stool behind the counter. The colored man swore he was all right. "Just a glancing blow, that kick. I seen it coming and was rollin' away from it." He patted Brun's shoulder. "Brun sure gave him a whole lot worse than he gave me. Couple of teeth there on the ground, and they wasn't mine."

"Nevertheless," Stark said. "You are going to let Dr. Overstreet look you over. Brun, go along and make sure he gets there safely, then take off for the day. I'll close up. Isaac, I'll take Belinda upstairs with me, Sarah will look after her. But I think we'd better get her out of town for a while."

Isaac nodded agreement. "After supper, I'll take her on out to my sister's in Smithton."

"After *dark*," said Stark. "And *we'll* take her."

Chapter Eight

Sedalia
Saturday, July 22, 1899, afternoon

Walter Overstreet watched the new boy lead Stark's man outside. Once they'd crossed Ohio, the doctor trudged back into his office, plopped into his leather chair, sighed, shook his head, and reached into the little cabinet. He poured from the bottle, knocked down a swallow, refilled his glass.

He drank his seconds more slowly. Good thing Isaac was all right. Most of Overstreet's colleagues would tell him that was because the skulls of colored are thicker than those of whites, but one day in anatomy lab, Overstreet had put that precept to test and found it wanting. Isaac likely owed his escape to his own agility and the braveness of that boy, what was his name? The doctor hoped the boy would be all right, working at Stark's. John Stark could be stubborn and hotheaded, and there was never a time when somebody or other in town wasn't muttering about the way he behaved toward colored. Why he'd chosen to settle in Missouri, not Kansas, Overstreet couldn't begin to understand. Something about Stark...he seemed always troubled. Overstreet had known other such men, and made it a point to be on guard around them. They could go through their lives as model citizens, but let something happen that stirred up a memory long tucked away, and all hell would break loose. Fortunately, this time, when push really did come to shove, those Alteneder morons, Marty Browne, and that Freitag dandy had cut and run. Otherwise, Overstreet figured, he'd now be in the middle of East Fifth Street, trying to handle simultaneous medical and civic emergencies. Damn and blast, a man has limits. He picked up the bottle and poured thirds.

No sooner did Brun and the Higdons sit down to supper when Higdon announced that a dead woman had been found early Wednesday morning on Washington Street by a policeman making early morning rounds. Brun smiled to himself at the way Belle and Luella made every appearance of being properly shocked, but not quite so badly that Higdon wouldn't tell them more. Who was the woman? How had she been killed? Do they know who did it? Do they know why?

Higdon looked at Brun. "*You* don't seem very interested."

"Oh, well, sure I am," Brun said. "But Miss Belle and Miss Luella asked every question before I could even think about it."

"Well, then, to answer you all," said Higdon. "We don't know who the woman was. She wasn't local, but she did have on a wedding ring and diamond engagement ring. It's possible her husband ran off, and she was looking for him. And she was strangled."

The two women made terrible faces. Miss Belle moved a hand up to her neck.

"Did they find a rope, or something like that?" Brun asked.

Higdon shook his head. "No. Doc Overstreet said from the look of it, it was done by hands. Finger marks on the neck, and her spine was broken...Brun, your face is gone so pale."

Belle drew a glass of water, and passed it to Brun, who took a long swallow. So that was why her head had flopped all around when he tried to lift it. "Sorry, Mr. Higdon. I was just thinking what it must be like to get your neck cracked like that. It had to have been a pretty strong man."

Higdon made a sour face. "That's a very good point. The man they're holding in the County Jail isn't big, and he doesn't look at all strong. But the police went around to the hotels with

pictures and a description of the dead woman, and they hit pay
dirt today at Kaiser's. John Kaiser told them a man brought her
in there Tuesday evening, got her a room, took her upstairs, and
John never saw either one of them again. According to John,
the woman was badly upset or drunk, and he gave the police a
to-the-T description of the man. They picked him right up and
arraigned him, and he'll probably go to trial week after next. He's
not a local, so Bud Hastain contrived to throw a little work to
his former clerk." Higdon chuckled. "Ladies, your brother and
uncle are the man's attorney. He's an odd duck, to say the least.
Says he lives in Buffalo, New York, and works for the Procter
and Gamble Company. But he talks like an unreconstructed
Virginia plantation owner."

Brun coughed and choked on a mouthful of chicken, grabbed
for his water glass, swallowed hard. Tears ran down his face. By
the time he recovered himself, everyone at the table was staring
at him. "Oh, he couldn't have done that," Brun said. "I'd warrant
he couldn't have strangled a woman and broken her neck."

Higdon put down his fork and knife, stared at his young boarder.
"But Brun…I haven't even mentioned the man's name."

"It's Fitzgerald. Mr. Edward Fitzgerald."

Higdon leaned across the table. "That's right. But how did
you know that? And just how can you be so sure Mr. Fitzgerald
couldn't have done it?"

Sure as a person can be, Brun thought. But he was careful to
limit himself to recounting Mr. Fitzgerald's kindnesses to him,
and how Fitzgerald had told him he was in town to set up a large
subsidiary plant for Procter and Gamble. "It's not just that he's
way too gentle to ever do a thing like that. It's that he's too…"

"Ineffectual? Is that the word you're looking for, Brun?"

The boy nodded. "I just plain know Mr. Fitzgerald couldn't
have done it. You've got to get him off."

Higdon gave the boy a curious look, then said, "Well, Brun,
tell you what. If you have any information that might help me
help Mr. Fitzgerald, I hope you'll give it to me."

Brun thought of the time, years before, when he watched an older boy catch a darning-needle bug, then stick a pin through its body, making the poor thing squirm and flap its wings something awful. "I haven't, sir. Or I would for certain, kind as Mr. Fitzgerald was to me."

Before Brun finished talking, the understanding hit home that it was up to him to find information that would get Mr. Fitzgerald off the hook without getting Scott Joplin on. Because if either Fitzgerald or Joplin went to the gallows, Brun doubted he'd ever again sleep through a night.

The Central Presbyterian Church stood on Sixth and Lamine, just a couple of blocks from Higdon's. As soon as Luella and Brun were out of view of the house, the girl linked her hand into Brun's arm. Crossing Ohio, Brun cast a glance toward Main Street, where he wished he could be on this Saturday evening, his first in Sedalia. But when Luella said, "It really is very nice of you to escort me, Brun. I hope you don't mind," the boy gave her the best smile he could manage, and said, "Why ever should I mind? You've all made me feel right at home, and I'm glad to be asked." Two out of three weren't lies, he thought, not so bad.

The Social was in the church basement, gray and dreary in the paltry light of coal-oil lamps. The minute Brun and Luella walked in, the mustiness sent the boy into a sneezing fit. Up front, a long table held plates of cookies and a cut-glass bowl full of some kind of pink, over-sweet fruit punch. The young people sat around little tables and talked, all the while under the eyes of six vinegar-faced chaperones, three men and three women. There was no music, and certainly no dancing—Satan get thee far from Central Presbyterian. Brun thought the boys were mostly milksops and sissies with exaggerated manners; many of them wore spectacles. The girls were much like Luella, prim and very proper. There was a good deal of prattle about Colonel Robert Ingersoll, who'd died suddenly the day before. "Serves him right," one of the girls said. "Old Mister Pagan Bob, always trying to get people to believe the Bible is wrong, and Jesus wasn't the son of God. I wonder if he thinks there isn't any hell now." Everyone at the table, Brun excepted, laughed.

After a while, Brun became the center of attention, not surprising, considering that he was new in town and a runaway. He went on at considerable length, knowing that if he stopped talking, there would be further palaver over divine retribution and other matters holy and spiritual. The sissy boys and proper girls goggled as he told his story of riding the rails to Sedalia, and taking lessons in colored piano music from an actual colored man. The chaperones got more ugly-mugged by the minute. Every now and again, Brun caught the eye of a boy he knew envied him, or of a girl he thought might prove an interesting companion once outside sacred walls. He tried to catch the names of a couple of those.

At the stroke of ten o'clock, the chaperones announced with obvious relief that the pleasant evening was at an end. Brun and Luella walked a block back across Sixth with Fred Vollrath and Mabel Horton, seventeen-year-olds who had an understanding, which meant they'd agreed when Fred finished his schooling at Missouri University, he would come back to Sedalia, join his father's insurance firm, and he and Mabel would be married. Brun could not for the life of him understand how they could talk that way and sound so happy about it. He pictured the couple in twenty years, thirty, forty, fifty, but finally forced himself to stop, as the images made him sadder than he cared to feel.

At Ohio, Fred and Mabel went off, hand in arm, toward the big houses on Broadway. Luella smiled up at her escort. "Thank you, Brun, it's been such a lovely evening. But it's gone by so fast, hasn't it?"

Something about her face put a lump into Brun's throat. "Well, then, let's not have it end so fast." Words spoken before considered. "Suppose we go back up Ohio to the Boston Café, and have us an ice-cream soda."

Like he'd offered her the moon and stars.

By that hour, Ohio Avenue's Saturday evening festivities were winding on down, but there were still a fair number of people on the sidewalks and the pavement, talking, arguing politics, courting. An hour or two earlier, Ohio would have been a sea of men, women and children, and Brun regretted not having been there to share in the fun. He and Luella walked past a street corner where four young blades were harmonizing on "In the Evening by the Moonlight," one of them strumming a guitar, another rattling a pair of rib bones, setting a livelier rhythm than one usually heard for that drippy old tune. The shrill whistle of the popcorn and peanut wagon on the corner of Fourth cut the air. And from a few blocks beyond, the sounds of revelry on Main Street came louder and clearer with each step. Brassy music, shouting. Luella obviously heard it, too, and clear she didn't approve.

Brun steered her past a fiddler and a banjo man doing a fair job on "Old Zip Coon," then past four boys, a clarinet, two trumpets and a banjo, so bad Brun couldn't even tell what tune they thought they were playing. Just outside the Boston Café, a loud bang set Luella to shrieking and throwing both arms around Brun's neck. "It's okay." The boy pointed at two men a few steps past the doorway, one with his hands on his knees and laughing to beat the band, the other holding a cigar stump and sporting a scowl that said his friend might be lucky to go back home that night without a blackened eye. Luella giggled, "Sorry." Brun noticed she was not quick to pull back her arms.

They walked inside and up to the counter, and Brun asked what flavor Luella would like. Strawberry, no uncertainty. Brun ordered a strawberry ice-cream soda with two straws and two spoons. As he sat head-to-head with Luella over the glass, he caught a raised eyebrow and a sly wink from goatish Mr. Balch, behind the counter. If Luella looked any happier, Brun thought, she might bust wide open, and he felt a sadness deep in his stomach. Girls like Luella should go for sissy boys like the ones at the Social, but she hadn't paid a one of those boys a moment's notice, and here she was, flirting with Brun Campbell for all the world to see. Not fair. At least one of them was going to end up getting hurt.

Walking hand-in-arm back to Higdon's, Luella let her head rest against Brun's shoulder. Watch out, Brun thought, this could get dangerous in a hurry. He tried to walk faster, but it's not easy to put on speed with a girl's head resting right next to your own. Luella sighed. "Oh, Brun, I just love the way the air smells at night this time of year. Like a million flowers." Brun told her, yes, the smell was most agreeable, but he wished he were smelling the perfume from the women and the smoke from the cigars and cigarettes in Miss Nellie Hall's place on West Main.

Belle, sitting by herself on the front-porch glider, gave the young couple a pleasant hello and said she hoped they'd had a nice evening. Luella assured her she'd had at least that, and Brun didn't argue. Then, Luella asked Brun whether he might be willing to escort her to church next morning.

Brun had no wish to offend his host's niece, nor hurt the poor girl's feelings, but he knew there was no such thing as agreeing to go to church with a woman only once. "I'm sorry," he said. "But I have another engagement for the morning. And also, Miss Luella, truth be known, I am not a churchgoer by nature."

She didn't look upset, just smiled and said, "Well, maybe over time I can help you become one."

If a boy wants to live to become a man, he learns when he's over-matched, and does not push certain matters. Brun smiled back at the women, excused himself, walked inside and up to his room.

But not to go to sleep. The stroll down Ohio with its glimpse of life on Main Street had been a brain tonic for the boy. He thought about Nellie Hall's, perfume and tobacco smoke, Big Froggy at the piano. But how was he going to get past the women who were still probably sitting on that glider, Luella telling Belle about her lovely evening? And where was he going to get a little scratch? You didn't go to a house without some money in your pocket for liquor, or maybe even for a girl. But he'd be foolish to spend his first paycheck for that, then go wanting, the whole week ahead.

There were twenty-eight dollars, though, weren't there, in Scott Joplin's money-clip. It wouldn't be right to spend that money, but why not consider it a loan? Pay it back after he'd collected another few paychecks, or worked another night or two at Boutell's. He ran to the closet, pulled the money-clip from its hiding place and removed five dollars, which he stuffed into his pocket. From there, it was easy. Change into his old clothes, then out the window, shinny down the downspout—just like at home—and he was past the side of the house in an instant, off on the run to West Main Street. The big street clock in front of Bichsel's Jewelry Store on Ohio read twenty minutes before twelve as he hightailed past it.

Sarah Ann Stark heard her husband coming up the stairs. She rushed to the door, opened it, laughed as she saw the surprise on his face. Johnny always said he loved the way she laughed. He told friends that was the first thing he'd noticed about her, when she and her mother came to the barracks to sell molasses cookies to the soldiers. And when anyone asked what was the second thing he'd noticed, he only smiled.

Stark stood his rifle against the wall, then put his arms around her. "It's after two in the morning, Sarah. What are you doing up?"

"Waiting for you, of course. What else?"

"But you needn't have."

"Now, stop that. What sort of wife would I be if I could sleep a wink before I knew all went well for you and Isaac?"

Stark patted her arm. "It all went well. Belinda is safely at her aunt's, and as you see, I'm here with you. Isaac took the horse back to the stable, he'll be with us shortly. I thought better to have him sleep here tonight than in his own house."

She saw his face tighten. "What is it, Johnny? There's something you're not telling me. I saw it in your eyes before you left, and I see it still." She watched emotions move across his face like clouds in a windy winter sky, uncertainty…concern…anger.

And one she was unaccustomed to seeing. Fear. She knew he could neither lie to her nor put her off. "It's about this Freitag, Johnny, isn't it?"

Nod. "He's an odd one. Deucedly clever, but something's terribly wrong with the man. Setting up a colored troupe to work like an antebellum plantation? He really believes that nonsense, Sarah, that the colored are a lower grade of man and it's an act of Christian goodness to treat them like an organ grinder treats his monkey. And now with those two Alteneder hellkites in the picture, he's got his overseers. I'm afraid this business with Belinda and Isaac is only the beginning."

She folded her arms around him, patted his back. "We've been through much in our lives that hasn't been easy, but we've always come through. And we will this time."

He drew partway back. She could hardly bear to look into his anguished eyes, but knew she mustn't turn away.

"Sarah, it's been more than thirty-five years that the colored haven't been slaves, but are they any better off? Having to give way on a public sidewalk to the likes of Fritz Alteneder? Having to be sure they don't look cross-eyed at a white woman? Having to stand by quietly when men like Freitag steal from them, because they know if they make any complaint, they'll be found in the morning hanging from a tree, burned and mutilated? I fought nearly five years in a terrible war, and the slaves were freed. But only on paper."

She'd heard it before, many times. "You've always made certain nothing happened to Isaac. In 1865, again today, and how many times in between?"

"But Isaac is only one. And I'm nearly sixty years old. It doesn't end."

"No, Johnny, it doesn't. It will be here after you and I are no longer even a memory. It stole out the courthouse door at Appomattox, and took command of a whole new army of confederates. We'll never be mustered out from this war, and so long as we don't desert, no one can properly fault us." She took him by the arm, guided him toward the kitchen. "There's fresh coffee, let's have a cup." She smoothed back a thick lock of hair from his brow, as much gray now as black. "Then I'll go make up the couch for Isaac."

The sun was high next morning when Brun pried himself off his bed, winced, shaded his eyes, then staggered downstairs and outside, first to the privy, then to the pump, where he held his head under a stream of cold water for two minutes by the count. Back in his room, he squirmed and wriggled into shirt, tie and pants, and told himself he was heading straight for perdition. Two nights in a row, throwing-up drunk, not getting into bed until after three in the morning. Was it worth it? To his surprise, he smiled. Yes. It certain-sure was. More than two hours of Big Froggy banging those piano keys, then an hour upstairs in Rita Hodges' room, doing what Luella wouldn't imagine doing until she was firmly and legally married...well, a lot of what Rita and Brun did, Luella would never imagine, let alone actually do.

But now Brun had something to do. The talk at dinner the evening before had started him thinking, and his excuse to Luella that he had another engagement for the morning had set a plan into motion in his mind. He'd visit Mr. Fitzgerald in the County Jail, see whether he could learn anything which might help get that poor man out and away from the danger of a noose.

Downstairs, he checked the longcase clock in the living room. Past ten. He knew he ought to be thoroughly ashamed, but couldn't quite manage. The Higdons were no doubt gone to worship, but Belle had left him half a peach pie and the remains of a pot of coffee. By the time the boy finished his meal, his head still hurt some and his mouth was a dust bowl, but he believed he was thinking straight. He washed and dried his dishes, threw the towel on the little hook above the sink, skipped to the front door, and ran outside.

Before he got so far as the corner, he saw the Higdons on the other side, about to cross. He considered ducking away and running, but too late—there was Luella, waving a hand. Then they all waved.

"On your way somewhere, Brun?" Higdon made a show of looking at his watch. The ladies smiled just enough to let on that they were in on the joke.

Brun considered lying, but what with Higdon being Fitzgerald's lawyer, he'd likely be found out, and then it would be considerably harder to explain himself. "Yes, sir. I'm going to talk to Mr. Fitzgerald, in the jail. Maybe I can figure how to repay some of his kindness."

Higdon scratched at his cheek, and looked off into the distance. "Tell you what. As soon as I see the ladies home, I'm going to talk to Mr. Fitzgerald myself. You can come along, if you'd like."

Brun felt a flash of disappointment, but then reconsidered. Fitzgerald might say something to Higdon that he wouldn't say to Brun, and Brun might just see more in one particular comment or another than Higdon would. "That sounds fine to me, sir." He turned to start walking with the family back to the house, but Belle told her brother she really thought she and Luella could get themselves half a block without an escort. "The two of you go right along," she said. "We'll see you for dinner."

Uh-oh. Brun suddenly remembered. "Miss Belle, I'm sorry, but with all the commotion yesterday, I forgot to tell you. Mr. Stark invited me for dinner at his house today."

Higdon looked surprised, then laughed. "You constantly amaze me, Brun. I don't think I've ever known such a fast mover. Well, all right then, let's go. I'll be back in plenty of time, Belle."

The Pettis County Jail was a red-stone building on Lamine, between Second and Third. Higdon led Brun inside and down a dark, damp corridor. The boy tried holding his breath against the stink of unwashed bodies and chamber pots not emptied nearly often enough. At the end of the corridor, a young policeman sat with his feet up on a desk, eyes half-closed. "Hey, there Calvin," Higdon said. "I'd like to talk to my client."

The young copper practically jumped to attention. His face showed relief to the point of gratitude that if he'd had to get caught on the loaf, it had been by a civilian, not by the captain or, worse, one of the sergeants. "Sure, Mr. Higdon."

Calvin clearly couldn't figure out where Brun fit in, but he picked up the big ring of keys from the desk and started walking back through the cell block. "Sheriff Williams and the Missus're out to her mother's," he said. "They always go there Sunday after church, and stay to dinner, so it's just me here right now." The smirk on Higdon's face said he knew that. Brun wondered whether that just might explain why the lawyer had scheduled his visit for right then.

They walked between rows of cells, most of them occupied, which made sense to Brun. Saturday night was the likeliest time for being drunk and disorderly. Other prisoners would be in for theft, assault or murder. Most of the inmates slept curled on their small beds; one man lay stretched out on the dirt floor of his cell. A few stared at the short parade going past. A big ebony-black man in a torn shirt and patched pants rattled the bars of his cell. The man's muddy eyes bulged; a trickle of blood ran down his left cheek. "When'sa doctor comin'?" he shouted. "Mah haid hurts fit to bust."

"You shoulda thought of that before you decided to run outa Scally's with that armful of groceries," Calvin snapped. "Doc'll be here when he gets here. Now sit down and shut the hell up."

Brun made a new vow to lay off the sauce. He looked all around for Fitzgerald, but didn't see him until they came up to the last cell on the left. The Southern gentleman looked very different from the two times Brun had seen him at Boutell's. His face was stubbly, trousers badly wrinkled, shirt dingy and open at the neck. No attempt to hide his suspenders. At Boutell's he'd been immaculate; here, he looked like just another gutter bum picked up drunk and pitched into a jail cell to dry out. The perplexity all over his face, probably from trying to figure where Brun fit in, didn't help his overall appearance. He stood, then walked quickly to the front of his cell. "Mr. Higdon!" he called. "Did you straighten this terrible business out? Am I going to be set free?"

Calvin snickered, but the look Higdon turned on him wiped the comedy off his phiz in nothing flat. "Not yet," Higdon said. "I need to talk to you for a few minutes."

Calvin opened the cell door, and as Higdon and Brun walked inside, locked the door behind them. Brun felt a stab of panic. The cell was furnished only with a small cot at the back, under a tiny barred window ten feet up the wall, the sole source of light.

"Call me when you're done, Mr. Higdon," Calvin said. Then he was gone back up front.

Higdon called a thanks, and turned to Fitzgerald. "I believe you've met my young friend."

"Brun Campbell." The boy extended a hand. "At Boutell's. You were very kind, got me a room at the Y. I'm sorry to see you in this situation, sir."

Fitzgerald gave a courtly nod, then shook Brun's hand gravely. "Of course I remember."

"Brun is now my lodger," said Higdon. "When I told him about your arrest, he insisted you could not possibly be guilty. He was determined to come and see you this morning, and since I was coming anyway, I asked him along. Is that all right with you?"

"Oh, yes," said Fitzgerald. "Absolutely. And, Master Campbell, I am grateful without bounds for your confidence in my character." He drew himself straight up to attention. "As God is my witness, Mr. Higdon, I am totally innocent of the charge against me."

If the man's situation were not so distressful, Brun might well have laughed at his Southern formality of speech and manner. But the sadness that seemed draped across his shoulders like a heavy cloak brought tears to the boy's eyes.

"That's very well," said Higdon. "For what it's worth, I believe you. But we're going to need to convince a judge and a jury to feel as we do. And I'll need your help doing that."

"Whatever is necessary, sir, that I will do."

"All right." Higdon sat on the edge of the cot, and looked up at Fitzgerald. "Please tell me about your encounter with the dead woman. All about it. Every detail you can remember, the entire story. Leave nothing out, no matter how insignificant it may seem."

Fitzgerald sank onto the edge of the cot, next to Higdon, and lowered his face into his hands. "Well, now, let's see," he drawled. "Tuesday evening, I stopped for a couple of drinks at Boutell's—"

"What time was that?"

Fitzgerald studied the ceiling as if the answer might have been written there. "Oh, between six and seven, I should say."

"Is that as close as you can get?"

Back to reading the ceiling. "Just before six-thirty, yes. According to the clock there."

"Good. The closer we can pin down times, the better. Please go ahead."

"All right, sir. I decided to have a bit of supper, so I walked over to Mr. Pehl's Restaurant on Second Street, was taken to a small corner table, ordered my supper, and ate. I left, oh, I should say, at about half-past eight, and as I went outside, I practically bumped into this young woman on the walkway. She was attractive, and rather well turned out. I dare say that white silk dress on her cost some man a pretty penny. She looked…well, confused. Frightened? Casting glances everywhere. It even occurred to me she could be mad. I asked whether I might be of assistance, perhaps escort her to her home, but for some reason that seemed to upset her no end. She began to cry, and passersby started to stare…well, sir, you can surely understand. I thought perhaps if I could get her out of public scrutiny, she might calm down, so I led her across Ohio, into the lobby of the Kaiser Hotel, and to a sofa off to the side of the hotel restaurant and behind a row of potted plants. I asked repeatedly what was the matter, but if anything, that only made her cry the harder. I asked her name; she said Sallie Rudolph."

Maybe that's what she said, Brun thought. But I bet her name was really Freitag.

"I told her again that I'd be most happy to escort her home, but she said, 'No, thank you, that would be much farther than either of us could walk.' I asked her where she was from, and what had brought her here, which seemed a quite reasonable thing to do, wouldn't you say? But that only got her worked up all over again, and I began to fear she might become hysterical. So I went to the desk clerk, explained the situation, and said I'd pay her night's lodging. I thought of going for a doctor, but in the end decided perhaps just a night's rest would permit her to gather her emotions. I signed her in, and asked the clerk to be so kind as to show the lady to the room, but he said the bellhop was off for a break, and he couldn't leave the desk unattended. So I told him I'd show her to the room myself. He gave me the key; I led her to the stairs—"

"One minute." Higdon held up a hand. "Did this woman, who was presumably from out of town, have a suitcase?"

Fitzgerald looked back to the ceiling. "Oh yes. Of course. I *am* sorry, Mr. Higdon, I'd forgotten. She had indeed been carrying a small case, cardboard, brown imitation leather. Rather a cheap one, I'm afraid. I took it from her as we started up the stairs. Her room was to be on the second floor, and as we were walking along the hall, she began to act as if she were faint, so I left the suitcase, assisted her into her room, and then helped her off with her shoes and onto the bed. After that, I went back for the suitcase. So it did take a bit longer than I'd expected to get her to the room, and comfortably situated. But I assure you, sir, I left the door open the entire time. I do believe that's the entire story."

Higdon tapped a finger on the soft red-stone wall. "While you were in the woman's room, did you notice anything unusual there? For that matter, what *did* you see?"

Fitzgerald half-closed his eyes, then slowly shook his head. "I really don't recall anything out of the ordinary. Just a hotel room, a bed, a couple of chairs, a washbasin—"

"Did you see any clothing hanging in the closet? Any *men's* clothing, in particular?"

"No, sir. The closet door was closed, and I most assuredly did not go snooping inside."

Brun thought that remark and the tone in which it was made tickled Higdon as much as it did him. But the lawyer just said, "All right. Did you happen to notice a name engraved on that suitcase? Or initials?"

"No, sir, I didn't. But we do know her name, don't we? Sallie Rudolph?"

"Maybe," Higdon said. "There's no proof of the last name, but Doc Overstreet found a gold heart inscribed 'Sallie' on a chain through a piercing in her navel."

A considerable number of women did such, and it gave Brun creeps. To punch a hole in *his* bellybutton, they'd have to tie him down pretty tight. So, all right, her first name was Sallie. And come to think about it, maybe her last name really was Rudolph. An awful lot of drummers did have lady friends along their sales routes, and not all those ladies were single. If Freitag's picture was in the woman's locket, that didn't necessarily mean the wedding ring on her finger came from him.

"We also don't know whether that was her suitcase, rather than a companion's," Higdon said. "Or one borrowed from a friend—someone who might be able to shed some light about who she was and why she was here."

Fitzgerald put up a finger, like he was on the verge of spouting a bright idea, but then he stopped and murmured, "Oh, of course. I see. Those possibilities never occurred to me. I'm sorry, Mr. Higdon, but I really saw no need to take particular notice of anything in that room. And quite frankly, sir, I was eager to get out and into the hallway, for it did occur to me that this attractive young woman might have been involved in some sort of…illegal activity."

Higdon pursed lips. "All right. How long do you estimate it was between the time you left the registration desk and went upstairs, until you returned?"

Fitzgerald started off like a house afire. "Oh, certainly not more than five minutes…" But then, of a sudden, he looked like someone who'd just taken a shot to the side of his head from a sap. "I don't know whether the desk clerk will be able to corroborate that. When I came downstairs, he was quite busy, talking to another couple checking in, and with two more people waiting behind *them*. I don't know that he saw me."

"We'll check it out," said Higdon. "Just one more thing for now."

Fitzgerald's jaw drooped. Brun thought the poor man might just melt onto the floor. Higdon's last question and his own clumsy response seemed to have unglued him. The man had no backbone, Brun thought and kind as he'd been to Brun, the boy felt an embarrassing inclination to slap him across the cheek.

"Have you notified your family about this situation?"

That activated Fitzgerald in a hurry. "Oh, no. No, I haven't." He waved both hands, as if trying to brush off a particularly pesky flock of gnats. "I mustn't…you mustn't… My wife comes from a very fine family, quite well-to-do. I'm afraid she…they… wouldn't understand."

"But Mr. Fitzgerald. Soon or late, you are going to have to tell them. Don't you think it would be best—"

"No!" The gnats around Fitzgerald's head suddenly became hornets. "Mr. Higdon, I'm completely innocent of these terrible charges, and I pray you will move quickly to have me exonerated, such that my wife and her family—and my employer—will never hear these sordid details."

Mr. Higdon stood a moment and stared. Finally, he said, "I'll do my best."

Fitzgerald stepped forward and took his hand between his own two. "I shall be forever grateful, sir."

As they walked away from the jail, Higdon asked Brun whether he'd heard anything that struck him as possibly important. The boy shook his head. "Nothing particular. But I think I'm even surer he didn't kill that woman."

Higdon muttered something about not being able to understand the workings of the mind of the Southern gentry. "I don't
know whether I ought to give that man a pat on the shoulder or
a swift, hard kick to the behind." Brun told him he understood.
The boy felt considerably better about having wanted to slap
Fitzgerald's face just a few minutes before.

Higdon slowed his pace, then stopped and scratched at his chin.
"What time are you supposed to be at Mr. Stark's for dinner?"

"He said one o'clock."

Higdon checked his pocket watch. "It's getting on to that, so
you'd better be on your way. Don't want to make a bad impression, do you?"

"No, sir. And thank you."

"I'll walk down to Fifth with you."

At the corner of Fifth, Brun stood a moment and watched
Higdon go off southward on Ohio. He regretted his dinner
appointment, thought whatever Higdon was up to would be
interesting. On the other hand, no way to know whether the
lawyer would have asked him along. In any event, getting into
music publishing on the ground floor wasn't anything to turn
your nose up at. Sometimes, you can't lose for winning. He
turned onto Fifth, walked briskly down the block to Stark's.

Ten minutes later, Higdon turned off Ohio onto Broadway
Boulevard, a wide thoroughfare lined by the large and elegant
houses of the well-to-do. Half a block east, he turned again, this
time onto a slate walkway, then up six marble stairs to the colon-
nade entryway of a grand home of stone and marble. Around the
corner, he could see a shiny Studebaker carriage under shelter
at the turning point of a circular drive. He knew as well as he
knew his own name that Higdon, rather than Hastain, would
never be cut in script above the knocker on the door of this
sort of house. Money makes the world go round, as his fiancée
so often reminded him, and getting involved in the affairs of

unfortunates didn't pay the rent or put food on the table. He smiled, then rapped the knocker.

A man-servant, a slim, hairless fellow with the face of a beagle, opened the door and greeted Higdon with considerable warmth. "Mr. Higdon, always a pleasure to see you. I suppose you'd like to talk with Mr. Hastain."

"If he's back from church, Jennings. And not busy."

"He'd rarely be too busy to talk to you, Mr. Higdon. He's in his library. Why don't you just come along, and I'll tell him you're here."

Higdon followed the butler past a wide marble stairway, then down a long paneled hallway, past paintings of sourpussed Hastain ancestors. They stopped before an open doorway, stained glass to either side. Jennings walked in, and a few seconds later, out charged Bud Hastain, the servant behind him. Bud always put Higdon in mind of a grownup version of the boy in that book by Mark Twain, *Huckleberry Finn*. Hastain grinned, then gave Higdon's hand a vigorous shake. "Well, Bob, this is an unexpected pleasure to brighten a tedious Sunday. What brings you here?"

"I need some help, Bud. With that Fitzgerald case."

"Of course. Come on in."

Hastain and Higdon walked into the library. Jennings shut the door behind them. Hastain strode to the big mahogany desk and lowered himself into his armchair; Higdon took a chair opposite. The early afternoon sun coming through the stained glass window to Hastain's left set colored lights dancing across the papers on the desk.

"All right, then, Bob. What's going on?" Hastain's tone was somewhere between the growl of a bear and the purr of a mountain cat.

Pleasantries now clearly at an end, Higdon told Hastain about his recent talk with Fitzgerald, then said, "Bud, I really don't think he did it. And there may be more to the situation than we've considered. That new boy in town, Brun Campbell, who's boarding with me and working for John Stark? He told me

Fitzgerald doesn't just work for Procter and Gamble. He's here to evaluate whether P and G should set up a subsidiary plant, a big one, in Sedalia."

Hastain had been leaning back comfortably in his chair, but now he sat straight up.

"So we might do well to get him out as soon as possible," Higdon continued. "He's said nothing to his family yet, or to his employer. But how long can that go on? What's going to happen when P and G gets wind that the man they sent to Sedalia is in jail and charged, probably falsely, with murdering a young woman?"

Hastain slammed a fist onto the desk; a letter-opener jumped to the floor. "Christ Almighty, it won't be just P and G either, will it? That sort of word gets around in a hurry. Let something like this get out, and a dozen State Fairs won't do us any good." Hastain put a hand to his temple. "All the businesses John Bothwell's been courting like fair maidens will run like hell, and Sedalia will be just another word for Podunk. I'd go down to the jail myself and get the man out, but I'm not mayor any more. And if I even mention that notion to Walter, he'd have a fit, probably in public, and we'd have a scandal on our hands beyond containment."

"That's not what I was thinking," said Higdon. "Look, Bud—the woman was found early Wednesday morning on a roadside near the train terminal. Walter estimated the time of death as between eight and eleven the evening before, but a patrolman walked that beat about eleven-thirty, and didn't find the body. So she might have been killed somewhere else. And she was registered at the Kaiser Hotel."

Hastain's grin started a comeback.

Higdon leaned forward to press his point. "All I want is to look around the Kaiser for a bit. See whether I can find anything that might help my client, maybe even exonerate him. But John Kaiser's bristly enough that I don't think he'll want me snooping around his place, as he'd probably put it. Afraid it'll hurt his business."

"No question there." Hastain pointed a finger like a school-teacher making sure a snappy but careless student really did get the point. "But what if you find something at Kaiser's that implicates the man?"

"That might not be so bad either. If Fitzgerald really is guilty, the onus is no longer on the city, which would put P and G on the defensive. They'd probably lean over backward to make it right with us."

Hastain smiled. "Bob, I trained you well." He pushed away from the desk and got to his feet. "We do want to see justice done, don't we? Let's go."

◇◇◇

Hastain and Higdon walked up to the reception desk at Kaiser's Hotel, where a man about Hastain's age but half his weight perched on a stool. Green garters held up his shirt sleeves; he peered at his visitors through wire-rim glasses balanced on a long narrow nose. A huge Adam's-apple bobbed up, down, up again in his throat. "'Afternoon, Mr. Hastain," the man squeaked.

"Good afternoon, John," Hastain rumbled.

John Kaiser's Adam's-apple took another trip up, then down. Higdon thought he looked like a nearsighted possum, trapped by dogs. "What can I do for you gentlemen?"

Hastain swept an arm in Higdon's direction. "You know Bob Higdon, I'm sure. My former associate."

"Oh, yes. Yes. Of course." If Kaiser's hands were flint and steel, he'd have had a blaze going on his counter.

"Well, Bob is representing Mr. Fitzgerald, the man they've accused of murdering that unfortunate woman in your hotel. He wants to look around the room she was in."

"Oh. Well, I can certainly understand… But don't you think perhaps…" Higdon hoped the man wouldn't swallow his tongue. "I mean… Don't you need a warrant to search a hotel room? And wouldn't this properly be a police matter? Perhaps you ought to speak with Captain Love."

Hastain's bearing put Higdon in mind of a cat catching sight of a small white rabbit. But the lawyer's speech was friendly as could be, Missouri drawl broadening with every line he spoke. "Well, John, sure. Bob could get a warrant. But there would be some delays then, don't you think?"

Hastain paused long enough to force an answer. Kaiser swallowed again, then nodded his head and said, "Yeah…yep. Guess I'd have to say there would be. Papers to fill out and all that."

"And the longer the delay, the colder the trail to a killer gets. Now, John, I want you to suppose Mr. Fitzgerald is innocent. He's rushed to trial, convicted, and executed. And then the killer strikes a second time, maybe more than once. What do you suppose that would do to business in Sedalia, having some nut loose, strangling women right and left? What would it do to the hotel business? Not to mention what would happen to business at one particular hotel, if word got out that the proprietor refused to let Fitzgerald's lawyer look the place over when there was still time to find the real killer. That was a respectable woman who was killed—the way she was dressed? And she was wearing a wedding ring. Hell, John, that could have been *your* wife. And it still could be, if we've got the wrong man in the county cooler. You ever think of that?"

Kaiser worked his rear end back on his stool, as far as he could from Hastain, but the lawyer propped his hands on the counter, leaned forward, and barked, "What room was the woman in?"

"Two-oh-four." Higdon could hardly hear Kaiser's voice. The hotel-keeper reached back toward a row of pigeonholes behind him, some with message slips, some with keys, but halfway there, it stopped. "What am I supposed to say to Captain Love if he complains I shouldn't have let Mr. Higdon up there?"

"Just send him to me," Hastain said.

Kaiser handed the room key to Higdon like it was a dead mouse he'd picked up out of the corner. Hastain thanked him, then said goodbye to Higdon, and went off through the lobby and out the door.

Higdon took the stairs two at a time, opened the door to Room 204, walked in, looked around. The floor was dark wood, nicely polished. To his left, a neatly made iron-frame bed, just this side of a cedar clothes closet. To the right, a small pine desk and chair, and a pine dresser. On the far wall, between two windows, stood the customary wash table and basin, towels on a rack. Higdon cleared his throat. Nothing unusual.

The lawyer walked slowly around the room, lifted the mattress off the bed, peered into the empty clothes closet, inspected the far corners. He opened, then shut, the four desk drawers, then the three dresser drawers. Nothing. He squatted to peer under the bed. Not even dust balls. He walked to the window, pulled it open, peered out. Nothing. The fire escape was at the corner of the building, some twenty yards down. He shook his head, pulled the window shut, and went back to the lobby. Seeing him, Kaiser put on his twisted smile. "Find anything?"

Higdon shrugged. "Not really. But let me just check a couple of points. Friday night, when all this happened, were you at the desk, or was the night clerk here?"

"It was me," Kaiser said. "Ed Sawyer was supposed to work, but he claimed he was sick. A man owns a business, what's he going to do, huh?"

Higdon was all sympathy. "The buck always stops with the owner, doesn't it?"

"You ain't a-kidding, Bob. Busier'n hell that night—"

"That's what Mr. Fitzgerald said. He told me that was why he took the young woman up to the room himself."

Kaiser's face said he wasn't going to sit still and be accused of neglecting his duties. "He didn't have to do it. If he could've waited a minute or two, Pee Wee would've been back, the bellhop. Then him or I would've taken her upstairs just fine. But what I think is, he *wanted* to do it himself—figured once he got her into the room he could stop her crying and get on with whatever his business was. But she must've turned him down, or made him some kind of trouble, so he killed her. That's the way I see it."

"That's a possibility," Higdon said, smooth and cool as custard. "How long do you think he was up there altogether?"

"Well, that I don't know, running back and forth the way I was. I'm betting when he came back down, he watched and waited 'til I was out of the way or not lookin'. Then he ran on out, the little fancy-pants."

"Did you see anyone acting funny, John? In the lobby or around the desk?"

"Funny?" Kaiser gave Higdon the fish eye. "God almighty, didn't I already tell you I was running my bee-hind off? When do you think I'd have had any time to see funny business?"

"You saw Mr. Fitzgerald, and thought what he did was a little different."

Kaiser slammed a pencil down to the counter. His glasses fell forward to near the end of his nose; his purse-string lips twitched. "Judas Priest, Bob—how many times I gotta tell you I can't help you any? Now, would you please be so kind as to let a man get his work done? You've already taken up more of my time than I can afford."

"All right, John. Thanks for letting me look around."

Kaiser wiped his lips with a finger, then said, "Don't thank me, Bob. Thank Bud Hastain."

"I did," said Higdon. "And I will again." He tipped his Panama, and turned.

"Maybe some day you'll stand on your own two feet," Kaiser shouted after him. "'Stead of hiding under Bud Hastain's skirts."

Higdon told himself no point getting into a pissing contest with a skunk. Better use of his time to stop at Walter Overstreet's on the way home, ask a couple of questions.

From his bedroom, Isaac heard his dog bark, then a scraping sound from out back of the house. He left off tying his tie, grabbed his old Smith and Wesson from the night-table, tiptoed to the edge of the doorway and flattened himself against the wall, pistol up and ready. Probably just an animal looking for food, but a colored man who wanted to see the next sunrise didn't take much of anything for granted.

For the thousandth time he told himself he was a fool to leave all that growth behind his little back yard to shelter any varmint, human or otherwise, that might want to sneak into his place. But when he'd brought Mae here and bought the house for her, she wouldn't hear of cutting down the trees and clearing the brush. She called it their own private forest, told him it put her in mind of the woods she loved walking through near her childhood house in Kentucky. Eight years now since she died having Belinda, but Isaac still couldn't bring himself to cut down a single tree.

One tap, then a second, then Isaac heard the outside door open. He peered around the corner into the kitchen. Emil Alteneder stood in the middle of the room, looking every which way, all the while holding a nasty wooden club at the ready. As he began to move in Isaac's direction, the colored man leveled the pistol and stepped quickly into the doorway. Alteneder's eyes bugged at the point-blank Smith and Wesson. He staggered back a step.

"Drop it," Isaac said. "Now."

Alteneder's surprise passed quickly. He raised the club. "You ain't gonna shoot me," he said. "Nigger shoots a white man, he don't get further'n the next tree."

"Not if no other white man ever knows." Isaac tightened his finger on the trigger. "You're the only white man for blocks around. You make me shoot you, I get my neighbors real fast, and inside of an hour you be hog food, nothing left of you. Now, put down that club, turn yourself around, and get your sorry face out of here. I'm countin'. One—"

Alteneder dropped the club and glared at Isaac.

Isaac gestured with the pistol toward the door. "I said turn around and go."

"You messed up my boy's face," Alteneder snarled.

"Next time he even look crooked at my child, I mess him up so bad he ain't never gonna get unmessed." Isaac's voice rose. "Now go on, get the hell outa my house. Don't say one more word."

Alteneder shot Isaac a glance of pure hate, then stomped back through the doorway and outside. Isaac moved quickly to the doorway and watched his enemy give a wide berth to the beagle tethered to a post, as he retreated through the yard, into Mae's forest, and finally out to the road, on his way back to white Sedalia. Only then did the colored man go back to his bedroom, slide his pistol into its holster, strap it on, and cover it with his dark suit jacket. On his way out, he stopped just long enough to pick up Alteneder's club like it was something contaminated.

Chapter Nine

Sedalia
Sunday, July 23, 1899

Brun raced past the Stark and Son display windows, put on the brakes, backed up, and took a few seconds in front of the glass to straighten his tie and smooth down his hair. First impressions. He was going to be on trial, the judge a woman. Hornswoggling his old man had never been much of a problem, but when wool had to be pulled over eyes, Brun's Ma was the devil's very own. The boy set his chin, then walked on past the shop, through a doorway into a small vestibule and up the staircase to the Starks' flat.

Stark greeted him at the top of the stairs. Behind his boss, Brun saw a spacious living room furnished with hardback chairs, a red tufted sofa, and a couple of stuffed armchairs a bit past their prime. A grand piano, music on the rack and spread over the bench, took pride of place. Stark patted Brun's shoulder. "Glad you could come."

"I'm glad to be invited."

"I'd like for you to meet Will, but he's still in St. Louis, and couldn't…"

Whatever Stark was going to say never did get said, because just then, two women, both red-faced and perspiring, walked into the room. The older woman carried a tray with a pitcher at least as sweaty as she was, and four tumblers. "Ah," said Mr.

Stark. "Let me introduce you to my wife and daughter. My dears, this is the new clerk I've been talking about, Mr. Brun Campbell. Brun, my wife, and my daughter, Nell."

Brun politely allowed how pleased he was to make the ladies' acquaintance. Mrs. Stark, the one carrying the tray, said, "Let's go sit on the porch and have some lemonade. We must get better acquainted."

More than a touch of Irish in her voice, her smile warm, genuine. The boy gulped back a sudden bolus of Sunday-afternoon homesickness as he followed the Starks through the dining room and out onto a covered, screened-in porch. The building across the alley, fronting on East Sixth, was only one story high, so Brun could see several blocks down Lamine. It was cool and quiet, and as the boy sat in a wicker chair, sipping at Mrs. Stark's perfect lemonade, just the right mix of sweet and tart, the leaves on the maples along Lamine rustled in the mild breeze, and he suddenly realized not only had the homesickness vanished, he was happy in every fiber of his being. He felt so much at home, sitting on the Starks' back porch on Sunday afternoon, that the notion of being a traveling piano man came to sound downright mean. How nice it might be to settle in Sedalia, work with Mr. Stark and Will, publishing and selling music.

But woolgathering wouldn't do, not right then. Brun told himself he'd best show interest and initiative in the proper direction. Nell Stark had a lovely head of black hair, piled up on top and set off by a white blouse, but it was her hands that caught and held Brun's attention. He couldn't take his eyes off those long delicate fingers which never stopped moving in her lap, as though all the while they talked, she rehearsed a piano piece. "Miss Nell, Mr. Stark tells me you've been to Europe to study with Moszkowski."

Nell's ice-blue eyes, from the very mold that had produced her father's, projected an intensity that told Brun in no uncertain terms she would not suffer a fool gladly, if at all. "Twice," she said. "First in Berlin for two years, and then for just a few months in Paris." She turned a look on Stark that made Brun wonder whether he'd have done better to keep his trap shut. "But Papa was concerned for my safety, you know, the Spanish-American War. So I had to come home."

If she was casting bait, Stark didn't bite. He just smiled, which seemed to irritate his daughter. "Papa fought in a war," she said. "And Mother, all of sixteen years old, came up the Mississippi from New Orleans to Indiana, not four months after the war was over. But even with the whole of the Pyrenees mountains separating me from those hordes of rampaging Spaniards, they were concerned for my safety."

Brun thought his question had been innocent enough, but pretty clear Nell was one of those people who aren't much affected by usual polite conventions. The boy readied himself for a word-storm.

But Mrs. Stark straightway sent the squall off in another direction. She was smaller than Brun's Ma, five feet tall at the outside, in a white dress with frilly lace down the front. No question where Nell's beautiful black hair came from. Smile lines played at the corners of Mrs. Stark's green eyes, and around her mouth. To this point, she hadn't said much beyond that she was pleased to make Brun's acquaintance, but now as she began to speak, the boy saw respect scribed cleanly over both her husband's face and her daughter's. "Mr. Stark had no choice but to fight for his country and his beliefs." Again, the hint of Ireland in her voice. "And as for me, I would not have chosen to make my way up the Mississippi in times such as those, certainly not as a girl of sixteen. But it was safer for me than staying in New Orleans, married as I was to a Yankee." She looked squarely at Brun, who worked his face to consider her in the most serious fashion he could manage. "Those were difficult times, Mr. Campbell."

Exultation surged in the boy's chest. Not Master Campbell. *Mister* Campbell.

"New Orleans was captured and occupied by Union forces. My father was dead, and my mother made our living selling cakes and cookies to the soldiers. I went with her to help." She fired a wicked glance Mr. Stark's way, the kind of flash Brun hoped a pretty girl might one day turn on him. "And I met this dashing and handsome bugler boy."

Against her will, Nell laughed.

Stark rubbed his hand over his face. "Her mother carried the tray, and she sang, to get our attention." Stark's voice was half an octave lower than his usual, the words husky. "I'd never heard a more beautiful singing voice before, and have not heard one since."

"We were married in February, 1865," Mrs. Stark said. "And then Mr. Stark's regiment was transferred to occupy Mobile Bay. Without him there with us, not only was I in danger, so were my mother and my younger sister and brother. So off I went, up the river to Gosport, Indiana, and I lived there with Mr. Stark's older brother Etilmon and his family until Mr. Stark joined me after he was mustered out, January of the next year."

"Let's not get too far off the subject, Mother." Nell, her father's daughter, not easily gotten around. "I know your tricks, don't I? You were still in far more danger on that voyage than I ever was in Paris."

"Oh, I don't know about that." Mrs. Stark, close on to fifty, suddenly looked to Brun like a mischievous schoolgirl. "Did you have a leprechaun with you in Paris, as I did all the way up the Mississippi River? Making sure every minute that I would have no trouble."

Brun watched her eyes, where Irish humor shows itself. Nell and Stark burst out laughing; Nell wiped at her eyes. "Mr. Campbell, I hope you won't draw hasty conclusions about Mother. She and her leprechauns… When we were children, she was forever telling us stories about little Irish fairy folk, how they'd show you a hidden pot of gold, if only you could catch them. Never two stories the same. She made them up as she went along."

"Well, and didn't I have a leprechaun along on that trip?" said Mrs. Stark. She waved both hands grandly. "Look, my pot of gold. Husband, children, grandchildren. My lovely home. Never as a child did I expect to have such riches."

Brun began to think he might be all right with Mrs. Stark. She went on talking to him like he was one of her own children, rather than a young stranger who'd ridden a rail into town not a week before. Nell was a first-class pianist, her mother said, who played in concerts and gave lessons, and now that she'd studied with Professor Moszkowski, she wanted to move to St. Louis to open a studio. "And then, if Will decides to go off to St. Louis or Kansas City to publish music, we'll have no one left here at home. No one even to help Mr. Stark in the store."

Every nerve in Brun's body twitched. He didn't dare look at Stark.

"Now, Mother." Nell laughed so hard she could barely say the words. "You should go on the stage, you know that?"

Mrs. Stark humphed, then stood, and smoothed her skirt. As if on a signal, Nell picked up the tray, with its empty pitcher and tumblers, and the two women marched out toward the kitchen.

Just as they sat down to dinner, Brun heard the stairwell door open, then footfalls in the living room. Mrs. Stark's face lit. "Oh, good, that will be Isaac. Right on the dot."

For the first time, Brun noticed the place setting in front of an empty chair between Nell and Stark.

As Isaac walked into the room, Mrs. Stark's face lit. The colored man smiled, and wished all a good afternoon. "Sorry I be late," he added. "Some things needed doing."

In his spotless black suit, white shirt, and dark, sober tie, Isaac looked very different today from the way Brun had seen him in the shop. Mrs. Stark reached to pat his arm. "You're never late, Isaac, you know that, dear. Whenever you come, you're welcome, and glad we are to see you."

A colored man, walking into a white house, cool as you please, to sit down to dinner with the family and their guest? Brun had never heard of such. The boy stared, thoroughly confused, until Mrs. Stark shut down his gawk by passing him a heaped platter of fragrant sliced meat.

◇◇◇

What the meal lacked in fancy, it more than made up in generous, a joint of spring lamb with potatoes, and beans which probably were still on the vine on a nearby farm the day before. Cold beer in a pitcher, lemonade in another. Brun was careful to not touch his fork before grace, but to his surprise, grace was not said. Stark simply picked up his utensils, and the party set to. Mrs. Stark took a small taste of meat, potatoes and vegetable, seemed to find them acceptable, then turned to her guest. "Mr. Stark tells me you're recently arrived in town, Mr. Campbell."

"Yes, ma'am."

"Where did you come from—if I'm not being too inquisitive."

Brun took advantage of a mouthful of potatoes to think before he answered. "Mostly, I grew up in Kansas."

She looked impressed. "Oh my. That's pretty wild country."

"Well, that's for sure, ma'am. People there still keep one eye peeled for Quantrill's raiders, or Jesse James. Or Old John Brown."

All around the table, forks and knives hung in the air. Sounds of chewing vanished. Then everyone picked right up and went on eating like nothing had happened. But something *had* happened. Brun remembered Stark's reaction to "John Brown's Body" the day before, and cursed himself for a triple-plated fool. "Actually, my folks and I lived all over Kansas and Oklahoma," he said, talking faster than his usual. "Presently, they're in Arkansas City."

Mrs. Stark's face said a clear thank-you. "Have you brothers and sisters, Mr. Campbell?"

"Yes, ma'am. A brother, younger by six years."

"Mr. Stark and I have three children, Nell, Will, and Etilmon—Till, we call him. He teaches music and violin at the Marmaduke Military Academy near St. Louis. I'm grateful that my children live close, and I see them often. I do hope you send *your* mother a letter from time to time."

Brun almost said yes, once a week without fail, but held back long enough to try to figure which falsehood would get him out of a kettle of fish and which would leave him there to be cooked along with the evening meal. Mrs. Stark, with her gentle smile, could have been feeding him a little chitter-chat about her three children by way setting a trap. Likely, Mr. Stark had told his wife the boy was a runaway, and not a lot of runaways send letters home to their parents.

So Brun looked down at his plate, then back up, and stared directly into those earnest green eyes. "Sorry, ma'am," he said, contrite as he could possibly manage. "I ran away from home. Truth, I wasn't home all that much of late, anyhow, because like as not on any particular night I'd get a beating from Pop, and they were getting worse all the time. If you'll excuse me, ma'am, and not to offend you ladies…" He pushed his chair back from the table, stood, and very cautiously raised the right side of his shirt, just far enough to show the raggedy bruise, now all purple and yellow, from the encounter he'd had on the train with that crate of lead shot. Then, he quickly lowered his shirt. "The night I ran away was right after Pop gave me that medal."

Stark shook his head. Nell's jaw fell open. Isaac let out a low, soft whistle. Only Mrs. Stark spoke. Brun would not have believed that small woman could house such indignation. "You mean to say your mother never stopped him doing that?"

"No, ma'am, she didn't. She couldn't have. Pop's a big man, easy twice as big as Ma. Bad enough for me to get a beating, but let her *or* me say a word against him when he'd been drinking, and neither one of us'd ever see the light of day again. She often did try talking to him the next day, and Pop would say how he was sorry, sometimes even cry. But that night he'd get himself all full of the sauce again, and then there was no reasoning with him. Most nights the last year or so, I've been sleeping in the kitchen in the restaurant I played piano at."

"Playing piano in a restaurant…" Judging by Mrs. Stark's expression, Brun thought she might be wondering whether it really had been a restaurant he'd played in, and he was trying to be polite. "At your age."

"Well, ma'am, I've always had a knack. And when I heard Scott Joplin's music, I knew I wouldn't rest until I mastered it. That's why I came here when I ran away, and ever since I got here, I've had nothing but the best luck. Mr. Joplin said he'd take me on for lessons, and I got me a good job with Mr. Stark, and a good place to live, boarding with Mr. Higdon."

Brun had no trouble seeing that his "Mr. Joplin" had scored him points with Mrs. Stark, and probably double points from Isaac. "Mr. Joplin is a fine gentleman," said Mrs. Stark.

"He's also a fine musician," said Nell, a little sharply, Brun thought. "You're fortunate to have him take you on. You'll need to work hard if you expect him to keep you on."

"I know that, Miss Nell, and I'll do whatever's required. Ragtime's not easy to play. Have you ever tried it?"

He couldn't have missed the glance that flew between Mr. and Mrs. Stark. "Here at home," she said. "Not in recitals…yet."

"Maybe after dinner you and Nell can play for us," said Stark. He picked up his fork, shoveled in a mouthful of potatoes. But Mrs. Stark wasn't finished. "Still, Mr. Campbell…you do know, don't you, there are ways you can send a letter without anyone knowing where you are. Please send one to your mother. It would mean so much to her, just to know you're safe. Promise me you'll do it."

He could handle that. If Mrs. Stark ever asked again, he'd tell her how he'd sent a letter, all addressed and ready, inside another envelope, to the postmaster in Seattle, Washington, with instructions to redirect the inside envelope, addressed to Mrs. Campbell in Arkansas City. No return address on either message. "All right," Brun said. "I promise."

"Very good, dear," said Mrs. Stark. "And should you find yourself in temporary need of a mother, I would be glad to stand in."

"That's a comfort, ma'am," Brun said, and pointed at his plate. "If dinner's any indication, I couldn't be in better hands."

"You spread blarney thicker than I spread butter on bread," said Mrs. Stark, but she was smiling.

Isaac gave Stark a light poke in the ribs, then leaned toward Brun. The boy never had seen such familiarity between a white man and a colored, not even between Scott Joplin and Professor Weiss. "Where you learn to get around a woman so good?" Isaac asked.

"I guess I really don't know, Mr..." Brun broke the pause as quickly as he could. "...Stark."

Now, Isaac and John Stark exchanged glances. Brun hurriedly added, "Maybe I just come by it naturally."

"I be predictin' a happy life for you, young sir," Isaac said. "Keep talkin' that fine, maybe one day you be a congressman, even a senator. And I do give you thanks for your consideration, but best you don't call me Mr. Stark. Just Isaac will do. Or, if you want, Uncle Isaac."

After the festivities in the street outside the music store the day before, Brun thought not many Sedalia whites would be inclined to call Isaac "Uncle."

The same notion must have occurred to Isaac himself, because he said, "Like yesterday afternoon. That's the world, and the older you get, the more you see there's things you best be careful about. I ain't gonna say it don't bother me any, but it's the way things be. I wouldn't care to be wearin' Scott Joplin's shoes the day somebody go and put a tab in his hand, make him pay dear for every time a white man called him Mister."

Stark slammed down his fork and knife and sat bolt-straight in his chair. "Not if I can help it."

The silence around that table was like heavy fog. Nobody moved, let alone said a word. Lower lip out, Isaac nodded in thought. Then he smiled, just the tiniest bit. "That's 'not if *we* can help it,' Mr. Stark."

One after the other, every head at that dinner table turned Brun Campbell's way. If the boy had felt right at home a minute before, now he felt as much an outsider as a person possibly could. He cleared his throat, getting ready to apologize for something he might have said, but Mrs. Stark was quicker to speak. "I'm sorry, Mr. Campbell. We are being rude. The fact is, Isaac and Mr. Stark go back a very long way, and some people don't take too well to that. Which means the Starks have never been the most highly regarded citizens of any town we've lived in. Mr. Stark told me about the way you punched that boy who was kicking Isaac, and that was very good and brave of you. But we've not seen the end of the matter. You likely don't know just what you've let yourself in for, coming to work for Mr. Stark."

She turned to look at her husband, said nothing, didn't need to. Brun had seen that look pass many times between his mother and father. A response was expected.

Stark sighed. "You tell him, Sarah. You're the story teller in this family."

Mrs. Stark's face lit. "Well, then. Here's the way it was. I've already told you, Mr. Stark courted and married me in New Orleans, and then his regiment was sent to guard Mobile Bay. The war was almost over then, everyone knew it, but the worse it looked for the Southerners, the more determined they were to spill every drop of Yankee blood they could. Even after the war ended, there were those who would not lay down their arms. One day, Mr. Stark's regiment went out on maneuvers outside Mobile, and what should happen but a young Negro boy ran up and told them they were walking into an ambush. A bunch of rebels were hiding behind a knoll down the way, waiting to gun down every last Union soldier. So the troops changed their course, snuck up behind those rebels, and the ones they didn't kill, they took prisoner. Not a single Union soldier was even hurt. They started to march the prisoners back to Mobile, but couldn't decide what to do about the colored boy. If they let him march back into Mobile with them, they'd have stirred up the population something awful. And if they sent him away, they were afraid he might fall into the hands of other raiders who'd force him to betray the Union regiment. So the captain ordered Mr. Stark to take the boy out into the woods and shoot him."

Just what Freitag had said. Brun gasped. Mrs. Stark's eyes commenced to shine. "But Mr. Stark would have none of that. He couldn't refuse the order, of course, but he was not about to shoot down a boy who'd saved his life and those of his comrades. So, he took Isaac out into the woods, told him the situation, fired a few shots, and then they both ran. They trooped all the way to New Orleans, more than a hundred miles, traveled mostly at night, slept in fields and forests during daytime, shot game or stole food. They came into the city under cover of darkness, and went straight to my mother's house. Mama was sitting up with a shotgun because we didn't dare sleep all at the same time. It was only a month after Appomattox, and there were those in our neighborhood who called me traitor and made threats. The steamboats had just starting running up the Mississippi again, so next morning, Mama got dressed in her Sunday finest to go talk to the captain of one of the steamers…" Mrs. Stark took a few seconds to enjoy the scene she'd just painted. "Mama was never short on blarney herself, not by any manner of means. She paid my passage and Isaac's—"

Brun laughed. "Your leprechaun."

Mrs. Stark laughed along. "Yes, that's right. Mother told the captain he was my servant, and we needed to go to Indiana for me to join my husband. So the next day, we boarded the steamer George Jackson." Mrs. Stark looked at Isaac, who'd begun to laugh quietly. "There I was, all got up as a fine young Southern woman of sixteen, with my fifteen-year-old leprechaun-servant carrying my husband's pistol under his shirt in case trouble found us. But early that morning, before we went…" She paused, not laughing now. "Mr. Stark gave Isaac that gun, and told him to shoot him in the leg, just give him a flesh wound. Isaac didn't want to do it, but I've never known anyone who could say no and make it stick when Mr. Stark said yes. My brother and sister helped Mr. Stark get to the army hospital. He told them he'd been ambushed by rebels near Mobile, that they'd taken away a colored boy and hung him, and forced Mr. Stark to come to New Orleans, where the rebs were going to use him as a decoy to ambush a Union patrol, just like what almost happened at Mobile. But right outside the city, he managed to get away, though the rebs shot him in the leg. He stayed in the hospital for a couple of weeks, and once he was healed, they sent him back to his regiment. The next January, when he was mustered out, he came right up to Etilmon's, and we have all been together since—which is why our neighbors have always told stories about us, better ones by far than I could ever make up. And after the way you behaved yesterday, Mr. Campbell, you likely will soon find yourself included in those stories."

In the privacy of his mind, Brun cursed Freitag. The boy considered what a marvel it was, the way two people could tell the exact same story, and have it come out so different. Just because something's a fact doesn't necessarily make it truth. "I'd be honored to be included, ma'am."

Mrs. Stark beamed. "We're pleased to have you, just so long as you come in with your eyes open." She pushed away from the table. "Well, then, Mr. Campbell, I hope you've saved room for coffee, and a piece of my apple pie and vanilla ice cream."

"If it's anything like my mother's," Brun said, "I'd never say no to a second slice. And Mrs. Stark, it would please me most mightily if you'd call me Brun."

Isaac pounded one fist into the other. "Sen-a-tor Brun. I do believe you are elected."

Brun thanked him, but the boy had no wish to be elected senator. Vice-president of Stark and Son Music Publishers would do just fine. Even better, vice-president of Stark and Campbell.

After coffee and two helpings of apple pie, the company repaired to the living room. A small black spring-powered fan on an oak table did its best to keep the close, muggy air moving, but the poor thing was overmatched. The men sweated, the women perspired, and everyone just went on with their business. Mr. and Mrs. Stark and Isaac listened to Nell and Brun take turns at the piano. It occurred to the boy that in most homes, whether in Sedalia or just about anyplace else, playing the piano on the Lord's day was ample cause for a whipping. But in most homes then, one of the hostess' first questions of a guest would have been which church did he attend, and no Stark had posed him that question. Nor did the boy see a Bible on a table, or an image of a crucified man surrounded by winged creatures hanging on a wall.

Brun thought Nell played a beautiful piano, but especially on ragtime did her skill surprise him. She seemed to let the music play *her*. Like Joplin did. Listening to Nell follow his own playing of "Maple Leaf Rag," Brun felt humbled, and when she finished, he applauded with gusto. "Miss Nell, you take the cake for fair. You've cut me so bad, I don't think I have any blood left. Where did you ever learn to play that music?"

Nell laughed. Most young women would have said, "Oh, Mr. Campbell, you are flattering me shamelessly. My piano playing can't hold a candle to your own." But Nell didn't pretend modesty. "We came here to Sedalia just after I turned eleven, so I grew up right along with ragtime. But don't be discouraged. When you've been playing ragtime for as long as I have, I'm sure you'll be just as good."

Stark cleared his throat. "Nell, it didn't hurt that you got lessons from Scott Joplin, on and off for four years. Whenever he and you both happened to be in town."

"I'd never deny that, Papa. Mr. Joplin helped me tremendously. And I'm sure he'll be just as much help to Mr. Campbell."

This Miss Nell was some handful, Brun thought. Coming up on thirty, still a spinster, maybe no wonder about that. She'd not only taken ragtime piano lessons, she'd taken them from a colored man. "Miss Nell, how on earth did you ever…I mean, you didn't go down to the Maple Leaf Club—"

She cut him off with an unladylike guffaw. "The Maple Leaf Club started up only last year. Mr. Joplin came to our home to give me lessons."

So a colored man had come regularly to a white house to give piano lessons to the young daughter. Not as far outside the proprieties as the idea of that girl going to a colored club for lessons, but still way beyond what was conventionally thought seemly those days. But then, here was Isaac, sitting in the parlor after dinner, a family member who lived in another house only because maybe there were limits that even the Starks needed to observe.

By the time Brun had made thanks to his hosts and set off for Higdon's, it was near on seven o'clock, a warm summer Sunday evening, laziest time of the week. Full of good food and beer, the boy walked slowly down Fifth to Ohio, then turned north. Any other time of the week, there would be bustle on that street, all the sights and noises of commerce, but right now the town looked dead. The only sounds of human activity Brun heard came through the open windows of churches he strolled past. Evening services, vespers.

At Third, he turned left and started walking toward Liberty Park. Every step raised clouds of tan roadside dirt. One of the little yellow streetcars rumbled past, chock-full of young people on their way back from an afternoon at the park. Through the open windows, Brun heard raucous singing: "Sometimes Pa says with a frown, soon you'll have to settle down, have to wear your wedding gown, be the strictest wife in town...Ta-ra-ra boom-de-ay." A laughing girl his age gripped the window edge and leaned far out to wave a bright blue hat at him. He waved back, but with less than full enthusiasm. Sunday night seemed the worst time to be by yourself in a new town.

Not many people still in the park when Brun got there. He walked through a stand of maples to a small grassy hillside near the lake, folded his jacket on the ground and stretched out, his head on the jacket, and watched clouds drift across the pale blue sky. Unlike those clouds, Brun Campbell was moving fast, and with a particular direction in mind. Mrs. Stark had asked him back to dinner the next Sunday, as good a sign as he could've hoped for. Mr. Stark was giving him a great opportunity, but he needed to watch his step; no-nonsense men like Mr. Stark generally expect other people to behave as well as they do. Generous with opportunities, such men are miserly with second chances. Brun wondered whether he might be able to get Scott Joplin to let Stark and Son publish his music, but then the clouds took over, and the boy fell sound asleep.

After Brun left Stark's, Isaac walked out and down to the vestibule, then came back brandishing a dark, heavy club. Three pairs of eyes widened. "This's why I be late to dinner." Then he told the Starks about his set-to with Emil Alteneder earlier that afternoon.

Stark shook his head sadly. "This is not going to end well, at least for someone."

"You'll stay here tonight!"

Isaac looked at Sarah Stark, seemed about to say something, then chuckled. "Ain't no point, me tryin' to argue, is there?"

"No," Sarah said. "None at all."

Walter Overstreet heard the knock, tried to pretend he hadn't, but knew it was no use. "I'm coming," he shouted, then pushed himself out of the soft armchair, trudged to the door, let Bob Higdon in. Without a word, the doctor ushered his visitor into his office, flopped into his desk chair, and pulled the bottle and two glasses from the little cabinet. "Join me?"

Higdon nodded. From across the desk, the lawyer studied Overstreet's bloodshot eyes, his fluttering lids. "Sorry to have to bother you, Doc."

Overstreet leaned across the desk to hand Higdon the glass, two inches of brown liquid at its bottom. "I couldn't talk to you earlier because I had to get over to the Katy Hospital, one of the yard men got his leg and pelvis crushed."

"Anyone I know?"

"Luther Jensen?"

Higdon shook his head. "No. Did you get him through?"

Overstreet downed his drink in one swallow. Higdon wondered how the man managed to get through one day after another after another, running full tilt, but always a half-step behind Death. He took a sip from his glass, then said, "Sorry."

The doctor poured himself another drink. "Left a wife, two months pregnant, and a little girl, three. No family to take them in. I can get her a job in the kitchen at Sicher's Hotel, but then, when she starts showing… Well, we've got a month or two to think about that. I gave her twenty dollars for now." He slammed down the second drink, poured a third.

Higdon thought about Fitzgerald, that pathetic, ineffectual bag of Southern manners. He also had a wife and a small child—what would happen to them? The lawyer imagined himself looking up at a scaffold as the sheriff fitted a noose around Edward Fitzgerald's neck. At least Jensen's family could count on some charity from the yard workers and their families. Who ever tried to help the family of a convicted murderer?

Higdon set down his glass. "I'll try not to keep you too long, Doc. I'm representing the man they picked up in connection with that young woman who was strangled last Tuesday night. Can you tell me what you found when you examined her?"

Overstreet slowly sank back into his chair, closed his eyes, then blinked them open. "Somebody did a real job on her. Bruises all around the neck, and her trachea and larynx were shattered. Whoever killed her was strong as the deuce."

"And that's all you found?"

"I'm afraid so…but wait a minute. Talking about Mrs. Jensen reminds me. The dead woman was two months pregnant."

Higdon sat up straight. "You're sure of that? Two months?"

"Easy enough to tell." Hoarse laugh. "Ed Love was a little more difficult. He wanted to know what color the baby was. But yes, you can figure two months, though I don't know how that would help your client. He could have been with her in some other town, two months ago."

Higdon made a wry face. "You ever think of taking up the law, Doc?"

Overstreet's reply was instant. "I'd take my life first."

◇◇◇

When Brun woke, it was dark. Cotton in his head, a dry, salty taste in his mouth. He stumbled to his feet, then picked up his jacket, made his way down the hill to the lake, washed his face, and headed back up the hill and into town. As he came up on Ohio, he heard noise, loud shouting, and stepped up his pace. From the corner of Ohio and Third, he saw a crowd up a few blocks, on Main Street, and past the knot of people, an orange light in the sky. Fire. In Lincolnville, north of Main.

He ran up the street to the mob. Everyone he saw was white, and as the group shifted and pulsated, it took care to stay on the proper side of the railroad tracks. "What happened?" Brun shouted, but the only answer he got was "Fire in Lincolnville." No one seemed to know what was burning. When he asked whether the fire department had gone out, a man he took for a drummer stranded in Sedalia over a Sunday, laughed and said, "Fire department? Whatever are you thinkin', boy? You suppose a white volunteer fireman oughta go'n risk his life for a nigger's house?" A woman at his side spoke up. "We've got a paid fire department in Sedalia, and they go to any fire, anyplace." "Well," said the drummer. "Then you're a bigger bunch of fools than I took you for."

Brun turned to leave, but at the edge of the crowd, he almost walked straight into Elmo Freitag, grinning to show all the teeth in his mouth. "Well, now, if it ain't young Master Campbell. You got a pretty mean right cross, you know that? That boy you hit yesterday still ain't eating or saying a whole lot."

Brun looked around. Emil Alteneder stood like a stone statue just to Freitag's left, and he wasn't close to smiling. Arms crossed over his chest, eyes sizzling, he glared at Brun. "Fat pig that kid is, it won't hurt him to go without food a while," Brun said, keeping a good eye on Alteneder. "And considering what-all he likes to say, it won't be so bad for him to keep his trap shut a while, either."

Freitag looked like Brun had just barely managed to amuse him. "You've got a good mouth on you, all right, Master Campbell. Just you better keep watch nobody messes *it* up."

Brun glanced at Alteneder. "That a threat?"

"No, boy. Just a little warning, friend to friend."

"I don't think you're my friend."

Freitag shrugged. "Your loss." He jerked a finger back toward the fire. "Too bad about that nigger's house—it's gonna burn right to the ground. Won't be a thing left, inside or out, and his dog's gonna get cooked up nice and juicy. It's a real mistake to tie up a dog inside of a house, 'cause you never can tell, can you, when there's gonna be a fire. But then, a nigger'll eat anything he can get into a stew pot, possum, squirrel, 'coon, whatever. Bet he'll think roasted dog is damn fine eatin'."

Alteneder let out a gargle of a laugh. In the dim streetlight, Freitag's face was aglow. His eyes fairly shone. Despite the warm night air, the joy on the man's face set Brun to shivering.

"Good thing the nigger and his li'l girl weren't in there when the fire hit, ain't it? Otherwise, they'd be just as cooked as their dog."

"Isaac…" It was out of Brun's mouth before he realized he'd even thought it.

"Oh, yes. Yes indeed. Mr. Isaac Stark. That's his house burning. You didn't know that, huh?"

"Nobody here seems to," Brun said. "Except you. I wonder how it is you know."

Freitag threw back his head and laughed like a maniac. A well-dressed man and woman stared at him a moment, then quickly moved away. Alteneder stepped forward; Brun got a whiff of coal oil and smoke. Freitag coughed his guffaw down to a snide chuckle, then said, "Well, now, Master Campbell, is *that* some kind of threat."

Brun thought about telling him, no, just a warning, but he was already off and running, down Ohio to Fifth, to Stark's, up the stairs, banging at the door, shouting. John Stark let him in and took him directly to the back porch; at the sight of him, Isaac's eyes opened wide, and Mrs. Stark clutched at her throat. By the time the boy finished his story, Isaac was halfway to the door, but Stark told the colored man to sit tight and cool down.

"Nothing to do now." Each word clipped cleanly, right at the edge. "Going into that crowd would be foolish at best."

Isaac took a moment to think matters through, then slowly went back to his chair. "He burn' my dog! I never tie Buster up in the house, he was in the yard like always. What kind of a man is it, do a thing like that?"

Mrs. Stark walked over to Isaac and rested a hand on his shoulder. Brun thought if they were giving out guns before a battle, Mrs. Stark would be at the head of the line.

"A man like this Freitag tends to run up pretty long tabs himself," Stark said. "Soon or late, I believe we're going to have to collect."

Chapter Ten

Sedalia
Monday, July 24, 1899

Joplin and Weiss were so engaged in their discourse as they walked out of Myers' Drug Store, they bumped square into Emil and Fritz Alteneder. Emil shoved Joplin to the side, and growled, "Hey, nigger, watch where you're going. You better learn and learn fast about givin' way to a white man." He turned a hot-eye on Weiss. "Same goes for fat old white fools who like to go walkin' with niggers."

Joplin thought they'd been set up, the whole business staged, but no matter. Emil obviously expected a reply, though his son appeared to be more interested in getting inside the store to find relief for his swollen eye and bruised mouth. Most people hurried past, but a few waited to see what was going to happen. "I beg your pardon," Joplin said. "I wasn't looking, and I'm sorry I bumped you."

He watched the wind go out of Emil's sails. Whatever the man had expected was not what he'd got. "Well, okay, then," he grumbled. "See you don't let it happen again."

"Come on, Pa." Fritz's plea was somewhere between whining and mumbling.

Joplin and Weiss began to move off, but Alteneder called after them, "I ain't done with you yet. One way or another, you're gonna sell that music of yours to Mr. Freitag. If you're smart, you'll get paid decent. If not…" Emil shrugged, and showed his few teeth in a nasty smile.

Joplin took a step away, but Emil went after him. "Nigger, a white man talks to you, you don't just up and walk off." He grabbed at Joplin's coat, but Weiss moved with surprising speed to get between the two. Joplin heard a torrent of angry German words, the only one of which he recognized was *schwein*. Then, Weiss took him by the arm. "Let's go, Scott."

Joplin had never seen his teacher so angry. When they got to the next corner, he asked what Weiss had said to Alteneder. Weiss reddened. "Just that he was a pig, a disgrace to Germany. And if he ever puts a hand on you again, I will cut off his penis and his testicles and feed them to dogs in the street."

At Stark's that afternoon, Brun had an abundance of time to play the piano. He thought the lively tunes he knocked out ought to bring crowds into the store, but most passersby just stopped briefly, tightened their lips or shook their heads, and walked along. Shortly before closing, six or seven little boys came up to the doorway, stuck their thumbs in their ears, wiggled their fingers, crossed their eyes, and yelled, "Yah, Stark! Nigger-lover!" Brun took a step toward them, and they scattered.

About four o'clock, Stark told Isaac to take off the rest of the day. Not long after he'd left, a sunburned pear of a man in farmer's overalls, bald-headed and unshaved, duckwalked through the doorway. Brun asked could he be of help, but the man pushed past him like he wasn't standing there. Just ambled up to the counter, and shouted through the open door to Stark's office, "Hey, Stark, know what I just heard? They lynched that nigger, Embree. Took him away from the sheriff was bringin' him back from Kansas, stripped off his clothes, laid on the lash 'til he was all over bloody welts, and then put a rope 'round his neck, threw the other end over a tree limb and raised him up so he choked real slow. Had more'n five hundred people watchin'. What do you think of that, huh?"

Brun's stomach rocked. He tried to remember where he'd herad about that business. Stark turned in his chair to face the man. "I thought Governor Stephens gave the Kansas governor assurance the man would be brought back safely to stand trial."

Now it came back to Brun. The newspaper article he'd read in the Boston Café at breakfast.

The big man laughed. "Jeez, Stark, you are a daisy. Waste all that time and money on a trial? An' then what if he breaks jail? Ain't but one way to deal with bad niggers, 'cause if they don't know for God's truth they're gonna get themselves strung up, no white woman'll be safe anywhere, never mind little girls. Damn good thing you ain't responsible for nothing except runnin' a music store."

Stark got up slowly, walked to the counter, reached underneath, and came up pointing the shotgun at the big man. He waggled the barrel in the direction of the door. "Get out."

The man looked like he might call Stark's bluff, but moved away, probably a smart call, considering the look on Stark's face.

"Come in here and talk like that again, you won't walk away," Stark called to the man's back. He replaced the gun, walked back into his office and sat at his desk. Brun quickly found some music sheets that needed to be put into the racks.

Back at Higdon's after work, Brun spotted Luella in the yard, taking down the wash. Just like his mother, a wooden clothespin in her mouth, folding a towel with one hand, while the other hand pulled a sheet off the line. Meanwhile, clothespins, one after the last, dropped neatly into a little wooden box on the ground. A trick women were born knowing how to do? Brun believed he could practice 'til the cows came home and he'd still have clean wash all over the ground and clothespins across hell's half acre.

When Luella noticed her audience, she got the clothespin out of her mouth in jig time. "Hi, Brun." She waved the towel like a flag. "I got you all nice, clean towels and sheets—this is Monday."

Just one more funny way of women. Sleep on a sheet for a week, or use a towel for that long, a man won't see anything wrong with it, but to a woman's eye it's dirty, no room for discussion. Brun said a proper thank-you, then waited until Luella had all the wash down, and carried the basket inside for her. She looked up at him like he'd pulled a sword and killed a dragon that was going to eat up all the sheets and towels.

At dinner, talk turned to the previous night's Lincolnville fire, after which Brun told about the goings-on at the store that afternoon. Higdon looked grim. "I'm concerned for Isaac," he said. "And John Stark, for that matter. Rabble-rousers like Freitag know just how to get others to do their dirty work for them, while they keep their own hands nice and clean."

Luella, who hadn't said a word to that point, put down her fork, and said, "Brun..." in that tone women use that tells a man trouble's moving in fast. "Let's you and me walk over to church after supper, and say a prayer for Mr. Stark and Isaac."

Brun scratched at his head. "Well, truth, Miss Luella, I'm really not much for praying. Last time I was in church was when I was baptized."

"But you *were* baptized."

But I was only a month old, Brun thought, so I couldn't do a whole lot about it. But neither could he manage to say that to Luella. Her face had gone all bright and smiling. "I know what, Brun. You walk me to the church, and *I'll* say a prayer."

Belle's expression and Higdon's told Brun they both were on to Luella's game. He felt sorry for the girl. "All right," he said. "I'm game to do that." At which, Higdon's body relaxed, and Brun thought Belle wanted to put her arms around him and give him a hug.

After dinner and after the dishes were cleaned, off the young couple went across Sixth, Luella's hand linked into Brun's elbow, while she prattled away about what a comfort it was for a person to know they were saved, and that whatever happened in this life, all would be well afterwards when Jesus himself would personally welcome them into his kingdom. Brun listened politely.

In front of the Central Presbyterian Church, he made ready to wait outside, but Luella would have none of that. "Oh, Brun, come on in with me. You can just sit there, you don't have to pray. Why, you look like you're afraid."

"Well, 'course I'm not afraid."

Brun took her arm and escorted her up the walk and into the church. It was dark, cool and quiet, and the boy admitted to himself, if with some considerable reluctance, that it gave him kind of a peaceful feeling. Luella led him up to the back pew, and he sat and listened while she went through the rigmarole, addressing Jesus like he was some kind of old friend, then invoking his blessing and protection on Mr. John Stark and his whole family, and Isaac Stark and little Belinda, colored though they were. Brun couldn't help but think of Jesus being like an operator on one of those telephone switchboards, headphones over his ears, hooking up one supplicant after another to God, local and long-distance, world without end. Brun's Ma always told him to trust in the Lord, and the boy considered that if a person could believe in the Lord in the first place, it probably did make sense to figure He'd call the best shot, and put all that praying time to more practical use.

Luella prayed not more than five minutes, and as Brun led her back outside, he asked whether she'd like to take another walk through town. The look on her face caused him to wonder if that actually might've been what she was praying for. "Let's go up Lamine to Second," he said. "Then we can cut over to Ohio, and walk back to Sixth."

He'd rather have gone as far as Main, but knew there would be hell to pay back at Higdon's if Luella burbled about how they'd gone walking across Main Street, especially coming on dark. In any case, the girl seemed to have gotten the religion out of her system for the time being, and as they strolled up Lamine, she talked on about how she really didn't want to go back to Kansas City in the fall, and maybe she'd ask Uncle Bob to talk to her father and let her stay on in Sedalia. "Sedalia's lots nicer than Kansas City, and Uncle Bob and Aunt Belle are so good to me. And now that you're here…"

Brun commenced to shed considerably more sweat than the weather could have justified. Going for walks, hand in arm, two nights out of three, put him close to being a beau. Stay away from Liberty Park, he told himself. Don't let her even think you might want to take her sparking. Thirteen was old enough to be married, and breach of promise was a serious affair. A young man could get himself a life sentence, no parole, by saying something he didn't really mean, or intended a different way.

As the young couple came up on Third Street, a rough voice startled Brun out of his thoughts. "Hey-a, young mister and young lady. No you go walkin' down in that alley."

It was Romulus Marcantonio, a raggedy Italian with a big bushy mustache and dark eyes that made him look sorry he'd ever left Italy. Romulus pushed a wagon around town all day, hollering, "Ice-kadeem, ice-kadeem." He leaned against the wall of Glass' Wholesale Liquors, wobbling, weaving, as he waved a wine bottle to punctuate his warning. Luella moved closer to Brun, whether out of genuine fear or just opportunity. "He's all right," Brun whispered. "He wouldn't hurt anybody." Brun cupped his hands around his mouth. "What'd you say, Romulus?"

The Italian tipped a stained brown fedora toward Luella. "I wisha you a good-evening, young lady." Then he wagged a finger at Brun. "You no take-a this nice young lady walkin' down da alley-there. Not safe. Got ghosts."

Luella put a hand to her mouth. "Come on, Romulus," Brun said. "There's no such thing as ghosts."

The Italian came right back. "What you say, boy, there ain't no ghosts? Well, you wrong. That place, there, it's-a haunted. Once-a time I'm standin' right here an' I see those ghosts, an' I run for my life. I no mess-a with no ghosts, no sir. No more I go over there after dark, not for nothin'."

"Probably got the DTs and has himself scared silly," Brun whispered to Luella. Romulus took a stagger-step, came close to dropping his bottle, and in recovering it, nearly went face-down in the street. If he had, Brun thought, he'd tell the next people by that a ghost had pushed him. "Okay, Romulus, thanks," Brun said. "We're not going down that alley, not for nothing. We'll go up and walk across Second."

"You welcome. An' stay this side of the street," Romulus called after them.

"Thanks, we will," Brun shouted over his shoulder.

They strolled past the Post Office, crossed at the corner of Second and walked past Kaiser's Hotel. After a quick look into Mr. Bard's jewelry-store window, they went along to Ohio, then turned south. As they passed the Boston Café, Luella flashed such a look of longing that Brun told himself what the hell, steered her inside, and bought her another ice-cream soda. The way she looked at him, face to face over their straws, reminded him of Wendell, the little cocker pup his parents gave him on his seventh birthday. Wendell got run over by a wagon when Brun was nine.

Back at Higdon's, Belle took Luella off to the kitchen to pit cherries. Higdon was nowhere to be seen. Brun went out back to the screened porch, rolled a cigarette and lit up. Thinking about Romulus Marcantonio and his ghosts, he laughed. Italians are so superstitious, anyone could tell you that, and they can be as hysterical as women. Besides, Romulus had been drunk. Maybe he had a bad dream and didn't even know he was sleeping.

Next day at the end of Brun's lesson, Scott Joplin allowed that he was pleased with his pupil's progress, but still wasn't altogether satisfied. "When you keep watch on yourself, you come close. But then you get into the music, and you sound like any barrelhouse player, da-d'-*da*, da-d'-*da*, da-d'-*da*. Your technique is good, but if you want to play my ragtime, you need to develop a better feeling for the music."

Professor Weiss had sat quietly through the lesson, but now he spoke up. "What you gotta do, Brunnie, is to develop that ear inside of your head. Scott says you play like a barrelhouse pianist, and that's because maybe you *hear* the barrelhouse players in your own head. Have you ever been to a concert with a classical pianist?"

Brun shook his head. "No, sir. Never."

"Ah, see!" Weiss turned to Joplin. "That's the problem. You never was at a concert either, Scott, but you heard me all the time play classical music at Rodgerses'. I would play Brahms and Beethoven, remember? And then you would learn them yourself. Listen, Brunnie, I tell you what. You have a piano where you live, yes? To practice on?"

"Sure."

"Good. Then I will come there tonight, say, eight o'clock? It's all right? I'll bring music and play for you, and then maybe your ear can start hearing classical instead of barrelhouse."

"I'll ask Mr. Higdon," Brun said. "But I'm pretty sure he won't mind."

As Brun put two quarters into Joplin's right hand, the Negro slowly raised his left hand, all the while squeezing a rubber ball, one-two, one-two. "And meanwhile, remember—"

Brun pulled his own rubber ball from his pocket. "I haven't forgotten, Mr. Joplin. And I won't."

The dark man nodded. "Good."

Brun stopped by Higdon's office to tell him of Weiss' offer. Higdon smiled. "I'll let Belle and Luella know. A European musical salon in their own house, they'll be thrilled." He winked at the boy. "I suspect we'll benefit by more than the music."

Just past twelve, enough time for Brun to get in a little practicing before lunch. On his way to Higdon's, he squeezed his rubber ball, right, left, right, left. Keep this up, he'd have some real muscle in his hands and arms. He thought how strong Scott Joplin's hands and arms must be after years of squeezing a ball. Strong enough, he wondered, to strangle a woman and break her neck?

Higdon was right on target about the side benefits of the evening concert. When Weiss arrived at Higdon's, there was a tray of gorgeous iced cakes and a pot of coffee on the low table in the living room. Brun introduced Weiss all around, they had refreshments, and then the German arranged himself on the piano bench and began to play. Brahms and Beethoven, as promised, also Chopin, Bach and Liszt. In between selections, Weiss dispensed bits of advice. "You see, my boy, every pianist plays the same notes from the score, but in spite of that, every player does sound different, yes? So, how can this be? For one thing, they use different dynamics, that gives the music color and flavor, sometimes even surprises. They try variations of tempo. And for a repeat passage—Scott's ragtime has got lots of those—you can go up an octave, see? Makes it sound lighter, like in an orchestra where a whole different group of instruments comes in."

Through the hour-long concert, Luella sat at Brun's side, eyes like pie plates, her mouth open fit to catch flies. After Weiss finished the last piece, a hectic Chopin polonaise, the company applauded, and the girl leaned and whispered into Brun's ear, "Oh, Brun…isn't it beautiful?"

He could hear the unsaid part of the comment: "Not like that trashy ragtime you play all the time." He gave the girl a smile he knew would settle the matter, but he also knew classical music would never touch his heart anywhere near the way ragtime did. Still, he vowed he'd do his best while he practiced his trashy ragtime to think of how Mr. Weiss played Beethoven's piano sonata and Bach's Toccata. Not that he cared whether Luella might like it better. But Scott Joplin might.

Chapter Eleven

Sedalia
Tuesday, July 25, 1899

A little before one next afternoon, Brun walked up to the front door of Stark and Son, but before he could get inside, Fritz Alteneder, sucking on a half-lemon, rushed up to plant himself in Brun's path. Fritz pulled the lemon from his mouth and threw it on the ground. "You think you're pretty hot stuff, don't you, kid? Well, you're gonna be feelin' a lot different when we get done takin' care of you and your pet nigger."

Brun thought of telling the clod he didn't look so good without two of his front teeth, but considering he had on his business suit, he decided to keep shut. He started forward, but Fritz moved over so as to block him from the doorway. "Excuse me," Brun said. "I'm going in to work."

Fritz's face bent into a sneer. "Oh, excuse me, I'm going in to work," falsetto mimic. Then back to his usual voice. "Guess you're just gonna have to get past me first, ain't you?"

Brun stepped sideways; Fritz moved right along with him. Brun was on the point of delivering a quick shot to the bread basket, double the stupid jay over and run past him into the store, but just then, John Stark walked outside. Fritz spat on the ground next to his shoes. "Go on back inside, old man," he snarled. "Me and your kid here have some talkin' to do."

Stark didn't say a word, just stood there, hot-eyeing Fritz for all the boy was worth. A half-minute, maybe more, and Fritz appeared to shrivel. He spat again, but with a whole lot less conviction. "Okay for now, kid," he said to Brun. "But don't worry, I'll be seein' you."

"That'll be your problem," said Brun, bold as brass.

Stark took his clerk by the elbow and led him inside. Isaac stood near the counter, looking worried. A few customers browsed in the sheets; a man examined a saxophone. "Brun, I think we all need to be careful," Stark said. "You're going to have to watch yourself, particularly your back."

Brun did feel concerned. Not that he worried about handling Fritz Alteneder in a fair fight, but he knew Stark was right, that he likely would not get a chance at a fair fight. So during his afternoon break, he walked down to Messerly's General Store and spent a half-buck on a good sturdy jackknife.

When he got back to the store, High Henry was waiting for him, face split wide by a grin. "Hey, Young Mr. Piano Man— Scott Joplin says tell you come on by the Maple Leaf after work. Don't be wastin' no time."

The money-clip—could Joplin have found out? But how? "What's up, Henry?"

"Ohhhhh." Henry's grin went sly. "You see. He gon' have a big treat for you."

Brun worked the rest of the afternoon with only part of his mind on the job, then directly after closing, he beat leather down to the Maple Leaf and up the stairs to the big hall. Just inside the door, he stopped and stared.

There was a crowd around the piano the likes of which he'd not seen before. Weiss was there, and Scott Joplin; so were Otis Saunders, Big Froggy, Arthur Marshall, Scott Hayden and five or six other colored men Brun didn't know. They stood in a rough circle behind the piano, watching another colored man play. And what he played set Brun's fingers tingling. It was ragtime, but not like Scott Joplin's, and not really like barrelhouse either. Maybe I *am* getting an ear inside my head, Brun thought.

Weiss waved his arms like a windmill. "Brunnie, why you standing in the doorway like a dummy? Come on over here."

The pianist stopped playing, and turned half-around. He was a round colored man with a large head shaved bald, and a fine-trimmed mustache. Even though it was only five o'clock on a Wednesday afternoon, he was dressed as if for an evening out, a nicely tailored three-piece gray suit, spotless white shirt and bow tie. On the left lapel of his vest hung two impressive medals, with a heavy gold watch chain running below them. As Brun came close, he noticed the man's eyelids, tightly closed under bushy eyebrows. "Gee-manie," the boy breathed. "Blind Boone."

Boone smiled up at Brun. "I fear you have the advantage on me, sir." For such a big man, his tone was surprisingly high-pitched and thin. "Your voice tells me you're young, and probably from Kansas or Oklahoma, but I don't think I've had the pleasure of making your acquaintance."

"No, sir. My name is Brun Campbell, and I recognized you from your pictures in newspapers and on posters. You never performed any place I was living, but if you did, I would have come for sure."

"Do you play, then?"

Before the boy could answer, Scott Joplin spoke up. "Brun is my pupil. He ran off from Ark-City to take lessons from me."

"Hmmm." Boone looked surprised. "Do you mind if I touch your face, young man?"

"No, sir. I don't mind at all."

Boone ran fingers lightly over Brun's cheeks, then smiled and said, "So you ran off to study piano with Scott Joplin, did you? That's not at all usual, a white boy running away to take piano lessons from a Negro."

Brun looked hard at Boone's eyelids, sewed tight-shut. No way did he have eyes behind there, peeking through slits. "You know I'm white on account of the way I talk?"

"That's a part of it, but only a part. I can see with my fingers and my mind; I tell color by touch." He reached to rub the sleeve of Brun's suit between his fingers. "Your suit is quite dark. Sober, temperate. You wouldn't happen to work in a funeral parlor, Mr. Campbell, would you?"

His face told the boy he was joking. "No, sir, in a music store. But my boss is very proper."

"Boone, now, how you ever do that?" Big Froggy shook his head in wonder. "Tell color by touching."

"It's something I always could do, I think mostly thanks to my mama. When I was a little boy, she was always telling me what things looked like. Flowers, water in a lake, stones and trees. She made me to touch them. Music is like that, too…listen." Boone swung around to the piano. "This is the *Hungarian Rhapsody Number Six*, by Franz Lizst. Listen here." He played a bit, then stopped and quickly replayed a short passage. "Hear that glorious chord? It's a bright yellow." He played another few seconds. "Hear that, now, how it just glows with fire, like a coal? That's a rich, red part. How do I know that, Mr. Froggy? How is it you look with your eyes at the sky, and can say it's blue? Now, Mr. Campbell, I would like to hear just why it was you left your home to come all this way to study with Scott Joplin."

"To learn colored ragtime," Brun said. "The way he plays it."

"Was there no one in Arkansas City could've taught you?"

"No, sir. The colored wouldn't, and white people didn't even know the music."

"Now, that's a sad thing," Boone said, "very sad. All my early piano teachers were white. They taught me proper technique, and the music of the European classical masters. If it were not for those white men and boys who taught me, I would likely be standing on a street corner with a cup in my hand." Then, Boone swung back to the piano and played for a few minutes, that same ragtime music so different from Joplin's, but not like barrelhouse. He looked over his shoulder, asked Brun what he thought.

The boy couldn't shake the weirdest feeling that this eyeless man could actually see him. "I do like it," he said. "What is it?"

Boone smiled. "Just a little something I've been fooling with, a medley of some southern rag-tunes. Do you think you can play it?"

"Not like that," Brun said. "But I can try."

Boone shifted to the end of the bench to make room for Brun. The boy sat, stretched his fingers, moved them toward the keys, then pulled them back. "Here, now," Boone said, and reached over in front of Brun to play a short passage. "There's the beginning for you."

Which helped considerably. Given the start, and allowing that it was a first try and without music to read, Brun thought he did a creditable job. Boone flashed a broad smile. "Not bad at all, young man. You have ability, and I hope you'll work to develop it. Scott Joplin can teach you what you need to know."

"He picks up your music faster than he does mine." Joplin didn't sound sore, just matter-of-fact.

"The way he plays, he'd probably pick up easy from Turpin." Boone turned his sightless face back to Brun. "When you go to St. Louis, go on by the Rosebud Saloon and listen to Tom Turpin play."

"That's the man wrote 'Harlem Rag.'"

"And a whole lot more. He plays his own ragtime pretty much the way he wrote it, like Joplin here, but the music itself is closer to what you and I just played—nothing more than some tunes been around the south ever since the colored first came in. I set them into ragtime, but I leave plenty of space so a performer can fiddle them any way he sees fit. But your teacher's up to something different altogether. He takes those folky tunes and he cleans them up, polishes them 'til they shine, and *then* he makes them over into ragged time. He's turning ragtime into a whole new form of classical music. Now, this *Ragtime Dance*, Joplin? Not a whole lot of help I or anybody else can give you for it. Little things, that's all. Remember that part from the 'Dude Walk,' comes right after the 'Backstep Prance'?" Boone played a few bars, then another few. "Hear the clash there? But that won't be hard to fix."

Joplin moved toward the bench, Brun quickly got up and out of the way, and then everyone started talking at once. Joplin's fingers flew, played a short musical passage, then another. Every now and again he stopped to scratch out notes on his manuscript and write others down. This went on for a good half-hour, at which point Joplin played a long stretch without interruption, the entire "Dude Walk" portion, which sounded very good to Brun. And from all appearances, also to Boone and the others.

And to somebody else. Loud clapping from behind, then a voice familiar to Brun. "Bravo, maestro, bravo. That should knock those Emancipation Day dudes smack on their ears."

Along with everybody else, Brun turned, and there was Freitag, Maisie McAllister at his side. Maisie winked at Brun, which under other circumstances would have pleased him no end, but right there and in that place, he hoped no one noticed. No such luck. Otis Saunders, standing right next to the boy, chuckled and gave him a sharp elbow to the ribs.

"We were passing by," Freitag said, "and we couldn't help but hear the fine music through the open windows." He looked closely at Boone; Brun saw the light go on. "And my, my, who have we here but Blind Boone. I am honored to meet you."

Boone didn't look like he felt the least bit honored, didn't say a word. Nor did anyone else. Finally Freitag spoke. "I'm Elmo Freitag, formerly of Carl Hoffman Music Publishers, now sole proprietor and impresario of Freitag Enterprises, devoted to the publication and performance of colored music, both in the United States and abroad." He stuck a hand under Boone's nose, then chuckled. "Oh yes, I forgot," and grasped Boone's hand where it rested on the piano keys. Boone pulled his hand away.

Which didn't appear to bother Freitag, who shifted his attention to Joplin. "Well, Scott, how about yourself? Have you had any change of heart? Performing your score at Emancipation Day festivities in Sedalia is one thing. Having it published nation-wide and performed on-stage is something else altogether."

Joplin turned a frozen face to Freitag. "I've had no change, sir, not of heart, mind, or anything else. Now, please, I need to excuse myself. I have work to do."

Looking at Freitag, you'd have thought Joplin had told him it was a nice day out. He laughed lightly. "You know, I just can't help thinking...can you imagine Blind Boone and Scott Joplin playing their music on the same stage? Why, no one would even think about Bob Cole and Will Marion Cook any more, you'd run 'em into the ground. We'd be booked a year in advance, sellout crowds all over the country. Then maybe a European tour—"

"Thank you, but I have a manager. Mr. Lange." Boone pointed to a light colored man with close-cut hair, an amazing pair of mutton-chop whiskers, and a severe expression, standing very straight between Froggy and Scott Hayden. "He does very well for me, thank you."

"Oh, I'm sure he does," Freitag boomed. "And considering what fine skills I know he's got, I would find a right place for him in my company. But for managing your career, there's no question I can do even better for you. I can get you bookings that no colored man could ever get. And I can take the bother of money troubles off Mr. Lange's shoulders and yours. We'd all be doing what the Lord intended. You colored would make music, sing and dance, I'd look after the business, and we'd all come out on top."

Brun wasn't sure who was going to blow first, Lange or Froggy. Both colored men seemed to be holding themselves in check with difficulty. Lange's hands trembled, though not, Brun thought, from any weakness. But it was Boone who answered Freitag. "I thank you for your consideration, sir, but I'm completely satisfied with my situation." There was an edge to his voice you could have cut a finger on. "And now, as Mr. Joplin said, we need to get back to work. Joplin, let's go on to that 'Stop Time' dance."

Boone raised his hands over the keyboard. Freitag's cheeks deepened to the color of ripe plums. All the colored men turned back to the piano, and began to talk, but softer now, Brun noticed.

Freitag sniffed. "Some people, you just can't do a thing to help them. You're being foolish, the both of you, and you'll live to regret it." Then, Freitag swiveled like a soldier, took Maisie by the arm, and walked to the doorway and out.

When the stomp on the stairs died away, Boone let up playing the theme from "Stop Time," and turned his face toward Joplin. Brun again marveled at the way that blind man could tell where everyone stood, even as they shifted and moved around. "Joplin," he said, very gravely. "That is a bad man."

"I know. He came by last month with Mr. Daniels, from Hoffman. They wanted me to give them *Ragtime Dance*. Daniels did most of the talking, but he didn't get anywhere, so maybe he sent Freitag around to see what he could do with that sleigh ride about happy darkies on the music plantation."

Mr. Daniels, from Hoffman? Brun took care to file that scrap of information in his mind.

"Today was the first I met the man," Boone said. "But I did hear him once before, down at the train depot after I was by to work with you last Tuesday. I was waiting on the platform to catch the train back to Columbia, and I heard him tell a woman to get out of town and stay out, that if she thought she was going to make trouble for him, she'd find out in a hurry what real trouble was. She had a beautiful voice, and if she hadn't been so upset, it would've been pure pleasure just listening to her." Boone shook his head. "Don't have any truck with that man, Joplin. Don't let him near your music."

"A woman with a beautiful voice, you say?" At Joplin's question, the whole room went still.

"Oh, just lovely," said Boone. "She could have sung for me any time."

"She was here," Joplin said. "Last Tuesday, that's right—while I was having lunch at Cleary's. She told me she was desperate to find Freitag, had heard him mention my name, and thought I might be able to help. I'll admit, I was a little short with her.

She said she was sorry to interrupt my meal, and could she come back later? I told her not to bother, that I had no idea where Freitag was."

"Did she?" Question out before Brun even knew he was thinking it.

"Did she what?" Joplin looked confused.

"Come back later. Like she said she was going to do?"

Joplin couldn't seem to figure the why of Brun's question.

"Just asking," Brun said.

"Some questions a man don't ask," Big Froggy rumbled.

Brun started to say he was sorry, but Joplin beat him to the punch. "No, she didn't. I never saw her again. But I certainly do remember her voice." Then he looked around at the group. "Let's go on," he said. "Now that I've got Boone here, I'd be a fool not to take full advantage."

Everybody laughed, except, of course, Joplin.

Next morning, when Brun came downstairs for breakfast and piano practice, Belle and Luella ran out of the kitchen and up to him. "Mr. Higdon is over at the jail," Belle said. "There was a break. He says you can go over there and meet him, if you want."

The boy was halfway outside when Luella called, "Brun, Brun…You haven't had breakfast. I can make you some eggs real quick."

"Thanks, Miss Luella," Brun shouted back. "I'll just get something later."

Outside the jail, men stood in groups, talking. Brun pushed his way through them and ran inside, where he saw Mr. Williams, the sheriff, talking to six men. Brun figured he was deputizing them and they were going to chase after the escaped prisoners. He started past the group, but the sheriff shouted, "Hey, you—boy. Where do you think you're going?"

"Mr. Higdon sent for me," Brun said, polite as he possibly could sound. "Can you please tell me where I'll find him."

A couple of the deputies started to laugh, but shut up in a hurry when Sheriff Williams looked at them. The sheriff jerked his thumb toward the cells. "He's back there with Robert E. Lee. Last cell on the left."

Which is where Brun found Higdon and Fitzgerald, sitting side-by-side on the cot. Fitzgerald looked like he'd crawled home on his eyebrows. "Who got out?" Brun called through the bars.

Higdon reached a key through the bars and opened the door. "A couple of bad ones, a thief and a murderer. Somebody got them a hammer and a chisel." He pointed at the next cell over. "This red stone is soft as mud. They chipped away around the bars, then pulled them free, and bashed enough stone to get out through the window." He glanced toward Fitzgerald. "When they had it all clear and were on the way out, they tossed the tools over here for Mr. Fitzgerald to use."

"But you didn't," Brun said.

Fitzgerald pulled his back straight and raised his head so he was looking down at Brun. "No, sir. I certainly did not." He looked insulted that the boy had gone so far as to even think he might've gone out a jail window. "When a man sacrifices his honor and good name to expediency, then he's not worth his space on earth."

"If he had run, he would have convinced everyone he *was* guilty," Higdon added.

"I am innocent of the charges against me, and I intend to clear my good name."

He sounds like a politician on a soapbox, Brun thought, then wondered what he would have done in Fitzgerald's place. The man could have hopped the next train to Buffalo and been gone. Or hid out for a while somewhere down south. But it takes considerable gumption to break jail, even more to stay out, and Brun did not think Fitzgerald was long on gumption. If he'd gone out the window the night before, like as not he'd already be back behind bars, and as Higdon said, he'd then have everyone convinced he was guilty. And the longer Brun looked at Fitzgerald, slumped on the edge of the cot, tired lines and

creases around his eyes deeper than ever, the guiltier he felt for
his own behavior.

Toward four o'clock that afternoon, Brun heard a commotion
at the back of the store. Isaac looked up from the register, where
he had just finished ringing up some music sheets for a heavy,
sweaty-faced man. A small crowd, everyone shouting at once,
moved toward the front. Stark came at the run out of his office,
dropped the papers in his hand onto the counter, but before he
could take more than a few steps, four people burst into full view,
three grownups and a little boy. Two of the adults were Mrs.
Stark and Higdon; the lawyer held a large carpetbag suitcase in
one hand. The third adult was a woman Brun had never seen
before. With one hand, she clutched to her skirts a beautiful
little boy, chunky and blond, with eyes like pools of melted
emeralds. While the three grownups ran off at the mouth, the
child stared from one to the other, like he was trying to make
some sense out of their loud chatter.

It seemed to Brun that the woman was unhappy about
something, and Higdon and Mrs. Stark were trying to calm her
down. But she would have none of it. They all stood in front of
the counter, words flying back and forth like bullets, arms going
every which way, until Stark slammed a fist onto the counter,
and shouted fit to rouse a man from a coma, "What in the name
of Sam Hill is going on here?"

That shut everyone up. A girl who'd been looking through
the music sheets stopped, then rushed up front, passed by on the
other side of the piano, and got herself out of the store about as
fast as a person could move. Higdon and Mrs. Stark both started
to talk, then went quiet and glanced at the woman with the
little boy like they were afraid given half a chance, she'd be off
and spouting again. Finally, Mrs. Stark nodded at Higdon: go
ahead. Butterfly motions at the corners of her mouth tempered
her usual warm smile.

Higdon set down the carpetbag. "Mr. Stark, this is Mrs. Edward Fitzgerald—"

"*Mollie* Fitzgerald," the woman barked. "Mollie McQuillan Fitzgerald."

Stark and Brun stood shoulder-to-shoulder, agog at Mrs. Fitzgerald. The boy had seen some odd women, but never one such as this. Mr. Fitzgerald was neat, trim, and well decked out; before he got locked up, you could've called him a dandy. But Mrs. Fitzgerald had skin like library paste, dark circles underneath her eyes. Thin, pale lips, both corners turned down in a sour frown. Her hat was a marvel of terrible taste, big, black, and floppy, with a spray of feathers that could've been plucked off a giant turkey. From beneath the edges of the hat, tight frizzy black curls, starting to go gray, ran down her back, and covered her ears and forehead. She wore a plain black dress, buttoned up in front, which appeared to have been made for a woman wider in the beam and smaller in the chest. Her high-button shoes were open at the top, laces dragging. Brun looked twice to be sure he was right, and yes he was: one shoe was black, the other, brown. And on this sunny, cloudless day, she carried an umbrella over her left wrist. Not a white parasol, a big black umbrella. She couldn't seem to take her eyes off Isaac, who finally walked to the back of the store and found something to do there.

The little boy pulled his thumb out of his mouth, and said, "Mama—"

"Be quiet, Frankie," the woman snapped. "Mind your manners. Don't talk when grownups are talking."

Thumb back in his mouth in a hurry. He made sucking noises, and went back to studying the company.

Higdon gave it another try. "Mrs. Fitzgerald just came in by train—"

"I did not *just* come in," Mrs. Fitzgerald corrected. "I have been here for more than two hours. When my husband is on the road, he always calls me, every evening, regular as your finest clock. And when I'd not heard from him between Saturday and Monday, I knew something was the matter, so I called his hotel.

Neither the desk clerk nor the manager would tell me a thing—a fine bunch of mealy-mouthed weasels you have in this city. So I packed my bag, put my pistol into my purse, got myself and my child onto a train, and came down, all the way from Buffalo, New York. And where do I find my husband? In jail, accused of murdering a woman. A fine kettle of fish!"

Higdon looked as if he'd like to grab the umbrella off Mrs. Fitzgerald's arm and clout her a good one over the ear. He forced a smile. "I've taken Mrs. Fitzgerald to see her husband—"

"And a splendid sight *he* is. Sitting in your jailhouse, unbathed and wearing the same clothing for nigh-onto a week. Do you people have no idea of sanitation out here?"

Her speech was as rum as her clothes, slow, with big rolling inflections and vowels prolonged to ridiculous lengths. Brun thought she looked and sounded like someone you'd expect to see in the Sunday funny papers. She flipped her umbrella into her free hand, and pointed it at Higdon. "And *you* are his lawyer. What have you done for him? Why is he still locked up in jail? If I don't see him freed very shortly, I am going to call the governor of this misbegotten, out-of-the-way state."

Brun thought no one could have criticized Higdon for dragging the terrible woman into Stark's office, sitting her down in front of the telephone, and telling her to go ahead, call the gov. But Higdon kept calm. "Mrs. Fitzgerald, I've told you, this is going to take a little time. I'm doing everything for your husband that can be done."

Mrs. Stark laid a hand lightly on her husband's arm. "Johnny, dear, these last few days have been a terrible trial for poor Mrs. Fitzgerald. First, she hears nothing from her husband, then she rides here on a train, how many miles is it from Buffalo? And all the while fearing the worst. Then when she gets here—"

"I went straight to the *po*lice, that's what I did. And what do I find, but my husband sitting in a jail cell, charged with choking a young woman to death. Ridiculous!" Mrs. Fitzgerald stamped her umbrella onto the wooden floor. "Edward, strangling a woman? What a bunch of nonsense. Edward doesn't have the nerve to kill a housefly."

Stark put a hand over his mouth, whether to hide a smile or hold in a word, Brun couldn't tell. The boy figured that right then, poor Mr. Fitzgerald was likely better off in jail than out. "The police captain took me over to Mr. Higdon's law office." Mrs. Fitzgerald paused long enough to give Higdon the kind of glance she might turn on a worm that had crawled up onto one of her untied, mismatched shoes. "He doesn't look to me as if he's been out of diapers long enough to be a lawyer."

"Now, Mrs. Fitzgerald." Brun heard sinew in Mrs. Stark's voice. "You're upset, my dear. Young, Mr. Higdon may be, but people in Sedalia hold him very high indeed in their regard. Now, let's not dither any longer." She looked back to Stark. "I've offered the hospitality of our home to Mrs. Fitzgerald and little Frankie. It would not do to have them stay in a hotel room during such a trying time. They can have the room where we put up Etilmon when he's in town."

Brun pictured this crazy woman in a hotel room downtown, stomping back and forth, banging on walls, rushing up and down hallways, walking up to strangers in the lobby, poking her umbrella into their chests, and he commenced to wonder whether after all, Fitzgerald really *might* be guilty. With such a wife at home, maybe he did have ladies on the road, and maybe something went wrong with one of them the other night, and poor Fitzgerald just went bughouse, grabbed her by the throat and squeezed. But then, he thought, how to explain Joplin's money-clip next to the body?

John Stark bowed slightly, and said, "Mrs. Fitzgerald, you and your son are welcome to stay with us for as long as needed. We'll do what we can to make you comfortable."

Mrs. Fitzgerald tilted her head back a bit to take Stark in from beneath the brow of that ridiculous hat. "Thank you," she said. "I'm grateful for your offer. But I must ask, before we stay in your house. You and your family are not Jews, are you?"

Nobody breathed except little Frankie, who took advantage of the silence to sing past his thumb, "Jews, Jews, Jews…"

His mother pulled the child closer; he leaned against her leg. "You see, I must consider the safety of my son. There is a Jewish man named Stark in Buffalo who owns a men's clothing store, and he has a beard like yours. And I know for a fact that he tries to get little Christian boys into his shop, especially in the spring." She leaned forward, then continued in a hoarse whisper, "I've heard it from the priest himself. He tells all the mothers in the parish to keep their children safe around Easter."

Mrs. Stark didn't blink an eye. "Oh, now, Mrs. Fitzgerald," she said, and Brun almost laughed out loud at the thick layer of Irish that suddenly coated each of her words. "Should Mollie McQuillan Fitzgerald have any reason to fear for her son's safety or her own in the home of Sarah Ann Casey Stark? Let's have no more nonsense. I'll take you and Frankie upstairs, and by the time my husband is done with work…" She stopped just long enough to give Stark a hard look. "And finished having his beer, why you'll be feeling as safe and comfortable as in your very own house." She reached for Frankie's hand. "Come along, little Irishman. I have sugar cookies, nice big ones. I baked them just this morning."

Higdon reached for the carpetbag, but Mrs. Fitzgerald was quicker, and snapped it up. "I can carry it, thank you," she snapped. "You can put your time and effort to better use by attending to my husband's predicament. I trust the next time I see you, you will have some good news."

"I'll do my best," Higdon said, very politely. If she heard him, she gave no sign.

Isaac quietly moved forward along the opposite side of the store from the retreating Mrs. Fitzgerald. For a minute or two, he, Higdon, Stark and Brun stood there like men surveying the scene right after a tornado had unexpectedly blown through. Finally, Isaac said, "Somehow, I don't think that woman's gonna cotton to havin' a colored man sleepin' in the same house as her."

"Well, she'll just have to, won't she?" Stark was furious.

Isaac held up a hand. "Plenty of room in the shop—we can put a cot in the office." Stark opened his mouth, but Isaac cut off whatever he might have been going to say. "Mr. Stark, some things just ain't worth the fuss. B'sides, this particular colored man's gonna be a lot happier not sleepin' in the same place as that crazy woman."

Higdon said, "I'm sorry, John. I owe you an apology."

Stark grimaced. "I don't think that's necessary, but perhaps a short explanation might do. I will admit to more than a little curiosity."

Higdon cleared his throat. "I was at the office just a few hours ago, and all of a sudden it sounded like the circus was coming through my door. It was Ed Love, with Mrs. Fitzgerald and the little boy. She'd come in on the two-sixteen, gone straight to the police, told the desk sergeant who she was, and asked him if he had any information about her husband's whereabouts. When the sergeant said she'd have to talk to the captain, she got pretty rough with the man, and he managed to find Ed in a hurry. Ed told her the story, and you'd have thought she'd ask to be taken directly to her husband, but no. 'That's utterly ridiculous,' she told Ed. 'My husband does not consort with women when he's away from home—I doubt he's got the nerve, and I know he does not have that sort of need. Why, that man can't even kill a chicken for our Sunday dinner. Now, I demand his instant release!'"

Brun, Stark and Isaac laughed that little laugh that sneaks out when you're walking home alone late at night through a graveyard.

"Poor Ed Love tried to reason with her, but you can imagine how much good that did. Somehow, he got through to her that I was Mr. Fitzgerald's lawyer, and she really ought to talk to me. So he brought her by and introduced her, and while she and the boy were using a toilet, he told me what had been going on. Then he got himself out of the office in quick time, which I guess I can't really blame him for doing. I thought I'd need to call Doc Overstreet to give her a sedative, she was that worked up. She read every one of my diplomas on the wall, told me I was a gossoon and a stripling, and insisted on having a real lawyer for her husband. All the while, that little boy just hung on to her hand or her leg, didn't say a word, just watched. He didn't seem at all bothered."

Stark snorted. "He must be used to it."

Higdon looked unconvinced. "The way that kid watches, those great big eyes… I was getting nowhere in a hurry, so finally I called Bud Hastain, and bless him, he came right over, sat down in front of that woman, and gave her the most tactful what-for you can imagine. Told her she should be pleased to have my services for her husband, that I was the smartest young lawyer to come up the pike in a lot of years, and I had the time and the ambition to do full justice to her husband's case. 'That's all very well,' she said, 'but I still think I should call Buffalo and get an experienced lawyer to come down.' 'That's fine, Mrs. Fitzgerald,' Bud told her. 'You can call in a lawyer from New York…' You know the way he says 'New York,' John. 'And he may be a fine lawyer, but I'll guarantee he does not know our local customs and behavior. Which means he's going to have real trouble with a jury. My advice to you is to avail yourself of Mr. Higdon's excellent services, with the understanding that whenever he might want to speak with a more experienced attorney, he can call on me. I've practiced law in Sedalia for fifteen years.' Then, he raised the one eyebrow."

Stark laughed. "I can just see him."

"'And I have served four years as mayor of this city.' Of course, that got her attention. 'Oh, well, then, Mr… I beg your pardon, I did not catch your name.'

"'Hastain. P. D. Hastain.'

"'P. D.?' She gave him that odd look of hers, the way she peers out from under the brim of her hat. 'I don't think I can trust a man whose Christian name I do not know.'"

Stark took the name of the Lord in vain.

"So Bud said, 'My Christian name is Pleasant, but most people other than my mother call me Bud.'

"'Pleasant?' I swear, John, that woman rolled the word around in her mouth like she was tasting it. '*Pleasant?* I must say, Mr. Hastain, that's a most peculiar name. Is it perhaps your mother's maiden name? Or some other family name?'

"'No, indeed,' Bud said. 'That was my mother's wish for me, and my father went along. You've no doubt met girls named Prudence, or Constance, or Patience, or Faith, or Hope, or Charity. Well, long before I made my appearance, it had been decided, boy or girl, I was going to be Pleasant.'"

Higdon laughed, but Brun heard an edge to his merriment. "He *was* pleasant with her, all right—finally had the woman eating out of his hand and saying it was delicious. But it's not going to be pleasant for me if I foul up Fitzgerald's defense, and Procter and Gamble pulls out of Sedalia."

Stark turned his head to launch a direct hit on the spittoon. "Bud's a good man, but he's caught a big dose of Bothwell's booster germ."

"He's been nothing but good to me ever since I got to town," Higdon said. "And I'm bound in any case to make Fitzgerald a good defense, so I guess I really don't have room for honest complaint. Anyway, after Bud left, I realized I'd better find a place for Mrs. Fitzgerald and the boy to stay, but the way that woman carries on, can you imagine her in any of our hotels? Or a boarding house, even one as nice as Leila Wallace's? I don't think it would take her a day to make sure I wouldn't stand a chance of getting an impartial jury anywhere within fifty miles. I need to keep her close at hand where I can get to her, but no one else can. And I need somebody I can trust to keep an eye on her and make sure she doesn't go around shooting off her husband's feet, and mine with them."

"I guess I know who that somebody is." Stark sounded just a bit weary.

"Can you think of anyone better? I left Mrs. Fitzgerald and the little boy with my secretary while I came and talked to Mrs. Stark. Then, I brought them over here, and took them upstairs for introductions."

Mr. Stark chuckled. "I guess I can't fault you, Bob, nor will I complain. As hard a row to hoe as that Fitzgerald woman may be for me, she'll be far worse for you. And as for Sarah, I'm sure she's just tickled. A little boy like that? We'll be listening to a whole new bunch of her fairy stories for a while."

"If she's got an extra leprechaun, ask her to please send him my way." Brun thought Higdon sounded not at all like a man making a joke.

◇◇◇

As they closed up for the day, Apple John, his basket empty, sauntered up and told Brun that Mr. Boutell would like him to play an hour or two the next night, that his regular piano man was going to be late. "But you're gonna have to go tell him yourself, 'cause I ain't no messenger boy."

"I'll tell him for you, Brun." Stark's face was wry, teasing. "Mrs. Stark did say I was going to have a beer after work, didn't she?"

Stark didn't sound at all in a hurry to get home, for which Brun owned he could hardly fault him. He thanked his boss, then fell in next to Higdon. The lawyer looked anything but happy. "I didn't want to do that, and if I didn't know the Starks so well, I never would have. But if anyone can keep that Fitzgerald woman under wraps, it's Mrs. Stark. She just might give me a fighting chance to come up with a decent defense. Right now, I don't have much to hang my hat on."

Brun swallowed the bubble that rose into his throat as he again thought about the locket and the money-clip. If Higdon ever found out Brun had been hiding those clues all this time, it would go very badly for him. He tried not to think along those lines. He wanted never to leave Sedalia.

Chapter Twelve

Sedalia
Friday, July 28, 1899

When Brun got to the Maple Leaf Club for his morning lesson, he found Joplin in a brown study, alone at the piano, staring at papers on the music rack. No other students, no Mr. Weiss. Brun tiptoed up, but Joplin either noticed his student's movements or sensed the boy behind him. He whipped around, then quickly pulled his watch. "You're six minutes early."

"Couldn't wait any longer." Brun pointed at the music. "Are you getting it to where you want it?"

"Not quite. Emancipation Day's only a week away…" Joplin sighed, then folded the manuscript, laid it carefully on the floor next to the piano, and got up. "All right, sit down. Play me what I've taught you. 'Maple Leaf,' then 'Original Rags,' 'Sunflower' and 'Swipesey.' Play them as a medley."

When the boy finished, he was covered in sweat. Joplin nodded. "Better."

"But it's still not like you play it."

Joplin shook his head. "If you'd learned ragtime from me from the beginning, it would have been easier. Once you get into bad playing habits, you need to get rid of them before you can pick up good ones. Maybe we should give you something new…all right, here. This is a part of a tune I'm just starting to work on."

Brun got off the piano bench. How many tunes did this man have in his head, all being worked on at once? As Joplin took his seat, the boy noticed a small piece of paper on the floor next to *The Ragtime Dance* manuscript; he bent to pick it up. It was a business card for The Maple Leaf Club, Sedalia, Missouri, 121 East Main Street, W.J. Williams, Prop. Joplin began to play. Brun flipped the card in his hand, and read, "The Good Time Boys will give a good time, for instance Master Scott Joplin, the Entertainer." Below were a bunch of other names, but before Brun could read them, Joplin suddenly lifted his hands from the keyboard and said, "All right, then. Now, you play it. Just the way I did."

Brun wanted to ask for another listen, but was scared at what Joplin might say. The boy palmed the card into his pocket, then sat at the keyboard, and asked, "Can you please give me a start?"

Joplin took up Brun's hands, set his fingers on the keys. "Go on, now. I know you've never heard this tune before, and I want to hear how you do with it."

Brun barely had heard it then, and he stumbled his way through, never mind showing proper feeling for the music. When he finished, he thought his teacher looked like someone who'd just taken a length of two-by-four to the head. "I'm sorry, Mr. Joplin," he said, moving to the side as he talked. "Play it once more and let me watch closer. Please."

Without taking his eyes off Brun, or saying a single word, Joplin sat back down and played the passage. "All right?"

Brun burned with shame and embarrassment. "Yes." He moved his hands toward the keys, then began to play. This go-round, he got through the music nicely, and Joplin nodded approval. "Better. Your expression is more accurate. Maybe we need to concentrate on music you haven't heard before."

"What's the name of this one?" Brun asked.

"No name. So far it's just what you heard, some bits and pieces."

"I like it. Is there any more of it you can play for me?"

Joplin sat and knocked out some fifteen seconds of music. There's something about whatever he composes, Brun thought. Even bits and pieces sound like music nobody else could have written. "You've already got 'Scott Joplin's Original Rags,'" the boy said. "You could call this one 'The Entertainer.'"

"'The Entertainer'? Where did you get that from?" Brun pulled the card back out of his pocket. Joplin raised his eyebrows. "Keeping up with you is a challenge—but yes, that's what they call me here. All right, enough of that. Your lesson time is passing, and we need to do some exercises."

Later, before Brun left, Joplin took out his rubber ball, squeezed it left-handed, then right. Brun quickly worked his ball out of his pocket and began to squeeze it in time with Joplin. "Good," Joplin said. "Before you know it, your hands will have such strength and endurance, you won't be able to stop them playing."

Sarah Stark thought a walk around town might be a good diversion for Mrs. Fitzgerald, so after lunch she herded the strange woman and little Frankie down the stairs and over to Ohio. Saturday afternoon, the street was bustling, wagons rolling past like a parade. Every hitching post was taken. Horses in too-close quarters snorted and pawed the air, shook their manes and switched their tails against the fierce, persistent horseflies. The sidewalks were packed with shoppers, but they fell away to clear a path for Mrs. Fitzgerald as she marched, stone-faced, waving her black umbrella before her like a sword. Frankie couldn't decide where to look first, and when he spotted the little popcorn wagon at the corner of Fourth Street, he jabbed a finger and commenced to jump up and down. Mrs. Stark asked Mrs. Fitzgerald's permission, then bought the child a small bag of popcorn.

As the women and the little boy approached Boutell's Saloon, a heavy blond man in a preposterous light-gray suit moved out from a small group of loafers. Mrs. Stark thought he smiled like the Cheshire cat in *Alice in Wonderland*, and though he tipped his straw boater and said, "Good afternoon, ladies," his attention clearly centered on Frankie. "What a beautiful little boy," the man boomed, then leaned into Frankie's face. "What's your name, little guy?"

Frankie hid his face in his mother's skirts. The man laughed. "Bashful, eh?" He reached into his pants pocket, then held out his hand. "Bet you like horehound drops."

When Mrs. Stark saw the expression on Mrs. Fitzgerald's face, she spoke quickly. "Thank you, sir. My friend and her son are newly arrived in town, and I'm afraid the little man's a bit shy." She tugged on Mrs. Fitzgerald's arm.

"You're welcome, Mrs. Stark," the man called after them. "Maybe after your friend and her boy get more comfortable, we can all become friends." He rejoined the group of men he'd been talking to. Mrs. Stark looked over her shoulder. She'd never seen the man. How was it he knew her name?

At Boutell's that evening, it occurred to Brun that if he played around with some of the practice exercises Scott Joplin had given him, they might just come across as ragtime tunes. Like what Blind Boone did, that southern rag medley. It took only a few minutes for the boy to really get it going, ragging those exercises for all they were worth. He'd been at it a good half-hour when who should glide up to the piano but Otis Saunders, a smile big as Everest painted on his face. "Well, hello there, Mr. Brun Campbell," Saunders said. "Here I be, walkin' past the door, just mindin' my own business, and all of a sudden I say to myself, 'Is that Scott Joplin playin' piano at Boutell's? Nah, nah…'" Silly idea, he pushed it away with his hand. "But then I say, 'Sure do sound like Scott, I gotta go see for myself.' An' just looky what I find."

Brun's fingers didn't slow. A piano player who couldn't carry on a conversation while he performed didn't hold his job for very long. "Thanks, Otis," he said. "I appreciate the compliment, but I know I don't really sound anything like Mr. Joplin. Maybe some day."

"Oh, well, now, Brun—you know I was just ragging on *you* a little bit. But you want to remember something. Scott Joplin, he a mighty fine piano player, an' he write music like he got an angel sittin' on his shoulder, whispering notes in his ear. But he not the be-all and the end-all. Everybody who play ragtime got his own way, and there ain't no two players with just the same touch. 'Course I knowed that wasn't Scott Joplin in here, it was Brun Campbell. Just like recognizing your face. Now…"

Saunders pushed Brun to the left, stood next to him at the keyboard, and said, "You just keep right on playin'." Then he swung into a lively accompaniment to Brun's ragged-up syncopated exercise. The room went so quiet, Brun could hear from somewhere past the bar, "Godamighty—izzat a white man and a colored, playin' on the same piano?" "No, you damn fool. Anybody can see they're both white."

When Brun and Saunders finished, note-perfect and dead-on with each other, people clapped and whistled. A few dropped coins into Brun's hat on top of the piano. "See there, now," Saunders said. "You play Brun and I play Otis, and it be like two people having a pleasant li'l talk. Ain't that the way?"

"Try another one," Brun said, and swung into the few lines of what he'd called "The Entertainer." Saunders rested a hand on his arm. "Wait just a minute, now. Where you get that tune?"

Uh-oh. Did Saunders recognize the music? Better play safe. "That's one of the exercises Mr. Joplin gave me, and I've been fooling around with it."

"Do tell." Saunders' eyes widened. "So that ain't no tune been published?"

"Just an exercise from Mr. Joplin." Brun started to play "Harlem Rag," but Saunders went right on talking. "Don't you see what you got there, boy? You got yourself a brand-new ragtime tune. Put it down on paper, and next you know, you be seein' it on the cover of a music sheet, an' your name right underneath." Saunders laughed at the expression on Brun's face.

"You lucky, boy, can't you see that? You in the right place an' at just the right time, what with there bein' a man in town, lookin' to buy up all the ragtime he can get a hand on. So…" Saunders cupped a hand to an ear, and leaned to the side. "Don't I just hear Mr. Opportunity, a-knockin' hard at Brun Campbell's door? I think the boy be a fool, he don't open up that door an' let the man in." Saunders made a show of looking at his watch, then grinned. "Got to go now—got a special appointment, if you catch my meaning."

Which left Brun mightily distracted. For the next hour, the boy improvised on every exercise Scott Joplin had given him, played rings around every melody fragment he could dredge up from what he'd heard other players play in other places. Write them down? Well, why not? Wasn't that what Boone did? But not to sell to Freitag. Stark and Son would need some good tunes for *their* catalog, wouldn't they?

Arthur Marshall came in at ten o'clock, and Brun headed out, his pocket heavy with more than two dollars in change. Paltry compared to what he could make writing down music to publish. The boy was so busy running numbers through his head that as he came up on the alleyway next to Boutell's, he nearly plowed directly into a woman. "Well, Mr. Campbell," she said. "You ought to watch better where you're going. And you might just say hello to a friend."

Maisie McAllister, in summery cotton and lace, lit up the night with her smile. "Or maybe you're mad at me?"

"No…no, 'course not," Brun stammered. "Why should I be mad at you? I was just thinking about something."

He looked around, but didn't see Freitag or any other man nearby. Maisie pointed toward the swinging doors. "Mr. Freitag went inside for a beer. Didn't you see him?"

Brun shook his head. "It was pretty crowded."

"And so hot—and all the cigars. That's why I decided to wait for him out here. But tell me, Mr. Campbell. What's so very interesting that it's got your mind to where you didn't even notice me?"

By way of apology, Brun executed a little bow. "Miss McAllister, I am sorry for my behavior. Since I've come to town, I've had uncommon good luck, and I was just thinking about my future. That's why I didn't take proper notice of you."

"Perhaps you should."

That smile, those eyes... Even in the out-of-doors, there was no missing the fragrance of her scent. Other girls had given Brun that particular look, and what came afterward was always very pleasant. "Mr. Campbell, you know what?" Maisie's eyelashes fluttered. "I'm tired of standing here. Why don't you see me back to my house, and on the way, you can tell me what you've been thinking." She slipped a hand into the crook of his arm.

Brun looked around, which brought a snicker from Maisie. "Don't worry about Mr. Freitag. If he wants the company of a glass of beer more than mine, he can just enjoy it." She gave a little tug at Brun's elbow.

The idea of seeing Maisie home was more than agreeable to Brun, and the thought of Freitag coming out of Boutell's, looking all around for the girl and not finding her, was icing on a very tasty cake. So, off they went down Ohio, past Fourth and Fifth. The streets grew darker, the sounds of night life further away. Brun told Maisie about his piano lessons with Scott Joplin, job with John Stark, lodgings with the Higdons. "It's a swell start, but a man needs to strike while the iron's hot. I think music publishing is going to be big, and I want to get in on it."

They turned onto East Sixth. Moonlight gleamed off Maisie's hair. Her wide eyes seemed to take in every word he said. "Are you thinking as a publisher? Or do you want to write music to publish?"

"Maybe both." He told himself he'd be smart not to mention anything to do with John Stark. "But for now, anyway, I want to write the music. It shouldn't be all that hard. Why, the tunes are right there—piano men play them every day, and the first to write a tune down is the legal owner. Not like it's stealing."

She squeezed his arm. "Flowers growing in a field are just there for the picking, aren't they?"

"That's the way I see it." Then he began to hum "The Entertainer" fragment. Maisie picked right up. "That's a catchy one."

"Shouldn't be all that hard to stretch it into a tune," Brun said.

They stopped in front of a little yellow clapboard house between Washington and Harrison, its front yard filled with ivy, save for a narrow winding path to the front door. Maisie tugged at Brun's arm. "Why don't you see me inside, we can talk some more." She looked at his face and laughed, a lovely musical sound. "Don't worry, I won't hurt you. And I won't tell your mother."

Brun commenced to feel foolish and just a bit insulted. Maisie ran her fingers playfully through his hair. "Oh, come on, now. I just baked a cake this afternoon. We can sit in the living room, have cake and coffee, and you can tell me more about your plans. I'm interested. I really am."

Brun waited in the living room while Maisie went into the kitchen. The room was neater than he'd expected, furniture definitely not bought on the cheap, a horsehair sofa, two overstuffed chairs with lace antimacassars on the arms and headrests, a floor lamp between the chairs, and a low wooden table in front of the sofa. Against the back wall sat a nice Bush and Gerts upright piano. Brun walked over and commenced to play.

When Maisie came in, carrying a tray with a chocolate cake and a coffee pot, he was midway through "Good Old Wagon." Maisie set the tray on a little table, clasped her hands in front of her chest, and sang along with the last lines of the tune. "Bye-bye my honey, if you call it gone, O Babe. Bye-bye my honey, if you call it gone. You've been a good ol' wagon, but you done broke down."

Brun was surprised no end. "I didn't think you'd know that."

"Huh!" Maisie pretended to be affronted. "Well, of course I know it. Why shouldn't I?" She set to slicing cake and pouring coffee. Brun moved over to sit on the sofa. Maisie set two china coffee cups and two plates with cake onto the table, then positioned herself next to the boy. She brushed hair back behind her ear. "Brun…is it all right for me to call you Brun?"

"Sure. I don't mind."

Big smile. "Good. Then we're friends. You can call me Maisie."

Brun couldn't bear to look at his slice of cake an instant longer, picked up his fork, took a large bite. Maisie turned a pout on him. "Didn't you think I sang that song all right?"

"Oh, now, sure I did," he said through a mouthful of chocolate. "I mean, you sang it more than just all right. You knew all the words right on, and you've got a very nice voice."

She grabbed his hand like she hoped to squeeze more compliments out of it. "You really think so? Do you mean that?"

"I wouldn't have said it otherwise."

She let go of him and leaned back against the sofa cushion. "My mama and dad got me music lessons so I could sing and play, first for them, then for my husband, like a proper girl is supposed to do. But what I really wanted was to go on the stage, and my parents wouldn't ever have let me do that. When I turned eighteen, they wanted me to marry Hugh Menton, one of those nice young men in Daddy's bank, so I…I ran away. With a circus that was in the next town."

Now that's a capper, Brun thought. Running away to Sedalia was small pumpkins next to running away with a circus. Maybe that explained some things, like how much face powder and perfume Maisie used. And why she lived on her own, a young woman, supporting herself by giving piano lessons.

"I wanted to become a singing performer, but they needed an aerialist-girl, so I agreed to do that, at least at first. They taught me the tricks, and oh, I'll admit, it was fun for a while. But I wanted to sing. I worked out a routine with the clowns, something I thought I might be able to develop into a vaudeville act, but the manager just kept putting me off, 'Maybe soon, maybe soon.' I was with them more than two years, and then one night when we were in Kansas City, I went to the theater to see Ben Harney—"

"So, that's how you knew…he's who wrote 'Good Old Wagon.'"

"Well, of course. He played all his songs, and I don't think there's been a day since that I haven't thought about it. He did a blackface routine with his wife, he played piano, and she sang and danced. They did 'Wagon,' and 'Mr. Johnson, Turn Me Loose,' and 'I Love One Sweet Black Man'…oh, it was wonderful. I wanted to be right up there with them. Well, I knew by that time I was never going to get anywhere with the circus, so next day, I left. I couldn't go home—my parents would've thrown me right back out, ruined as I was." She caught Brun looking from his empty plate to the cake, smiled, cut another piece and slid it onto his plate. "At first I thought to stay in Kansas City and give piano lessons, but I couldn't find any kind of decent living quarters with a piano. Then I heard about Sedalia, all the music here, so I decided to give it a try. Right off, I found this little house, and your Mr. Stark was kind enough to give me time payments on this second-hand piano out of one of the Broadway mansions, where an old woman had died and her children were cleaning out. I save every penny I can, and one day I'll have enough of a stake so I can try a vaudeville circuit. But meanwhile, I keep my eyes open for possibilities—"

"Like being Freitag's assistant?"

The instant the words were out, Brun realized how unkind they might have sounded. But Maisie didn't seem to take offense. "Well, of course. His pay is all right, and it's that much more than I'd make just giving piano lessons." She leaned toward Brun, face close to his, eyes sparkling. "But I think I can see a better opportunity, and not just for me. The way you play piano? Why, if you really can write music like you say, *we* could be in vaudeville, you and I. Just like the Harneys."

Brun wondered whether she might have taken leave of her mind. He'd seen the Harney show himself. Ben was a first-rate piano man, maybe white, maybe just a touch of the brush; his wife Jessie was a gorgeous songbird, a Kentucky girl, most definitely white. Brun could not for his life see how he and Maisie could make it with that kind of an act, and he told her so.

Which got him a pretty little laugh. She patted his hand. "Oh, Brun, think a little, would you. We've got the talent. And I've got a little money, enough to get us started. What we need is music. This is my dream, ever since I was a little girl, and I'm not about to just follow around after Mr. Freitag or anybody else until I'm too old to ever have a singing career. How about you? Do you want to sell sheet music for Mr. Stark until you're forty or fifty, then he dies and his family closes down the store? How old are you, Brun? Really."

"Sixteen. Seventeen later this year."

"And I'm twenty-two. That's not such a big difference. Brun and Maisie, The Ragtime Sweethearts. We'd play St. Louis, Kansas City, Baltimore, New York…" All of a sudden, she jumped off the sofa, grabbed Brun by the hand, and pulled him toward the piano. "Sit down. Do you know 'At a Georgia Camp Meeting'?"

"Well, 'course I do. I've been playing it over a year now."

"Go ahead, then. I'll follow you."

She practically pushed Brun onto the piano stool. He executed a little flourish, then went into the actual tune, watching Maisie, wondering what was she going to do. The girl bowed toward the middle of the room, turned her eyes on her audience, and began to sing.

> *"A campmeeting took place by the colored race*
> *Way down in Georgia.*
> *Foolish coons large and small,*
> *Lanky, lean, fat and tall…"*

For all the times he'd played that tune, Brun had never given a thought to the lyrics, but now as he conjured up that great gathering of foolish coons of all different shapes and sizes, he caught sight of Scott Joplin's unsmiling face in the the crowd, and straightway lost his place in the music. Maisie brought him back in a hurry. "What's the matter? I thought you said you knew this tune."

She stood over him, hands on hips, and her face told him that his professional reputation was on the line. He rubbed at an eye. "Sorry, Miss Maisie—I must've got something in my eye." He blinked. "Okay, now. Let's just start it over."

He waited while she got herself back in position. She really does have a voice, Brun thought, every note like a bell. "Here we go," he called to her, and off he shot, playing with a vengeance. She didn't miss a beat.

> *"A campmeeting took place by the colored race*
> *Way down in Georgia.*
> *Foolish coons large and small,*
> *Lanky, lean, fat and tall...*
> *In that great coon campmeeting.*
> *When church was out, how the sisters did shout,*
> *They were so happy."*

Maisie danced across the room and back as she sang, every now and again bending forward like she was singing to a man in the first row of her theater.

> *"But the young folks were tired,*
> *And wished to be inspired,*
> *And hired a big brass band."*

Brun played and Maisie sang, chorus and both verses, and by the time they finished, singer and pianist were soaking in sweat. Maisie, laughing, dropped down to the bench next to Brun. A lock of yellow hair covered her left eye. She slipped a hand behind his neck, and kissed him.

At fifteen, Brun had done some sparking. He'd meet Taffy, his girl friend, on Saturday afternoons, when his parents and hers thought their children were in town, in proper company of the same sex. They'd run out behind Old Mr. Rasmussen's barn and lie down together in the tall weeds, and kiss and kiss and kiss. They must have kissed hundreds of times, but never like Maisie kissed Brun on that piano bench. Her lips pressed onto his like a lid on one of his mother's jars of preserved fruit, and her tongue moved inside his mouth like a snail having the epileptic seizures. For a second, Brun thought he tasted Sen-Sen, but then his mind moved back to the matters at hand. Maisie held the back of his neck firmly enough to make sure the only way he might be able to pull back was to stamp on her foot.

When Maisie finally popped her lips free, Brun swallowed such a gulp as could be heard out on the street. Maisie slid a small, warm hand into his, laid her head on his shoulder, then sighed, "Oh, Brun," a breathy whisper. "Please forgive me for being forward, but I got so happy and excited. We *were* good, weren't we?"

Brun coughed his throat clear. "Truth, Miss Maisie, I didn't have any idea you had such a voice."

She picked strands of his hair between a couple of her fingers, and twisted. "Why, I'll bet if we had some real ragtime numbers, we could bring down any house. And if we had our own music, not just have to sing other peoples' songs…" She leaned forward again, and Brun prepared himself for another whopper kiss, but to his disappointment, she just kept on talking. "Just think what a start we'd get off to if we had Scott Joplin's *Ragtime Dance*. You could write words to those tunes, and we'd be a sensation."

Brun was up like a shot, but Maisie grabbed his hand and pulled him back down, then put a finger to his lips and shushed him. "Just listen for a minute, Brun, all right? Can you imagine the act we could put together with that music? Thirteen different tunes, isn't it?"

"Something like that. I didn't count them. But a lot."

"Enough for a couple of acts, easy. You'll play, I'll sing and dance. We'll sell the music to a publisher, and I don't mean Freitag. We'll go big time, right to the top, New York. Witmark? Or Stern and Marks? Why not?"

"Why not is that when Scott Joplin found out, he'd know exactly what happened. And how many people here already know the music is his?"

Maisie shrugged. "What of it? What's some colored man in Sedalia going to do, take us to court?" She giggled, then took Brun's hand between both of hers, squeezed it, and looked squarely at the boy from not more than four inches away. He thought he might fall into those blue eyes and drown. "Oh, Brun, please don't think badly of me. Maybe it's not exactly a nice thing to do, but this is my chance—*our* chance. People who don't take a chance usually die without ever having their dreams come true, and I'm not going to do that. You shouldn't, either. This is perfect for the two of us. The minute I saw you the other day at that piano in Mr. Stark's, I knew."

"And you're going to just up and tell Freitag to get lost?"

"Faster than you can blink your eyes. Think what it would be like for us. The Ragtime Sweethearts, topping bills for Keith-Albee, or the Orpheum. Tony Pastor's. Then we'd go off to tour Europe."

All of a sudden, being part-time clerk and future vice-president at Stark and Son didn't look like such great shakes anymore. Not next to the notion of playing hell out of a piano while a theater full of people clapped and cheered, then waking up next morning with a certain face on the pillow next to his. Was stealing written music really that far past stealing another man's tune off a piano performance? Brun knew he should've just up and walked out the door, but Maisie's face a few inches away was as effective at keeping him in the room as if she'd been holding a revolver. Maybe more so. He shook his head, chuckled deep in his throat. "You sure don't do things by halves."

She squinched her eyes. "I don't do anything by halves, Brun." She got up and stretched, then took a couple of steps toward the back of the house. "Too hot tonight to be wearing all these clothes. I'm going to get out of them."

"Okay," Brun said, and started back to the piano. "I'll wait for you here."

"Brun!"

She was halfway to the door, hokey displeasure all over her face. "What kind of a gentleman are you, anyway? Aren't you going to come help me out of all these hot clothes?"

Fifty years later, Brun could recall every detail of that night. With no clothes on, Maisie put her experience as a circus aerialist to amazing use on the mattress, put poor Rita Hodges all to shame. Afterward, Brun slept like a dead man, and when he woke the next morning, it was broad daylight and the house was full of the smell of eggs and bacon. He stretched, and as he rolled over, he noticed a purple discoloration on his left arm, just below the shoulder. He grinned, then hustled into his clothes and ran out and into the kitchen.

Over breakfast, Maisie asked whether she'd convinced him to be her ragtime sweetheart. Brun told her she'd made a strong case. "But just thinking about stealing Mr. Joplin's music makes me feel so bad, I can't even imagine how I'd feel if I actually did it."

One more time, he thought of the money-clip hidden in his closet. If that ever came to light, Scott Joplin would have no further use for his music, nor would there be any accusations when *The Ragtime Dance*, by Brun Campbell, sold thousands of copies and had them dancing in the aisles in New York. He actually had to stop eating for a moment.

"Well…" Maisie squeezed his hand. "I thought you might not just say yes right off, but I was hoping, and I still am. At least think about it, would you, Brun? Please?"

He nodded. "Truth, Miss Maisie, I don't think I could help doing that."

She leaned over and kissed his cheek. "O-kay. Just don't think too long and miss the train."

Or run too fast, stumble and fall underneath, Brun thought. "And, Brun…"

He looked at her. Those blue eyes. Maybe before he left, she'd like to do a little more persuading.

"I think we're well enough acquainted now, you can forget the Miss."

Maisie had a ten o'clock piano student, so directly after breakfast, she walked Brun outside. He wondered whether he should say anything at Higdon's about his night-long absence, but decided no point bringing up an awkward situation. Better to just wait and see whether anyone asked about it. Maisie gave him a good solid kiss to send him on his way. As he started down the path to the street through the ivy, she called after him, "Don't forget, now. You get the music and we'll set vaudeville on its ear."

Brun turned, and straightway saw he wouldn't have to worry about making excuses to the Higdons. There stood Luella, a basket of eggs on her arm, staring smack-dab at him. She must have gone to Tobrich's, a block further across Sixth, where they kept chickens and sold fresh eggs. The look on the girl's face as she took off toward home made it more than clear she didn't care to have him accompany her.

Chapter Thirteen

Sedalia
Saturday, July 29, 1899

Back at Higdon's, Brun went straight for the piano, and practiced until just before one. Mr. Higdon was nowhere to be seen, and both Luella and Belle gave the living room a wide berth, whether out of consideration or because Luella had spilled the beans the instant she got home. Brun's mind labored through heavy weather. He felt bad about upsetting Luella, had hoped to disabuse her of her illusions a bit more gently. Then, there was the matter of stealing music from Scott Joplin, which he knew he shouldn't even be thinking on. And how about abandoning John Stark for Maisie McAllister, never mind that most fifteen-year-old boys would make that trade in the blink of an eye? Worst of all, he still hadn't figured out what to do about the locket and the money-clip hidden in his closet. More and more, it looked like the choice of whether to send Edward Fitzgerald or Scott Joplin to the gallows was going to be Brun Campbell's.

Business was brisk that afternoon at Stark's, but not quite up to the Saturday usual. Brun noticed that several customers were more reserved than he'd known them to be, not so much inclined to chat over their purchases. Toward midafternoon, lardy, frowzy Mrs. Wilkins walked up to the doorway, stood with her hands on her hips, and harrumphed until she had Stark's, Isaac's and Brun's full attention. Then she wheeled around and stalked away. Brun scratched his head. "What's eating *her*?"

"Judging by her expression, I'd say her hemorrhoids are acting up," said Stark.

Brun laughed, but Isaac looked almost grim. "I think somebody be tellin' stories."

Stark shrugged. "Probably so. And that battle-ax would be the first to believe them."

A bit later, during a lull, Stark and Isaac told Brun more about Mrs. Fitzgerald. When Isaac's status in the house came clear to her, she grabbed little Frankie and started to stomp out, all the while delivering a world-class harangue about how she was not about to stay in a place which catered to white and colored alike, nor sit next to a nigger at the dinner table. It took a good bit of Mrs. Stark's blarney to convince her guest that she was not at a boarding house, and that white and colored alike who needed sanctuary would find it within Sarah Ann Casey Stark's walls. "I was all for just getting out of her way and closing the door behind her," Stark grumbled. "But you know Sarah."

Isaac laughed lightly.

Stark gave him the hard eye, then turned to Brun. "The woman's not in her right mind. Do you know what she did at supper last night? Just set down her fork, and said, 'Mrs. Stark, I spent a great deal of time this afternoon at the mirror, trying to see how I would look in mourning. How do you suppose I'd appear?' Can you imagine that? Mrs. Stark just told her she imagined Mrs. Fitzgerald would look somber and sad as any mourner, but she shouldn't worry her head because Mr. Higdon would get her husband safely back to her." Stark shook his head.

Late in the afternoon, Professor Weiss waddled into the shop. Brun hustled by to see what he needed. "Music paper, if you please, Brunnie. Scott makes changes, changes, changes. I tell him, the music's good, leave it be, but no. He needs it better, always better, change this, change that. He's used up all his paper, but he still won't stop with his changing. Better give me two packages."

Brun pulled two pads of music manuscript paper from the rack, and handed them to Weiss. The old German's dark eyes looked weighted with the cares of the world. "I don't know if Scott is going to finish before the performance so he's satisfied. Never have I seen him so uncertain. You know what he says, Brunnie? That it's because he lost the money-clip I gave him. He says all the years he had it, he had good luck, and now he feels like maybe he can't write music no more." Weiss cocked a finger at Brun. "You see how strange is the workings of the mind? Scott thinks the money-clip was bringing him luck, so he says to himself, 'I lost the money-clip, and now I can't no more write music…' Brunnie, are you okay? You're so pale, maybe you should lay down."

The boy shook his head. "I'm all right." He rang up the purchase and took Weiss' money.

Weiss didn't look convinced. "You sure you're all right, Brunnie? You look like you saw a ghost—mein Gott, you are going to fall down on your face. Here, let me help you." The German reached stubby arms across the counter; Brun waved him off. "Don't worry, Mr. Weiss, I'm all right. I guess I just feel bad on Mr. Joplin's account."

At dinner, Brun picked at his food, and now and again wondered whether Belle and Higdon were looking cross-eyed at him. Higdon's fiancée, Miss Gertrude Selover, was there, and it seemed to Brun that all the Higdons were taking care to not say anything out of turn. Everything about Miss Gertie seemed sharp: the angles of her thin body, her slim nose, thin lips showing just a slit of tooth at the middle. Every word she spoke sounded like it had been snipped off with well-honed shears. And she showed not the least reluctance about telling Mr. Higdon how he should manage his business. "Bob, I think it's a mistake for you to defend that Fitzgerald man. The whole town's talking, everyone thinks he's guilty. I'm afraid you're going to end up losing a lot of good clients."

Higdon smiled. "Not if I get him off. Let me get an acquittal for a man everyone thinks is guilty, and I'll have a line outside my door two blocks down Ohio."

Miss Gertie said she didn't think that was at all funny.

Brun ground his teeth so hard, a pain from the corner of his jaw shot down his neck. He knew just how to settle the whole matter, didn't he—set Mr. Fitzgerald free, make sure Mr. Higdon had no problem, and put every note of Scott Joplin's music up for grabs. One stone, three birds. Brun felt his dinner rise up like boiling water into his throat. He didn't say another word the entire meal, just sat and chewed his cud.

After supper, Higdon and Miss Gertie took off for the Saturday night dance in the big hall over the St. Louis Clothing Store. Brun followed them out, but where they turned off Sixth onto Ohio, the boy continued straight. He walked four blocks to Lafayette, looking up and down the avenues as he crossed, then went north a block on Lafayette and started westward on Fifth.

Early Saturday evening, the work week done. People sat in small groups on porches, gossiping. A boy of about eight shot out from between two houses, crossed Brun's path, darted across the street and vanished up between two houses on the other side; he was followed closely by a gang of eight or ten boys about the same age, all of them laughing and shouting, "Go, Sheepy, go!"

Brun walked on, passed a vacant lot where some teenaged boys played a loud and lively game of base ball. Brun figured he had a year or two on them, not more, but they seemed ages younger than himself, and he felt a curious sensation of superiority, sadness and envy, all mixed up together.

Back across Ohio on Fifth as far as Moniteau, looking every which way, then up Moniteau to Fourth. A little fellow on an iron-wheeled tricycle shot past him, piping, "Whoo-whoo…MoPac Special, clear the tracks." Brun smiled, but his eyes filled.

At the next corner, just a little way up Kentucky, Brun saw what he'd been looking for, a crowd of small boys and girls at the edge of the street, pushing, shouting, arms out. He heard the familiar cry, "Ice-kadeem. Ice-kadeem," and started to run. As he came up to the little push-wagon, raggedy Romulus Marcantonio scooped a serving into a paper cup and put it carefully into the hand of a little girl, then took the nickel from her other hand. "There-a you are, Missy. Bes' ice-kadeem in Sedal', vanill'. Maybe tomorra choc'late, who know?" Then he caught sight of Brun, and flashed a sly grin. "Hey-a, young mister. Where's-a da pretty girl tonight, huh?"

Brun tried a smile, wasn't at all sure he'd pulled it off. "That's for later, Romulus. Right now, I just need to talk to you."

By the time Brun finished with the ice-cream peddler, it was growing dark. The boy felt at sixes and sevens. He had to talk to someone, but who? John Stark? Then he could forget about any future he might ever have with Stark Music Publishing. Higdon? He might just as well get on the next train back to El Reno. The cops? Sure, if he wanted to share a cell and a chamberpot with some drunk bum. He could think of only one person who might possibly give him a sympathetic ear.

He hustled back to Ohio, then up to Second. From the open windows above the St. Louis Clothing Store, he heard piano music, no question who was playing it. He took the stairs two at a time, paid his quarter at the door.

At first, he didn't see Higdon or Miss Gertie, but spotted Scott Joplin at the piano, the gaiety of the *Fledermaus* waltz he played as far from the impassiveness of his face as black is from white. Mr. Weiss stood at his side. Some fifty couples were on the dance floor, while a few others sat at small tables, sipping drinks and talking. As Brun caught sight of Higdon and Miss Gertie across the room, he did a quick doubletake. He'd have sworn that woman was too much a sobersides to dance at all, but there she was, gliding easily around the room in Higdon's arms, smiling, and every now and again saying a few words up into his face.

Then Joplin surprised Brun by throwing a little bridge into the music and crossing it, right out of *Fledermaus* into "Echoes of the Snowball Club." One of the dancing couples stopped, looked at each other in clear confusion, and walked to the sidelines, shaking their heads. But the rest went right on dancing. Brun walked toward the piano, and when Weiss saw him, he put an arm around the boy's shoulders. "Brunnie, hello!" He made a show of looking around. "What is this? You don't have yourself a pretty girl with you?"

Brun shook his head. "Just here by myself."

"So you come to hear Scott play, yes?" Weiss didn't wait for an answer. "You see, then, what he does? Two lovely waltzes, one from Europe, one from America. One with syncopation, one without, but look." He waved a hand, covering the entire range of the dance floor. "They can dance to one, they can dance to the other. Is waltzes, that's all."

During Mr. Weiss' speech, Joplin played his way across another short bridge back to *Fledermaus*, but now syncopating it. Then he transitioned to an unsyncopated "Echoes," and finally he put the two together, a phrase from one, then the other, never missing the waltztime beat. When he finished the tune, the couples stood and applauded for over a minute.

"So, Brunnie," said Mr. Weiss. "You see now what a genius he's got."

Joplin looked pleased, but as always, no smile came over his face. He stood, made an awkward bow, then sat back down and swung right into "Sidewalks of New York." The boy stared at the composer, off in his own world of music, and tried to figure how to tell him and Professor Weiss that for a whole week, Brun had been hiding the one material object that bound them together. Sure, the idea was to save Joplin's neck, but Brun had no trouble imagining Joplin, unreadable as any Chinaman, turning that unsmiling face on him, and saying, "So you thought I was guilty of murder," then cutting him dead. "Yes, I see," Brun said quietly, then left the dancers and went back to Higdon's, to his room, to bed.

Sunday morning, the courthouse bell and the rail yard whistle didn't blow, and turning a deaf ear to church bells had never been a problem for Brun. By the time he blinked his eyes open, the house was quiet, near ten by the clock in the kitchen. No doubt the Higdons were gone off to church, fine with Brun. He'd awakened with the makings of a plan in his head, and was grateful for solitude to work it through. He fried a couple of eggs, made coffee, and as he ate, he thought. By the time he washed and dried his dishes, he figured he might just have the matter in hand.

But it was only about eleven, too early to turn thought into action. Best, though, to be away before the Higdons got back. He went to his room, took the locket out of the cubby, and headed out toward Liberty Park. All through town, a clangor of Methodist bells, Presbyterian bells, Catholic bells, each trying to shout down the others. Another few hours, the park would be mobbed with picnickers, but right now it was near-empty. Brun strolled around the lake, one hand on the locket in his trouser pocket, thinking his idea through and through. After an hour and a half, he turned off the path and made tracks to Stark's.

John Stark looked surprised as he opened the door to Brun. "I know it's early, Mr. Stark," the boy said. "Sorry to intrude on the Sabbath."

Stark's eyes opened wide. He took a moment to regard Brun from over the upper rim of his reading spectacles. "Sabbath or not, the world has a habit of intruding. And somehow, I suspect there's a degree of urgency to your visit."

"Yes, sir. I think there is."

"Then don't just stand there, come in."

Stark led Brun to the back porch, where Mrs. Stark and Nell sat with Isaac. Mrs. Stark gave the boy her customary warm greeting, but he saw suspicion in Nell's eyes.

"Brun's come to talk to me about a problem," Stark said. "Do you wish privacy, Brun?"

The boy shook his head, took a chair. "Not from anyone in your family, sir. It's about Mr. Freitag—and that woman who was murdered last week. I was walking along the road this morning, out where they found the body, and I saw the sun shining off something in the grass." He pulled out the locket, gave it to Mr. Stark. "Look inside."

Stark grunted, then popped the locket open. His eyes bugged. "Jesus, Mary and Joseph!"

Everyone was around him in an instant. Brun heard Isaac murmur something, but couldn't quite pick up on it. Mrs. Stark asked who the man was.

A hoarse staccato from Stark. "That Freitag nut." He looked back to Brun. "You say you found this where the woman's body was discovered?"

"Yes, sir. The weeds were still trampled down."

"Why did you bring it here? Why didn't you go to the police with it?"

Brun was prepared. "Truth, I'd rather be answering your questions than the coppers', especially what with me being a runaway. But if you want me to go there, I will."

Stark's smile would have been sly, if not for the troubled way his brows beetled. "No, I don't want you to do that, at least not until I've had more time to think about it. I'm sure Ed Love would wonder why you found this locket so readily, when his men had already combed the whole area and missed it."

"I thought of that," said Brun. "I own, it does seem queer. But when I saw the sun shine off it, it was just for a second, then it was gone. I almost went on walking, but figured maybe somebody had dropped a gold piece in the grass, so I went to see. I was surprised when I saw what it was."

"But you thought right off about the murdered woman."

"No, sir, not exactly right off. What I first thought was just that some lady had lost it, and then I wondered what she would have been doing in the grass by the side of the road."

Stark smiled. Isaac chuckled. The women took care to look in another direction.

"Then I remembered that was where Mr. Higdon said they'd found the woman. The weeds were knocked every which way to Sunday, so maybe the cops tromped the locket down underneath, and I just happened to see it from where I was standing right then."

Stark studied the photo. "Hmmm. Could the woman have been Freitag's wife?"

"Mr. Fitzgerald said she told him her name was Sallie Rudolph. Not Freitag."

Now, Mrs. Stark spoke up. "He wouldn't be the only man, married or not, to have a lady friend, now, would he? And a man like him? Perhaps the poor thing showed up in town at an awkward moment. Or with a troublesome demand."

"Mother, you have a wicked mind."

Nell was teasing, and Mrs. Stark knew it. "We'll wait until you've been on this earth as long as I," she said. "Then, you can make judgments as to the wickedness of my mind."

"Wicked your mind may be, my dear," said Mr. Stark. "But I've never known it to be unfair, unkind, or off the mark." Stark got to his feet with such suddenness that Brun jumped. "I think I'll have a talk with Bob Higdon, and see whether there was a chain on the woman's body, one that the locket could have been torn away from. I'd guess he ought to be home from church by now." He bent to kiss his wife. "I'll be back for dinner, my dear. Brun will be staying."

"Well, of course he will," said Mrs. Stark. "I invited him when he was here last Sunday. Or have you forgotten?"

Not half an hour later, John Stark marched through the living room and onto the porch. Conversation stopped as if cut off by a sharp knife. Stark chuckled. "Bob thought something was up, what with my coming over before dinner on a Sunday, and he was curious, to say the least, as to why I was asking such a question about a locket chain. But he said yes, the police did find a small torn chain at the roadside, near the woman's body." Stark sat, surveyed his audience. "Now, suppose we take this locket to the police. They'll call in Freitag, who'll swear up and down he knows nothing about the dead woman. He'll ask what evidence there is to suggest the locket was in fact hers. And would you doubt that Miss McAllister, close as she's become to Freitag, might swear that the locket, with Freitag's picture, belonged to her, and she just happened to notice last night that she had lost it somewhere? It leaves us in a difficult position."

"I've got an idea, Mr. Stark."

Everyone looked at Brun.

"I heard Mr. Joplin say Freitag used to work for Carl Hoffman in Kansas City, and he was here last month with a man named Daniels, trying to get Mr. Joplin to let them publish his *Ragtime Dance*…"

Brun stopped talking as he saw the look that passed between Stark and Isaac. "That's Charles Daniels," Stark said. "A little bit of a hot shot, but a capable young man, and I think decent enough. The two of them also came to our store that day. Well, all right, Brun. Just what are you considering?"

Brun's stomach felt like a half-full jug on the deck of a boat during a heavy storm. He licked his lips. "I was thinking I could take the early train to Kansas City tomorrow morning, go to Carl Hoffman's, talk to Daniels and see what I can find out about Freitag. I'd work the line around to how a woman named Sallie Rudolph found herself a whole mess of trouble in Sedalia. I could probably do that and get back to work on time, but in case I don't, I wouldn't want you thinking I was dogging it. That's why I'm telling you now."

Smiles came over all the faces in the company, the women's warm, the men's tight. Stark said, "I believe we can manage to get along without you in the store for at least part of a day. Let's talk more over dinner. I for one have worked up a hearty appetite."

◇◇◇

Six o'clock before Brun left Stark's. He had a double sawbuck in his pocket, and a paper with Carl Hoffman's address, both courtesy of John Stark. The boy had eaten considerably more of Mrs. Stark's roasted chicken and cherry pie with rich vanilla ice cream than his mother would have considered polite, and now he felt logy. At the corner of Sixth and Ohio, he decided he wasn't in the right frame of mind to deal with the Higdons, whether over the locket or his behavior with Maisie, so he changed direction and wandered out to Liberty Park, found a comfortable spot under a huge old maple, stretched himself on the grass and stared at the sky. A flock of wild geese passed overhead, partly blotting out the sun. Their honking call set off the same lonesome tug below the boy's ribs that he'd felt during his long ride to Sedalia, when he heard the train's whistle long and low in the night. He closed his eyes.

Next he knew, it was full darkness. He blinked, then pulled himself to his feet, stretched, brushed at his trousers, and started hoofing back to town. At Third, corner of Osage, he thought he heard a sound coming out of a patch of brier bushes, so he walked up, carefully spread branches, and peered through. Now, he definitely heard a moan. "He'p me."

The stickers pulled at his pants and shirt, and he had to cover his face with his arms to get down and look at the body in the middle of the brier patch. When he reached to touch the person, there came a scream of such pain and fear as to cover the boy's body with goosebumps. "I won't hurt you," Brun said. "What happened?"

"They beat me turrible." The voice was familiar; Brun bent for a closer look. A colored man, head curled tightly to his chest, upper body rocking back and forth, long legs lying stretched and motionless. "Henry?" Brun asked. "High Henry?"

The moaning and screaming stopped. "Who you be?"

"Brun Campbell. Scott Joplin's young piano man. What happened to you?"

"They beat me," Henry said again. "He'p me, please. My head hurts somethin' awful, an' I don't feel nothin' in my legs at all. I think I gonna die."

No way for Brun to get the Negro out of those briers by himself. "Henry, listen up. I'm going for Doc Overstreet—"

"Do he treat colored?"

"Mr. Stark sent Isaac there when he got hurt by the Alteneders—"

"Them's who did it to me."

"The Alteneders?"

"The very same. I was goin' along to Lincolnville, mindin' my own business, an' I hear somebody say, 'That him.' Then Mist' Alteneder an' his boy, they grab me, pull me out back of Adams' blacksmith shop, an' say where is that music I tol' Mr. Freitag I'd give him. I say I ain't got it on me, gotta go home an' get it, but then they start hittin' me with clubs an' kickin' me an' sayin' this what happens to a lyin' nigger who tell Mr. Freitag he gonna give him some music, then never do. The boy punch my face an' say I done missed my chance 'cause Mist' Freitag gonna get all the music he want later tonight outa the Maple Leaf Club."

That seemed to exhaust Henry; he closed his eyes and his head lolled. Brun bent over him. "Just hang on, Henry, okay? Be right back with the doc."

When Overstreet opened the door to Brun's pounding, the boy quickly apologized for making such a racket late on a Sunday evening. "But there's a man down the street, needs your help in a hurry. He got beat up and thrown in the briers, and he's hurt real bad. Please, will you come?"

The doctor's Adam's apple bobbed; his shoulders slumped. "I'll get my bag," he said, through a cloud of recycled whiskey.

No sound as Brun and Overstreet approached the briers. The doctor put down his bag, then he and Brun broke their way in to Henry, who now lay still. "He's not...dead, is he, Doc?" Brun asked.

Dr. Overstreet had already reached his hand along the side of Henry's neck. "No, just unconscious. Let's get him out of here, where I can get a better look at him. Take his feet, I'll carry his head and neck."

They lifted Henry slowly, carefully. As the long body unfurled, Overstreet whistled low. "God blast me—it's High Henry Ramberg. What happened to him?"

"He said Fritz and Emil Alteneder gave him what-for 'cause he wouldn't sell his music to Mr. Freitag."

"Christ Almighty!" Overstreet turned his head and spat. He opened his bag, poked the Negro here and there, tapped him with a little hammer, listened at his chest. After a couple of minutes, the doctor stood, his face grim. "Can you help me get him back to my office?"

For answer, Brun bent, but before he could lift Henry's feet, Overstreet tapped his shoulder. "You've got to be careful. We both do. His back's broken, and we don't want to make it worse. Handle him as if he were a bag of dynamite."

As Brun and the doctor came up to Overstreet's office, two men and their wives approached from the opposite direction. The small group rubbernecked, then Brun heard one of the men say, "Doc Overstreet and some kid, carrying a nigger." Whereupon one of the women said, loud enough to be sure of being heard, "Hmph! He'd do better to go to Sunday vespers than go scratching around town looking for drunk niggers to treat."

Overstreet called out, "Jack, Ernie, one of you please be so good as to open the door."

The men looked at each other, then one moved forward, opened the door, and held it long enough for Brun and the doctor to carry Henry through. "Thank you, Ernie," Overstreet called back over his shoulder.

They laid Henry gently on the table in the examining room, then peeled off his shirt and trousers. The sight moved Brun to near-sickness. Bruises covered Henry's body, cuts everywhere, scratches from the briers. That beautiful chocolate face was a mass of lumps and patches of dark discoloration; one eye was swollen shut. His legs lay at strange angles to each other. Overstreet shucked off his vest and tossed it on the back of a chair, then rolled up his sleeves and went to work on Henry, who showed no sign of life beyond breathing and letting out an occasional, "Oooooooo." Brun wanted to tell the doctor about the plan Henry had overheard, but didn't dare interrupt him. The little clock on the wall next to the examination table chimed ten-thirty. Brun fidgeted. "Is he going to live?"

Overstreet grunted. "If I have anything to say about it. But even if he does, he's never going to dance again."

"I'm going to *kill* them." Brun's rage tore out of his mouth without ever passing through his mind.

Overstreet half-turned, raised a finger to the boy and snapped, "You stay away from them."

"But what they did—"

"You heard me. Don't you go near those thugs, not for anything."

Without another word, Brun whirled and ran out of the room. A couple of seconds later, Overstreet heard the office door slam. He sighed, then turned back to his work.

Outside, Brun ran a few steps in the direction of Stark's, but then pulled up. Nearly eleven, and he had no idea, did he, just when the Alteneders and Freitag would be going in at the Maple Leaf Club. And once they'd made off with Joplin's music, he'd never get it back. Freitag would publish it all, probably with a phony name as composer, and what court could Joplin go to for help? Brun had no time to wake Mr. Stark, even less to try to convince the cops what was about to happen. Like Dr. Overstreet was doing his best to save Henry's life, it was up to Brun to do the same to try and save Joplin's music.

He took off on the run along Ohio, down to Main, up to the Maple Leaf Club. Any other night of the week, the street would be alive, all the customary activities of the sporting district in full swing. But this was the Lord's Day, or at least His Night. The sports had gone to church, enjoyed a good dinner, then hit the rack early to enjoy dreams about the week past and the week before them. Only an occasional reprobate went weaving along the side of the road, and Brun took care none of them saw him slip up to the door of the club and inside.

Dead quiet. Brun went up the stairs on tiptoes, stopping to listen every time he made a stairboard creak. Once in the club, he went directly to the piano, scooped all the music off the rack, set it on the bench. By the light of a lucifer, he spotted several more papers on the top of the piano, others on the floor to the left of the bench; he added them to the pile. Then back downstairs, a quick glance both ways at the door to be sure the Alteneders weren't on their way in, and down Lamine he flew, taking caution not to lose a single page of music to the wind.

Dark at Higdon's. Brun muttered a quiet thanks, then ran in through the living room, and up the stairs. But as he scurried along the corridor toward his room, he noticed something odd. All the other bedroom doors were open, Higdon's, Belle's, Luella's. He reversed course, went back downstairs, turned on a lamp in the living room, and looked around. Nothing unusual. But in the kitchen, he found a note on the little pine table across from the stove. "Dear Brun," it said. "Our mother was taken ill this morning, and we are going out to the farm to see her. It's coming on four in the afternoon, and I doubt we'll be back tonight. There is cold chicken in the icebox, and some salad and fruit, and half a berry pie on the window sill. Just help yourself." The note was signed "Belle."

He set the music next to the note, and took a moment to catch his breath. He felt dizzy, and, suddenly, hungry, so he set up at the kitchen table, and while he made short work of the cold chicken, salad, fruit, and a hefty slice of berry pie, he thumbed through the sheets of music.

What a treasure of ragtime in a small pile of paper. Best Brun could tell, he had the entire score of *The Ragtime Dance*, and full copies of "Maple Leaf Rag," "Swipesey Cake Walk," and "Sunflower Slow Drag." Beyond that were partials on pieces called "Peacherine Rag" and "Easy Winners." He recognized an untitled partial as "The Entertainer." Several unnamed fragments, he'd never seen before. He wiped his hands on his pants, then took the music, all of it, to the piano, and commenced to play.

No churchgoer ever found in any Lord's Day worship what Brun Campbell discovered that Sunday night at Higdon's piano, playing his way through every note of that music by Scott Joplin. It occurred to Brun that if by some strange chance he eventually found his way to heaven, he would never be happier than he was right then. He didn't think to look at a clock until he'd played through the entire pile, and then he saw it was nearly one in the morning.

Now, what was he supposed to do with that music? Scott Joplin lived in Lincolnville, but Brun had no idea just where. Besides, he had to be on a train to Kansas City in not that many hours, and right now he was bushed. Maybe best to hide the music somewhere safe, grab a few hours of sleep, then as soon as he got back from Kay Cee, take the music directly to Joplin and explain.

He cleaned up his dishes, then went to his room and looked around. The cubby where he'd put Joplin's money-clip and the gold locket was nowhere near big enough for a pile of music manuscripts. He thought of putting them under his shirts and underwear in the dresser drawer, but in the end decided to slip them under his mattress, all the way to the middle. Once that was done, he got undressed and lay on top of the bed, and until the bell atop the courthouse clanged out six a.m., Brun played Scott Joplin's ragtime music over and over in his sleep.

Chapter Fourteen

Sedalia
Monday, July 31, 1899

Brun's feet hit the floor before the courthouse bell was done ringing. He washed and dressed at double-time, and before the railroad shop whistle blasted out seven, Mr. S. Brun Campbell, decked out in his business suit and tie, hair pomaded to the nines, was sitting like a swell in the dining car of a Katy passenger train, white linen and nice silver on the table, shoveling down a hefty plate of ham, biscuits and gravy. Before eight-thirty, he was on the platform in Kansas City, asking a redcap for directions to 1012 Walnut Street.

By the time he walked up to the great white-stone Hoffman Building, the day had warmed considerably. Sweat poured off the boy's forehead, into his eyes, and down from under both arms. Mr. Stark had said Daniels would be in the office Monday morning, reviewing the past week's sales. But would Daniels see him, what with him not having an appointment?

"Yes," Brun said out loud. By hook or crook, Daniels would see him. He walked inside like he owned the place, then swaggered up to the receptionist, not a looker by any stretch, big buck teeth, and forty if she was a day. He gave the woman his best smile, and told her he was looking for Mr. Charles Daniels.

She didn't smile back. "Is he expecting you?"

"Well, if he's not, he ought to be."

The receptionist's face said she knew *his* type, and didn't think a whole lot of it. But she pointed down the hallway and said, "Take the first left, and go as far as you can."

The glass-paneled door at the end of the corridor stood half-open. Brun peered around the edge. A man sat at an upright piano, his back to the door. Brun knocked. "Mr. Daniels?"

Charles Daniels wheeled around on the stool and stared at the boy with a smile more confused than friendly. He waved Brun inside. "Yes?"

Brun hadn't imagined Daniels would look so young. The cuffs of his blue-pinstriped shirt lay open, sleeves rolled up to near his elbows. Collar unbuttoned, dark tie knotted loosely, flapping free. Brun took a second to get himself in hand, then announced, "I need to talk to you for a few minutes, Mr. Daniels."

Daniels swung all the way around on the piano stool and leveled a heavy fish eye on Brun.

The boy took a deep breath, then spoke the lines Stark had told him to use. "My name's Brun Campbell, I study piano with Scott Joplin. I'm his only white pupil. He calls me The Ragtime Kid."

Daniels laughed out loud, but not like he was making fun. "The Ragtime Kid, huh? How old are you, Kid?"

"I guess not more'n three years younger than you."

Now Daniels laughed to beat the band. "More like five or six, I'd guess, but all right. What is it Joplin sent you about? The man's a damned fine composer, but he's got some ideas that're just plain crazy. There's no way he's going to get a royalties contract from anybody until he gets a whole lot more famous or a whole lot more white…but okay, let me shut up a minute and listen. What is it you and Joplin want?"

"Mr. Joplin didn't send me. I'm here on my own screw, and it's important. I want to talk to you about Mr. Freitag—"

"*Freitag*? What about Freitag?"

Daniels wasn't laughing now, not even smiling. "I'm sorry, Mr. Daniels," Brun said. "There's a lot happening in Sedalia on his account, and I'm hoping you can help. Mr. Freitag is trying to get his hands on all the colored ragtime he can, but especially Mr. Joplin's. He says he's going to publish it and also set up a road company to perform it."

Daniels shrugged. "Freitag hasn't been with Hoffman for more than a month now, so I can't see where whatever he does is any concern of mine."

Brun thought the man was trying to look a lot less interested than he really was. "Well, for one thing, there's talk that Freitag's actually fronting for you. I heard him say such myself—that with a big company like Hoffman behind him, he can't miss."

Pure fabrication, and Brun was the boy to carry it off. A blood vessel at Daniels' temple swelled up, thick and blue. "Well, there's nothing to that, absolutely nothing. I haven't seen Freitag since last month, and I don't care if I never see him again. Go back to Sedalia and tell people that. And while you're at it, tell your piano teacher that if Hoffman wants his music, *I'll* be talking to him. No one else."

Daniels started to swing back to face the piano, but Brun stopped him with, "That's not all. Mr. Freitag's got himself a couple of yahoos to scare the colored and beat them up, and steal their music. I work in Mr. John Stark's store—"

Daniels jumped off the stool to face Brun directly. "So Stark sent you. I should've figured."

"No sir, that's wrong." With a face that could melt butter. "I told you I'm here on my own screw, and I am. What I'm trying to say is that for some reason, Mr. Freitag's got it in for Mr. Stark and Isaac. You know Isaac, don't you?"

"The colored man, works in Stark's store."

Brun nodded. "The same. Freitag's telling people that Isaac and Mr. Stark are actually brothers. That their father...you know."

"Damn that Freitag." Daniels' voice was soft, but there was no missing the anger. "He's still fighting the Civil War, always will be."

"There's more."

Brun thought Daniels looked like he was sorry he hadn't just stood in bed that morning.

"Mr. Freitag's yahoos went and picked on Isaac's little girl, just for fun. They rubbed horse shit all over her dress, and then, afterward, they burned down Isaac's house."

"Oh, no. You're not going to tell me he was inside. He and the girl?"

"No, they're both all right. But Freitag's bashers tied up Isaac's dog in the house before they set the fire." Talking faster now. "And about two weeks ago, a woman was murdered in Sedalia, strangled. I think Freitag had something to do with it."

Daniels shot a look behind Brun, then charged to the door and pushed it firmly closed. "What did you say your name was again?"

"Campbell. Brun Campbell."

Daniels wiped his hand over his mouth, as if what was about to come out was not to his liking. Then he walked to the side of his desk and brought his fist down, slam! Papers shook, piles rearranged themselves. "God damn Elmo Freitag. I should've fired him a year ago. Only salesman at Hoffman with expense accounts bigger than his sales. He spent more time pitching girls than music store owners. I wouldn't trust him to hold my dog's leash while I went to piss. That scene he made in Stark's store last month was the last straw. I didn't see you there, but I'm guessing you heard about it."

If someone gives you a gift, Brun thought, take it. "Oh, you bet. Mr. Stark told me all about it. He was really in a state."

"I figured. Stark's a damned good customer, and Freitag was out of a job before we ever got back to Kansas City. But my God, Campbell, you're saying you think he's involved in murdering a woman?"

Stark had warned Brun not to mention the locket on any account, so he said, "Somebody heard Freitag yelling at her, making threats. Telling her she better get the hell out of town and quit bothering him. But the dead woman's name wasn't Freitag. Maybe she could have been his sweetheart."

Daniels picked up a pencil, tapped it on the desk top while he thought. "Freitag does have a wife, but that wouldn't stop him having a hotel full of sweethearts. All right. I want it to be good and goddamn clear to everyone in Sedalia that he has no connection with Hoffman or me. I'll get his address from the receptionist, and then you and I will go and have a talk with Mrs. Freitag, make sure she understands that if her husband causes me any problems, Hoffman and I will file a suit that he and his family will never recover from. You'll be my witness, someone who heard Freitag claim he's acting as my right-hand man. Two dollars for your time and help. What do you say?"

To the chance to meet Mrs. Freitag, hear what she'd have to say, and get a couple of bucks in the bargain? Brun laughed. "What are we waiting for?"

Daniels extended a hand. "I'm sorry I was short with you before. Looks as if we both need to deal with that jackass, and I think we can do it better together than separately."

As he talked, Daniels rolled down his sleeves, fastened his cuffs, straightened his tie. Then he grabbed a slick boater off a hook behind the door, and slapped the hat onto his head at an angle that made him look natty and sharp, especially when he smiled like he did right then. "Okay, Campbell," he said. "Let's get on with it."

Freitag's neighborhood was not one Brun thought he'd have cared to find himself alone in at night. Once he and Daniels left the industrial area, they walked along dirt roads, no paving, no sidewalks. The houses looked ashamed to be located there, like once-respectable men now in old age, slumped and crippled by disabilities they know will never be set right, and likely will get worse.

Half a block along Arden Street, Daniels pointed at a small frame house, surrounded by scrub grass and weeds. The roof sagged. Separating the house from the road was a picket fence, which, like the siding on the house, had once been painted a pale peach color, but now was near-bare wood, paint peelings lying on the ground like shed snakeskin.

Daniels opened the gate. He and Brun walked into the yard, and up three creaking stairs to the small front porch. At other houses in the neighborhood, children played in yards, and most doors were open for ventilation. No children at Freitag's, though, and the door was shut. Daniels rapped hard, no answer. He rapped again, harder, but with the same result.

"Sure this is it?" Brun asked.

Daniels pulled a scrap of paper out of his pocket. "This is the address we've got at Hoffman's, but I wouldn't put it past Freitag to leave a fake address." He shaded his eyes to peer through the glass panels on the door, then muttered, "No one."

"She could be out shopping," Brun said.

Daniels nodded, then pointed to the front yard next door, where two small children, a boy and a girl, sat in a sandbox, playing with little pails, shovels, and sifters. "Let's go ask."

As the men walked by, the children regarded them with open-mouthed kid-curiosity. "Hello," Daniels called through the open front door. Then he cupped his hands around his mouth and called louder.

"Yeah, hold your horses." A woman's voice.

A moment later, the owner of the voice appeared at the door. Pale, thin, eyes red and watery, shoulders slumped as if in defeat, final and permanent. Sandy hair hung stringy and lank. Brun doubted she was thirty, but she looked used up. She glanced at Daniels, then at Brun, then back to Daniels, all suspicion. Then she snapped, "What do you want?"

Brun noticed she had one hand on the edge of the open door.

"I'm sorry to bother you, ma'am," Daniels said, smooth as silk. "We're looking for the Freitags, but there's no one there."

Which seemed to annoy the woman. "Ha! You think you're telling me something? I know nobody's there, and that's just fine with me. Mrs., I feel sorry for, but him? A first-class bum, if there ever was one. One thing for a man to go with hoors, 'least they're grown-up women mostly, and they can do it or not as they please. But men who go lookin' for little boys, that's different. If I wasn't a lady, I'd tell you what I think they ought to do with men like that."

Brun looked at Daniels, who shook his head. "Had no idea."

The woman picked up. "Yeah, well I got more than an idea. Last month, he lost his job, so what does he go and do? Gets himself good and stinko, that's what. Next day, his wife's off at work up by the meat packers, and I'm standing inside by an open window, and I hear him telling my little Arnold he'll give him a nickel to come over to his house and play with him. So I run out in the yard and grab Arnold away, and I tell that creep if I ever see him near Arnold again, he's going to be dealing with my husband." She smiled, not an attractive sight. "Charlie's six-four and two-thirty, slaughters cattle in the stockyards. 'Oh, now, Mrs. Evans,' the bum has the crust to say to me, 'it's all a misunderstanding.' In a pig's eye, misunderstanding. 'I didn't misunderstand nothing,' I told him. When his wife got home that night, I told *her*, figured she had a right to know. But it was like talking to a wall. 'Oh yes,' she says. 'Poor Elmo. When he gets to feeling bad, he finds himself some little boys to play with, 'cause it makes him feel like when he was a boy himself, and takes his mind off his troubles.' Can you believe that? Well anyways, a couple of weeks ago, off he goes, his wife tells me he's got himself a job with some other music outfit, and he'll be on the road for a while. I say to myself the longer the better. But then, let's see, a week last Monday, here comes Mrs. F, and she's pretty upset. Says she's got to go see her husband, she lost her job at the meat packers, 'count of being sick every morning." Mrs. Evans snickered. "Didn't need to have a real big brain to figure that out, did I? She said she thought she'd be gone only a day or two, but just in case, she asked me would I water her plants." The woman shook her head. "Sallie and her plants, jeez!"

"Sallie?" Brun said.

Daniels gave him a curious look.

"Yeah, that's her Christian name," said Mrs. Evans. "Sallie, with an i-e, not a y. What's the big deal?"

"You don't have a picture of her, do you?"

Mrs. Evans looked Brun up and down. "What're you guys, cops or something? They in trouble someplace?"

Daniels laughed, then took off his boater and waved it at Mrs. Evans. "A cop? In this hat? No, ma'am. We're private, hired by a man in Sedalia whose daughter got bilked out of a fair bit of money by a couple who promised to get Carl Hoffman to publish her music. Hoffman gave us a picture of Freitag, and the girl identified him. But we don't know what Mrs. Freitag looks like, and that'd be a big help."

Mrs. Evans pointed at the house next door. "There's a wedding picture of the two of them, up on the living room wall. You want to see it?"

Brun let Daniels answer. "We'd really appreciate that." He pulled a small roll out of his pocket, then handed Mrs. Evans a fiver. She grinned wide enough to show every one of her few rotten teeth, then slid the bills into the pocket of her housedress. "Okay, let's go."

Inside Freitag's, it was hotter than Hades on Midsummer Day, and smelled like it does when you open an old leather suitcase that's been locked shut since your last trip a year ago. Mrs. Evans marched the men across the living room, then made a grand gesture toward a photograph in a dime-store frame. "Well, there they are. Hope it's worth your five bucks."

There they were, all right. Big, florid Elmo Freitag, and a woman in her middle thirties, dark-haired, with a sweet smile. Except for the smile, she looked just the way she did the last time Brun had seen her, lying at the side of the road, her head wobbly on her neck. "That's his wife?" Brun asked. "Mrs. Freitag?"

"One and the same. What's the problem?"

Daniels had questions smeared all over his face. No way could Brun say he'd ever seen this woman before, and he commenced to think as hard and fast as he could. "Well, the woman we've been, uh, looking for, her first name *is* Sallie. But she called herself Sallie Rudolph."

"Oh, pshaw." Mrs. Evans let out a laugh to shame a horse. "She does, does she? Rudolph was her name before she married

Freitag. Her 'stage name,' she calls it. She used to be a singer, got a beautiful voice, but he says no wife of his is gonna go on the stage or on the road. She just plain married trouble, the good-for-nothing bum! I bet he forced her to do that scam."

Daniels put his hand back into his pocket; it reappeared clutching a gold coin. "That's a really good picture, Mrs. Evans," he said. "I'd like to have it."

A crafty smile clawed one corner of the woman's mouth. She snatched the coin, slid it into her pocket. "Guess if you want it that bad, it wouldn't be nice of me to say no, now, would it?"

Brun and Daniels walked back to the Hoffman Building in silence, Daniels carrying the photograph. Inside, the rabbit-faced receptionist smiled at Daniels, but he didn't come close to returning it. "I've got to go to Sedalia, Lucille," he said. "I should be back tonight, but if I need to stay over, I'll telephone."

When Brun hopped aboard the train to Kansas City early that morning, it was like the beginning of most summer days in Sedalia, bright and clear, birds in full song, streets quiet. Too early for the hucksters and the oil man and the fresh fish peddler. Apple John would have been in Smithton, picking up his day's supply of merchandise. Shops were closed, most children still in bed. But Dr. Walter Overstreet was up. He'd been up all night, fighting what he really had known all along was a losing battle. Now, he pulled the sheet up over High Henry's battered face, trudged back into his office, and slumped in his chair, head down on the desk.

After some twenty minutes, he raised his head and blinked a couple of times. Short naps like these got him through the long days and longer nights. Short naps and... He took the bottle from the cabinet, poured himself a shot, knocked it down, then shook his head full-awake. He heard Emily Sewell's voice from the night before: "He'd do better to go to Sunday vespers than go scratching around town looking for drunk niggers to treat." There had been no smell of alcohol on High Henry, not a trace, but never mind. Emily Sewell also went around town telling people that men like Walter Overstreet who never do get married, well if you ask me, there's something wrong with them, if you know what I mean. Imagine having to look at that face and hear that voice over the breakfast table every day. A bachelor's life could be lonely, but Overstreet wouldn't have traded places with Charlie Sewell for any consideration.

Now, he had to report the case to Ed Love, who would say thank you, I'll take care of it, and then as soon as Overstreet was out the door, would give the report to the secretary and tell her to file it in the unsolved-cases drawer. Go chasing after a couple of thugs who'd beaten a colored man to death and dumped him in brambles, and the only living source of information was a runaway kid who hadn't even witnessed the attack, and for good measure, bore a healthy grudge against the alleged strong-arms? The Sedalia police had better things to do.

Overstreet poured another glass of scotch, downed it in a swallow, then trudged upstairs to shave and get himself clean and presentable, so he could go up to Lincolnville, to Big Henry and Mattie Ramberg's cottage on Morgan, and tell them why their son hadn't come home last night.

And while he was at it, better stop by the music store and have a word with John Stark about his boy. The look on that puppy's face when he said he was going to kill the Alteneders—he wasn't just whistling down the wind. The doctor had already pulled one too many bodies out of brier bushes.

By the time Overstreet put his backside onto a rickety wooden chair in the Ramberg living room, it was obvious the reason for his visit was no mystery to Henry's mother and father. They sat on a sofa opposite the doctor, Big Henry stone-faced, gripping his cane in his lap. Mattie cried into a red bandanna through the whole report. "I knew when he didn't come in before midnight," she wailed. "I jus' knew in my heart. Who done it, Doctor? An' why?"

"We're not sure," Overstreet said.

Now, Big Henry spoke. "Which mean, ain't nobody ever gonna pay for killin' my boy. That how it be when a white kill a colored. They never do have to pay."

Fear pushed grief off Mattie's face. She reached an arm to her husband. "Doctor didn't say it was a white man kill Henry."

Big Henry turned such a wicked eye on her, she moved away. "He didn' have to say—what colored man in this town would kill Henry? They all love him. B'sides, if it was a colored, they'd have him in the jail now." He looked back to Overstreet. "Henry was our onlies' chil', so what we got us now? Mattie and me was born slaves, and now we been set free, but I don't see the leas' difference. White men kill us on the plantation, they kill us now, an' it's no matter. They kill our chillun, take away our whole future, an' no one say a word for us. I be a father, an' I want me some justice. If the po-lice don't get it for me, I get it myself. You jus' tell me who kill my son, an' I do the rest."

"I can't—"

Overstreet was going to explain that he couldn't say because he didn't have proof, only a second-hand report from a boy who had not seen the crime committed. But Big Henry didn't want to hear any more. Up on his feet now, six feet six, waving his cane. "What good emancipation be for me, Doctor, huh? You tell me that. Friday, I suppose' to go over by Liberty Park, and sing and dance 'cause Mr. Charlie an' Miss Ann tell me I be free. 'Cept it still be all right they kill my son and jus' walk away. You a doctor, you the mayor of this city, an' you won't tell me what white man it was killed my son! You ain't worth shit."

Mattie rose, shaking all over. She extended her arms toward Overstreet; for a terrible moment the doctor thought she was going to fall to her knees. "Please, Mist' Doctor, don' be mad at my husban'. He don' really mean it, he jus' so powerful upset. Please." She took Big Henry by the arm, tried to persuade him back to his seat.

Overstreet stood, a little abruptly, said, "I'm sorry," then turned and started toward the door. Big Henry raised his cane, moved forward. Mattie grabbed his arm. "Henry, *no!*"

Overstreet spun around. Mattie screamed again. Big Henry lowered his cane and staggered back a step, struck dumb and petrified by the face on Overstreet and the single tear working its way down the doctor's cheek.

Daniels and Brun got off the Katy passenger train toward four o'clock. To avoid the late-Saturday afternoon crush of shoppers and hucksters on Ohio, they went along Washington Avenue to Fifth, and into Stark and Son—where they walked into a commotion of impressive proportions. Stark, Isaac, Joplin, Weiss, Freitag and the two Alteneders stood between the counter and the demonstration piano, all of them shouting, Emil Alteneder brandishing a fist. In the middle of the fuss stood Chief Love, a bear of a man with a face like a rough cut of raw beef. He looked like he was trying to bring some order, but without a whole lot of success. What surprised Brun most was Joplin, standing to the chief's left. For almost two weeks now, the only emotion the boy had ever seen the composer show came when he didn't like the way Brun played his music, and even that was mild enough. But now the composer was furious, his face twisted, body like a tight-wound spring. He aimed a finger at Freitag, and yelled, "You stole my music—you and your friends there." Then, he turned to the chief. "I demand you search this man's room."

The worry on Stark's face and Isaac's frightened Brun. Love's cheeks were scarlet; his hair seemed to bristle out from under his cap. "I'm chief of police here," he bellowed into Joplin's face. "Where're you coming from, telling me what I got to do."

"It's your job—"

"Oh, it's my job, is it? You're tellin' me what my job is? Now, you listen here, Scott, and listen good. You never been in any trouble, but keep this up, you're gonna be in way over your head in a big hurry."

Freitag and the Alteneders sported huge grins, but when Freitag looked at Brun and saw who was with him, his smile dissolved. He glanced back over his shoulder; Brun thought if there was any way he could've run, he'd have done it. Daniels held the photograph in one hand behind his back, and fixed a calm, level gaze on Freitag, who, for his part, made very sure to look anywhere but at Daniels.

Meanwhile, Joplin showed no sign of backing off. Weiss tried to pull him away from the chief, but Joplin yanked his arm free. "Are you telling me you are just going to let this thief get away with stealing my music?"

Chief Love stuck out his belly and roared into Joplin's face, "You have no proof that Mr. Freitag stole your music, and I have no legal reason to search his rooms. That's it, Scott. Now, you shut up your mouth, because if I hear any more, I'm gonna run you in for disturbing the peace. And if this stuff goes any further, I'll have you for inciting a riot. Do you understand me?"

Weiss put an arm around Joplin, tried to lead him off.

Fritz and Emil Alteneder were laughing now, and Freitag had got back some of his composure. Brun felt frantic. How fast could he get to Higdon's and back, give Joplin his music, and explain why he'd taken it? But right then, Daniels shouted, "Freitag, you scoundrel, you *are* a thief, and a liar to boot. You've never represented me, and you're not doing it now. If I ever hear again that you're saying you have any association with me or Carl Hoffman, I won't bother with police or lawyers. I'll take care of you myself. You'll be hustling music from a hospital bed for a good long while."

In the silence that followed this new development, Freitag seemed to rally his nerve. "You measly worm," he shouted at Daniels. "You think I'd ever have anything to do with a pipsqueak nobody like you. I've never told anyone that. And if you don't stop telling lies about me, *I'll* see *you* in court."

Brun didn't think, just came out with it. "That's all he *has* been doing. He told me lots of times how he was going to get Scott Joplin's tunes, Mr. Daniels would publish them at Hoffman's, and they'd be big hits in his road show. He even tried to sign up Blind Boone, I was right there and heard him. He said he could do better than any colored man at getting bookings and managing accounts, and the colored could just stick to writing music, singing and dancing. He'd take care of everything else for them, especially the money."

Every face in the room but John Stark's turned Brun's way. During the boy's speech, Stark's eyes had focused on a scene forty years back in his memory, a December day in 1859. He was out behind the cabin, splitting wood, when Etilmon tramped up through the snow. "They hung John Brown," Etilmon said. "And those who went with him and weren't killed will shortly get the same. Good we didn't go." Johnny said nothing in reply, just picked up his hammer and gave the wedge a blow that sent a fair-sized chunk of wood whizzing past his brother's ear. Etilmon quickly turned aside, took one look at Johnny's face and without another word, beat a path back to the cabin.

Johnny swung and swung and swung. Wood flew in every direction, but the young man took no notice. All his attention had come to bear on a moment a year and a half earlier, late on an afternoon in June, sunny and mild. But inside the Starks' little cabin, a fierce electrical storm bid fair to blow the place apart. The source of the wild weather was a skinny old coot with bristly white hair and the full beard of a biblical patriarch. He aimed a gnarled finger across the rough pine table at Etilmon Stark, then roared, "You've done good work, Mr. Stark. Many of our dark brethren owe you their lives. But it all comes to nothing so long as the abomination of slavery exists in our land. We must strike at the heart of the atrocity. I propose to carry out a bold attack on a major southern symbol, which will serve as a call to arms for all our countrymen now held in bonds. Negroes already free, here in the northern states and Canada, will rise in revolt as well. Then, when we have a goodly citizen base—"

"Mr. Brown!" Stark's voice was even, but his face, deeply tanned by this time of year, looked drained of color. "You'd be facing the force of the entire United States Army."

Brown leaned forward across the rough wooden table to bring his face within inches of his audience. Young Johnny Stark, seated to his brother's right, edged back into his chair. "We will make our strike, then retreat into nearby mountains where even small numbers of men can hold out almost indefinitely," Brown hissed. "And thanks to our good friends in New England, we will have arms a-plenty. But without capable soldiers, my weapons will be useless. I wish you to join with me."

Etilmon Stark's reply was quick and strong. "Sorry, Mr. Brown, but I can't go along with that. We need to talk to people, get 'em to where they see for themselves what's right and what's not. When they do, that'll be the end of slavery in this country."

Brown's face softened; Johnny breathed a little lighter. "You're a good and a gentle man, Mr. Stark," Brown said. "But I fear you are misguided. Peaceful emancipation is no longer possible. Daily, the southern heart gains resolve to oppose your counsel. What's happened in Kansas is, I fear, only a beginning, and the longer we wait, the worse will be the carnage. The crimes of this guilty land can now be purged only with blood, but perhaps if we act quickly, the curative dose will be small. Can I not convince you to be my lieutenant?"

"Only in spirit, sir."

Brown turned slightly to redirect his gaze into Johnny's eyes. Johnny gripped the edge of the table. "And what say you, young man?" Brown's tone became surprisingly gentle. "How old are you?"

"Seventeen, sir." Johnny hoped Brown didn't hear the quaver in his voice.

If he did, he didn't let on. "Seventeen, old enough. Will Etilmon Stark's brother Johnny join my army?"

As if in a dream, Johnny saw black faces, contorted in misery, washed by tears for wives, husbands, children, friends left behind on plantations or buried in forests between Mississippi and Indiana. Not a week earlier he'd tended to an emaciated woman, burning with fever, three-week-old lash-marks across her back oozing green and yellow fluid. She lay curled up on blankets on the floor of the Stark cabin, her shaking black hands over Johnny's on the metal cup of water he held to her lips. "Gar bless you," she whispered. "'Least I gets to die free."

That night Etilmon and Johnny buried her in the woods back of the cabin; the day after that, her husband and son went on toward Canada, disguised as women, led by a white man who pretended to be their owner.

Johnny worked to keep his gaze and his voice as level as Etilmon's. "sir, I've helped colored to get free, and I'm going to keep on doing that the best I can. But I don't think one wrong can make another wrong right. I'll stand with my brother."

Brown's razor-edged lips twisted into a crooked smile. "A well-spoken fellow," he said to Etilmon. "How came he to live with you?"

Etilmon cleared his throat. "Johnny was only three when Mother died, and he went to live with our sister Effie and her husband near Taylorville in Kentucky, where we were all born and raised. But Effie's husband keeps slaves…" As Etilmon paused, Johnny noticed his brother's face had more than regained its usual color, and when he spoke again, his words fairly throbbed with anger. "And I would not, by God, stand by and have my brother brought up in the house of a slaveowner. I rode down and brought him here, worked him heavy on the farm, made sure he got schooling over by Miss Wilkens'. I'm mightily satisfied with him."

Brown drew a deep breath, sprang to his feet, stepped in the direction of the open doorway. "Mr. Stark, since I cannot enlist your active assistance, I thank you most sincerely for your sympathy and your hospitality. Now, I must be on my way." He chuckled. "Our Mr. Buchanan has put a price on my head, so shorter visits are best for us all. Besides, I need to get to Kansas. There is much to do."

"Go in peace, Mr. Brown," said Etilmon. "I'll see you to your horse."

Brown's eyes flared, as if he might've considered Etilmon's benediction an insult. From the doorway, he stopped just long enough to look at Johnny. To the young man, it seemed as though Brown were taking his measure and finding he'd fallen short.

Ed Love's bellowing, as he tried to restore order, brought Stark back. For just an instant he stared at the small mob, then stepped forward and marched directly up to Joplin, who looked like a man with a bad case of St. Vitus' Dance. Stark rested a hand on Joplin's shoulder. "Forget about this nonsense," he roared for all to hear. "*I* am going to publish your music."

"But…but…" Joplin jabbed a spastic finger toward Freitag. "That man has stolen my music. How—"

Stark took just long enough to shoot Freitag a glance of pure contempt. "There won't be any problem. You'll sit down and copy out the music from memory, and I'll publish it."

"But *The Ragtime Dance* has thirteen tunes—"

"We'll start with your 'Maple Leaf Rag.' One tune's probably better anyway for a new publisher and a composer just getting started. For as long as you've been playing it, you ought to be able to get me a copy in a day, maybe less. After that, you can take your time with the rest of the music." Stark's eyes shot flames at Freitag. "And if that man ever tries to publish even one piece of your music, I will go to court on your behalf."

Freitag let out a howl, lowered his head and charged, but before he got halfway to Stark, the police chief had him in a hammerlock. "All right, that's it," he shouted. "Whoever don't belong in this store, out." He directed a very hairy eye toward the Alteneders, who backed up a step; then the chief gave Freitag a shove that sent the big man staggering toward the doorway. "Out," Love yelled. "All of you." He looked at John Stark, still standing with a hand on Scott Joplin's shoulder. "I'm gonna get those characters a couple of blocks away. Then I'll be back. And Scott, I'm gonna escort you to your house myself, and I want you to stay there. I'm confining you to Lincolnville 'til this business blows over." His voice softened. "For your own safety."

Julius Weiss pulled himself up straight. "I must be allowed to go with him."

Brun thought the chief was going to say no, but he nodded and said, "Suit yourself." Then he straightened his cap, went outdoors, and Brun heard him yell, "All right, the three of you, get moving. I see you on Fifth Street again today, you get a free room for the night."

Weiss said, "Brunnie, go get some music paper, yes? A lot. That way, Scott can start writing down his music as soon as we get back to his house. Is that all right with you, Mr. Stark?"

Stark motioned with his head toward the rack of manuscript paper. "I don't think you should go back to your own place, Joplin. Too easy for someone to find you. Is there another place you could stay, where you'd have someone to stand by you? Just in case?"

"Marshalls," Joplin murmured. "I once lived with them. They're good people."

During the exchange, Brun ran to the paper rack and quickly counted out five pads, then ran back with the pads and put them into Weiss' hand. Weiss smiled like a benevolent uncle.

In a few minutes, Chief Love was back. Brun ached to tell Joplin right there and then that it had all been a mistake about his music. But after what had just happened, the boy was not sure how Joplin and Stark, never mind the police chief, would take that information.

Halfway to the door with Joplin at his left, Weiss on his right, the chief turned around. "Better close up for today, John. Probably by tomorrow this'll all be blown over."

Stark shut and locked the door behind Love, then hung out the CLOSED sign. "Tangle with a pig in his trough, you're going to get filthy." He waved toward the stairway in back. "Let's go take a load off. Sounds like we need to do some talking."

Stark's back porch was shady and cool, if a bit crowded. Isaac, Daniels and Brun sat with Stark in a circle of chairs. After making sure everyone had a glass of lemonade, Mrs. Stark and Nell sat off to one side with Mrs. Fitzgerald, odd-looking as ever in her mismatched shoes. Little Frankie curled in his mother's lap, tried to play patty-cake with her.

Stark looked at Brun and Daniels. "We've had quite a day. Somebody—I don't have much doubt it was Freitag and his pair of halfwits—broke into the Maple Leaf Club during the night. When Joplin got there this morning, all his music was gone, and the place was pretty badly worked over. Chairs broken, top of the piano smashed, all the strings cut and the sounding board a mess of splinters. Maybe with all that's been happening, Joplin shouldn't have left that music sitting there in the club, but the way he worked at it, coming in at all hours whenever he was free, I can't rightly fault him. In any case, he went clear off his head, ran all around town yelling about how Freitag had stolen his music. Freitag heard and decided to beard Joplin, told him he was being pretty loose with his tongue, and he'd better mind his manners, starting with an apology right then. From down on his knees."

Brun closed his eyes.

"The only thing that saved Joplin was that Mr. Weiss was along." Stark chuckled, not humorously. "He let Freitag know that Joplin was not going to do any such thing, and then he got Joplin away and over here. I thought we had matters in hand, but then Freitag and his bully-boys showed up. Fortunately, there was a policeman up at the corner. He sent Ben Helminck's boy running up to the station, and kept things under control here until the chief got himself over."

"Mr. Daniels and I went to Freitag's house in Kay Cee," Brun said. "And the lady next door told us what a bad egg he is. He's a lush, and besides that, he…" Brun glanced backward at the women, decided to go on, but carefully. "Well, he likes to play with little boys."

Mrs. Fitzgerald's black umbrella clattered to the floor; she didn't make a move to pick it up. Mrs. Stark looked like she'd tasted curdled milk.

"And that woman who was killed here week before last? Freitag's neighbor said she *was* Mrs. Freitag, but she used to be a singer, and Sallie Rudolph was her stage name. The neighbor said she came to Sedalia because she was getting sick from being in the family way, and lost her job."

Daniels, who hadn't said a word to that point, bent to pick up the photograph he'd set on the floor, and handed it to Stark. Mrs. Stark peered over his shoulder. "Oh, my, what a lovely woman. Johnny, dear, is she the one?"

Brun bit down hard on his tongue.

"I can't know that, Sarah, but I'll bet Bob Higdon will. He'd give a lot to see this picture, and he will see it."

"If I'm stepping out of bounds, I apologize," said Daniels. "But do you really intend to publish Joplin's music?"

"I'm not in the habit of dealing in taradiddle." Stark's tone and face said that was the end of the discussion.

But Daniels persisted. "Joplin won't agree to anything unless it includes royalties."

"I know that," Stark said. "And not to be impertinent, but I don't believe I ought to discuss Joplin's business and mine with you."

Daniels gulped loud enough for Brun to hear. Then he said, "I apologize if you think I was trying to impugn your honesty. That wasn't my intent."

"Your intent, I'm sure, was to find out whether you still had any chance of getting that music for yourself, though I don't doubt through honest means," said Stark. "And if you can convince Joplin he'd be better off publishing with you, then I would have no objection. But I do mean what I say."

"I hope you believe I've had nothing to do with Freitag, though."

Stark nodded. "I don't think you or Mr. Hoffman would ever stoop to such behavior."

Daniels chewed at his upper lip. "I've had no dealings with Freitag since he left Hoffman, and I never will."

"Good," Stark said. "Now, then. I'll warrant Freitag stole Joplin's music just so what happened did happen. He knew Joplin would accuse him, probably in public, a dangerous thing for a colored man to do. And unfortunately, I don't think Ed Love is right. This is not all going to cool off overnight, Freitag will see to that. But if that murdered woman really was Freitag's wife, it puts a whole new light on the case."

"But it wouldn't prove he killed her."

Everyone turned to Nell.

Stark said, "That's correct. The information would open up a whole new line of inquiry for Bob Higdon, as well as for the police, but that line wouldn't necessarily weaken the case against Mr. Fitzgerald. In fact, there's a possibility it might strengthen that case."

"Mr. Stark!" Mrs. Fitzgerald was on her feet, holding Frankie by the hand. The little boy jammed his free thumb into his mouth. "My husband does not have dealings with strange women while he's on the road."

He sure does when he's at home, Brun thought, and judging from the looks on most faces right then, he was not alone in that idea.

Mrs. Stark took Mrs. Fitzgerald by the hand, murmured to her, eased her back into her chair. Then came a call, "Yoo-hoo. Mr. Stark?"

In the alley below, Professor Weiss waved a hand. Stark called down to him to go around front, and he'd open the door.

By the time the two men came back up, there was a chair set for Weiss. When Sarah Stark handed him a glass of lemonade, he thanked her with a great profusion of words and bows, then took a long swallow. "Ach!" He looked around the group. "Such a time."

"Is he all right?" Brun asked. "Mr. Joplin?"

"Ja. He is at Marshalls', they will make sure he stays the night. But why I come—Brunnie, he wants for you to go there before dark and tell him what happened in Kansas City."

Stark nodded toward Brun. "I told Joplin you went to try to find out why Freitag was here." He pulled his pocket watch. "After five already. Brun, go ahead, why don't you. If it'll make Joplin feel any better, it's worth it."

Brun wondered whether High Henry had told anyone else what had happened to him, and about the plan to steal Joplin's music. For that matter, was Henry still alive? Brun was this close to asking whether Stark or Isaac knew how Henry was doing, but figured better not to open another door; Stark would be through and inside instantly. And then Brun likely would be on the receiving end of some harsh judgments. So he kept shut, and followed Weiss toward the door.

As Weiss led Brun out, Stark said to Daniels, "Would you be kind enough to give me the photograph? And by the way, I hope you'll join us for dinner this evening."

"I'd be pleased, thank you," said Daniels.

"We'd be glad to have you stay the night," said Mrs. Stark. "But I fear we are full right now."

"That's all right." Daniels cast a sidelong glance at Mrs. Fitzgerald. "Once we have everything sorted out, I'll take an evening train back to Kansas City. And since you're determined to publish Joplin's music, I'll stay out of the way."

"I am not just determined to publish that music," said Stark. "I am *fully* determined."

Daniel smiled. "I'll be interested to hear how your negotiations come out."

The Marshall house, on Henry Street, six blocks past the railroad tracks into Lincolnville, was a small white frame building with a neat front yard and flowers all along the front and sides. Joplin had the door open for his visitors before they'd covered half the cement path from the street.

The living room put Brun at ease. Comfortable. The rug on the floor was threadbare, but not dirty; the chairs were the overstuffed kind that a person could sink into and get lost. Arthur Marshall and Scott Hayden sat at an upright piano against the far wall, looking like they were working at writing music. Joplin introduced Brun to the elder Marshall, a dark brown burl about fifty years old, with a shaved head and an easy smile. "Wife's in the kitchen," he said. "And my daughter."

"I can tell," Brun said. "Pork chops, if I'm not wrong."

Marshall laughed. "You be welcome to stay to dinner. Mr. Weiss, there, he eat with us all the time."

"I'd like that," Brun said. "But truth, after I talk to Mr. Joplin, I need to get back and see Mr. Higdon. But I do thank you."

"Some other time. Well, you go right ahead, Scott, Mr. Campbell. I just sit here and be a bump on a log."

Joplin and Brun sat face-to-face on the brown horsehair sofa, and Brun repeated what he'd learned from Daniels and Freitag's next-door neighbor, including the information about Freitag's wife. Joplin sighed. "She must be the one who came by Cleary's that day, looking for Freitag. I really do wonder whether that man might have killed his wife. He's got a vicious temper."

Brun pictured Joplin, just an hour before, blind with rage.

Marshall, across the room, was doing his best to be a bump on a log, but pretty clearly, a bump with ears. Well, if Mr. Joplin doesn't care, Brun thought, why should I?

"We may need to change the program for the Emancipation Day Concert," Joplin said. "Mr. Weiss is generous, but I'm not at all sure I can have *The Ragtime Dance* back down on paper inside three days, let alone have time to practice it."

Always right back to his music. Brun had never seen such a one-track mind. Again, the boy came inside a hair's-breadth of telling Joplin his music was safe, but he reminded himself that after the day's commotion, he was going to have to cobble an awfully good story to explain how he'd gotten his hands on the manuscripts. So he just said, "I'm sorry."

"I would like for you to play some ragtime."

Brun gave Joplin a curious look. The man didn't have a shred of a sense of humor, but was he pulling Brun's leg? "Now?" the boy asked. "Here?"

"No, no. At Emancipation Day. Scott and Arthur there will play, too, so I'll have all three of my students."

"But, Mr. Joplin. A white stu—"

"At an Emancipation Day concert? Is that what you're asking? But yes, that's exactly what I have in mind. Does it bother you?"

"No, sir. Just, well, it's so different. What tunes you got in mind?"

"I'll think about that. Tomorrow, at your lesson, we can decide."

Brun didn't tell him he'd forgotten about the lesson, and vowed he'd do some heavy practicing in the morning.

All the way back to Higdon's, Brun could think only of how to get Joplin's music back to him. The truth was just too awkward. Maybe tomorrow he'd tell Joplin that earlier in the morning, he'd waited until he was sure Freitag was out, then broke into his room and found the music. He could tell Mr. Stark the same. And if that made Brun look something of a hero, he guessed he wouldn't much mind.

He pulled in at Higdon's just as they were making ready to eat, and quickly asked how Mr. Higdon's mother was coming along. "Well enough, Brun, and thanks for asking," Higdon said. "It seems to be just a summer catarrh, but for a while yesterday she was having a little breathing trouble. So we thought we ought to stay over, and help look after her."

"Do we have long enough before dinner, I can tell you what I found out today? It's got to do with Freitag and that murdered woman."

"Can it be discussed over dinner?"

So as they ate, Brun told his story for the third time in as many hours. Considering the presence of the young women at table, he considered leaving out the part about Freitag and young boys, but decided best to tell it straight. Belle's eyes opened wide, and Luella dropped her fork onto the floor. Brun picked it up and passed it to her. Her thank-you was as icy as her hand.

Higdon cracked his knuckles. "Sallie Rudolph, eh? And she came to town to talk to her husband because she was expecting and feeling sick. That does put a new light on the situation. Now, Brun, just so we're all above board here, while you were at Joplin's, John Stark came by to show me that photograph. We talked a good while, about that and the locket you found." Brun felt his face color. Higdon smiled. "Neither of us feels comfortable about what might happen to Mr. Fitzgerald or you if Ed Love should get hold of the information. So, at least for now, we'll keep quiet." He looked around the table. "We'll *all* keep quiet."

"What are you going to do?" Brun asked.

"We're still thinking."

That was as far as Higdon went. The rest of dinner, Brun, Higdon and Belle chatted. Luella didn't say a word, nor did she eat a whole lot. Then, afterward, while they carried the dishes into the kitchen, Belle said, "Oh, Brun..."

The boy juggled a water tumbler, caught it just in time. "Yes, ma'am?"

"I almost forgot, you had someone looking for you this afternoon. Miss McAllister."

Luella burst into tears and ran out of the room.

Higdon worked at keeping a straight face.

"Did she say what she wanted?" Brun asked.

Belle shook her head. "She said you weren't at Stark's today, so she thought you might be here and maybe not feeling well. She said she'd look in on you later."

A bad notion popped into Brun's head. "And then she just left?"

Belle pursed her lips. "I guess so. Luella and I were on our way to do the grocery shopping, and Miss McAllister caught us out front. Then we went our way, and I suppose she went hers."

Brun had to fight himself to not just tear off upstairs and rip the mattress from his bed. He thanked Belle, then helped finish clearing the table. Before they were through, Luella came back, red-eyed, and the look she gave Brun would've frozen a runaway train.

Once the women fell to washing and drying, Brun made a move toward his room, but Higdon caught him by the arm and motioned him out to the back porch, where he told the boy to take a seat. "It may be none of my concern," he said. "But Luella is my niece, and I'm responsible for her well-being."

Brun had suspected he was in deep water. "Yes, sir," he said.

"The last couple of days, she's been spending more time crying than doing anything else. You saw what happened a few minutes ago. Up until Saturday, if anyone mentioned your name, she just glowed, but now she becomes hysterical. She won't talk about it, though, not a word. I hope you might be able to shed some light."

He didn't sound angry, only concerned, which heartened Brun. "Truth, Mr. Higdon," he said, "I'm afraid I can. Though I want to assure you, I've made no improper advances."

He smiled. "Perhaps at least not to Luella."

"Not to any woman. But Friday night, after I was done playing at Boutell's, I ran into Miss McAllister outside. She was waiting for Mr. Freitag. He'd gone inside for a drink, and left her standing out there like she was his horse. She asked me to please see her home, and when we got there, she invited me inside for some cake."

Higdon commenced to laugh. "And considering you never came in Friday night, I imagine you got more than a piece of cake."

"Two pieces of cake, actually," Brun said, which, as he hoped, made Higdon laugh harder. "But yes, sir, you're right. I didn't leave until morning, and when I did, Luella was just then coming back from Tobrich's with a basket of eggs, and she saw Miss McAllister give me a kiss. I was afraid she might not take it too well, but I didn't know what to do about it."

"Sometimes there's nothing to be done." Higdon's face went solemn. "The girl's sweet on you, she's only thirteen, and she's not had a happy childhood. I can't expect she'd take that sort of disillusionment terribly well."

"I'm sorry, Mr. Higdon, truth, I am. If there was any way I could make it right—"

"I know, Brun. You're a decent young man, and I'm sure you wouldn't intentionally hurt Luella. What happened was an unfortunate accident, and I don't hold you responsible in any way. Belle will talk to Luella, and she'll eventually get over it. In the meanwhile, you just continue to show her the same consideration I've always seen from you."

"I'll do that, Mr. Higdon, and thank you."

Brun started to get up, but Higdon wasn't done. "Just one more thing."

Brun held his breath.

"Young men will sow wild oats, but they need to be careful about the field they sow them in. I like Miss McAllister, I really do. She's got spunk, looking after herself as she has, but she doesn't seem particularly choosy about who she lets serenade her. If you do go hanging around her back door, I hope you'll be careful."

"I will, Mr. Higdon. I mean, I would. But I'm not going to be seeing her any more. At least not like that."

"All right, Brun," Mr. Higdon said. "Thank you. I appreciate your time."

"Thank you for taking interest in me, sir."

It didn't take a minute for Brun to get into his room, close the door, and throw the lock. He beelined for the bed, pulled up the side of the mattress, reached all the way in—and felt nothing. He wiggled his hand in all directions. Still nothing.

He told himself it wasn't for real, he'd just made a mistake. A heave, and the mattress was off the bedframe, its far end resting on the floor. Brun could see the entire frame, but not a single sheet of music.

He clamped a hand over his mouth to keep in the howl that tried to escape; then he sagged against the bedframe and slowly folded to the floor. How long he stayed there, he never could recall. Finally, he wrestled the mattress back onto the frame, plopped down on it and told himself to think.

It had to be Maisie. Had to. She came by to see whether she'd managed to convince him, then after Belle and Luella went off, she let herself into the house, found Brun's room, and searched it. Probably didn't have to search very long, either. Brun cussed himself in every direction for leaving the music where so many people hide valuables, and where any harebrained thief would look.

Then panic hit again. Joplin's money-clip! Brun tore into the closet, reached up and into the cubby, and there it was, safe. But once burned, twice cautious, as his mother used to say, and he slipped the money-clip into his pants pocket, down under his handkerchief. But then he stopped. Maybe once burned, twice cautious, but did lightning strike twice in one place? The clip had stayed safe through the raid that lost him the music, hadn't it? He blew out a slow mouthful of air, replaced the clip into the pigeonhole, then took off at a gallop for Maisie's house.

Chapter Fifteen

Sedalia
Monday, July 31, 1899, evening

Five minutes that felt like five hours, and Brun was at Maisie's. Unfortunately, neighbors sat talking on their porches on both sides of his target. Brun cursed them far out of proportion to their sin, and kept running, to the corner and around. Then he cut between two houses, no one there to see him, and flew through three back yards into the scrabbly crabgrass behind Maisie's house. He listened hard at the back door, then knocked. No answer. A quick look around to satisfy himself no one watched, then he opened the door and slipped into the kitchen. Not the likeliest room to hide a bunch of music manuscripts, but he checked the bread box, the icebox, the covered cake dish. He opened every cabinet, but no luck. Ditto for the dining room.

In the living room, he took a moment to stare at the couch and recollect what had gone on there a few nights earlier, then yanked the cushion away. He found a few coins, which he dropped into his pocket, but no music. Neither was there music in or under any piece of furniture. He rolled up the Oriental carpet, but got nothing other than dirty hands for his trouble.

That left the bathroom and the bedroom. The bathroom was a fast hunt, cupboards and cabinets too full of makeup and other female equipment to possibly hold manuscripts. On to the bedroom. It was growing dark. Brun checked that he had his lucifers.

He pulled back the mattress, nothing there. Then he dropped to the floor, crawled under the bed, struck a lucifer, but found only dust. He scrambled back out, brushed himself off, walked into the big closet and wasted a few lights to peer behind a row of dresses, check underneath shoes, and look up on a shelf. He felt everywhere for a cubby big enough to hold the music, but came away with only a couple of splinters. Which left the dresser drawers. If the music didn't turn up in them, he'd probably need to get into the attic crawl space. There was no basement, so at least he wouldn't have to fight off rats.

He walked out of the closet, took a step toward the dresser, then stopped in his tracks. Voices, Maisie's and a man's. Maisie said something; the man laughed. Inside the closet, Brun hadn't heard them.

He scanned the room like a drowning man searching the water around him for a piece of wood to float on. Two windows, both open, but screened. He thought about going back into the closet, but the other night, Maisie had made him hang up every piece of clothing he took off her, so they wouldn't get wrinkled. Now, Maisie's voice broke off his thoughts. "Don't you laugh... I *am* going to sing in vaudeville." Then the man spoke. "Well, 'course you are. I ain't laughin' at you. All that music...biggest thing in all of vaudeville."

They were right outside the bedroom door, no longer any choice. Brun launched himself at the nearer window, rolled up both fists, punched through the screen, and hit the ground balling the jack. He flew through Maisie's crabgrass into a patch of string beans and tomatoes in the yard behind, but as he danced out of the vegetables, the crack of a gunshot sent him face down in the grass. He felt no pain, didn't think he was hit, but resolved he'd never again laugh at any of those jokes about going through a bedroom window in a hurry. He heard shouting, raised his head, saw a skinny old coot in an undershirt and worn overalls racing toward him from the back porch of the house behind

Maisie's, waving a rifle in his right hand. "Don't shoot," Brun called. "Please. Don't shoot."

By then, the codger stood over him. "Dad blame you, boy, y'ain't got the brains God gave you. Go runnin' through a man's yard like that when he's shootin' rats, you're gonna get yourself killed." He waved the rifle toward Seventh. "Go on now, get yourself the hell outa here, and stay out."

More than enough encouragement for Brun, who got himself a good two blocks down Seventh before he slowed to a trot. He was home free, but without the music. Maisie had done a whole lot better job than he had of hiding it; he'd have to go back another time and really tear the place apart.

But wait a minute. Maisie was no dumbbell. If she really did get her hands on that music, she likely wouldn't have hidden it for long, if at all. She'd have wanted to turn it into money and probably a deal to sing in Freitag's shows. Maybe that's why the two of them were in her bedroom now, so Maisie could get into her best bargaining position.

Brun ransacked his memory: where was it that Freitag had told High Henry to bring his music? "Across from Miss Nellie's whorehouse, Commercial Hotel." The boy started running again.

The Commercial was at other end of the scale from Kaiser's, rooms two bits a night, sheets and towels changed once a week no matter how many different people had stayed in the room, and no extra charge for roaches and bedbugs. From the doorway, Brun did a quick survey of the lobby. No one there except for Jeb Johnson, the night clerk, perched on a high stool behind the counter, head down on the registration book. Brun could hear him snore all the way out in the street. You couldn't call Jeb a birdbrain without insulting the birds, and more, he was usually at least half-plastered. Brun figured he'd have no trouble sneaking past him, but then what? He didn't know Freitag's room number, and the register was under Jeb's face.

Still early in the evening, the boy thought, and Monday to boot. Ought to be quiet at Miss Nellie's. An eye-blink later, he was across the street and in the parlor, and no, it wasn't at all busy. The girls lounged on sofas and in chairs, bored and lazy, and when Brun came in, they proceeded to make much of him. Rita jumped onto his lap, ran fingers through his hair. "Froggy ain't here yet," she said. "Come on and play us a little ragtime." She winked. "Get us both in the right mood."

"If you sit there with me."

There being only a stool, Rita pushed herself up to sit on top of the piano, then bent one knee and clasped her hands around her leg. As Brun swung into "Maple Leaf," he looked up and saw the girl wore no underwear. "Rita," he said quickly, before he decided to change his immediate plans. "I need some help from you."

"My, my. We're in a little bit of a hurry tonight."

"Not that. Something else. I've got to get Jeb away from the front desk next door at the Commercial. I figure you can do it. I'll pay the freight."

The girl jumped down from the piano to deliver a solid whack to Brun's arm. She was furious. "You want to pay me to jazz that moron?"

Brun tried to keep his voice down, but all the other girls were watching the show. Nothing to do but go ahead. "That's about the size of it, but it's really, really important. I need him away from that desk for maybe half an hour. Go in there, tell him business is slow, and you got an itch you need to get scratched. I'll warrant he'll be off his seat in nothing flat. Rita, please won't you help me?"

Now he had her smiling. "You are a most deceitful young man. Here, and I thought you were a babe I could bring up to my own tastes."

A couple of the girls sauntered over. Brun went back to playing piano like nothing was the matter. Rita jerked a thumb his way. "You hear what this little Brun-baby wants? He's gonna pay me to go get Jeb Johnson away from the counter at the Commercial for half an hour."

One of the girls, a young blonde, mean-looking to start with, made a face even meaner. "That maggoty retard? Christ, it makes me sick to even think about it. I wouldn't touch him even if he took a bath in the perma'ganate."

Another girl, a hefty piece named Marsha, near forty, Brun figured, just laughed. "Hey, Rita, tell you what. I'll go with you. We'll tell him we're both gonna give him a good what-for. He'll have us back in a room in nothing flat." She leered at Brun. "Your boy can pay the both of us."

Brun knew when he was beat. "All right. Deal."

Marsha went off to check with Nellie, and was back in no time. "Miss Nellie says it's the funniest thing she's heard all year. Okay, Brun. You pay in advance for this one."

Brun dug into his pocket, put money into one girl's hand, then the other's. "Something a little different's kinda fun," Marsha said. Rita looked like she was considering throwing up.

As the girls went into the Commercial, Brun waited outside, rolled a cigarette and lit it. He couldn't hear what was being said, but saw Rita pinch Jeb's cheek. Then Marsha leaned across the counter and commenced to rub her bosom against Jeb's other cheek. Not two minutes, and the poor sap was on his feet, grabbing a key out of one of the boxes behind him and heading off top-speed with the two girls down the corridor to a first-story room. Brun felt just a bit sorry, conning him like that, but told himself Jeb's situation hardly warranted sympathy, going off to spend a little time with a couple of Miss Nellie's liveliest girls. At Brun's expense.

He strolled into the lobby and up to the counter like he owned the place, bent over the register, and there it was. Elmo Freitag, Kansas City, Room 215. He put a hand on the counter and vaulted over it, snatched the key out of its pigeonhole, then went back over the counter, and took the stairs two at a time. Down the corridor to Freitag's door, where he dropped the cigarette and ground it out on the dirty wood floor. He listened for a few seconds, heard nothing, knocked at the door. No answer. He turned the key in the lock, and went inside.

By the light from the hallway, he found his way to the coal-oil lamp and lit it. Then he closed the door, took up the lamp, and started walking around the room. The neatness surprised him. He'd figured Freitag for a real slob, but there was nothing out of place, no worn clothes or pajamas lying around, no stuff tossed onto the floor, no plates of half-eaten food. The light did send a bunch of cockroaches running for cover, but that was not something he could properly fault Freitag for.

The top of the desk was bare. One by one, Brun opened the drawers, found only a grimy dog-eared Bible. Next, he went through the scratched and gouged dresser, but nothing there besides Freitag's underwear and shirts. To get down and look under the bed took a firm resolve, like jumping into the river to swim on the first day of spring. No luck, though, and nothing under the mattress. In the closet, the boy ran his hands over the suits and pants on hangers, checked all the pockets, came away empty all around. But behind the hanging clothes, he lit upon a suitcase, which he wrestled out of the closet and threw onto the bed, no trouble, light as cardboard is. The boy snapped the case open, then stood and stared like an oaf.

That suitcase was more than half-full of papers covered with musical notes. Brun tried to examine them by the light from the lantern, but got concerned he might set them afire. Better to run, and look later. He jammed the sheets back into the suitcase, snapped it shut, and started for the door.

Downstairs, the reception counter was still unattended. Brun slid the key back into the right pigeonhole, then ran out with the suitcase, down Main to Ohio, keeping close to the buildings. At the corner of Third he saw four men talking outside Boutell's, a half-block down, and one of them, he swore, was Freitag. Fast worker, wham, bam, back for a drink. Brun turned and cut down Third to Osage, which was dark and quiet, then trotted along to Sixth and up to Higdon's. He stashed the suitcase behind the wide hedge in front of the living room window, and went inside. Voices from out back. The Higdons were sitting on the screened porch.

Up to his room he went on tiptoes, then shut the door and settled on the bed to wait. A couple of hours passed before he heard the family saying good-nights and closing doors. He forced himself to sit another fifteen or twenty minutes, then tiptoed back downstairs and outside to the hedge, where he picked up the suitcase and silently retraced the path back to his room.

He locked the door, laid the suitcase on his bed. Fitzgerald said he'd carried Sallie Rudolph's cheap cardboard suitcase into her room. Was this the very one? Brun checked around the handle, then on top, and on every panel, but no initials anywhere. That was as long as he could wait. He snapped the case open and started leafing through the music. On top of the pile was a piece titled "Sedalia Rag," by someone called Pushface Willie Lucas. Brun thought it didn't look very good. He found other tunes by other composers, some of whom he knew, some he didn't. But not a one of the manuscripts looked to be worth publishing.

Then he found one that did have promise, a lot, in fact. The title was "Maple Leaf Rag," but the composer was Otis Saunders. Brun hummed along as he read the music, and no doubt, it was Scott Joplin's tune of the same name. There were two other pieces with Saunders' name on them: "Peacherine Rag," same as the partial that Brun had taken from the Maple Leaf Club, and "Easy Winners."

Brun was taken so aback that it was some time before he realized he hadn't seen anything from *The Ragtime Dance*. When that thought finally came to him, he went back and thumbed through all the music, page by page, but still no *Ragtime Dance*, damn! He must have overlooked it. Why hadn't he taken the time to go through every possible hidey-hole in Freitag's room?

And then a string of memories hit Brun, one triggering the next, a cascade of remembrance that left him open-mouthed and staring into space. He'd thought he had this thing figured, but now saw he didn't, not altogether. He wiped his face on the bedsheet, gathered up the music and threw it back into the suitcase.

Just a few minutes later, he was pounding on John Stark's door. He woke the entire household. There they all stood, the Starks, Mrs. Fitzgerald and little Frankie, holding his mother's hand and sucking at his thumb. One look at Brun, and Sarah

Stark hustled Mrs. Fitzgerald and Frankie back to their room. Nell disappeared down the stairway to the store.

Stark considered the suitcase in the boy's grip. "Well, Brun, before you choke that poor thing to death, perhaps you'd like to sit down and tell us what's on your mind."

Brun set the suitcase on the sofa. "I thought you needed to see what I found, sir." He opened the suitcase and passed some of the papers to Stark.

Footsteps on the back stairway, then Nell appeared with Isaac. The colored man yawned and rubbed at his eyes. Brun gave each of them a handful of paper from the suitcase. "The pieces that have Saunders' name on them," he said. "I've played just about every one in my lessons with Mr. Joplin. They're his."

Nell had hold of "The Entertainer," and was reading the score, her hand beating time in the air, lips moving but making no sound. "Well, of course," she finally said. "Nobody but Scott Joplin could have written this."

Stark asked, "Where did you get these, Brun?"

"From Mr. Freitag's room, at the Commercial Hotel, down on West Main."

"Would it be too much to ask just what you were doing in Mr. Freitag's room?"

"I was looking for the music Mr. Joplin said Freitag stole last night. I figured that was where it had to be." Brun paused, judged it prudent not to mention who had helped him get into Freitag's room. "That fool Jeb Johnson was at the night desk, and when I saw he was asleep, I snuck in, checked the register, took the key to Freitag's room, and searched it. When I found the suitcase and saw the music in it, I scrammed in a hurry."

"I'm glad you came here, Brun. I really am. But what on earth possessed you to go off all on your own and pull a trick like that?"

"I wanted to help Mr. Joplin. He's been mighty good to me, and it made me sore to see a crumb-bun like Freitag steal his music."

"That was brave of you," Stark said. "But sometimes bravery can be difficult to distinguish from folly. Freitag's not right in his head, the man's dangerous. Promise me you won't take matters into your own hands again."

"But—"

"No buts. It's time to deal with him once and for all, and I have an idea. I'll need help from both Mr. Higdon and you. But I'll need to be able to count on you to do as I tell you, and only as I tell you. Otherwise, the plan may fail, and you may well endanger all of us. Oh, and by the way—you are to stay away from the Alteneders. Dr. Overstreet told me what you said the other night."

Brun felt as though he'd taken a punch under the ribs. "Henry? Is he...?"

Stark shook his head. "He never woke up, probably just as well." The boy's eyes filled; Stark reached a hand to his shoulder. "I intend that we will deal with the Alteneders as well as Freitag. But I must have your full cooperation. I can't have you rushing out and doing something foolish that might spoil the whole plan."

Brun looked at the three pairs of eyes trained on him. If Henry didn't wake up, then he couldn't have told anyone else about the plan to steal Joplin's music, or that he had told Brun about it. Safe on that score. The boy promised solemnly to mind his behavior.

Stark nodded. "All right, then. Here's your first assignment. Tomorrow morning, as quickly as you can, find Saunders. Don't come in to work until you've told him that I intend to publish Scott Joplin's music under a royalties contract. Be sure to mention the royalties."

"But you said that yesterday. At the store, before Chief Love broke up the ruckus."

"No, I didn't. I said only that I'd publish Joplin's music. I purposely didn't mention royalties. I gambled that Joplin was sufficiently upset that he wouldn't press the point."

"Is that the truth, then? You really are going to give him royalties?"

"Just do as I say, Brun. Then, go and find Joplin—"

"I'm supposed to have a lesson at eleven."

"Not on the Maple Leaf Club piano, you won't. Just you find Joplin, and give him these tunes with Saunders' name on them. Tell him I gave them to you. And if Joplin asks, you have no idea how I got them."

"Yes, sir. Then, what?"

"Then come to work, and we'll proceed from there."

"One more thing, Mr. Stark—that suitcase." Brun repeated Fitzgerald's story about carrying a cheap cardboard suitcase up the stairs for Sallie Rudolph.

Stark tugged at his beard. "First thing in the morning, I'll stop by Mr. Higdon's office, and give him the suitcase. I don't want you to be the one to explain to him how you happened to find it."

"Are *you* going to tell him, sir?"

"Yes, I will, so you should be prepared. But I think by the time I'm through talking to him, he won't be angry with you."

Brun didn't know just where he might find Otis Saunders, but since he did know most musicians are not early risers, he let himself sleep through the courthouse bell, the railway shop whistle, and the clatter of the milkman as he left the cans of milk on the back steps. When the boy came downstairs, a little past nine-thirty, the music sheets carefully folded into his shirt pocket, Belle asked whether he'd like some breakfast. He thanked her, said he had to run an errand for Mr. Stark, and would get something to eat in town.

He walked slowly down Ohio, looking all along the way for Saunders. Bruno Sneath, the popcorn man, hadn't seen him that day; neither had Luigi Vitale, playing his accordion on the corner of Ohio and Third, nor John Fischer, the rag-picker, pushing his cart across from the St. Louis Clothing Store. But as Brun came up on Main, he got lucky. Apple John nodded his head, and pointed west around the corner. "Saw him going into Lopp's just a bit ago. Probably by now he's behind a big stack of griddle cakes."

Lopp's was a small hash house directly downstairs from the Black 400 Club, and across the street from the Maple Leaf Club. Brun charged through the open doorway and inside, wrinkled his nose at the thick bouquet of days-old frying grease, and looked around. Saunders sat at a table by the window; he spotted Brun as fast as Brun spotted him, and waved the boy over. "Hey, there, young piano genius, come on and sit down. You have your breakfast yet?"

Brun thought of those chameleon lizards that actually change color depending on who and what are around them. "Don't mind if I do," he said, took the chair opposite Saunders, and called for coffee and a stack of griddle cakes. He and Saunders talked of this and that, just banter, until Saunders asked how the boy's piano lessons were going. Brun made haste to swallow his mouthful of pancake, then said, "Good enough, I think. But I hope Mr. Joplin will keep me on as a student after he gets famous."

Saunders laughed. "Well, now, Scott sure is a fine musician and a great composer. But I don't think I'd worry too much about him getting famous this week or next."

"You haven't heard?"

The smile died as if Brun had shot it. "Heard what?"

"About Mr. Stark. He's going to publish Mr. Joplin's music."

The smile revived itself. "'Less Scott gets royalties, he ain't never gonna let no publisher have his stuff. Ask me, he just could die without ever seein' another piece of his music for sale in a store."

"But Mr. Stark said he *is* going to give Mr. Joplin a royalties contract. When Mr. Joplin can get *The Ragtime Dance* down on paper again, Mr. Stark will publish it, but in the meantime, he's going to publish 'Maple Leaf.'" The boy told himself to shut up, that he'd said what Mr. Stark had told him to say, but what he had in mind was just too good to keep to himself. "And 'The Entertainer,' 'Peacherine,' and 'Easy Winners.'"

Now the mulatto's smile was dead for good. He forced a laugh. "Well, I'll be damn'. Mr. Stark ain't even a music publisher, just has the store. You know why he's doin' that?"

Some people just can't resist telling stories. "I think maybe because of Freitag," Brun said. "Mr. Stark was sore as a boil about how he stole Mr. Joplin's music. But isn't that the grandest thing for Mr. Joplin? Like I said, though, I hope he'll keep giving me lessons."

"I wouldn't worry, was I you." Saunders' heart was not in his words. He looked up at the clock over the counter, the glass so covered with grease Brun could barely see the hands. "Got an appointment." He pushed away from the table. "Sorry to run off on you like this."

"See you later." Brun shoveled in a forkful of pancake, and chewed hard to keep the grin from spreading across his face.

As Brun crossed Main Street, he saw Joplin and Professor Weiss in front of the door to the Maple Leaf Club. Joplin didn't even say hello, just pointed up at the building, and said, "We'll have to go somewhere else for your lesson today. No one will ever play on that piano again."

"If you'd rather skip it—"

"I didn't say that. I said only that we need to go somewhere else where there's a decent piano."

Brun suggested Boutell's, then Miss Nellie's place, but Joplin shook his head at both. "Do you think anyone at Higdon's would mind? There, no one will disturb us."

When the three trooped in, Belle and Luella were in the kitchen, Luella scrubbing the floor and Belle wiping down the cabinets. Brun explained the situation; Belle smiled. "Go right ahead, we've already done the living room." Luella gave Brun a look that said something very different.

Once at the piano, Joplin wasted no time. "I'm going to have you practice 'Original Rags' and 'Maple Leaf.' We'll go through them line by line, note by note. Then, as I told you yesterday, on Friday afternoon, you will play them at the Emancipation Day concert."

"You're really going to let me play 'Maple Leaf' for a colored audience?"

"I insist on it. And I also insist that you play it beautifully. I want them to see how well my student plays ragtime."

Was Joplin using him for a hustle? To show a bunch of colored that he could teach even a white boy how to play ragtime right? He'd have students lined up around the block.

"Brun, are you listening to me?"

Whatever Joplin had said, Brun missed it completely. "I'm sorry, Mr. Joplin. What you told me got me so sparked, I lost track of myself for a minute. But I'm with you now. Don't worry, I won't let you down."

Brun considered he was saying that a lot lately, and it was getting to be something of a heavy load.

When they finished the hour, Brun was dripping wet. He thought his fingers might never straighten again. Weiss patted his shoulder. "You are doing very much better, Brunnie. You must just practice, not worry, and all will be fine."

Brun took a half-dollar from his pocket, handed it to Joplin, then said, "I've got something else I need to give you."

"What might that be?"

Brun peered around the doorway, didn't hear voices. He pulled the music from his pocket and put it into Joplin's hand. To look at Joplin as he scanned the sheets of paper, you might've thought he was just giving a moment's attention to the daily newspaper. But when he held the pages out for Weiss to see, Brun saw they shook.

Weiss' face bloomed like a rose bush. "Brunnie, where did you get these musics?"

"Mr. Stark gave them to me. He said I should give them to Mr. Joplin."

"Well, then, thank you, Brun." Joplin refolded the papers and slipped them into his own pocket. "I guess I need to have a talk with Crackerjack, don't I? And with Mr. Stark."

◇◇◇

When Brun got to work at one o'clock, Stark and Joplin were in the office with the door closed, and by appearances they were having themselves a spirited discussion. Brun set right to work, helping Isaac set up a shipment of brass in the back. By the time they finished, Joplin was gone, and Stark was behind the counter, ringing up a sale. He said nothing to Brun about Joplin, and Brun didn't ask.

The heat was past oppressive, air close to drinkable. Only a few customers came in, and they walked slowly and without clear aim, the women fanning themselves with such vigor as to generate more heat than they dispelled. Some time after three, Brun sold a beautiful S.S. Stewart banjo, inlaid all over with mother-of-pearl, to a dapper colored man passing through with an hour to kill between trains. The man mopped his face with a handkerchief as he put his money on the counter. "You got you'selfs some real heat, here," he said. "Thermometer 'cross the street by the courthouse there say a hundred."

Brun whistled. "And that's in the shade."

As the colored man walked out, two white men in overalls came in, working men by their looks, blue shirts and dirty overalls. One of them wanted guitar strings and a pick. While Brun punched the sale into the cash register, he heard one of the men say, "They sure did some job on her. Ask me, that kinda thing just shouldn't happen to no woman, not even a whore."

Suddenly, Brun commenced to feel exceedingly uneasy. He asked the men what they were talking about. The one buying the goods, a walking beer barrel with a bald head, a week's growth of whiskers, and arms thicker than Brun's legs, shook his head. "They found one of Nellie Hall's girls layin' dead back of Lemp's new plant there on Moniteau. She was beat up something awful, clothes tore offa her, bruises and cigarette burns all over her body, and carved up like a piece of meat. I don't figure you're supposed to treat a whore like a lady, but that…?" He shook his head.

Brun gave the man his package. "Do they know who did it?"

The man shook his head. "Just a whore, cops won't waste much of their time. The guy did it's probably a hundred miles down the railway tracks now, anyway."

The minute the men were out the door, Brun heard Stark call his name. The boy turned around. He didn't care for the look on his boss' face. "Brun! What do you know about that?"

"You heard what they said?"

"Every word. And you know something about it. Your face, when that man said it was one of Nellie's girls... Now, you and I are going back into the office, and you're going to tell me what's going on. And don't you dare lie to me."

Brun felt like those eyes might bore holes in his head if he told even the smallest fib. So he told it straight, how Rita and Marsha had helped him get into Freitag's room the night before. By the time he finished, tears were streaming down both his cheeks. "I've got to go over there, sir," he wailed. "If that was because of what I did—"

Stark took hold of the boy by both shoulders. "If that was because of what you did, then you're likely in danger yourself. We don't know what that girl might have told them before they killed her. Now, promise me solemnly that you will not go anywhere near Nellie's house. Not within a block of it in any direction."

Brun hesitated, just couldn't speak. Stark loosened his grip a bit. "If this has anything to do with your adventure last night, whoever killed the girl may be watching the place. Who was it, Brun. What was her name?"

"Rita or Marsha. They both helped me. They're really nice girls, I don't want it to be one of them." Which started the tears up again.

Stark squeezed Brun's shoulder. "Get hold of yourself, then go back out there and work as if nothing ever happened. I'm going up to Nellie's myself. If I'm not back by closing, put up the sign, but stay here. Do not leave before I get back, not under any circumstances. Do I make myself plain."

"Yes, sir."

"Good. Now, promise me you will go nowhere near Nellie's until this business is finished. Not for any reason."

"I promise, sir."

Stark nodded, then reached into his desk, pulled out a pistol in a shoulder holster, and strapped them on. Then he worked a handkerchief between his collar and the back of his neck, put on his jacket, grabbed his hat off the hook on the wall, and walked out of the office, pausing just long enough to say a few words to Isaac. Brun thought he looked like a soldier marching into battle.

Isaac strolled into the office, and looked Brun up and down. "You don't mind me askin', what in hell is going on?"

Brun took a deep breath, then told the story yet another time. When he finished, Isaac said, "That Freitag be one bodacious sackful of trouble. You be sure and do what Mr. Stark tell you, hear? Don't even go thinkin' about crossin' him."

The idea of waiting until dark, then hopping a freight out of town to anywhere cut through Brun's mind, but he said, "I won't."

◇◇◇

All the way down Ohio to West Main, people moved off to let John Stark pass. When he walked through the front door and into Nellie Hall's parlor, a slovenly dark girl sprawled on the sofa across from the piano took one look at him and pulled her leg off the sofa arm, then sat straight as a schoolgirl after a severe tongue-lashing by the teacher. Self-consciously, she brushed a mop of hair back off her forehead and gathered it in behind her neck. "Yes sir?"

"I need to speak to Miss Nellie. Please be so good as to get her for me."

The girl looked uncertain. "Well, sir, right now she's kinda busy, and—"

"Please tell her that John Stark is here and needs to talk to her immediately."

Without another word, the girl scrambled off the sofa, and fled up the stairs to the second story. A moment later, she returned. "Miss Nellie says if you'll please come with me."

Stark followed the girl up the stairs, then to the right and half-way down the corridor, to where Nellie Hall stood outside a room. Nellie nodded to the girl, who turned on a dime and hustled back downstairs. "I'm sorry to disturb you," Stark said. "But I need to speak with you."

Nellie Hall nodded. She was an attractive woman, not yet forty, well-groomed and dressed. Passing her on the street, you'd never take her for a whoremarm. Stark often wondered how she'd gotten into the business. "I've paid regular on the piano, Mr. Stark," she said. "Every Monday without fail."

"That's not why I'm here, Nellie. I wish it were. There's been some trouble, and I need information. I don't know whether you've heard, but it sounds as if one of your girls has been murdered, and I'm concerned there might be another one in danger."

Understanding dawned in Nellie's eyes. "The kid, Brun—he works for you."

"He told me what he did last night, with help from two of your girls. By the way, you need to know that he wanted to come by himself and tell you how sorry he is, but I wouldn't let him."

"He's a decent kid," said Nellie. "Maybe just a little big for his britches."

"We all were at his age, weren't we? We learn, but it's too bad somebody else often has to pay for our lessons. I think I know who killed the girl, and if I'm right, they're not going to let the other one get away alive."

Nellie began to cry quietly. "It was a lark," she said. "The kid wanted to get into a room at the Commercial Hotel, and figured a girl could get that saphead Jeb Johnson away from the desk long enough for him to grab the key and get upstairs. He asked Rita Hodges, but Marsha Gordon heard what was coming off, and told Brun if he'd pay her *and* Rita, they'd keep Jeb busy plenty long enough. They did ask me." Nellie choked on a sob. "And

I told them sure, it wasn't busy, go ahead, make some money and have a little fun. I should have known better."

Stark tried to think of something comforting he might say. Nellie wiped at her eyes, then opened the door to the room she'd been standing in front of, and motioned Stark into the room. The only light came from around the pulled window shade. Stark heard crying. He followed the sound to the bed, where a fully dressed girl lay, sobbing hysterically. Nellie pulled the shade half-way up. "This is Rita," the madam said. "She's been like this since she got back a few hours ago. Rita, honey, you know Mr. Stark, he owns the music store. Can you tell him what happened?"

The girl looked up. Stark was appalled. Her hair was a mess, eyes swollen, face streaked with tears and mucus. "Hello," he said, a little roughly. "We heard in the store what happened to your friend, and—"

"Is she all right? Marsha?"

Stark glanced at Nellie, but got no more than a little shrug by way of reply. A mallet commenced to whack just below the crown of his head. "I'm sorry," he said. "She was murdered."

Rita shrieked. Nellie moved forward to sit on the edge of the bed and take the girl's head in her arms, but Rita pulled herself free. "Those goddamn coppers, fucking coppers! I hope some day they see their wives and daughters get the same."

"Rita, what do you mean?" Nellie looked at sea. "Was it cops who grabbed you? I thought you told me—"

"No, it was them Alteneders, Emil and his ugly kid. We went out, Marsha and me, to get some makeup, but they caught us right at the first corner, Moniteau."

Stark wondered why the girls had walked west from Nellie's, toward Moniteau, rather than east to Ohio, where most of the drugstores were. Then he realized: prostitutes generally kept to the quieter streets when they went out during the day, so as to lower the odds they'd get insulted or even spat upon by the respectable women of the town. "What happened then?"

"The kid started draggin' Marsha back behind the building, had his hand over her mouth. The old man had me the same way, but I wiggled my head loose to where I could bite his hand. That made him let up enough so I could give him a good kick where he'd know about it. While he was bent over, I ran fast as I could to the coppers, told 'em they had to come quick, before Marsha got hurt bad. But they just laughed at me, the son of a bitches. Said that everybody else in town gives to charity, so why not a whore? I told them it wasn't like that, and I was afraid Marsha was gonna get killed. But the coppers just kept on laughing. One of 'em said that Jews and whores are all the same, neither one ever gives something for free without a fight. Finally, they told me to get the hell out or else they'd put me in the cooler for makin' a public nuisance. I didn't know what to do then, so I ran over to the mayor's office, but he had a room full of patients, and said I should go back to the cops and tell 'em he said to help me. Some goddamn joke. I figured I'd better just come back here before those Alteneder creeps caught me again." She grabbed the pillow from the bed, threw it across the room. "Bastards!"

Stark's headache was now a full-grown plant with roots down into his shoulders and branches reaching forward to his temples. If he went to the police with Rita's story, they might bring in the Alteneders, but then what? Freitag would have an alibi for them, and it would be his word against Rita's. Emil and Fritz might say that Rita had tried to solicit them, that they'd turned her down, and she'd threatened to "fix them." A jury would have to choose whether to believe Rita Hodges or Freitag and the Alteneders, but more likely, Rita would never even get to the witness stand. She'd disappear before the trial ever started, and who was going to go digging around town for a missing prostitute?

Stark said to Nellie, "Clean up her face and get her into some proper clothes. I'll take care of it from there."

An hour later, Stark and Rita stood on the platform at the train depot. They could have been a father seeing his daughter off on a trip to visit Grandma in St. Louis. Rita wore a plain black skirt and jacket over a white silk blouse, and a modest black felt hat, simply and tastefully trimmed with a drape of black velveteen and black curled quills to the side. Her eyes were red, but Stark thought she could still easily enchant a drummer, or perhaps even a respectable young man, on the train. He kept the girl close by his side, until the conductor called all aboard, then handed her the ticket, along with a ten-dollar bill. Rita's eyes bulged at the sight of the money. "Oh, Mr. Stark…" She couldn't get further.

He patted her arm. "St. Louis is a big city, and there will be opportunities for you. I hope you'll use the money to get yourself a room in a proper boarding house, while you look for a job that might not be quite so dangerous."

To his surprise and dismay, she threw her arms around his neck and kissed his cheek. "Thank you," she whispered. "I ain't ever gonna forget how kind you've been."

To try to hide his embarrassment, Stark said, "I'll say good-bye to Brun for you."

A step away, she stopped long enough to fire back, "That goddamned little pipsqueak. Tell him I hope he burns in hell for what he done." Then, she marched onto the train. Stark's headache pounded away like a water hammer.

He stood on the platform until the train disappeared 'round the bend, then walked to Third Street and turned eastward. Five blocks along, he stopped in front of a tumbledown house with a sagging roof, and siding that hadn't seen paint in more years than he'd lived in Sedalia. A man sat on a broken-down sofa on the front porch, a woman beside him. Stark took a deep breath, then walked through the weeds up to the porch. From the neighbor's back yard, a rooster moved away from the coop and started in his direction, screeching at every step. To Stark, exasperated by the events of the afternoon, his patience cooked to a crisp in the blazing sun, it seemed the bird was cursing him. He picked up a stone and threw it. The rooster beat a quick retreat.

Jeb Johnson watched Stark every step of the way, as did the woman, a scrawny thing with scraggly dishwater hair and no teeth. Stark didn't think Jeb was married, but then realized the woman was some fifteen or twenty years older than the young man. His mother, Lord! Sickly trees do bear rotten fruit. Stark removed his hat and said hello.

The woman gave her son a curious glance. "Y're gettin' more visitors today than y' usually get in a year."

Jeb grunted. His mother stood. "I s'pose you want me to go on inside, like when that big talker in the ice cream suit came 'long." She looked at Stark. "I sure hope he ain't got himself in some kinda trouble."

"No, ma'am," Stark said. "I wouldn't worry, if I were you."

It took only a few minutes for Stark to confirm that yes, Freitag had come by a little past noon, asked whether Jeb had any idea how his room could have been gotten into and ransacked the night before, and Jeb, poor idiot, hadn't the sense to lie. Freitag had been real nice about it, Jeb said, even promised not to say anything to the hotel owner. Stark thanked him and left, maybe a little more abruptly than was polite.

Ed Love looked up as Stark entered his office. The police chief was no slouch, and Stark's bearing made no secret of the fact that there was trouble in the air. He motioned his visitor to a chair. "Have a seat, John. What's the problem?"

Stark wanted to tell him that the problem was the way his officers had behaved toward a frightened woman, but knew he'd get nowhere, no point riding that particular hobby. "We've been lucky so far with this Freitag nut," Stark said. "But before our luck runs out, I'm going to make sure his does. I can do it myself, but I'd rather have your help. I don't think you'd want to find yourself trying to explain to Senator Bothwell, Mayor Oversteet and Bud Hastain why you just sat around and let a lynching and a riot happen when you could've stopped them."

Love leaned forward in his chair. "Listen, John. I'm chief of police here, and I'm not going to have you talk to me like that."

"Fine. Have it your way." Stark sprang to his feet and started toward the door.

Love called him back. "All right, all right. Sit back down and talk, if you want. I'll listen, but I'm not making any promises."

◇◇◇

Almost closing time when Stark marched back into the room and up to Brun and Isaac. Brun saw the news written across his boss' face. "Rita's on her way to St. Louis," Stark said. "I gave her and Nellie your condolences, and made certain they knew that only my order had prevented you from delivering them yourself."

To Brun's intense embarrassment, he started crying again. He tried wiping his face on his sleeve, but as fast as he dried, it was wet again. "Was Rita sore at me?" he asked.

Stark put an arm around the boy, and patted his back. "I don't think so. She told me to wish you well." As baldfaced a lie as Stark had ever told, but he felt no regret. "What you did was both right and brave, but you didn't think about the consequences of your actions, and that was a serious error. I never fault a man for making a mistake, but when he makes the same one twice, that's another story."

Brun pulled out his handkerchief and blew his nose. "I'll attend to what you say, sir."

"Good," Stark said. "We're going to set a trap for our Mr. Freitag, but we've got to be careful." Stark glanced up at the clock. "Close enough to five. Let's go to Boutell's and get ourselves a table in the corner. I think a cold beer right now would do us both good. I'll tell you about my idea."

Brun looked at Isaac, who laughed. "Don't be worryin', Brun. I can't go and sit with you in Boutell's, but Mr. Stark's already talked to me."

◇◇◇

Stark and Brun got to Boutell's a little before the after-work crowd. They stopped at the bar, then carried their beer to a table all the way in back, and sat so they faced the wall. For a few minutes, silence; then Stark spoke. "Except for involving those poor girls, you did well to steal the music, Brun. You fired the first shot, square across Freitag's bow. Scott Joplin's fired the second, he's had it out with Saunders. And by now, Saunders will have gotten back to Freitag."

Brun thought back to the conversation he'd seen in Stark's office earlier that afternoon.

"I want to give Freitag and his thugs what looks like an easy shot at getting rid of all three of us—Isaac, Joplin and me—in one fell swoop. Do you know Walker Williams?"

"The owner of the Maple Leaf Club? I met him once. He was behind the bar while I took a lesson."

"Then you can imagine he's not terribly happy with Freitag, knowing who wrecked his piano. Williams will make certain someone tells Freitag that Bob Higdon's going to draw up a royalties contract, and Joplin and I are going to meet at my shop to sign it about ten tomorrow night, with Isaac as witness. I suspect that will bring the vermin out from behind the woodwork. And I promise, they'll find more than they will have bargained for."

"Why at ten o'clock?" Brun asked. "Seems late to be signing a contract."

"Freitag will hear that it's because Joplin has a band rehearsal until nine-thirty." Stark ran a finger up and down the frost on the outside of his mug. "Scum such as Freitag likes to work under cover of darkness. Now, listen carefully. You'll need to know the rest."

Stark was still talking when from the corner of his eye, Brun saw Freitag come up behind Stark. The boy jumped from his chair, looking for a gun or a knife. But as usual, Freitag had brought only his mouth and the Alteneders. Emil stood at Stark's left, young Fritz at his right. Fritz glared at Brun, who gave back as good as he got. "Well, Mr. Stark," Freitag said, with a grand gesture. "How do you do, sir?"

Men drifted away from the bar to gather behind Freitag and the Alteneders, coyotes waiting for blood to flow. Stark half-turned in his chair, stared at Freitag, didn't say a word. "Cat got your tongue?" Freitag mocked him. "Or maybe just a little pussy? Guess it's easier to go stop by Nellie Hall's in the middle of the afternoon than tryin' to get around the Missus at night, hey, Mr. Stark?"

Stark jumped to his feet. The Alteneders closed ranks around Freitag. "There's a strange thing, Stark," Freitag shouted into the small crowd. "I hear tell you're going to publish Scott Joplin's music, and give him royalties."

"Scott Joplin's business and mine are not your business," snapped Stark.

"Maybe not, but maybe so. Who ever heard of giving royalties to a nigger? Sounds mighty damn fishy to me. Here I offer him the chance to write and play all the music he wants, no worries about money, but he says he'd rather publish with a man who ain't even a music publisher, and is gonna give him a contract he probably can't even read, let alone understand. You're gonna squeeze that poor nigger dry, is what you're going to do, then when you've got all you can out of him, you'll dump him in the gutter. What else did you promise him, huh? What kind of lies did you tell him?"

Brun heard a couple of nervous little laughs from back in the crowd. He wondered how Stark managed to just stand there, cool as ice. "I'm doing more than publishing his music," Stark said. "First thing tomorrow morning, I'm going to put another piano into the Maple Leaf Club, to replace the one you hooligans destroyed when you stole his music. Then, they can practice for Emancipation Day. Joplin won't be able to get his *Ragtime Dance* manuscript back down on paper in time, but he's got a good replacement program; he's calling it *The School of Ragtime*. All his students will play rags. His colored students…" Stark looked at Brun, and one corner of his mouth turned upward, though not a bit of the ice in those clear blue eyes had melted. "And his white student."

Freitag looked like Stark had just said the world was going to end in twenty-four hours. "What're you saying? That there's gonna be white and colored on the same stage?"

"For some tunes, even on the same piano." Stark's tone was as level as if he were talking about the weather. "Four hands, two colored, two white."

"Ain't gonna be no such," said Emil Alteneder.

"No reason why not."

"Reason is, people don't play piano with monkeys."

Stark's little smile spread across his face. "I don't see any problem. You're not planning to be up on that stage, are you?" Alteneder let out a growl like a junkyard watchdog, and leaped at Stark. Fritz, of course, went straight for Brun, who took hold of both his attacker's arms and tried to butt his head on the edge of the table. But Fritz was too strong. The boys wrestled and tugged at each other until Fritz hooked a foot behind Brun's leg and they both fell to the floor, neither boy able to get an advantage. Then, Brun felt a hand on his collar, pulling him up, away from Fritz. As he got to his feet, he saw it was Boutell. "Hold still," the barkeep whispered.

Brun did as he was told.

Another man held Fritz by the shirt collar, and across the table, a third man stood in front of Stark. A huge farmer held Emil Alteneder in a hammerlock. "That's enough," Boutell shouted. "Get 'em the hell out of here." The two men wrestled the Alteneders toward the door. Boutell gave Freitag a look you might turn on a worm you found in an apple you were eating. "You too," he said, and jerked his thumb like a hitchhiker. "Get out and stay out. Take your business someplace else."

Freitag didn't move. His face darkened and twisted. "You heard all that, what they're gonna do? And it's just fine with you, huh?"

"None of it's any of my business." Boutell's voice was dead-level. He clutched Freitag by an arm and his shirt collar, and hauled him through the crowd toward the street. Someone in the crowd shouted, "Hey, Gaylord, that ain't right. Only throwin' out the half of them."

"It's my place, Clem," Boutell yelled over his shoulder. "And I'll manage it just fine without your help, thanks. You don't like it, you can take your business someplace else too. Now, let's break this up. Move."

Some of the crowd moved toward the door and outside, others drifted toward the bar. The muttering died out. When Boutell came back, wiping his hands on his apron like they were filthy with soot, Stark said, "Sorry, Gaylord. I guess I shouldn't have started a fracas in your place, but he pushed harder than I could sit still for."

"It's okay," said Boutell. "You and the boy was minding your business, faces to the wall. It was all that tinhorn and his pet animals." He looked around. "I'd let you out the back way but I don't want them to catch you in the alley."

Stark nodded. "You're right. Better for us to go out on Ohio with plenty of people around. We'll just finish our beer."

On their way back to Stark's there was no trouble, though Brun did see people pointing fingers at them and whispering to each other. He glanced sidewise at Stark, but if the old man noticed anything, he didn't let on. In front of the shop, Brun said good-bye and started off toward Higdon's. But Stark called him back. "Hold on, Brun. Come inside for a minute."

He unlocked the shop door, and led his clerk behind the counter and into his office, where he took off his jacket, unbuckled the holster, wriggled it off his shoulder, and handed it to Brun. "I trust you know how to handle one of these."

"I've done my share of shooting, sir. Mostly varmints, and tin cans on a fence post, and if I do say so myself, I'm not a bad shot."

"I'm sure of that."

"Just that you took me by surprise."

"That's why I want you to have this—in case someone else tries taking you by surprise. From now on, you stay where there are people around. Don't go any place they could bushwhack you. And though I regret imposing upon your freedom, I want you to go straight to Mr. Higdon's from here, and stay there tonight, all night. Do not go out. If I can't trust you, I'll have to take you upstairs with me and turn Mrs. Stark loose on you."

"I can't say I'd mind that, sir. But you can trust me. I promise."

"Good. We'll hope you have no problems between now and tomorrow evening, but Freitag and his boys just might pull something nasty out of their sleeves. You'll have the gun in case that happens, but I don't want you to use it unless it's absolutely necessary. The last thing we need right now is to have one of those vermin get shot dead in the street, and you end up in the jailhouse with your friend Mr. Fitzgerald."

"I don't want that to happen."

"Good. If your feet or your fists will do the job, you are to use them. And, Brun…"

"Yes, sir?"

"Keep that weapon out of sight at all times. I don't want it to end up in anyone else's hand."

Sometimes Walter Overstreet thought the weariness would just swamp him, send him down to the bottom of the world and keep him there forever. Dealing with human diseases was no walk in the park, but this endless political wrangling, getting maneuvered into doing what was expedient rather than what was right, would yet be the death of him. Knowing he'd be set free on the first of January, 1900, gave him a boost, the thought of a new start, almost like being reborn.

He poured another dose of whiskey into his glass, his third? Fourth? He'd lost count, no matter. As he lifted the glass to his mouth, Bud Hastain said, "All right, Walter? Are you on board?"

He hadn't been listening. Ed Love had gone on and on about John Stark and his plan to get to the bottom of that murder, the young woman from a couple of weeks ago. Decent man, Stark, but let him get his teeth into a notion and it was easier to separate a bulldog from a bone. Stark thought he had something on Freitag and those Alteneder thugs, but not enough to nail down the case, so he had asked Ed Love to help him set a trap that night. But Bud was concerned, didn't want to risk a major public scene, possibly a violent one. The shadow of Senator Bothwell hung heavy over anything that might embarrass his city, lose it the State Fair, reverse the growing influx of businesses. Hastain thought it would be better to just quietly get Freitag out of town.

Overstreet rubbed his chin and willed his eyes to focus on Hastain. "I don't know, Bud," the doctor said, taking a flyer. "What about that poor fish, Fitzgerald? I don't like the idea of condemning a man who's likely innocent, just to make sure the city doesn't get dirt on its face."

Hastain smiled benevolently, which set Overstreet on guard. "But you're the mayor. It's your job to see that Sedalia does not get dirt on its face."

"God damn it, Bud. Not by sending innocent men to the gallows. Why don't we try to talk some sense into John Stark, and get him to turn over his evidence. Isn't withholding evidence a crime?"

Ed Love shifted slightly in his seat. Overstreet looked at the man's paunch and smoldering cheeks, and thought ahead to the day he'd be treating Ed's stroke. "He didn't say he had evidence, just an idea. I can't do anything to a man who won't turn over an idea to the police."

"Besides," Hastain chirped. "We wouldn't be condemning Fitzgerald. Bob Higdon's a sharp young lawyer. I'll bet a dollar to a doughnut he gets Fitzgerald off."

Overstreet downed the rest of the whiskey. "You mean after the senator has a little talk with the prosecuting attorney."

Hastain's benign smile came back. "It's the way things work, Walter, you know that. Now, come on. You're the mayor. It's your obligation to go along with Ed here, and tell Freitag to get himself out of Sedalia. Fast."

Midway through pouring his next glass of anesthetic, Overstreet paused. *That's* what Bud wanted? For him to go with Love to chase Freitag out of town? Overstreet almost smiled. When it came to playing God, doctors had nothing on politicians. Did Bud really think men like Freitag stick their tails between their legs and take themselves off to their next happy hunting ground, just because a cop and a mayor tell them to? What could be a better way to make sure a belligerent loudmouth like Freitag *would* step into a trap, and the Alteneders right along with him? Stark's boy's threat had shamed Overstreet, Big Henry's speech had mortified him. The doctor wanted to see the Alteneders properly rewarded, and if John Stark carried out his plan, they would be, in spades. Overstreet lowered his glass to the desk. "All right, Bud. When do you want us to go?"

The look of puzzlement on Hastain's face almost made Overstreet laugh out loud. "The sooner the better."

"Sorry." Overstreet shook his head. "It's after midnight. I'm not about to go tramping around town until dawn, turning every bar and brothel upside-down. Morning will be soon enough."

Hastain nodded grudgingly. "That's another thing, the brothels. When the senator hears about that murdered prostitute, he'll have a fit. Especially after the Main Street merchants' meeting last Thursday. They're bound and determined to close down Battle Row, or at least move it north of the tracks into Lincolnville."

"I heard." Overstreet sounded played out. "Where it 'won't flaunt insult in the faces of reputable and religious people.' As if colored aren't respectable or religious…or people. What those pious hypocrites are really worried about is their property values."

Ed Love coughed, then smiled a bland apology. Hastain slammed his glass onto Overstreet's desk. "Damn, Walter! Even if you *would* run for a second term, I'd shoot you before I'd let it happen. Everything you say is right, and John Bothwell would tell you the same, but we've got a city to run, and one thing the colored are *not* is flush. We're between a rock and a hard place. If a bunch of Pecksniffs are worried about their property values, they're not going to pony up for a street fair, now, are they? And it only makes matters worse that a prostitute was murdered in broad daylight just a block away."

"Inconsiderate of her." Overstreet's tone was scathing, but the greatest part of his contempt was directed at himself. He probably would have been too late to help her, but he didn't even try, did he? Too many patients waiting in his office.

Hastain held up both hands, peace. "All right, Walter, enough. First thing in the morning."

Chapter Sixteen

Sedalia
Wednesday, August 2, 1899

At six-thirty the next morning, a nurse at the Katy Hospital called Overstreet to attend to a yard man who'd fallen across a track in front of an oncoming freight train, and lost a hand and part of his forearm. The doctor could hear the man's screams from out in front of the hospital. Once at the bedside, his first impression came by way of his nose: alcohol didn't go well with hazardous work. But he was hardly the one to cast the first stone, and set himself to the job. By nine o'clock he'd finished, got the bleeding stopped and the wound debrided and dressed.

When he walked into the police station, Ed Love was pacing. Before the chief could open his mouth, Overstreet said, "Didn't they call you from the hospital?"

"Well, yeah. But..."

But you don't want any visits from Bud and the senator, Overstreet thought. Already, he was late for his house calls, but nothing new or different about that. By the time he was through singing his duet with Ed to Freitag, he'd be a whole lot later. And no telling what might come up in the meanwhile.

How Apple John seemed to know the whereabouts of every person in Sedalia at any moment was beyond Overstreet, but the mayor

knew, as did Chief Love, the best way to find Elmo Freitag. They
spotted John in front of the courthouse; the skinny fruit peddler
didn't hesitate. "Just seen him, over to the Boston there." He
pointed across the street, then took off his hat and wiped a sleeve
over his brow. "Gonna be hotter today'n it was yesterday."

Love nodded grudgingly. "Heat like this, there's always
trouble. People get crazy."

Overstreet tried not to think of how many cases of heat
prostration he'd be called to see that day. He gave John a nickel,
took an apple, bit into it. Breakfast.

As the police chief and the mayor came up to the Boston
Café, Freitag walked out. Good, Overstreet thought, no one with
him. And better than making a scene inside. Freitag flashed his
toad-eating grin, special for the occasion. "Gentlemen," he said,
tipped his boater, and started off down the street.

"Mr. Freitag..." Ed Love called after him.

Freitag turned. "Yes, Chief. What can I do for you?" The smile
slowly twisted into a grimace. He smells it, Overstreet thought.
Like a cornered animal.

"You can get yourself out of town," Love said. "Now."

Freitag shammed shock. "Now, Chief, that surprises me no
end. What on earth would make you—"

Overstreet's tiny store of forbearance ran out. "What would
make him is that ever since you've been here, you've done nothing but stir up trouble. Now, as mayor—"

"Mr. Mayor, this is an outrage. I'm an honest businessman,
trying to make a living publishing music. I've got more than
half a mind to go talk to a lawyer. Or maybe the editor of the
Democrat."

The chief made a brave attempt to pull in his gut and stand
tall. "Okay, Mr. Freitag. I'll tell you something. A prostitute got
killed over by Lemp's yesterday, and one of our citizens—"

"Mr. John Stark, by name," said Overstreet.

From Love's face, you'd have thought the doctor had sprouted
a pair of horns. Love fired him a shut-up-and-let-me-handle-this
look. "Like I was saying, Mr. Freitag. This citizen has got some

evidence that wouldn't make you feel very good to hear. But we'd just as soon not have a big deal over it. So, sure, stay if you want, but if I see you in Sedalia after twelve o'clock today, I'll pick you up for murder. *Then* you can talk to a lawyer."

Freitag's reaction was surprisingly mild. "Well, now, Chief, be reasonable. You've got to give me just a little time. At least enough to wrap up my business."

Overstreet wanted to smile, both at the man's preposterous gall and his own sense of relief. The doctor spoke quickly, before Love could react. "All right. Wrap up your business today, then get on a train. If I see you here tomorrow, I'll have the Chief pick you up."

Chief Love stared at Overstreet as if the doctor had taken leave of his senses. But nothing he could say, not now.

"Very well." Freitag had his sense of dignity back in hand. "Rest assured, I'll be gone by morning. And when you read about Freitag Enterprises in the papers, and see how much money and attention it's bringing to some other city, I hope you'll remember this meeting, and realize that it all could have been yours."

"We'll try to survive the disappointment." Overstreet tipped his hat, then motioned Chief Love away with him. Love could barely contain himself; they'd barely cleared the first corner when he blew. "Jeez Almighty, Doc, why'd you do that?"

Overstreet shrugged. "Just a few hours one way or the other shouldn't make a big difference. But maybe you'd better stop by Stark's tonight, the way you were going to. Just in case."

Love dabbed at his forehead with a handkerchief. "If there's trouble, it ain't gonna be on *my* head."

He sounded so like a sulky child, Overstreet smiled. "I guess you'd better make sure there *is* no trouble, Ed."

A little before ten that night, Stark, Joplin and Higdon clustered around Stark's desk in the office, while Brun jockeyed with Isaac and Weiss to peer over shoulders at the piece of paper Higdon's receptionist had typed out that afternoon. Brun understood that once signed, the agreement would give John Stark and Son the exclusive right to publish "Maple Leaf Rag," with Scott Joplin, the composer, to receive royalties of a penny a copy, and ten free copies of the music. The signatures were done in a moment. Stark and Joplin shook hands.

Then there was nothing to do but wait, a tough assignment late in the evening of a day when the thermometer had hit a hundred and two, and people had dragged themselves around like overtired children, cranky and out of sorts. Isaac couldn't seem to hold still, got up, walked across the room, came back, sat down again. Higdon chewed at a fingernail, then looked up. "Did you hear? Governor Stanley got back to Topeka yesterday, and when he found out about the Embree lynching, he severed all official relations with Lon Stephens. Won't even mention Stephens' name."

Stark drummed rhythms with his fingers on the top of his desk. "Good for Stanley, I hope he makes it stick. Though I don't imagine it's much comfort to Embree."

Only Joplin seemed at all at ease. Brun figured he was working through a stubborn passage of music. For his own part, the boy worked hard to not look back at the doorway. Stark had thought to leave the outside door open, but Chief Love told him better to shut it, so there wouldn't be anything that looked at all out of the usual. The chief's presence was a comfort to Brun. With every man in the room armed, and Love crouched behind the big display case for harmonicas and jews' harps, the boy figured they were well covered. Still, he couldn't keep from rubbing his hand against the pistol Stark had given him the day before.

The big clock on the wall behind the counter chimed ten. Isaac coughed. Higdon cracked his knuckles. Then, Brun heard glass breaking. "Fools," Stark muttered. "Idiots." All they had to do was turn the knob.

"Some people ain't got the sense to turn a doorknob," said Isaac, and Brun noticed the colored man's hand moving toward his pocket. The boy followed suit.

Then four men wearing white hoods with cutouts for their eyes were around the counter and into the office. Two carried shotguns, the third a pistol. The man without a weapon held a pile of blankets, wrapped in a length of sturdy rope. He dropped the blanket pack, pushed his way to the desk, grabbed the contract, and laughed. Brun recognized the crazy hee-haw. The boy's hand itched to pull the gun from his pocket and let fire, but he'd been warned not to pull his weapon unless he absolutely had to. Better if Chief Love could handle the whole situation.

Freitag, still hooded, pulled a lighter out of a pocket, flipped it into flame, then held up the contract and set fire to the bottom edge. As he looked around to make sure everyone was enjoying his performance, he caught sight of Chief Love, blocking the only escape route, a pistol the size of Texas in each of his hands. "Police," Love said, calm and quiet. "Drop your weapons and put your hands over your heads. Now."

Two shotguns clattered to the floor. The man with the pistol made as if to take a stand, but when the chief turned his right-hand gun on the man, he dropped his firearm in a hurry. Stark pulled the hood off his head, then grunted with disgust.

"Crikey," Brun shouted. "Otis Saunders!"

Saunders looked away. From behind him, Brun heard, "Crackerjack..." as if spoken by a strangling man, followed by a screamed, "No!" from Saunders. Brun turned and saw Joplin aiming a pistol straight at Saunders' heart, a look on the composer's face that would have cleared the streets of hell. "Scott, don't shoot," Saunders shouted.

Weiss moved toward Joplin. "Scott, no!"

"You're trash," Joplin shouted. "Wearing a white hood. Giving my music to that man, and telling him *you* wrote it—"

Love shouldered Weiss aside to push downward on the barrel of Joplin's gun. The chief said one word. "Don't."

The minute Saunders was no longer staring into a gun barrel, he got brave. "Stole your music? Bool sheet! You 'n' me both know it was me wrote 'Maple Leaf'—an' it was a proper colored rag then, not one o' them pretty little fay tunes *you* write." He was spitting mad now, barking words like a Gatling gun. "Why you think I show it to this boy here when I see him playin' piano in Oklahoma City? 'Cause I figured even a li'l white boy could play the kinda pussy ragtime you write, an' he did. Your music ain't worth the paper you write it on."

Joplin shouted, "Where's my *Ragtime Dance?*" and took a step toward Saunders, but Weiss held him back. "Leave him be, Scott. They'll take care of him now."

Chief Love had collected the lynchers' guns and stacked them in the corner. Now, he yanked off the remaining three hoods, first Freitag's, then Fritz Alteneder's, finally Emil's. "Emil Alteneder," said Stark, as the man's piggy eyes blinked in the full light of the room. "Filth of the earth!"

Just like that, Alteneder pulled a knife and went for Stark, and then all Niagara broke loose. Isaac blasted a hole in Alteneder's chest from close range. Emil dropped the knife, stood in place for a moment, a look of wonder on his face, then folded, slow-motion, to the ground. Joplin stared like a man watching a play in a theater. Fritz shouted, "Pa!" then delivered a shot to Joplin's jaw that knocked him to the ground, and scrambled past the composer to get to the knife. But Weiss was quicker. The instant he saw Fritz swing, he went for the knife himself, and in the same motion, moved under Fritz's arm and drove the blade into the young man's chest. Fritz screamed with pain, but Weiss kept stabbing, shouting *"Schwein! Schwein!"* with every thrust, until Chief Love wrested the knife from his hand. Fritz, both hands to the side of his chest like he was trying to keep what was inside from leaking out, crumpled to the floor beside his father.

The room reeked of gunpowder. Brun looked through the haze to see Chief Love, guns back in his hands, charging like a bull through the office doorway. "Stop," Love yelled, then ducked around the counter, and out through the shop door. Only at that point did it hit Brun that Saunders and Freitag had taken advantage of the Alteneders' foolishness to run.

Stark put an ear to Emil's chest. Higdon felt at Fritz's neck. With encouragement from Weiss, Joplin staggered to his feet, shaking cobwebs out of his head. Then the chief lumbered back in, and no one bothered to ask whether the men had gotten away. Love wagged a finger toward the Alteneders. "Either of them alive?" Sounding like he'd be just as glad if they weren't, but both Stark and Higdon nodded yes.

The chief sighed. "All right, go get Doc Overstreet. I want to put a cover on the train station before those other two can hop a freight. If I don't find them, I'll go out with some men and dogs. They could've headed in any direction."

"I'm sorry, Ed," said Stark. The chief waved him off.

Sarah Stark appeared at the office door, Mrs. Fitzgerald right behind her with little Frankie, sucking a thumb, in tow. Mrs. Stark looked around. "You're all right, are you? We heard a gunshot."

Stark pointed at the Alteneders. "All of us are fine, my dear, but these two aren't doing so well. Brun, better go get Dr. Overstreet. You ladies, go back upstairs. I'll talk to you later."

Even under the best of conditions, no one in Sedalia would ever have described Walter Overstreet as a cheerful man, and the conditions in Stark's office were far from the best. Overstreet looked at the two bodies on the floor, blood puddled around them, and shook his head.

"They had a rope party in mind," Stark said. "There were two others, but they got away. Ed Love is going after them."

Wonderful, Overstreet thought. The idea had been to take them all alive, the whole gang, then get Freitag to implicate the Alteneders for murdering High Henry and the prostitute. The doctor cursed himself for a solid-brass idiot. Here were the two men he'd wanted to see on a gallows, pouring out their lifeblood instead onto the floor at Stark's. The fact that Sedalia would unquestionably be a better place without them was no consideration. Try to practice medicine based on an estimate of your patients' value to the world, and you'll be on the high road to a nuthouse yourself. You've got to treat them alike, millionaire and pauper, bank president and prostitute. Otherwise, you're doomed.

Overstreet sighed, then bent down, checked pulses, and ripped back shirts to listen to the two chests. Neither man responded. Emil breathed like a steam engine, huff, puff, huff, puff. He had a gaping hole in the front of his chest. Fritz looked like a chunk of meat pulled away from a hungry dog. Overstreet glanced back over his shoulder at Stark, muttered. "Christ Almighty," then slowly got to his feet and signaled with his hand. "Come on, let's get them over to my office before it's certain I can't do anything."

Joplin still looked glazed. Stark bent to peer into his face. "Maybe we'd better take you too. That was a pretty good shot you took to your jaw."

Joplin shook his head. "I'm all right. Those two need him a lot more than I do."

Overstreet peered into Joplin's eyes, gave him a quick once-over. "Take him upstairs, let him lie on the sofa. Ask Mrs. Stark to please give him something to drink. If he starts acting sleepy, get him right over to my office."

Weiss came close to snapping to attention. "Ja. You can count on me."

◇◇◇

Stark and Isaac carried Emil; Higdon and Brun lugged Fritz. Down Fifth, across Ohio, then a block to Dr. Overstreet's clinic. They passed no one on the way. Overstreet opened the door to his surgery, and the two pairs of men set their burdens down, Emil on the steel table, Fritz on a dark leather couch. By now, Emil was making horrible screeching noises with every breath, and Brun wasn't sure Fritz was breathing at all. Overstreet frowned and rolled his sleeves as he bent over Emil. "Sucking wound, his lung's collapsed," he muttered. Brun didn't know what that meant, but hoped with a religious fervor that he never would have one.

The doctor began to sew up Fritz's wounds. Brun noticed Higdon wasn't there, opened his mouth to ask Stark where he'd gone, but decided he'd be smarter just then to be seen and not heard. Along with everyone else, he watched and waited.

About twenty minutes later, Higdon came through the doorway with a man Brun knew he'd seen before, but couldn't place. By this time, Overstreet had thrown a sheet over Fritz's face, and was working at the hole in Emil's chest. Higdon and his companion stared at the body under the sheet; then the new man asked, "Can you do anything, Walter?"

By way of answer, Overstreet stood, walked to the closet, grabbed a sheet, and threw it over Emil. God damn them both, the doctor thought. They got off easy.

For a moment, no one said anything. Then the man with Higdon said, "Well, I'd say we've got some talking to do." He exchanged a long stare with Overstreet.

The doctor led the way out of the surgery, into his consultation room, and went directly for the little cabinet. In a moment, a bottle of whiskey and six glasses sat on the desk. Everyone, Brun included, picked up a glass and in turn held it under the bottle for Overstreet to fill. The men sat, nursing their drinks, until finally the new man said, "All right. These last two weeks, the city's been like a war field. And now, this. John, I've got a feeling you're the one to tell me what the hell happened here tonight."

Stark didn't hesitate. "That blasted Freitag was trying to set up a company to publish and perform music by colored, which he had in mind to run like an Alabama plantation. I imagine those two idiots in there had signed on as his overseers. They destroyed the piano in the Maple Leaf Club Sunday night, and stole a bunch of Scott Joplin's tunes in composition. Freitag and Joplin almost had it out a couple of times Monday. Then, Freitag got wind that I was going to sign a contract with Joplin to publish his music, and they broke in here with a rope and a pile of blankets. Chief Love was hiding outside and broke it up, but Emil there pulled a knife, and before it was over, Emil and his son were down and Freitag and another man escaped. The chief's gone off—"

The man threw a hand up in front of Stark's face. "Just a minute. Why was Freitag still in town tonight?" He glared at Overstreet. "You and Ed were supposed to get him on the road first thing this morning. "

Overstreet shrugged. "We told him. I guess he didn't go."

The angry man turned back to Stark. "What in hell was Ed doing there anyway, hiding while you and Joplin signed a contract?"

Stark didn't blink. "Well, Bud, I thought there just might be some trouble, so I asked him to stand by."

Bud, Brun thought. Bud Hastain. The lawyer Mr. Higdon clerked for.

Hastain glared at Stark. "I suppose that scene at Boutell's yesterday afternoon wasn't trouble enough."

Brun couldn't have said who looked grimmer, Stark or Hastain. Stark took another belt from his glass, then said, "Unfortunately not."

"And now, Ed's chasing after Freitag and the other man. Any idea who he is?"

"Otis Saunders," Stark said. "He was supposed to have been Joplin's friend, but he was in with Freitag, stealing music. But there's more yet I probably should tell you."

Hastain drained his glass. Overstreet leaned over to refill it.

"That woman who was found strangled, a couple of weeks ago? She was Freitag's wife. I don't know why she was in town, aside from the fact she was pregnant and looking all over for Freitag. And the man in jail now for murdering her—"

"Freitag's wife? How do you know that? And why doesn't anyone else?"

Brun held his breath. Stark cleared his throat. "Let's just say I decided it would be better to keep it to myself. I will tell you, though, I broke no laws getting the information."

Higdon went pale. "Just for the record, Bud, that's not quite right. John did tell me. And I agreed—"

"Bob is my attorney and I presented that information to him as privileged," said Stark. "So please don't hold him responsible."

"Privileged information? Christ in heaven, John." Hastain looked ready to explode. "This is a case of murder. You weren't Bob's client in respect to that."

Stark gestured with his head toward Overstreet's surgery. "I don't think there's any point going on along this line. Time's wasting."

Hastain spun away, walked out into the waiting room, then a few minutes later reappeared in the doorway, where he stood and looked from Stark to Higdon and back. Finally, he said, "All right. I throw in the sponge. Let's get on with it."

Higdon said, "My client—"

"The southern gentleman from Buffalo, New York."

"Yes. Mr. Fitzgerald. It leaves him in a bad situation. Part of our plan tonight was to get Freitag to say something that would have implicated him in his wife's murder. If it weren't for that, I'd say it's just as well he's run off. But unless they catch him, the best I can hope to do in court next week is try to convince a jury that the circumstantial evidence against Freitag is more convincing than that against Fitzgerald. It's not an approach I'd want to count on."

Hastain pushed with two fingers against his forehead, just above his eyes. "I think we might be able to get a trial delay for Fitzgerald on the basis of your information, along with the fact the police are looking for Freitag. But what in hell are we going to do about those two yahoos in there? Who actually killed them?"

No one spoke.

Hastain's cheeks flared. "God damn it, I asked a question. Somehow, I don't think the chief killed those men, and I want to know who did. It's going to come out, and better now and to me than later to someone else. Who was it?"

Isaac raised a hand. "I shot the old man when he pulled a knife and went after Mr. Stark."

Then Higdon said softly, "And when the kid slugged Joplin and went for the knife on the ground, Professor Weiss beat him to it."

Hastain sank into his chair. "Jesus Almighty Christ, what have we got here? A colored man shoots a white man, never mind it was in defense of another. And an old kraut carves up a boy like a dinner roast, never mind it was a kid who should've been suffocated at birth." Hastain looked up at Isaac. "I'm sorry, nothing personal, but two white men, killed by a colored man and a foreigner? A white businessman damn near gets lynched? This gets out, we could have riots. It'd be a circus, on the front page of every newspaper from Kansas City to Chicago. You think any businesses would ever dream of moving here when they read about that? At least Bothwell's away, we've got a little time." Hastain waved a hand in the direction of the corpses in the surgery. "Did anyone see you bring those baboons in here?"

"No." Higdon and Stark answered together.

"All right, then. We'll take them out the back way, get them out of town, and bury them. If anyone ever asks, they ran off with Freitag and…what's his name again?"

Brun raised a hand, permission to speak. "Saunders. Otis Saunders."

"Fine. When Ed gets back, I'll talk to him. I don't think he'll want to explain to Bothwell how and why all this happened. Ed can call off the hunt. All four of them got away, too bad. Bob, I'll sit down with you in the morning, you'll fill me in on details, and we'll see what we can do for Fitzgerald."

Overstreet stood behind his desk, swaying like a man on board a ship in heavy weather. He'd gone so gray, Brun felt frightened for him. "Bud, I'm sorry. You're pushing me too far. I can't go along with this."

To Brun's surprise, when Hastain spoke, his voice was gentle. "I'm sorry, Walter, but do you want to be responsible for what happens to Isaac there, and the old man? And if this business ever goes public, how many more people just might end up under sheets in your office? Is that the way you want it?"

Overstreet's hands shook something fierce. Hastain leaned across the desk toward him. "If you'd gotten Freitag out of town the way you were supposed to, this never would have happened. So don't go crying now like an old woman. You want to blame somebody, take a look in a mirror."

Overstreet dropped into his chair like he'd been shot.

"Tell you what, Bud."

Everyone turned to Stark.

"We'd do best not to bury them too near town—someone might happen to see us. I'm supposed to pick up a piano in Knob Noster tomorrow, so I'll go get my wagon, bring it around back, and we'll load them in. Then Isaac and I will head off toward Knob Noster, find some woods a good way off, and bury them deep. Afterward, we'll go on, pick up the piano, and bring it back."

Hastain thought it over, then said, "Hmmm, all right. But one thing. Isaac here isn't going to spill any beans, but that old German's an odd duck. Where'd he come here from?"

"Houston."

"Fine. I'll take the professor to the station, buy him a one-way ticket, and get him on the first train to Houston."

Stark frowned. "He's here working with Scott Joplin on the Emancipation Day program—"

"Well, damn it, Joplin will just have to make do on his own for Emancipation Day. One wrong word from that dippy old kraut, and we'll all be in the soup. Now, let's get moving."

Stark clearly was not pleased, but motioned to Brun and Isaac, who fell in behind him. "The wagon's in the hitching shed behind the store," he said. "And I usually get a horse from Bengley. But I don't think I want to wake him up and try to explain why I need a horse at this hour."

Hastain and Higdon looked at each other, then Higdon managed a lopsided grin. "My neighbor Elliot keeps a couple of horses. I know him well enough, he won't ask questions."

On the way back, Stark grumbled that he hated to see Freitag get away. "Maybe it's better all around, but I can't help wishing I could have dealt directly with him."

Brun only half-listened. He'd been thinking about Maisie. After she'd stolen *The Ragtime Dance* manuscript from under his mattress, could she have given it to Saunders to copy? First thing in the morning, he'd find where Saunders had been rooming, and tear the place apart.

"Let's stop upstairs a minute," Stark said. He gripped the doorknob. "We ought to let Joplin, Weiss and the women know what's happening."

Isaac said, "I'll go on to the shed and get the wagon ready. When Mr. Higdon gets back with the horse, we can be right on our way."

Stark opened the door and started clumping up the stairs to the flat, Brun in his wake. They walked into the living room, then stopped flat-footed.

Mrs. Stark, Nell and Mrs. Fitzgerald were tied round and round into straight-backed chairs, their hands bound together at the wrists. Joplin and Weiss lay on the floor, hands lashed behind their backs, ankles roped together. Maisie stood over them, pointing a Colt revolver at the new arrivals. No frilly dress tonight; she wore work-pants and a man's blue work-shirt, which, Brun couldn't help but notice, showed off her female figure most admirably. Freitag, decked out as usual in his pearl-gray trousers and vest, stood near the middle of the room, a Colt in one hand, his other hand gripping Frankie Fitzgerald by the shirt collar. Frankie wriggled and screamed; Freitag wrapped his free arm around the child's middle and pulled him close. "One move, he's dead." Like a dog, growling. Mrs. Fitzgerald sat straight and silent, lips bloodless. Brun thought her stare might melt a steel block.

"That's right, stand where you are, hands up," Freitag shouted at Stark and Brun. "Move apart more, just a few steps…good."

Maisie walked toward them, pistol up and ready. Freitag said, "Do the war hero first."

Maisie ran hands over Stark's chest, then up and down his legs. She pulled a pistol out of a holster, and stuck it into her belt. "I'm watching," Freitag snarled. "While she's tying him up, anybody moves, we got us a dead little shaver here."

Maisie herded Stark across to where Joplin and Weiss lay, motioned him down to the floor, then roped his hands behind his back and tied his ankles together.

"Now you." Freitag waved his pistol. "Little Chief Wet-behind-the-ears. Too bad you had to go and play with the big boys, Sonny." Brun stood still while Maisie checked him out and came away with his gun and a red rubber ball. She gave him a funny look, glanced at Joplin, then tossed the ball across the room. As it disappeared under the sofa, she pushed Brun to the floor next to Stark, Joplin and Weiss, and tied him up.

"Oh, that's a pretty sight," Freitag sneered and waved his gun. "Now, we can have us some fun."

"Fun?" Maisie was clearly in no mood to have fun. "Come on, Elmo. You said we'd get the money out of the safe and register, kill them, and be a hundred miles away before anybody found—"

Freitag laughed again, a high-pitched whinny. "Oh, you just be patient, Maisie. We got time, and I think I got a little something comin' to me. Listen here, Stark. I was all of seven years old when the Yanks come and occupied Mobile, and shot my daddy dead. Before my mama and me starved, she went and married Joe Freitag, which made matters even worse—'specially for me. Now it's my turn to give back. You thought it was pretty funny, hey, Stark? Playing me for a fool. When all the time, you had it in mind to publish that white nigger's music. Well, tell you what. Maybe I couldn't get the music, but I'll have your money instead, and your lives to boot. Who's gonna laugh the last, huh?"

"I gave them the money, Johnny," said Mrs. Stark, and pointed at a big carpetbag on the floor near the door. "They were going to shoot Frankie if I didn't."

"It's all right, Sarah."

Stark seemed about to say more, but Maisie spoke first. All the time Freitag talked, she'd been examining something in her hand; now she bent over Brun to hold a small gold object in front of his face. "Where did you get this from, Junior?"

While Brun tried to figure what to say, Freitag walked over, and when he saw the gold locket, all color drained from his face. He delivered a sharp blow to the side of Brun's head with the butt of his gun. "*You* had this? Where the hell'd you get it?"

"It was in his pocket, Elmo. And it's got your picture in it. What's going on?"

Freitag's clout wasn't hard enough or placed just right to knock Brun unconscious, but it did loosen up his tongue. "Found it in the weeds where Sallie Rudolph was lying, after you strangled her to death."

Freitag suddenly looked out of reason, eyes wild, foam flecking the corners of his mouth. His jaw jerked. "You killed her?" A hoarse whisper, like a child whining. "*Strangled* her? You told me Saunders went and talked to her, and got her to go back home."

"Oh, Elmo, you damn fool. All *you* could do was take her to the station and tell her to go home and see the doctor and get rid of the baby. You really thought I'd trust Saunders to get her out of our hair? He'd have just tried to talk her out of her drawers, that's the only thing he ever *was* any good at, that and pocket-prowling. I got him to go lift Joplin's money-clip, then we went over to Kaiser's, and I waited out back in the alley while he peeked at the hotel register and got her room number. Then I climbed up the building, through the window and into her room. You should have heard her. Nothing was going to stop her having that baby, and she was going to stay here in town until she had you with her on a train back to Kay Cee. So I shut her up, pushed her out the window, went down the fire escape, and Saunders helped me carry her down to the corner and through back yards over to Washington. We dropped her by the side of the road and left Joplin's money-clip next to the body where the cops couldn't help finding it. We figured with Joplin put away, Saunders could get his hands on every manuscript Joplin ever wrote—except it seems like they never did find that damn money-clip. Now, damn it, Elmo, get hold of yourself, would you. Forget about Sallie. Whole lot of good she ever did you."

Freitag's body shook. He sobbed and honked, and wrapped his arm tight around Frankie's neck. The little boy squalled; Mrs. Fitzgerald jumped to her feet, the chair tied to her back. "You let him go," she shrieked, and took a step toward her son.

Maisie pointed her gun at Frankie, then glanced at his mother, who quickly sat back down, her face nearly black.

"What the hell good did *you* ever do me?" Freitag bawled. His voice was shrill, a good octave higher than usual. "You were gonna sweet-talk a pile of music out of these niggers, but all you got was crap nobody would ever publish. You spent a whole night with that little punk there, telling him bedtime stories about going on the vaudeville stage, and you didn't get shit for that, either."

"Cut it out, Elmo. It was my house you came sniveling to after these yokels ran you off, but I'm not here out of the goodness of my heart. I don't give a hoot in hell about Mobile Bay, your old man, or your Sallie. Did you really figure I was going to spend the next twenty years thanking you for tossing me a song here and there on your way to the bank? You're even a bigger damn fool than I thought you were. First chance I had, I was going to be off and gone with the whole pile of music. Now, at least let's get out of here with some money." She pointed at the carpetbag. "That's my ticket to a vaudeville circuit. We'll get rid of these chumps, split the take, then you go your way and I'll go mine."

Freitag sobbed convulsively. With his gun pointed more or less at Frankie's chest, every time the man's hand jerked or shook, Brun's stomach did a barrel-roll. "You cheap floozie. There was more worth in Sallie's little finger than you've got in your whole body."

Maisie's eyes narrowed to slits. Her lips tightened. She turned the barrel of her gun toward Freitag and Frankie. Brun's eyes went big as dinner plates as he saw Isaac edging through the doorway. Shouting at each other like they were, neither Freitag nor Maisie had heard him. Isaac slipped a pistol out of his pocket, raised the gun, took aim. Brun drew a breath, held it. If Isaac shot at Freitag, his aim better be perfect. Anything less, he might hit Frankie.

Apparently, Isaac thought the same way, because when he pulled the trigger and the room filled with the sound of the gunshot, a look of amazement came over Maisie's face. Her gun fired once, then she toppled.

Just as fast, Freitag's gun was against Frankie's head. The little boy shrieked, kicked his legs and flailed his arms.

"God damn fool!" Freitag shouted. Brun wasn't sure whether the man was talking about Maisie, Isaac or himself. Frankie, hysterical, cried, "Mommy, Mommy!" Freitag tightened his finger on the trigger. "Put down your gun, nigger," he said to Isaac. "Otherwise, we got us a dead kid here."

Mrs. Fitzgerald loosed a scream that set gooseflesh onto every square inch of Brun's body. Isaac, however, kept his pistol trained on Freitag. "I don't think so," Isaac said. "That boy's all that's keepin' me from blowin' you to kingdom come. He ain't no good to you dead."

Freitag giggled. "Hey, pretty smart nigger you got here, Stark. He knows how to pull a Mexican standoff. Well, we're gonna play it just a little different." He bent to croon at the child, "Hey, now, don't you worry there, Frankie. How'd you like to come with me, huh? You like candy, right? You come with me, we're gonna take a nice train ride, and you'll get all the candy you want."

Brun looked at Mrs. Fitzgerald, thinking she'd be having a conniption, but she just sat quietly. Try and figure crazy people. Frankie reached his arms toward his mother and moaned, "Ma-ma."

"Me and little Frankie here, we're gonna walk right past that nigger, and Frankie's gonna be in between his gun and me, every step. Nigger shoots, the kid's dead—and so's the nigger, 'cause soon as he shoots, I shoot *him*." Freitag wrestled Frankie squarely in front of himself, and bent down to make the little boy a perfect cover. Then he started duckwalking toward the door, past Stark, Joplin, Brun and Weiss. "Easy, now, nigger…that's right. I said you were a smart one—"

An astonished Brun saw Scott Joplin launch himself toward Frankie, knock him down and away from Freitag, then grab at Freitag's ankles. Freitag pointed his gun toward Isaac and fired; Isaac's pistol flew out of his hand and clattered against the far wall. Then Freitag aimed down at Joplin, and Brun heard a shot.

Someone screamed, "No!" Who it was, Brun realized afterward, was himself. Joplin let out a cry of pain, and rubbed fiercely at his left hand. Freitag staggered backward, then fell like a poleaxed steer, and lay still next to Maisie.

Mrs. Fitzgerald called out, "Come here, Frankie. Right this minute." As the child ran to her, she looked around the room at the frozen faces, all turned on the tiny pearl-handled Derringer in her right hand, which was still tied at the wrist to her left. "Well, whatever did you expect?" she said. "That I would come all the way from Buffalo on a train, without the means to protect myself and my child?" She dropped the little gun into a front pocket of her dress.

Sarah Stark said, "I thank our good fortune that you and Frankie were in the bedroom when they came bursting in here."

Mrs. Fitzgerald favored her audience with a crooked smile. "Before that strumpet made us come out here, I took the gun out of my pocketbook, and put it into my dress pocket with one of Frankie's shirts over it. That way, she didn't feel the gun while she was pawing me."

All through the exchange, Joplin, eyes squinched, held his left hand in his right, trying to squeeze the hurt from it. Mrs. Fitzgerald lifted Frankie onto her lap, and only then commenced to bawl, "My baby, my baby… I lost two, but I'm not going to lose you."

Stark said, "Joplin, what happened to you?"

"He stomped on my hand when she shot him."

Isaac, shaking his right hand, stalked over to retrieve his gun. He said something Brun couldn't make out, then walked to the kitchen, came back with a knife, and cut Stark loose. Stark was instantly up and over to Joplin, took hold of the composer's hand. He frowned. "I think you've got a break there. Let's get the rest cut free, then I'll take you across to Doc Overstreet's."

As everyone stood and stretched their arms and legs, Mrs. Fitzgerald, holding Frankie by the hand, marched up to Sarah Stark. "Mrs. Stark, I'll need a hot bath for Frankie, right away.

An experience like this is a terrible shock for a young child." She shot a quick glance at Joplin, Stark's arm around one of his shoulders, Weiss' around the other, as they moved him toward the door. "A hot bath will calm his nerves."

Brun thought she was more concerned that a colored man had touched her child than anything else. She never even said a thank-you to Joplin.

Nell took Mrs. Fitzgerald by the hand. "Come on," she said. "I'll heat water for you."

They disappeared into the back of the apartment. Everyone else stood in place, not a word. From the doorway, Stark looked back. "I guess I'd better get Bud Hastain again. Soon as we're done at Doc Overstreet's—"

Right then, Higdon walked in. He got as far as "I've got the horse" before he spotted the two bodies in the middle of the floor. He stared at Stark and Weiss, supporting Joplin between them. Stark grabbed him by the arm. "Come along," Stark said. "I'll tell you on the way over to Doc's."

Brun followed Isaac and Mrs. Stark to the kitchen. His knees wobbled for a moment as he thought what might have happened if he'd followed his first inclination after the music had been stolen, and put the money-clip into his pocket.

When Nell returned from the bath room, Mrs. Stark, Isaac and Brun were sitting around a fresh pot of coffee on the kitchen table. Nell cocked her head sidewise at Brun. "Lucky you had that locket."

Not a question, but Brun knew an answer past "Yes" was in order. "Mr. Stark told me I should bring the locket along tonight when they were going to sign the contract, and maybe we could use it to smoke Freitag out. I knew Saunders and Miss McAllister were involved, and probably Miss McAllister actually did the murder."

"Why Miss McAllister?" Nell asked. "What made you think of her?"

"Well, for one thing, I knew how strong she was. I found that out when, er, when she and I…" Brun felt his cheeks catch fire. "That's all right." Nell's grin was a mile wide. "We'll just take your word."

"She'd been an aerialist in the circus—that's how she came to be so strong. I figured she got into the room by shinnying up the wall and through the window, just like she said before Isaac shot her. And then one night last week I was walking along Lamine, past Kaiser's, and Romulus, the ice-cream man, was standing outside the liquor store—"

"In his usual state for the evening, I imagine."

"Nell!" Mrs. Stark tried to sound severe, but couldn't carry it off.

"He was as drunk as ever. And he told me to stay out of the alley behind Kaiser's because it was haunted. He said the other night he'd seen a ghost there. I thought he was just having the DTs, but after I got to thinking about it, I went back and talked to him some more. He said he saw the ghost fly down to the ground, stay there for a minute or two, then float away off down the alley. I remembered that Mr. Fitzgerald told Mr. Higdon and me that the dead woman was wearing a white dress, so I figured Miss McAllister had thrown the body out of the window, and that was what Romulus thought was a ghost flying. Miss McAllister would have been wearing dark clothes to go up the wall into the room, and whoever was helping her, Freitag or Saunders, would've also dressed dark. There was a full moon that night—I remember because it was the same night I came into town—so when they carried the body off down the alley, Romulus must have seen the white dress again and thought it was the ghost floating away."

Nell narrowed her eyes. "It makes sense. They wanted to implicate Scott Joplin, but if they'd left his money-clip next to the body in a room of a whites-only hotel, people might have wondered. Strange that no one ever found that clip."

"I don't know," Brun said, angel-faced. "I'm just glad they didn't."

Isaac reached for the coffee-pot and refilled his cup. "How about Saunders? What put you on to him?"

"First thing was, I saw Saunders with Freitag and Mais—Miss McAllister one night at Boutell's, and then I remembered how the first time I ever met Freitag, he knew I was taking lessons from Scott Joplin, and I couldn't think of anybody but Saunders who could've known to tell him. Also, before I went through Freitag's room the other night, I was looking around in Miss McAllister's place for the music, but I had to get out in a hurry 'cause I heard her coming in with a man. I thought it was Freitag, but not all that long after, I saw him standing outside Boutell's, and it hit me that it was actually Saunders I heard with Miss McAllister. The corker was when I found the tunes Saunders stole off Mr. Joplin, in the suitcase in Freitag's closet."

"Well, now, Brun dear, that was all very clever of you." By the tone of Mrs. Stark's voice, Brun knew she was not quite paying him a compliment. "But why on earth didn't you tell any of that to Mr. Stark or Mr. Higdon, and get yourself some help?"

"Ma always used to say I had too much of an imagination for my own good. I was afraid I'd just sound foolish."

"Mothers can do that," said Nell.

Brun looked away from Mrs. Stark. "And after I found the music at Freitag's, things were happening so fast I just didn't have it in mind at the right time. Not until we were in there with the guns aimed at us."

"Well, then." Mrs. Stark leaned over to give him a kiss on the cheek. "However it happened, Brun, you were very brave to go snooping after the music. I think you are the hero of this story."

Brun started to say no, but Isaac broke in. "That's truth, Brun. Don't go tryin' to deny it."

Truth sure does look different, depending on where you're standing, Brun thought. "But I'm sorry I couldn't get back *The Ragtime Dance*."

"Oh, no worry there," said Nell. "Mr. Joplin can write it down again. I can help him."

◇◇◇

If Overstreet and Hastain had been disquieted before, when they came back in with Higdon, Stark, Joplin and Weiss, they were thoroughly disconcerted. Overstreet went directly to crouch over the two bodies. Joplin's right hand was covered with a white bandage. Brun asked if he was all right.

"Yes. The doctor gave me a shot, and it feels much better."

"But your hand… Will you be able to play piano?"

Overstreet dismissed the corpses with a back-handed wave, grunted and got to his feet. "Not for a little while. That stomp broke a couple of bones above the knuckles. I set them, and now we'll just have to hope no tendons were damaged. But his hands and arms are in remarkable condition, what with all those exercises he does. Once the bones are healed, I think he won't have trouble going back to piano work."

"It's my left hand," said Joplin. "I can still write music."

"Mr. Joplin…"

Everyone turned to look at Stark.

"How did you manage to get yourself free?"

"Those same exercises, the ones with the rubber ball. While she was tying the ropes down on my wrists, I kept the bottoms of my hands a little apart and tightened my arm and hand muscles. When she was done and I relaxed, the ropes were loose enough that I could work them off. Then, while they were arguing, it was easy to get the ropes off my ankles."

Hastain pointed down at Freitag and Maisie. "Is this the end of it, John? Or are you planning on more?"

Stark smiled with tight lips. "It's the end, unless Saunders really didn't run. But I'd bet a lot of money he did."

Overstreet lowered himself into a chair by degrees. His face was gaunt; again, Brun felt worried for him. "Four bodies," he murmured. "How can we just take four bodies out and bury them somewhere in the woods?"

Higdon looked ready to say something, but Hastain beat him to the punch. "I can't see we have a lot of choice. In fact, we've probably got twice as much reason as we did a couple of hours ago. And Bob, from what John tells me, it looks as if your client is in the clear now, but unfortunately his wife seems to have shot someone dead. How she managed to nail him square between the eyes with a puny little Derringer, never mind with her hands tied together, I can't begin to guess, but—"

"The Lord tempers the wind to the shorn lamb," Stark muttered.

Hastain looked like a kid whose mother had just forced a spoonful of castor oil down his throat. "John... All right, now. What if Ed Love takes that woman in and starts asking questions? Yes, she'd eventually get off, but can you imagine what might come out of that mouth of hers at a hearing?"

Higdon put a hand to his forehead.

"And there's something else. Who's going to explain to Ed why he never got to see that locket? Especially after he comes back in the morning, empty-handed, and finds Mrs. Fitzgerald in the cooler, and two more bodies on a slab?"

Amid nervous laughs, Overstreet heard the rumble of his father's voice, upright Dr. Overstreet, who wore a black suit in winter, white in summer, and never once to his son's memory ever wore gray. Just his way, the doctor thought, he didn't know any other. But those poor Fitzgeralds, old Mr. Weiss, Isaac—none of them was guilty of anything other than being human. Nor was that prostitute Overstreet hadn't had time to try to help because he was too busy in his medical office.

"Walter?" Hastain peered into the doctor's face.

"I've become the man my father feared I might," Overstreet murmured.

The lawyer blinked. "What say, Walter?"

"Nothing. Let's get moving."

"Fine." Hastain pounded one fist into the other. "As far as anyone's concerned, Freitag ran away with Saunders and the Alteneders, and left the McAllister woman waiting for them at her house. When they didn't show up, she came running over here to look for them, and we've got witnesses who'll swear she said she'd killed the woman to get her out of Freitag's way, but she wasn't about to take a fall for him. She had a gun, so no one tried to stop her running off." Hastain looked around the room. "Anybody have a problem with that?"

Silence. A couple of heads shook.

Hastain fixed an eye on Brun until the boy commenced to squirm in his chair. "Can we count on you?" Hastain asked.

"Well, sure," Brun piped. "Why—"

"Because sometimes a boy likes to show off a little, maybe when he's got a snootful. Or wants to impress a girl. We can't have that happen."

Brun held up his right hand. "I swear I won't say a word, not to anybody, cross my heart."

Hastain covered a laugh with a cough. "All right, then, it's settled. When Ed gets back, I'll tell him our story and get Fitzgerald out of the can, back with his wife and the little boy, and onto the first train toward St. Louis. And—"

Overstreet cut him off. "I'm the mayor, and Ed's away. *I'll* get Fitzgerald out. By morning, he and his family can be well on their way."

Hastain goggled, but recovered quickly. "All right, that's even better. And Mr. Weiss, I'm sorry, but you'll be on the next train to Houston."

Joplin got out one word, "But—" before Hastain broke back in. "I'm sorry, Scott, I know he's here to help you with your music. But considering what's happened tonight, and the mood this town's gotten into, I'm concerned for his safety. And while I'm at it, I'll also tell you that putting a white boy up on a stage with colored right now in Sedalia would be like holding tinder to flint." He pointed at Joplin's bandaged hand. "I think everything considered, you ought to let go of the program altogether. Isn't there a good band coming down from Lexington?"

Joplin nodded. He looked like a little boy promised some ice-cream, but the store was out.

"Let the Lexington boys take care of the music. That hand of yours gives you every reason to back off for now. Next year, things may be very different."

Mr. Weiss made a clucking sound. "He's right, Scott. Sometimes is necessary before you go forward to take a step back."

"Not necessarily."

Stark moved forward to put a hand on Joplin's undamaged arm. "Sometimes, you still move forward, but in a little different direction from what you'd planned. You and I have business to complete. Freitag burned our contract, but as soon as I get back from Knob Noster I'll have Bob Higdon draw up another copy." He looked at Higdon, who smiled and nodded yes. "'Maple Leaf Rag' is a fine tune. It will get your name out, we'll both make some money, and then we may be able to publish more of your work."

Joplin turned a questioning eye on the shopkeeper. "I owe you an apology, Mr. Stark. I admit, I did wonder whether all that talk about the contract was just a trap to catch Freitag."

Stark's eyes blazed; his beard seemed to bristle. "We are well-acquainted, but in time you'll get to know me better." He glanced at Freitag and Maisie. "John Brown *was* right, wasn't he? But bloodshed is only a beginning; the matter must be seen through to the end. I have always been equal to all requirements, and I intend to so continue."

Stark put out a hand toward Joplin, who inched his own hand forward. Finally, he gripped Stark's. Fifty years later, Brun said he could still see those clasped hands, one black, the other white, clear as the day he witnessed the handshake. Stark glanced at Isaac, then kissed the top of Mrs. Stark's head. "I'll see you late tomorrow, my dear. Isaac and I had better get on our way, if we're going to finish our work before dawn."

Chapter Seventeen

Sedalia
Thursday, August 3, 1899

After Stark and Isaac took away Freitag's and Maisie's bodies, rolled in the bloodstained rug they'd fallen on, Brun filled a pail with soapy water, took a scrub-brush and some rags, went down to the store and got rid of the mess Emil and Fritz had left on the floor of Stark's office. Then, back upstairs, the boy walked around the living room to make sure there were no splatters anywhere. He dug a bullet out of a strip of molding, probably the wild shot Maisie took when Isaac finished her. Then he dropped into the nearest armchair, opposite Joplin and Weiss. Not long after, Mrs. Stark and Nell came back from cleaning up in the kitchen, and they all sat silent, one of those awkward times when everything seems to have been said. They'd have wished each other good night, but they knew the night was not yet over.

At the first gray light of day, Higdon and Hastain came in with Edward Fitzgerald between them. Fitzgerald's skin hung loosely over his cheeks; dark bags sagged under his eyes. His fine suit was filthy and unpressed, and he badly needed the attention of a barber. But as his eyes scoured the room, he held himself straight as any soldier on parade. Mrs. Stark got up and started toward the back of the flat. "I'll get you what you're looking for."

When Fitzgerald laid eyes on Frankie, his smile could've broken hearts. The little boy, clean from his bath and fresh from a few hours' sleep, screamed, "Daddy!" and ran to his father, who swept him up and hoisted him onto his shoulders. Brun noticed that dirty as Fitzgerald looked, Mrs. Fitzgerald said nothing about Frankie needing another bath. But neither did she smile at her husband. When he came forward to kiss her, she turned her head so all he could do was peck her cheek. "I can only say," she announced, "that I hope you've learned your lesson. All you ever get from that fine Southern chivalry of yours is trouble. You came close to making me a widow."

Brun thought Fitzgerald might do well to consider making himself a widower. But he just said, "Yes, my dear. I will be more judicious in the future, I assure you."

"I would certainly hope so! You know how delicate Frankie is, and dragging him and me down here was an act of extreme irresponsibility. I will hold you responsible for Frankie's condition. After that horrible fright he had, if he grows up feebleminded, we will both know why."

Fitzgerald tried to shut down his wife's tongue. "Now, Mollie, dear, I understand. I'm sorry, and so I have said. But I think that's enough for now—"

Unfortunately, the effect of his remark was opposite to what he'd intended. "Enough?" his wife screamed. "'*Enough*,' you say?"

Frankie commenced to cry, and ducked down behind his father's head.

"When I'm through, it will be enough," Mrs. Fitzgerald shouted. "And I'm not nearly there. On account of your folly, I will have to remember for the rest of my days that my son owes his life to a colored man. How do you suppose I should feel about that?"

Said like Joplin wasn't even in the room. Weiss laid a hand on the composer's undamaged forearm.

Brun expected Mrs. Stark would move in and bring the performance to a stop, but she just stood with an arm around Nell, an odd little smile on her face. Neither did Higdon or Hastain look the least inclined to interfere. Mrs. Fitzgerald pointed at Joplin. "This colored man ran over and pulled Frankie away from that terrible creature who was trying to kidnap him. I don't even want to think about what might have happened."

As Fitzgerald looked at Joplin, his eyes filled. "Is that true?"

Joplin looked away. The room was silent. It suddenly registered with Brun, plain as paint. Fitzgerald was not asking a rhetorical question. The man simply could not put faith in his wife's version of any story. "It's true, all right," Brun shouted. "Every word. That's how Mr. Joplin got his hand hurt."

Fitzgerald blinked at Brun, as if realizing for the first time that the boy was there. Then, he turned back to Joplin. His mouth opened, but nothing came out. Finally, Joplin said, very quietly, "Would you not have done the same? If you'd seen a child in danger like that?"

Fitzgerald paused only a moment. "Yes…yes, of course. Oh, my dear man, I am forever in your debt. My son's life is more precious to me than my own. I hope you are not badly hurt."

"Just my hand. It will get better."

"What is your name?"

"Scott Joplin."

"Scott? Hmmm. Well, Scott, I just don't know how to thank you." The southerner extended a hand, which Joplin grasped.

"Edward!" Mrs. Fitzgerald was beyond fury. "Have you taken leave of all your senses? Shaking the hand of a colored man, as if he were a gentleman? A simple thank-you would have been both sufficient and proper."

Fitzgerald paid her no heed. When he spoke again, it was in a voice firmer by degrees than Brun had ever heard from him. "When a man saves my son's life, shaking his hand is not nearly sufficient. Whatever can I do for you, Scott, to show my gratitude? I fear I would offend you by offering a monetary reward."

Joplin nodded. "You fear correctly."

"Very well. But I want you to know that if I can ever be of help to you in any way, I sincerely hope you'll call on me." He pulled a business card out of his pocket and handed it to Joplin. "And in addition…"

Fitzgerald glanced at his wife, jaw forward, looking daggers. Brun half-expected to see smoke come curling out from her ears.

"From this day on, I will honor you by calling my son after you—"

"Edward!"

Sarah Stark hurried up from behind and took hold of Mrs. Fitzgerald, who wriggled and tugged, but Mrs. Stark held firm. Fitzgerald spoke on. "My son is named after my great-great granduncle, Francis Scott Key, the man who wrote 'The Star-Spangled Banner.' We've always called the boy Frankie, but now he will be Scott."

"Over my dead body," screamed his wife, still squirming something fierce in Mrs. Stark's hold.

Brun caught the expression on Hastain's and Higdon's faces and turned away, lest he burst out into some highly improper laughter.

Fitzgerald bowed to Scott Joplin. "I apologize for my wife's remarks, Scott. I fear this unpleasant business has unduly taxed her mind."

Was that a smile on Joplin's face, for just a split second? Brun couldn't be sure. "Of course, Mr. Fitzgerald. Please don't concern yourself."

"Thank you, Scott. I am grateful for your understanding."

Shortly thereafter, Higdon and Hastain left for the depot with Weiss and the Fitzgeralds. Joplin went back to Lincolnville; his story would be that someone had tried to rob him on the street, and had stomped his hand during the fight. Brun walked slowly back to Higdon's, enjoying the cool early-morning air. He considered dropping by Maisie's and looking again for Joplin's missing music, but didn't want to risk having to explain to the police chief or anyone else who might catch him there. In the end, fatigue won out. The boy went straight to Higdon's and directly to bed. Despite all the excitement, he fell asleep instantly and did not see daylight again until almost noon.

◇◇◇

Just about the time Brun crawled into his bed, Stark and Isaac, in a small clearing off the road halfway to Knob Noster, leaned on their shovels and looked over their work. "Should be fine, Mr. Stark," Isaac said. "We got 'em deep enough, no wild dog's gonna sniff 'em and dig 'em up. And the way we've covered it all over with leaves and moss, nobody's gonna see the fresh dirt."

Stark nodded, then gestured with his head, and the two men trudged back to the wagon at the side of the road. They pulled fresh clothing from a sack, changed, and put their grimy digging duds into the sack, which they tossed with the shovels into the wagon. "Come on, then," Stark said. "We can get to Knob Noster just about in time for breakfast."

Isaac grinned. "Sounds good to me, Mr. Stark. I think I worked up an appetite."

Stark's face went wry. "I don't suppose you're ever going to call me John, are you?"

The colored man's smile faded. "You know why—"

"But Isaac, there is no one anywhere near us right now to hear you."

"Best not to get into bad habits, an' then one day I'll forget and make a slip. I don't want that happenin', not for either of us." He hesitated a moment, then reached out, took the white man into his arms, and pulled him close. For a few seconds, the men stood in embrace. Stark patted Isaac's back. "I guess it doesn't really matter." The old man's voice was hoarse.

"Uh-uh, it don't." Isaac moved a step away to look Stark in the eye. "We both of us know what we be to each other. We both know why I took your name, all those thirty-four years ago."

Stark sighed, then climbed up to sit behind the horse. Isaac untied the animal from the tree they'd secured him to, got himself up beside Stark, clucked and shook the reins. The horse seemed to notice his lightened load, and moved off at a good clip toward Knob Noster. Stark cleared his throat. "After we finished back there, I said a little prayer."

Isaac looked like he wasn't sure whether to grin or keep a serious face. "Guess their souls could use any prayers come their way."

Stark leaned to the side, hawked, spat. "Who said anything about their souls? I prayed we'd never again see the likes of them in Sedalia or anywhere else."

Isaac kept his counsel. His experience was, prayers tend not to get answered. Still, he allowed, you can bet your sweet mama's life no prayer's gonna get an answer if you never do ask it.

While Brun washed and dressed, he saw his future clear and bright. Once Stark made it official that he was going to publish Joplin's music, Brun would be sitting pretty. Considering what he'd done over the past week, he could be sure of a good situation in the new firm. There was also every reason to expect that Mr. Joplin would treat his white pupil well, so that maybe after a while, Mr. Stark would also publish ragtime by Brun Campbell. By the time Brun went down to the kitchen, he was whistling as happily as ever he had.

Luella stood at the sink, washing a big black pot. Even the vinegary look on her face didn't faze Brun. He bid the girl a polite good-morning.

She tossed hair back off her face, and said, "Hmph. More like good afternoon, I'd say. Out carousing another night away with drink and loose women?"

He came just that close to telling her he'd been in the company of her uncle almost the whole time, but caught himself.

She sniffed. "I suppose you'd like some breakfast. I can make you some bacon, eggs, and coffee."

"I don't want to trouble you. I can just go over to the Boston."

She set the pot upside-down next to the sink. "I don't mind. I'm done here, and Belle's gone out to get groceries. Sit down." She opened the icebox and pulled out three eggs.

Brun sat. "That's really nice of you."

"Not at all. I want to talk to you, anyway."

Now, how about that? Maybe Belle or Higdon had somehow got through to her, and she wanted to say she was sorry for her recent bad behavior. Brun wasn't entirely sure he'd favor a reconciliation; all-out war with Luella did have its unpleasant side, but the idea of endless skirmishes over Saturday night church socials and Sunday morning religious services didn't have much to recommend it either.

When she set the plate of food and the coffee cup down in front of him, he readied himself to accept her apology in a gracious manner. But the girl didn't apologize, nor did she sit. Just said, "I'll be back directly," then walked out of the room.

Brun had eaten only a couple of mouthfuls when she swept back in, plopped into the chair beside him, smacked a pile of papers onto the table between them, and gently laid a Bible next to the stack.

Brun dropped his fork. Right on top, staring at him, was the manuscript of "Maple Leaf Rag." He snatched up the papers, thumbed through them like a crazy man. "Swipesey Cake Walk," "Sunflower Slow Drag." Partials of "Peacherine Rag" and "Easy Winners," and "The Entertainer" fragment. And on the bottom, *The Ragtime Dance,* the entire score, every note. He snatched it up, scraped his chair back and was on his feet, ready to run, but Luella stopped him cold. "Sit down," the girl said. "If you know what's good for you."

That thirteen-year-old skirt sounded exactly like Brun's mother when he'd done something to get himself in Dutch. Probably something else women are born with. Brun sat without a second thought.

"Now," Luella said. "What do you have to say about this?"

Right there and then, Brun told himself he would never marry. "What do you mean, 'what do I have to say?' What do *you* have to say?"

"I have to say that you're a thief. And thieves should be punished."

Brun pulled the music closer, such that Luella couldn't grab it back. "I see what you're trying to do," she snapped. "But you better not even think about running off. If you do, I'll tell my uncle you forced your attentions on me, and when he sees what I look like, he'll believe me." She tugged at the front of her dress; a seam came loose. Then she raked a fingernail down her left cheek, and a four-inch streak of blood welled up. "Stop," Brun shouted. He jumped forward, grabbed for her hand, but she pulled away. "Only if you sit down until I'm done. Take one step away from that chair, and I'll rip off all my clothes and put scratches all over my body."

Worse by far than anything Brun's mother ever had done. He sank back down. "All right. I'm listening."

"Well, that's smart of you, Mr. Smartypants. First of all, I'll tell you how I found this music. You hid it under your mattress, what a dumb thing to do. That's the first place any robber would look."

"Oh, so you were snooping in my room."

"Don't go high and mighty on me, Mr. Brun Campbell. It's not me who's the thief. I found it while I was making your bed."

Oh, Lord, he thought. Monday, laundry day. After I ran off to catch the train to Kansas City, she stripped the bed.

The girl held a warning finger toward Brun's face, then reached across and pulled the pile of music so it sat directly in front of her. "Now. Can you tell me why I shouldn't show this to my uncle? Or Scott Joplin? Or maybe even the police?"

Brun fell all over himself explaining how he came to have the music. "I was going to give it back to Mr. Joplin after I got back from Kansas City, and in fact, I came back here to look for it right after the dustup at Stark's that afternoon. But it wasn't here. Now, please, you've made a big mistake. Let me take it back to him."

They say smiles warm the heart, but Luella's chilled Brun to the bone. "You've got it all wrong, Mr. Fast Talker. It wasn't *me* who made a mistake. I don't believe a word you're saying. Your mistake was hiding it in such a stupid place. You knew exactly what you were doing. You were stealing your teacher's music to give it to that hussy of yours, so you and she could go on the stage together."

Brun's mouth fell open. Luella clapped her hands. "See? I'm right, aren't I?"

"No, no. Wait, listen—"

"Uncle Bob told Belle and me at breakfast what happened last night before you went out on the town. About how Mr. Freitag and Miss McAllister and Emil and Fritz Alteneder and that Otis man tried to carry off Scott Joplin and lynch Mr. Stark and Isaac. But you all fought them off, and they ran. Uncle Bob said how Miss McAllister was probably 'using her charms' to get Otis to steal Scott Joplin's music, telling him she'd go on the stage with him if he did. That's when I knew for sure. You stayed a whole night at that Jezebel's house, and then she gave you a great big kiss when you were leaving, and said the two of you were going to set vaudeville on its ear. I heard! She was doing the same with you as with Otis. She didn't care who got her the music, just as long as she got it. So off you went and stole your teacher's music, and it would've worked, too, if I hadn't found it."

"No, listen, would you? You've got it all wrong—"

"No, *you* listen. Because you're the one who's got everything wrong. You think you can talk your way around everyone, but not me, wise guy. I've got your number. You committed a very serious crime, and you need to be punished. What I really ought to do is take the music to the police and turn you in. Then you'd go to jail, like you deserve. But I'll show you some Christian charity…maybe."

To Brun's amazement, she pushed the music back over to him. "Here. Take this music back to your teacher, and confess to him and ask his pardon. After that, get yourself on the next train out of town, and don't ever come back. If you do that, I'll forgive you, and I'll pray for your soul. But if you do anything else, I'm going to tell my uncle and everybody in town that you took the music back from me by force, and worse."

Her eyes were wild. Brun felt scared silly. He saw what was coming, lunged for her hand, but she jumped aside, then ripped the front of her dress open, tore away the slip underneath, and dug scratches and gouges with her fingernails across both breasts.

"Stop!" Brun shouted, and started after her, but she ran to the stove, picked up a small knife, held it with both hands to her belly, and screamed, "Don't you lay a hand on me. Move one more inch, and I'll do it. Then when they find my body, you can just try to explain. Now, go do what I told you. I'll change my dress, and if anybody asks about my cheek, I'll tell them I scratched it by accident. But if I see you in Sedalia after this afternoon, I'll show my dress and my body to Belle, and tell her you did it when you took back the music. Then you'll go to jail for thievery *and* attacking a young girl. Quick, what do you say? And stop looking at my breasts."

You're not trying real hard to cover them up, Brun thought. But he said, "Okay, you win. I'll do it." Whatever it took to get away from her. Then he'd have to figure what to do next.

Her eyes went shifty. "You'd better not be lying, or you're going to be the sorriest person on earth. Now…" She picked up the Bible. "Put your hand on."

Brun did as she said.

"Now, swear that you will do exactly what I said, and nothing else."

"I swear I will do exactly what you said, and nothing else."

"Say what you're going to do. Exactly. Swear it."

"I swear I will return the music to Scott Joplin, and then get out of town on the next train."

"And you'll confess to Scott Joplin how you got it."

"And I will confess to Scott Joplin how I got it."

"And you petition the Lord, if you say or do anything else, He should strike your mother and father dead right on the spot."

Brun hesitated.

"Say it," she barked.

"And I petition the Lord, if I say or do anything else, He should strike my mother and father dead."

"On the spot."

"On the spot. All right? Now, can I go?"

She pulled back the Bible. "Go get all your things together, and I'll put on a new dress. Then I'll see you out the door."

The scratch on her cheek was nasty, a line of dark red with small drips where blood had run down. "Better wash your face, too," he said. "You don't want that to get infected."

"Don't you worry about me," she said. "You'll do better to worry about yourself, especially if you don't do what you've sworn. Mend your ways. I'll pray for you."

The way she looked at him, he thought he'd rather she didn't send any prayers of any sort in his direction. But he said nothing, just went to his room, gathered his clothes into a bundle, came downstairs, and started for the door. Luella waited for him in the hallway. She wore a different dress, and had washed the blood off her face. "I'd like to at least say good-bye to your uncle," Brun said. "He's treated me well."

"Better by far than you deserve."

"And I'd like to thank him."

"You just do what you swore. I'll tell him you had to leave, and you send him regards."

She opened the door, and watched him all the way down the street.

Brun did not hold much truck with swearing on Bibles, and in any case thought if God was truly fair-minded, He'd set aside such swearing when it was done under compulsion. As he walked up Ohio, he racked his brain for ideas about how he could set matters right. But every thought ended with a picture in his head of Luella showing that dress and her bosom to Belle. No person in her right mind would have scratched herself up like Luella did, and Brun wasn't sure her uncle and aunt knew how far she was out of her right mind.

As he crossed Fifth, an idea came to him. Maybe Mrs. Stark had a leprechaun to spare. With Stark and Isaac off to Knob Noster, the store would be shut and Mrs. Stark likely would be upstairs. But as he hustled past the Stark and Son display window, he saw the shop door was wide open, and there stood Mrs. Stark at the front counter, looking for all the world like nothing had ever happened the night before. She smiled when he came in. "Well, Brun, right on time, you are. But what's that bundle you're carrying?"

He looked up at the clock behind her. One in the afternoon, he'd clean forgotten about coming to work. "Mrs. Stark," he said. "I need to talk to you, bad."

She looked around, then half-whispered, "Does it have anything to do with last night?"

"Sort of."

"All right, dear. Don't fret." She walked to the front door, shut it, and hung the CLOSED sign. "Let's just wait until those people in the back are done. Then, we'll sit in Mr. Stark's office."

"If it's the same to you, ma'am," Brun said, "I'll go in there now and wait. Best if no one sees me."

"As you say. I'll be there just as soon as I can."

A few minutes later, she walked in, sat in her husband's chair, smoothed her skirt, made a church steeple with her fingers, and looked the boy over. "All right, then. Tell me what's on your mind."

Brun always said that ever since that day, whenever he heard somebody talk about spilling their guts, he knew what it meant. His story poured out of him like he was throwing up some bad-tasting liquid. Mrs. Stark sat quietly the whole time. "I'd give anything to be here when Mr. Stark gets back," Brun wailed. "If I could see him and Scott Joplin sign that contract, it'd be something I'd remember my whole life."

She sighed. "You heard Mr. Stark make the promise. I assure you, it will happen."

"But I thought…I was hoping that I could be a part of it. That there'd be a place for me, publishing music with Mr. Stark. It's just not right, Mrs. Stark. That girl is crazy."

"She's gone through a lot in her few years, Brun. It's no easy row to hoe, being an orphan. As I'm sure it wasn't for Mr. Freitag."

"But Mr. Stark was an orphan, wasn't he? And look at him."

"Oh, well, yes, I suppose, strictly speaking. But he was fortunate enough to have had Etilmon and his wife take him in.

They brought him up as a son. Lord only knows what might have happened to him otherwise. That poor little girl hasn't been nearly as lucky. Her aunt and uncle do the best they can for her, but she needs a home where she feels as if she really belongs. And for that, she was looking to you, Brun, and lucky you were it didn't work out. The only hell more fearsome than the one she'll put her husband through is the one she lives in herself. I'll make it my business to talk to her. But I think you'd best leave Sedalia, as you promised her."

"Don't you believe me, Mrs. Stark?"

She tapped a finger on Stark's desk as a funny little smile came over her face. "Well, yes, Brun, I do, at least about this business. You have a fair bit of blarney in you, not uncommon in a Scotsman, and all considered, not so very bad. And if I don't believe every word you've ever spoken to me, I do believe you've not done anything wrong. If you'd had designs on that girl's virtue, you'd have used blarney, and I suspect it would have worked. But force? No. Your heart is good, that I know. But whether or not *I* believe you isn't what matters now. I have no doubt that if you do stay, that girl *will* show her body to her aunt and the devil knows who-all else. And before you know it, everyone in Sedalia will be talking about you. Every man with a teenaged daughter will have his gun ready, and if you're not shot to death, you'll get a nasty bath in a tar pot. Or, worst of all, you'll end up in church saying, 'I do.'"

"But Mr. Stark and Mr. Higdon—"

"I will speak to them both, and you have my solemn word they will understand and send blessings to speed your way."

"But just to run away? I feel like a coward."

"Soldiers sometimes need to retreat so as not to be slaughtered, and there's no shame in that, just good common sense. You remember the story I told you about Mr. Stark and Isaac, the first time we met…my, that was not even two weeks ago. It seems I've known you forever.

"Yes, ma'am, I do recall it. But, please, can I ask you something?"

"Of course you may."

"Was it all really true? None of it was blarney?"

She laughed to beat all. "Yes, dear, it's true, every word." Then her expression hardened a bit, but her voice remained soft. "And now, my dear, I think you should be on your way. If that girl sees you and takes a notion to have her revenge, it won't go well with you. Experience may be a good teacher, but she does go heavy with the hickory. I hope you'll learn from this experience, Brun."

"You can be sure of that, ma'am."

"And do keep in touch with your parents. There won't be a day they'll not be thinking of you. Let them know you are alive and happy." Sly smile. "Even if you're not terribly happy right at that moment. And let us hear from you as well." She paused. "This is not for anyone else to know, but before the end of the year, we'll be in St. Louis. Since Mr. Stark has decided to put his all into publishing, it seems a move would be best for everyone. Nell can have her studio—"

"But Mrs. Stark. The store. If you go to St. Louie… What about how Mr. Stark feels about the store?"

"Well, let's put it this way. Mr. Stark is quite certain that before too much longer, the establishments on West Main Street will be closed down to make the city more respectable. And when that happens, many musical people will move on, and then the store would likely have its problems." She got to her feet. "Come upstairs a moment, and I'll get you a couple of sandwiches and some nice fresh cake. You will always and forever be in my heart, dear. The last couple of years, I've worried considerably about Mr. Stark, what with all his talk about his day being almost done. You've helped him get back his fire. He's my Johnny again. My lovely soldier-boy."

Mrs. Stark sent Brun off with a hug and a kiss on the cheek. He started up Lamine toward the Maple Leaf Club, but then remembered there was no piano there. Where was he going to find Joplin? He didn't dare look for Apple John up and down Ohio. Maybe Marshall's? They had a piano.

He crossed the tracks into Lincolnville, hurried past seven blocks of small houses, shacks and downright shanties. When he finally pulled up, sweating, in front of Marshall's, he heard halting piano music from inside, one-handed notes and chords. Scott Joplin answered his knock.

The composer looked confused. "Brun?" He checked his watch. "This is Thursday, your lesson's not until tomorrow morning."

"I know. How's your hand feeling?"

Joplin held up the bandaged hand. "I do have some pain, but nothing I can't bear. Mostly, I worry about whether I really will be able to play again."

Brun wanted to reassure him, but knew whatever he might say would be hopelessly lame, and decided to go directly to the business at hand. "I need to talk to you—is there a place we can go?"

Joplin couldn't take his eyes off the stack of papers in the boy's hand. "I'm here alone. Come in."

Brun walked past the piano, littered with music manuscript, and sat in a sagging easy chair. Joplin pulled the piano stool over. Without a word, the boy handed his teacher the pile of music, then watched Joplin leaf through it. With every page, the composer turned, his eyes grew wider, and when he finally looked up at Brun, they were brimming. Brun coughed. "Where… How did you get these?" Joplin asked. He sounded like he'd got himself a bad case of bronchitis.

"I figured they had to be in Maisie's house, and that the coppers wouldn't be getting there until morning. So right after the fuss last night I went back myself, and I poked around 'til I found them under the mattress."

Joplin didn't speak for a long while. Then he looked into Brun's eyes. Brun had to look away.

"I am in your debt," Joplin said quietly, and of a sudden the boy felt guilty as sin itself, like he really *had* stolen the music to give to Maisie. And then he knew Mrs. Stark was right, that he did have to leave Sedalia. If *he* could imagine what Luella said might be true, why shouldn't the whole damn town believe it?

"It's me who owes you," Brun said. "I haven't had a lot of lessons, but I'm most grateful for what you've done for me."

"But we're not finished, certainly."

"I'm afraid we are. I'm on my way out of town. Let's just say I've had some trouble with a woman."

"At your tender age." Joplin shook his head sadly.

"I've learned my lesson," Brun said. "And I hope to be back some day and learn more piano from you."

"You'll always be welcome."

The boy was halfway to his feet when his hand went to his pocket. "Here's something else for you, Mr. Joplin."

Joplin stared at the musical money-clip like he'd never seen it before. "There's twenty-eight dollars there," Brun said. "Same as when you lost it."

He wasn't sure Joplin heard. The composer turned the money-clip over and pushed the button; music played. When he finally looked up, his face was as confused as his voice. "How did you come to have this?"

"I found it on the ground next to Mrs. Freitag's body, the night she was killed. I was going to turn it in, but when I heard you and Mr. Weiss talk about it, I knew it was yours, so I hid it away."

Brun was giving Joplin the bad stammers, but when he finally did get words out, they weren't exactly the expression of gratitude Brun had expected. "Why didn't you come to me sooner with it? Why not until now?"

Brun's turn to stammer.

"I'd have hoped you'd have more faith in me." Joplin's voice was quiet but accusing.

Brun looked the colored man square in the eye. "I'm sorry."

Very slowly, Joplin's face relaxed. "Well, perhaps I'm the one who should apologize. After all, you really didn't know me very well, did you? Thank you for protecting me…and for returning the clip to me now."

"I only figured it out in the last couple of days," Brun said. "Last fall in Oklahoma City, Saunders picked my pocket, slick as a wink, just for fun. He gave me back my money and told me to be careful in a big city. It made sense that he picked your pocket so he could leave the money-clip with Mrs. Freitag's body and then steal your music."

"We were all at Miss Nellie's until late that night. Crackerjack did leave for a while and then came back, but not for long. I remember thinking he had ants in his pants, but he was always on the move, so I didn't make a lot of it. It wasn't until I got home that I found the clip missing. But have you told anyone about this? Anyone at all?"

"No one. Not Mr. Stark or Mr. Higdon. Just you."

"We'll keep it that way."

"You bet." Brun stood. "I'd better get to the station."

Joplin stood, then took a silver coin from his pocket, which he handed to Brun. "Here's something for you to take along. This half-dollar is dated 1897, the year I wrote 'Original Rags,' my first. Carry it as a good-luck pocket-piece, a remembrance of Scott Joplin and the piano lessons you took from him."

When Brun's train rolled into the depot, he had to wait while a good number of colored got off, early arrivals for the Emancipation Day program next day. As they pushed past Brun, laughing, talking, humming tunes, the boy had to work hard at not crying like a sissy. But later, in the passenger coach, when he took Joplin's half-dollar from his pocket and remembered the sadness around his teacher's eyes as he'd given Brun the coin, there was no holding back. He just let the waterworks run.

By the time the train pulled into St. Louis, though, Brun had eaten his sandwiches and cake, and was feeling considerably more upbeat. Didn't Boone say he ought to go to the Rosebud Saloon and listen to Tom Turpin play? Maybe Turpin hadn't left yet for Sedalia. Brun could tell Mr. Turpin he'd been a pupil of Scott Joplin's, maybe even play the man a little of "Harlem Rag," and who could say what just might come out of that? Before the train even came to a full stop, first off was Mr. Brun Campbell, looking around for a porter to point him in the direction of the Rosebud.

Walter Overstreet walked slowly up the path to the little cottage on Morgan Street. He'd sworn an oath of silence regarding what had happened the night before, but many years earlier he'd sworn another oath, to Hippocrates. He hoped Big Henry and Mattie would take some comfort from the assurance that those responsible for their son's death were now dead themselves, the result of action by men and women—white men and women—who did not want them to get away with what they'd done. But that wasn't the whole ball of wax. The doctor knew he'd crossed a line to invade a dangerous neck of woods beyond the farthest reach of sympathy and justice. He shrugged, shook his head. Enough thinking. He raised a fist to the door.

The Last Word

Seattle, Washington
February, 2006

In 1899, people called ragtime nigger-music, as if only a black could write, play or appreciate ragtime, and a white could not and shouldn't even try. As if blacks and whites are born tone-deaf to each other's music, can't hear the rhythms of the others' hearts or the melodies in their souls. That's the legacy of slavery in our land. It cuts both ways, and it cuts deep.

But it's the bunk.

Consider this. Musicians and historians now refer to Scott Joplin and two other composers, James Scott and Joseph Lamb, as the Big Three of classic ragtime. At the time of the ragtime revival some sixty years ago, Scott was known to live in Kansas City and to be black, but Lamb had dropped entirely from sight. He was finally located in Brooklyn, New York, in 1949, and when he opened his door to the ragtime enthusiasts who had run him to ground, the scholars were astonished to find themselves staring at a man indisputably white.

And this. The great majority of composers, musicians and historians of the ragtime renaissance were white.

And this. In his 1936 book *The Negro and His Music*, the black philosopher Alain Locke mentioned Scott Joplin only to include him in a short discussion of white ragtime pioneers, whose work, once properly refined and polished, reached its quintessence in Irving Berlin's "Alexander's Ragtime Band."

And this. In his *Biographical Dictionary of American Music*, published in 1973, Charles Eugene Claghorn, a white man, referred to S. Brun Campbell, The Ragtime Kid, as a black itinerant pianist.

And this. Tom Ireland, who played along with Joplin in the Queen City Band, remembered Otis Saunders, an active and prominent ragtime musician, as a white man.

So much for racial separatism in musical aptitude and appreciation.

So much for infallibility of historical records.

History is generous with who, what, where and when, but often stingy with why. There's no disputing that on August 10, 1899, a white man named John Stark signed a contract with a young black composer, Scott Joplin, to publish Joplin's tune "Maple Leaf Rag." Remarkably, this contract stipulated that Joplin would receive royalties on sales of the music, a penny a copy. Those days, with the exception of a few vaudeville top-liners, black composers were lucky to get ten or twenty dollars outright from a publisher for a piece of music.

"Maple Leaf Rag" took the country by storm. Historical accounts vary, but over the years it probably sold more than a million copies. In any case, it provided both Stark and Joplin with significant income throughout their lives. But then along came jazz, and for a generation or more, ragtime, Scott Joplin and John Stark were forgotten.

During the 1940s, some serious music people—historians, college professors, professional musicians—rediscovered ragtime. They wrote articles in prominent music magazines, describing ragtime as our first truly American music form. They wondered just how John Stark and Scott Joplin had happened to get together to publish "Maple Leaf Rag," and raced the clock to find and talk with people still around who had been there.

But those ragtime revivalists got as many versions of the anecdote as they did interviews. Even immediate members of the Stark family told different stories. Stark went to the Maple Leaf Club for a beer on a hot August afternoon, heard Scott Joplin play "Maple Leaf Rag," and signed him up on the spot. Wait, that's wrong. Joplin taught a little colored boy to play "Maple Leaf," then brought him into Stark's place to show Stark that anybody could play his catchy tune. No, that's not how it went. Joplin walked into the Stark and Son Music Store one day with the "Maple Leaf" manuscript under his arm, and though John Stark wasn't impressed, his son Will convinced him to take it. Hey, that's not right. Robert Higdon, a young attorney and a friend of both Joplin and Will Stark, told Joplin he ought to get his music published, wrote out a contract, negotiated with Stark, and that was that. On and on went the interviews. But no interviewee seems to have mentioned those penny-a-sheet royalties for the black composer.

Why did a man nearly sixty years old, proprietor of a successful music store, who'd done no more than dabble in music publishing by printing copies of a few very conventional pieces, decide to bring out the work of an unknown young black composer? Why did that composer, so determined to write "respectable" music, entrust his work to such an inexperienced publisher? And above all, why did John Stark agree to a royalties contract, such a striking exception to common practice of the time?

The most carefully drawn historical accounts have holes you can drive a truck through. Or better, a story. Because where the facts of history are incomplete, fiction provides an opportunity to gain insight and understanding by uncovering a truth ignored or even hidden by history—perhaps a truth more striking and wondrous than any historical reality.

In writing this story, I did my best not to alter or contradict well-established historical data. Rather, I wanted to use history as a framework for a fictional attempt to illuminate and comprehend the motives of the people involved.

I accepted that Scott Joplin was a single-minded composer of music, a serious and sober man who rarely smiled, but gave generously of his time to help young musicians and composers. As a teenager in Texarkana, Joplin was discovered and tutored by an immigrant German teacher named Julius Weiss. Joplin's demeanor inspired respect from blacks and whites alike. He wanted his work to be regarded with similar respect, and was displeased that the publisher of his "Original Rags," Carl Hoffman, had put Charles Daniels' name on the sheet-music cover as arranger. The young composer's best friend between 1893 and 1899 was Otis (Crackerjack) Saunders, but they had a critical falling-out in or shortly after 1899, allegedly over authorship of "Maple Leaf Rag."

According to Brun Campbell's own account, he met Saunders in Oklahoma City in 1898, played "Maple Leaf Rag" from the original manuscript, and then the following year ran off to Sedalia to study piano with Joplin. But it's not at all clear just when in 1899 Brun did go to Sedalia, how long he stayed, or how many lessons Joplin gave him.

John Stark fought for the Union throughout the Civil War, was based for a time in New Orleans, where he married Sarah Ann Casey (who was sixteen and a half at the time, not thirteen, as has been stated in a number of histories) in 1865, and sent her up the Mississippi to his brother's farm in Indiana. There is in Stark's army record an unexplained six-weeks' desertion during the spring of 1865. After the war, he went from farming to ice-cream manufacturing to peddling organs; finally, during the mid-1880s, he settled in Sedalia to operate a music store.

John William (Blind) Boone was at the height of his fame as a touring piano virtuoso and composer, giving concerts of American and European music, and inviting people to come up on-stage and play tunes of their choice, which he then would reproduce, note-perfect, mistakes and all. In his infancy, Boone had become ill with a "brain fever," and the doctors said the only way to save him was to take out his eyes, which they did. All the skills I attributed to Boone, including the ability to tell color by touch, are supported by historical accounts of his life.

Dr. Walter Overstreet was mayor of Sedalia between 1898 and 1900. P. D. Hastain and John Bothwell were prominent in city and state politics and were strong civic boosters; though they lost out on the State Capital, they did succeed in bringing the State Fair to Sedalia. Robert Higdon read law in Hastain's office in 1898, and opened his own practice the following year. He became highly successful and quite wealthy, though his wife remained critical of his generosity in providing *pro bono* legal services for indigent clients. One of his six sisters died in childbirth in 1888, leaving a two-year-old daughter. Charles Daniels, at the Carl Hoffman Music Company, was on his way to becoming an accomplished and well-regarded composer and publisher. Apple John Reynolds had recently begun what developed into a half-century of walking the streets of Sedalia, selling fruit and—far ahead of his time—warning people of the dangers of tobacco and alcohol. Walker Williams was part-owner of the Maple Leaf Club. G. Tom Ireland was a well-regarded black newspaperman and musician.

Some persons in my story began as no more than names on a yellowed page: High Henry, Belle Higdon, Police Chief J. Edward Love, Sheriff J. C. Williams, Gaylord Boutell and his saloon. Other persons were entirely fictional, including Elmo Freitag, Maisie McAllister, Emil and Fritz Alteneder, Big Henry and Mattie Ramberg, and Isaac Stark.

There's no suggestion that Edward and Mollie Fitzgerald were ever in Sedalia, let alone in 1899, but based upon extensive, consistent information presented by many of Frankie's biographers, I feel certain I've drawn the Fitzgeralds' characters faithfully, and I believe that if they had in fact found themselves in the predicament I put them into, they would have behaved just the way they did in my story.

We should be grateful John Stark was not chloroformed at sixty. For the remaining twenty-eight years of his life after he and Joplin signed their contract, he was the most prominent publisher of ragtime music in the United States, and earned a reputation for fairness and generosity in his dealings with ragtime composers, whether black or white. Stark was far and away the most vigorous promoter and champion of classic ragtime; his advertising statements and claims bear witness to his unwavering commitment to the music of Scott Joplin and other composers of first-rate ragtime music. Stark's last professional accomplishment, in 1927, was to secure renewal of the "Maple Leaf Rag" copyright for the Stark Music Company, as it was then called.

Walter Overstreet left the mayor's office in 1900, and continued to practice medicine in Sedalia until 1916, when he died following a bizarre psychotic episode. In his obituary, the *Sedalia Democrat* reported that Dr. Overstreet, "although a member of no church, lived a life that won for him the close friendship and high regard of all who knew him."

S. Brun Campbell, The Ragtime Kid, spent many years as an itinerant pianist in the midwest, then married and settled down to raise a family and work as a barber in Venice, California. Unfortunately, it seems Brun did not learn from his fictional experience; his wife was vehemently opposed to ragtime music, and would not permit him to play it in their house, so he kept pianos in his garage and barbershop. When ragtime was rediscovered, Brun did much to make certain Scott Joplin achieved his rightful place in music history (though many of Brun's recollections were, to put it mildly, touched up or embellished). During Brun's last years (he died in 1952), he recorded a number of ragtime pieces, some written by other composers, some by himself. Historians have referred to his performance as a time capsule of sorts, a first-hand demonstration of the style of most piano professors of fifty years earlier. The recordings reveal that Brun's ear remained faithful to the barrelhouse manner of playing, closer to what now is called folk ragtime than to Joplin's classic ragtime. Interestingly, Brun's only published rag is named "Barrelhouse Rag."

Scott Joplin died in 1917, at the age of forty-nine, frustrated, and exhausted physically and emotionally. Back in Sedalia, Joplin had told Arthur Marshall that "Maple Leaf" would make him King of Ragtime, as indeed it did. But Joplin's success seems never to have satisfied him. He wanted respect for his music, and to that end spent years writing extended ragtime pieces, including two operas. But those days, no one would produce an opera or a ballet by a black man; in fact, many refused to believe that a black man could write "serious" music. After his death, America embraced The Jazz Age, and forgot all about Scott Joplin.

John Stark's body lies a-mouldering in the grave.

But his work goes soldiering on.

With the mid-century rekindling of interest in ragtime, and changing social attitudes, Scott Joplin's music finally was accorded the respect the composer had hoped for, and more. As if in fulfillment of his Sedalia-days prediction that his music would be appreciated in fifty years, Rudi Blesh and Harriet Janis published *They All Played Ragtime*, the first major publication on ragtime music, in 1950. The authors dedicated their book to Joplin with a line written many years before by John Stark, proclaiming Joplin's towering originality and genius.

That was the beginning. In 1970, playing closely by the score, musicologist Joshua Rifkin recorded Joplin's rags; since then, record stores have most commonly displayed Joplin's work on classical-music shelves. On January 28, 1972, the Joplin opera *Treemonisha* premiered before a wildly enthusiastic audience at the Atlanta Memorial Arts Center. In 1974, "The Entertainer" was used as the musical theme of the movie *The Sting*, and Scott Joplin suddenly became the hottest composer in the United States. In 1976, he was awarded a Bicentennial Pulitzer Prize for his lifetime of accomplishment in American music.

And on June 1, 1999, the centenary of the publication of "Maple Leaf Rag," attendees at the annual Scott Joplin Ragtime

Festival in Sedalia took time to dedicate the Joplin Memorial Park, at the corner of East Main Street and Lamine. They heard the Reverend Dr. Marvin Albright deliver this invocation/dedication prayer:

> *"O Holy God,*
> *You have called us to sing a new song,*
> *to rejoice over the creativity and ingenuity of the human*
> *spirit which You have planted deep within the soul.*
> *This place, O God, calls to mind one soul.*
> *From a segregated moment in history, there arose one who*
> *spoke the universal language of the heart.*
> *From the pathos of pauperism there emerged a giant who*
> *enriched us with sounds that make us glad to be alive.*
> *From the dives of a dance hall, a new song swept over the*
> *land to set our toes to tapping and our feet to dancing.*
> *Today, we dedicate this place to the memory of Scott*
> *Joplin, father of ragtime, mother of a new musical art form,*
> *child of God."*

Glory hallelujah an' a-men, brother.

Selected Bibliography

History of Ragtime and Its Pioneers

Affeldt, Paul A. "The Saga of Brun Campbell." *The Mississippi Rag*, January 1988.

Albrecht, Theodore. "Julius Weiss: Scott Joplin's First Piano Teacher." *College Symposium*, Vol. 19, Fall 1979.

Berlin, Edward A. *Ragtime, A Musical and Cultural History.* University of California Press, Berkeley, 1980.

Berlin, Edward A. *King of Ragtime.* Oxford University Press, New York, 1994.

Berlin, Edward A. "A Biography of Scott Joplin." Electronic publication, written for the exclusive use of the Scott Joplin International Foundation, 1998.

Blesh, Rudi, and Janis, Harriet. *They All Played Ragtime.* Grove Press, New York, 1959. (Originally published by Knopf, 1950.)

Campbell, Brun. "From Rags to Ragtime and Riches." *Jazz Journal*, Vol. 2, No. 7, July 1949.

Campbell, S. Brun. "From Rags to Ragtime, A Eulogy." *Jazz Report,* Vol. 6, 1967.

Campbell, S. Brunson. "The Ragtime Kid (An Autobiography)." *Jazz Report,* Vol. 6, 1967-68.

Campbell, S. Brunson, and Carew, R. J. "Sedalia, Cradle of Ragtime." *The Record Changer,* June 1945.

Claghorn, Charles Eugene. *Biographical Dictionary of American Music.* Parker Publishing Company, West Nyack, NY, 1973.

Curtis, Susan. *Dancing to a Black Man's Tune.* University of Missouri Press, Columbia, MO, 1994.

Darch, Robert R. "Blind Boone, A Sensational Missourian Forgotten." *The Ragtimer,* Vol. 6, No. 5-6, 1967.

Egan, Richard. "Brun Campbell, The Rag-Time Warp." Electronic publication, undated.

Egan, Richard A., Jr. *Brun Campbell, The Music of "The Ragtime Kid."* Morgan Publishing, St. Louis, 1993.

Gammond, Peter. *Scott Joplin and the Ragtime Era.* St. Martin's Press, New York, 1976.

Harrah, Madge. "The Incomparable Blind Boone." *The Ragtimer,* July-August, 1969.

Harrah, Madge. *Blind Boone, Piano Prodigy.* CarolRhoda Books, Minneapolis, 2004.

Haskins, James. *Scott Joplin.* Doubleday, New York, 1978.

Hasse, John Edward, ed. *Ragtime, Its History, Composers and Music.* Schirmer Books, New York, 1985.

Jasen, David A., and Jones, Gene. *That American Rag.* Schirmer Books, New York, 2000.

Jasen, David A., and Tichenor, Trebor Jay. *Rags and Ragtime.* Dover Publications Inc., New York, 1978.

Levin, Floyd. "Brun Campbell, The Original Ragtime Kid of the 1890s." *Jazz Journal,* Vol. 23, December 1970.

Parrish, William. "Blind Boone's Ragtime." *Missouri Life,* November-December 1979.

Rice, Patricia. "Blind Boone, Link to Ragtime Origins." *The Rag Times,* Vol. 11, March 1978.

Schafer, William J., and Riedel, Johannes. *The Art of Ragtime.* Louisiana State University Press, Baton Rouge, 1973.

Thompson, Kay C. "Reminiscing in Ragtime, An Interview with Brun Campbell." *Jazz Journal,* Vol. 3, No. 4, April 1950.

Waldo, Terry. *This Is Ragtime.* Da Capo Press, New York, 1991.

John Brown, Slavery and Abolitionism

Anonymous. *John Brown's Raid.* Office of Publications, National Park Service, Washington DC, 1973.

Du Bois, W.E.B. *John Brown.* The Modern Library, 2001.

Hurmence, Belinda, ed. *My Folks Don't Want Me To Talk About Slavery.* John F. Blair, Winston-Salem, 1984.

Reynolds, David S. *John Brown, Abolitionist.* Knopf, New York, 2005.

Sorin, Gerald. *Abolitionism.* Praeger Publishers, New York, 1972.

Waters, Andrew, ed. *On Jordan's Stormy Banks.* John F. Blair, Winston-Salem, 2000.

Nineteenth-Century American Music

Courlander, Harold. *Negro Folk Music, U.S.A.* Dover Publications, New York, 1972.

Finson, Jon W. *The Voices That Are Gone.* Oxford University Press, 1994.

Locke, Alain. *The Negro and His Music.* Arno Press and The New York Times, New York, 1969. (Originally published by the Associates in Negro Folk Education, Washington, DC, 1936.)

Shaw, Arnold. *Black Popular Music in America.* Schirmer Books, New York, 1986.

Southern, Eileen. *The Music of Black Americans.* Norton and Company, New York, 1983.

Social, Political, and Historical Aspects of Life in Sedalia in 1899

Anonymous. *Portrait and Biographical Record of Johnson and Pettis Counties MO.* Chapman Publishing Company, Chicago, 1895.

Anonymous. *Sears Roebuck and Co. Consumers Guide, Fall 1900.* DBI Books, Northfield, IL, 1970.

———*Sedalia Democrat* and *Sedalia Sentinel,* daily newspapers. Articles printed between July 4 and August 4, 1899.

———*McCoy's City Directory for Sedalia, MO,* 1899.

Chalfant, Rhonda. "Sedalia's Ladies of the Evening." In *Women in Missouri History*, LeeAnn Whites, Mary C. Neth and Gary R. Kremer, eds. University of Missouri Press, Columbia, MO, 2004.

Claycomb, William B. *Pettis County Missouri, A Pictorial History.* The Donning Company Publishers, Virginia Beach.

Cassity, Michael. *Defending a Way of Life.* State University of New York Press, Albany, 1989.

Lang, Hazel N. *Life In Pettis County, 1815-1973.* Privately published, 1975.

McVey, W.A. *History of Pettis County, and Sedalia, MO.* Privately published, 1985.

Nolen, Rose M., ed. *Lost on the Prairie: George R. Smith College Methodist School for Blacks, Sedalia, MO, 1888-1925.* Privately printed, undated.

To receive a free catalog of Poisoned Pen Press titles, please contact us in one of the following ways:

Phone: 1-800-421-3976
Facsimile: 1-480-949-1707
Email: info@poisonedpenpress.com
Website: www.poisonedpenpress.com

Poisoned Pen Press
6962 E. First Ave. Ste. 103
Scottsdale, AZ 85251